IF I SHOULD DIE TONIGHT

A Novel

C. C. Avram

wordeee
where words connect

Published in the United States by Wordeee 2018

ISBN 13: 978-1-946274-24-3

Cataloging-in-Publication data available from Library of Congress

Published by Wordeee

Website: www.wordeee.com

Twitter: @wordeeeupdates

Facebook: wordeee

E-Mail: contact@wordeee.com

Photo Credit: Kelly Mahoney

[10 9 8 7 6 5 4 3 2 1]

IF I SHOULD DIE TONIGHT

The earth is soft and fresh as it sifts through my bare feet. The double rainbow in the sky arches its way to infinity. Along the footpath, a great waterfall gushes seamlessly cascading down, down, down, down into the lake becoming one with it as it meanders to God only knows where. It is my place of respite. A place where God must have walked to make it so beautiful…that peaceful place often dreamed of and wished for in my life.

-Randy Austin, June 1969

CHAPTER ONE
Randy

New York, Monday, September 10, 2001, 5:55 a.m.

"HEY UP LADY, is it too early to call?"

"When is it ever too early for you to call?" Randy said, placing the phone in the crook of her neck. "What's up Amelie?" she asked, pausing before the armoire.

"You'll never guess who I just got off the phone with."

Randy shifted the phone to her other ear. "Let me see now…mmmm…at this time of the morning, the ghost of Schumann past?"

"Close, but no."

"Okay. That's all I've got. No twenty guesses today. Not in the mood."

"Mummy."

"Sod off. You're bloody kidding, right?"

"I'm not."

"What did she want?"

"She's passing through New York in two weeks."

"Good for her. She calls to tell you this at," Randy looked at her watch, "five minutes to six? Does that woman ever sleep?"

"Isn't she's the reason we're early risers?" Amelie reminded her sister.

"Yep, another reason to keep our distance but still isn't it way too early for this conversation," Randy reached inside the linen chest. The towels felt like she imagined cumulus clouds, warm, soft and fluffy. Throwing the towel over her shoulder she went to the small kitchen off her bedroom, pulled open the refrigerator and dropped three cubes of ice into a glass. Pressing against a paneled wall she pulled out a bottle of Ketel One. "Uh-uh," Randy said, in response to Amelie's continuous prattle. More than anything, she wanted to get off the phone and get on with her morning routine. For this conversation, she needed more than vodka.

"Can you at least try to make time to have dinner?"

Randy inhaled, dropping her shoulders as a sigh left her lips. "Why would I do that?"

"Just give it a try," Amelie encouraged.

"It'll only end up as usual."

"Please," Amelie begged.

"You really can't be serious. Mother and I haven't spoken in years! Why all of a sudden does she wants to mend fences and start all over again? Amelie, as you well know I'm in no state to fight with Mother. Plus, there is absolutely nothing I want to say to that woman now or in the future." Randy poured vodka over ice and added a splash of tonic water. Passing the full-length mirror on the way to the bathroom, she gave herself a once over. She needed to stop drinking. Been telling herself the same thing since she took her first drink at the age of thirteen. From that first sip of the Black Label Scotch she'd found hidden at the back of her mother's closet, she knew they'd become good friends.

"Randy…"

"Amelie," Randy interrupted her sister, "You and Ashley have dinner with Mom. Tell her I'll be out of town. She couldn't possibly miss me after all this time and let's face it, two out of three ain't bad." She grinned at her clever Meatloaf reference from his song of the same name. He was one of her favorite singers.

"It's you who she wants to see. Give her a chance."

"To do what? To tell me how self-indulgent I am? What a bad mother I am? For Christ, sakes talk about the pot calling the bloody kettle black! Or maybe I should give her another chance to remind me how good a life I have in spite of everything? I'll pass."

"Just think about it," Amelie pleaded.

"Yep. I will. I sure will. Bye." Randy dropped the phone onto the counter. Just the thought of her mother made her want to get drunk. Randy had vowed never to set eyes on that woman again after their last blow up five years before. And nothing, nothing in this bloody life would make her change her mind.

• • •

Throughout the years, Randy's choice of drink changed to fit her upper-crust lifestyle. (The fancier her lifestyle got, the fancier her drinks. She'd graduated from Black Label Scotch to the vodka and cocktails that now ruled her life.) But she was no common drunk. She was an Eastside drunk; chic, edgy, controlled women whose lives centered around lunches and cocktails, dinners and cocktails, charity events and cocktails, and then the necessary bedtime cocktail that helped them moan convincingly under husbands who offered nothing but money.

Sweeping her gaze downward she ignored the years of alcohol abuse etched on her face; the dark circles under her eyes, the cheeks that were a little too sunken, and the paunch sticking out from her otherwise svelte five-feet-eight frame. Her betrayers were easily camouflaged by make-up and custom clothes. What wasn't easy to ignore this morning, however, was the slight tremor of her hands. How did her life get this twisted and unhappy? Randy hadn't known when Lawrence brought her as his new bride to the high-rise building with rubbish piled out front and more chains on the door than a linked-fence, that theirs was a life to be coveted. She'd felt imprisoned. It hadn't taken long to find out that living at 70th and Park raised eyebrows and opened doors and checkbooks. It was considered the gold coast of New York. Still, the vapid group she hung around was tiring at best. Today she was every bit of an East Side woman living the life her mother thought was beyond compare. Randy sucked air through her teeth as she placed her glass on the ledge of the inlaid tub. Plugging the tub, she spun the taps on. Emptying a sachet of bath salts, she watched as crystals seeped orange pigment into the clear water and when the water began rising, she squeezed in a generous amount of bubble bath. Orange foam popped and wiggled.

In deft movements, Randy twisted her hair atop her head, shed her robe and skivvies, tilted the television to the perfect angle, and climbed into the deep whirlpool tub where turbo jets bubbled the perfumed water. Sinking inch by inch, she could feel the heat evaporating leftover alcohol from her pores. Settling in, she picked up the remote and began scanning channels on the overhead T.V. Her edges were raw, to begin with, and the discussion about her mother's visit had made it worse.

Randy flicked the remote control to find a mindless, (which wasn't hard to do) television show to watch as she contemplated yet another day in her hell of a life. Commercials! Randy poured vodka. Oh hell, she groaned as the Cialis commercial started right after the Cymbalta one ended. This damn nation was becoming a bunch of hypochondriacs! 'Yumm,' she closed her eyes. Nothing tasted better than the first sip of a morning 'cocktail.' It was, as usual, the beginning of her escape to her fantasyland where double rainbows promised a new beginning. She'd written those words in 1969 and they were still very much her rock today and had seen her through some pretty challenging times. The hope of an escape to wonderland was her promise for the crummy cards she'd drawn in this life. Randy suppressed a smile, lifted her glass in a cheer and said, "To me."

She was about to hit the TV's off button when the Big O, who was handing out copious amounts of tissues to the man in front of her, loomed on the screen. It had to be some kind of special because the time slot for the Oprah Show was all wrong.

"I didn't know…I still don't know…we were just playing house and…"

"How can a grown man play house with a child?"

Randy bolted upright and turned up the volume. Emotionally taxing subjects were usually off limits for her fragile mind but she was riveted…and without warning, down…down…down she went falling head first into a memory she'd buried under years of denial.

Leicester, East Midlands, England 1969

"There's a brown girl in the ring, tra la," they all sang, everyone reluctantly, except Randy whose robust voice was loud and committed.

"I'm done playing this stupid game," Randy interrupted mid-song annoyed at the lackluster efforts her sisters, Ashley and Amelie, were making to participate in her Heritage Program. As a part of the only

black family in Leicester, though it had a rapidly growingly South Asian population, Randy had taken it upon herself to indoctrinate her sisters in Jamaican culture in the form of childhood rhymes she held onto for dear life. Of all the childhood ditties, "I've Come to see Janie, Carry Mi Ackee Go a Linstead Market, Clap Hands till Mama Comes Home, Brown Girl in the Ring" was her favorite and she believed it would build cultural confidence in her sisters as it had in her. Now even the songs were of no more interest to her sisters. She supposed, just as Jamaica had grown distant to her with each passing year in England, so had the little songs Sadie, her nanny back in Jamaica had taught her…all was fading.

"C'mon. Let's at least get to the 'show me your motion' part," Ashley said.

"Nope. Not me. Not another second."

"You've something better to do?" Ashley asked.

"Maybe, maybe not. But, from this day forward I'm through with childish games. No more trying to remind you where we come from. You are both very ungrateful and I don't need this anymore. As far as I'm concerned you can become as British as the Queen. You can, in fact, become Ladies of the East Midlands!" Randy folded her arms across her budding breasts.

At thirteen, on the cusp of being neither woman nor child, the daily routine of playing with her sisters bored her more than it did them. But, it was better than hanging out at the Leicester Neighborhood Park or at the pool where kids were forever trying to touch their curly hair, something, which at best, was tedious.

"That's not fair," Ashley yelled looking to her sister Amelie for support. Amelie shrugged her shoulders wishing she was home playing the piano. Unfortunately, their Grandpa had accompanied Aunt Clarissa to some function or the other and since they couldn't be home without adult supervision they had to remain at the park or the pool where there were always adult supervision until someone picked them up.

"Let's push on over to the pool then," Ashley said, stirring Randy from revere.

"I'm not doing that either. I can't be around noisy kids today. Don't you get it?" Randy snapped. "Tell Mummy I went to my room to read."

"I'll come home with you and play the piano," Amelie said, perking up. She too disliked these nonsense games. All the culture she needed was listening to her grandpa's piano.

For sisters, none of them were alike in spirit or looks. Each as unique as a snowflake, they were the best of friends and each other's safe haven.

"How am I to read with you banging on that noise box?" Randy was losing her patience. "I want to be alone," she said dramatically.

"It's an instrument," Amelie corrected. "A beautiful instrument."

"You have no choice but to come to the pool," Ashley insisted.

"We can stop for ice-cream. Plus, Grandpa isn't home so who wants to be alone with crazy old Uncle Joe?"

"Uncle Joe isn't crazy. He's just not right upstairs," Randy said tapping her hand to her forehead. "I'll be fine." Apart from Grandpa, Randy was the only one who bothered to notice Uncle Joe. He was slow…not right in the head as her mother often said. Randy would sit with him and with the utmost patience explain simple things to him. She'd even let him brush her hair, a task he never seems to tire of.

"You know how Mother feels. She doesn't want us alone with Uncle Joe. He can't look after us."

"If Mother cared that much about us, she'd have taken us with her or stayed home," Randy snapped. "Anyway, go on now and Ashley," Randy warned her sister, "make sure you keep close to Amelie. If anything happens to her, Mummy will kill you."

"But we're all grown up," Amelie, all of seven said proudly. "We can take care of ourselves."

"Oh, stop jabbering and run along to the pool, will you," Randy said shooing her sisters. None of them wanted to admit that Amelie was their Mother's and Grandpa's favorite. She was a gentle spirit who felt

no need to fight except for her Grandpa's lap and the old piano he introduced her to before she could say a single word.

• • •

It was summer and the sense of freedom, solitude, and adolescence was intoxicating. Like any other teenager, Randy simply wanted to sit in her room and read a good book or listen to the music of her new obsession, Rod Stewart. She wasn't into boys yet like some of her friends…she preferred books.

"I'll tell Mummy you had a headache," Amelie offered.

"Brilliant! Good girl," Randy patted her sister's head. "Hurry on now to the pool and don't forget your lifejacket."

Randy walked the short distance home. Their house was a typical Victorian terrace on Morton Street which was always teeming with activity. Randy greeted neighbors and friends all the way to her front door. As usual, the door was open so she dropped her books on the sofa, darted to the bathroom to wash her hands and then to the kitchen to quell her hunger. Randy opened the refrigerator door and pulled out a plate of cold chicken. She sliced the hard dough bread (the one thing Jamaican her mother could never give up) and peeled a ripe avocado which she sliced into half-moons onto the bread. Carving into the leg of chicken she layered her sandwich and chewed on the chicken bone (though she had no talent for pulverizing it into calcium the way her mother did). She, who had learned from Aunt Clarissa to be the perfect hostess, was in her element acting like a grown up. She set the table with a floral mat and napkin and settled herself with her sandwich and a cup of tea.

For some unknown reason, her first home in Jamaica came floating into her thoughts. How different it was from their little house in the middle of England. The massive estate was dotted with Austin Rose hedges. Mangoes, tamarind, star-apple, cashew trees and a rambling old almond tree, all majestic and fruitful, laid claim to acres of land.

She didn't remember as much about Jamaica as she used to, often having to close her eyes to hear the sounds and remember the smells she'd cherished as a child; the whistle of the peanut cart, the tinkle of the milkman's bell, the shaving sound of ice from the snow cone man, or the distinctive smell of ripe June plums and naseberries. The one thing she did remember only too well was her fear of tropical lizards that crawled along her bedroom wall, always glad that she was under a mosquito net. But, most of all, she missed her father's lunchtime visits and the Bustamante toffees he'd bring her and Ashley as treats. She hadn't realized then that her father was English. She thought his accent was simply his until she came to England and everyone sounded like him. Time had faded some of the pain she'd felt about the loss of her father and today, at thirteen, she felt all grown up and was ready to put childish things behind her…including any more questions about her Dad.

Heading to her room after her afternoon snack, Randy stripped off her clothes and readied herself for a long, luxurious bath. It was probably foolish to eat and then bathe but she wasn't worried about indigestion like old folks. Before getting into the tub, she scanned the bookshelf for a good read, deciding on 'The Good Earth.' She'd read it countless times but she simply loved the book. As she leaned over to pull it out, she was aware that her young body had entered a new phase of development. Her breasts were the first to reach the bookcase. The once little nubs on her chest seemed to have sprung up overnight and still, too shy to look at them she plunged into the tub feeling particularly liberated about her decision to stay home. "There's a brown girl in the ring, tra la let me show you mi motion, tra la," Randy began singing in a beautiful falsetto voice, her Jamaican accent no longer as distinguishable as Sadie's. Cigarette smoke! Randy jumped from the tub and was about to wrap a towel around her when in the mirror, her eyes met a pair staring at her through a veil of cigarette smoke.

"Uncle Joseph! What are you doing?" Randy screamed at him. Can't you see I'm naked? Get out of here now! Remember what Mummy says, you have to knock on a closed door."

"I just wanted to see you," her uncle said coming into the bathroom and closing the door. Randy backed away covering her nakedness with the towel. "Mother will be quite mad when I tell her about this. Get out right now!" Randy tried to sound stern. "When I'm out we'll go to the park and sing our songs."

Uncle Joseph, though dimwitted, was her favorite uncle. He would never hurt her. Yet looking into his eyes, she could see that he was wrestling with something deep and dark and talk as she did, he seemed given over to another matter entirely.

"You're such a big girl now," he said, backing her into a corner. "I want to brush your hair…big girls need things right Randy." His smile disappeared and his expression hardened.

• • •

The voice came through the fog. Fog. Yep. That's the way she'd been living for twenty-seven years…in a fog and inside her pain. His steps were getting closer. Randy emptied her drink into the whirlpool and hurriedly sunk the glass into the sudsy water, holding it firm beneath her thigh. Such a waste, she flipped the tap and gulped a mouthful of water, switched off the T.V., sprayed a little more Penhaligon's air freshener and waited. She was a pro at concealment. Vodka, her preferred drink, was colorless, odorless and easy on the taste buds yet it delivered the punch she needed to face each day.

"Randy, Randy…RANDY," the voice was closer.

In here," she gargled exhaling into her hand, no smell. She'd never, ever smell like a drunk the way her mother used to when braiding her hair for school.

The double glass doors of her bedroom, now frosted with steam flung open and her husband, framed in the diffuse lighting and looking natty in his custom jacket stood fuming. He was tall, well-built and impeccable. Though his face had elements of fine features, the perfect flair to his nose, he was not a handsome man. But he was successful and offered stability, purpose and he was in love with Randy, the three things her mother Emily, who desperately wanted to marry her off at age twenty-one, was happy with. He was eight years her senior, already established by the time she'd graduated from Vassar and went to work at the Metropolitan where they had met. He'd courted her hard, told her of the jolt to his heart and his instant attraction to her from the moment their eyes met across the room. She remembered no such thing. She's dated him and then took him home. After Emily conducted her inquisition it was decided that he was to be her husband.

The light framed Lawrence's body like the angel he was who had saved her soul and mended her wounded heart. If only the walls could talk. Randy smiled at Lawrence. They were as different as North and South. Randy eyes narrowed. She gazed through him, her smile firmly in place. He had no idea of her disillusionment with life. No idea that she daydreamed of life without him and their daughter. Each time Randy thought of June she was riddled with guilt. She loved her daughter the best she could but it was clearly not enough. Even now she was never quite sure she'd recovered from bringing a child into the world. Her guilt was not only about her dead emotions but that they had no idea that with each passing day, a road trip to nowhere was looking better and better to her. Her rainbow was coming into view.

"Why don't you answer me when I call you Randy?"

" 'Cause, I didn't hear you, honey. I'm sorry." She wasn't sorry at all.

"Tell me," Lawrence repeated, "why don't you ever answer me the first time I call you?" He knew she'd heard him. It was a game she played to control. He looked around the confounded garden bathroom he hated. There was a time when Lawrence would have done anything to please his wife.

When her shenanigans would have earned her a planted kiss on her forehead instead of the impatience he now felt. Over the years their life had dulled and the ache for his unavailable wife had metered. Unlike Lawrence's dreary tomb with uncapped toothpaste tubes, rows of spicy cologne and used towels strewn on the floor, Randy's bathroom was a place of respite. Large and airy with Italian armoires stuffed full of colorful Egyptian cotton towels, the room was centered by an inlaid slate, claw foot tub, with candles and scented oils in cornices along its length. A large skylight served as diffused lighting for rows of breathtaking orchids. The prima donnas of the floral world, in a spectacular array of rainbow colors, lifted the sanctuary to a place of spiritual renewal. White Phalaenopsis floated on spindly stems while Dancing Ladies arched and dangled, flaunting their curiously golden, speckled flowers. A rare, delicate, pink Lady Slipper preened and swayed as the central attraction of the bathroom greenhouse. It was a room of fantasy, like stepping into a rainbow. The fragrance of the orchids mixed with Randy's expensive perfumes was intoxicating. Randy, surrounded by the beauty of the room, found it the only place where her life could pretend to be in bloom.

"Maybe if you didn't shout so much, I could hear you better," Randy said turning on the faucets, first hot and then cold, to warm up her water and create more bubbles. A mystery why she did it that way but it surely reflected the natural rhythms of life. First things are hot and then cold. She, personally, could remember nothing but the cold, dark corners of her fears.

"I wouldn't shout if you answered me," Lawrence gruffed. "You do remember that we have a dinner party tonight, right?"

"Ah Lawrence, is dinner really necessary? Why can't you take those people out to a pub or something?" Randy said mechanically pouring more Penhaligon's exfoliating body bubbles into the water. Fragrance permeated the room.

"What's wrong with you?" Lawrence demanded. "Something's gotten into you lately. Ever since you started hanging around those loony women. And for your information, we have no pubs in America, only bars. Can't you try to at least be American for once? You've been here for twenty-six goddam years!"

"Now why would anyone want to do that? Because American's are so enlightened?" Randy snapped. He had some nerve calling her friends whacks. Had he never stopped to listen to the idiots he brought to her home? By loony women, Lawrence meant her friends, Sheila and Adrienne, whom he detested because they refused to let him get away with some of the asinine things that fell from his lips.

"Anyway," Randy added, "dinner parties are out of vogue in America, you know. Everyone dines out these days."

"Not in this house. Dinner. Eight o'clock," Lawrence said with finality. "I'll call you with the number of guests."

"As you wish," Randy said.

She could hear him bouncing down the stairs like a damn ball. The man never walked like normal people. As soon as he left Randy got out of the tub, wrapped herself in an oversized towel, slammed the door shut and poured more vodka. She filled her glass with the clear liquid to an imaginary mark. Up to that mark, the vodka took the edge off and kept her from the dark edges of memory, anything more and she'd be incoherent. Lately, however, it took more vodka to reach calm.

CHAPTER TWO
Ashley

Philadelphia, September 10, 2001, 5:00 a.m.

NOT A FREAKIN' thing was working in her life, not the Kabbalah classes, or the evil eye bracelet. Not the guided meditations that implored her to find love for every living thing; the trees, the frogs, the dog, the bastards called men, the racist assholes at her job, nor the silly little Eat, Drink and be Happy book the world was going gaga over. Nothing had worked! Until Frederick, she hadn't been steeped in anger about colour, now like the Americans, she was stuck in hues and pop psychology. Ashley threw the book across the room. She was done with all this shit. Last night was the final straw. She'd gone to some School of Life event with her friend Marcia and while everyone was going Zen on her, she was acutely aware that her behind was lonely and worse, horny. She was a woman of forty-three and she was damn well entitled to be horny.

But poor Marcia, a magnet for the worst kind of men for whom she had born children and who she was forever dragging to court for child support, was still convinced that the red string she wore on her wrist, the white sage she burned all over the house and her *om nerenge* chants would cure all. Ashley had left her chanting, gone home, eaten ice cream and then curled up in her 800 thread count sheets. The monotony of her life was pushing her stress button.

The morning was proving no better. Sal, Ashley brightened. He was the best lay she'd had in years. Their last encounter, however, was too brutal for her to be the first to call. "There is no pleasing you," Sal had shouted as she'd stormed from his presence in a huff. The more Sal gave the less she wanted.

"That's the problem." She had shouted louder than him. "I don't want to be pleased. Why can't you accept things the way they are? It's such a bore for people to push for more than others want to give. Your love is a choking kind. Why? Why? Why?" she'd demanded. "I have no idea why I stay in these dead relationships."

As far as Ashley was concerned, she had a propensity to draw out relationship deaths like the opera singer in *La Traviata* who sang her death song for an hour. "Die already," Ashley had murmured under her breath at the theater, earning a scolding from Sal. An hour was way too long to die. She had sacked him that very night.

She found herself agitated all over again just thinking about Sal. That idiot had called her every kind of bitch in the dictionary and then some. It seemed relationships were not the only dead-end thing she was dragging out. She was clearly dragging her feet on quitting her meaningless job at WNCB affiliate in Philadelphia. It was five-fifteen a.m. Ashley punched out the number to her psychiatrist instead of Sal's.

"Mitch, I'm having a panic attack."

"Jesus Ashley. It's five-fifteen a.m.!"

"And? You're on call, no? And I'm having a panic attack!"

"Look, until you're ready to deal with your fears, nothing will change. It's that trust issue again, Ashley. That's all. All your issues are with trust no matter how they present," Mitchell, with his sedate voice and candor said.

What kind of poppycock is that? "Give me a better answer for once, Mitchell. Trust me, dear, if you grew up in my household with a stark raving mad ass mother or if you were a brilliant woman among backstabbing mediocre men, trust would be an issue for you too. What you are supposed to do, is help me find out how to get it back." *Asshole.*

"I want you to try staying in a relationship for more than two wee…" She hadn't let him finish.

"Don't be a twit, Mitchell. Why the hell do you think I pay you all this money if I didn't want to learn to trust? Of course, I want to be in a relationship for more than two weeks but am I to ruin my life again over some idiot man? Plus, I've watched my mother ruin her life over and over again and, in the process, she screwed up all our lives. I didn't beg for that you know. No, I can't be bothered, Mitch."

"But Ashley, it was only…"

Ashley slammed down the phone. She knew what he was going to say. The dumb ass. It's always only something! The dial tone left her lonelier but as much as she wanted to, she knew it would be a mistake to call Sal. In the short time they had dated, Sal had never understood her. It lasted for four weeks. She was making progress. She hoped Mitch was not offended by her dumb ass comment. She should really be more sensitive. Grabbing her keys off the hall table Ashley was heading for the door when the phone rang.

"What!" she barked into the phone expecting Mitchell.

"Who are you trying to kill this early in the morning," retorted her sister Amelie's who like her, was up and in place before the preverbal cock crowed. In fact, they were all early risers. It was a habit from having to play their own caretakers when their mother was too drunk to get them ready for school. Good things come from bad situations though because they were close and protective of each other.

"My wonky therapist. What's up?"

"Mom's coming to town."

"Hell no, not today, I'm busy."

"In a couple of weeks on her way back from Corfu."

"Amelie! Why must you always be the bearer of bad news? Why after all this time is Mother coming to town?"

"It's obvious. She wants to make amends."

"Call me then. I'll see how I'm feeling. You okay?"

"Fine."

"Good, then I've got to go."

Traffic was sparse as Ashley merged onto the breezeway. Maybe Mitchell was right after all. She should try staying in a long-term relationship. Unfortunately, she didn't know how. She watched the phone on her passenger seat vibrate. She could care less about driving and yapping on her phone. The vibrating screen, however, said unknown caller. She only knew two people with blocked numbers. It could only be a) Her sister Randy, ready to spew venom at her for not showing up for their Wednesday lunch b) Phillip making sure she'd get to the set on time or a third possibility c) confounded telemarketers who she'd scream at to lose her f-ing number. Well scrap telemarketers; they can't call until eight a.m. Though she wanted to speak with none of them, her curious, some would say nosy personality, made it a struggle not to answer. Testing her habit breaking technique, she finally sent the call to voicemail. Pulling into her designated parking space at six-thirty a.m., Ashley Freeman fluffed her feathered hair and made her way to make-up.

"Morning Clare. Where's Phillip this morning?"

"Just went to his dressing room."

Ashley flopped down in the chair and wrapped herself in a plastic bib to protect her clothes from specks of makeup that could smudge her pristine look. Make up done, gray as usual, she buttoned her jacket, clipped on her mic holder and strode down the corridor to her dressing room. The irony was she had that *je ne sais quoi* that had men running behind her. The fact did not escape her, but who at WNCB could be worthy of her time? She felt like weeping as not one man at WNCB-TV Philadelphia. even piqued her interest. On the other hand, they were always tempted to touch, but she was sure that like Frederick, they weren't ready to take her home to Mamie.

The newsroom was full of Jew boys, Ivy League snobbery, WASPS, the general poor white scrapper who'd made good working his way up the corporate ladder and a sprinkling of "diversity." She fell into the last group as one of three women anchors and the only black. She filled a double quota. Unlike the other women, Ashley didn't play by the women rules or any rules for that matter. She was considered a rogue employee who they couldn't fire because her show ratings were through the roof, so they tolerated her. Ashley, not into doing any 'dance' always came off as brash and that might well have been the reason, she was in the dead-end job of entertainment news and not elevated to the hard news, which was what she was trained to do.

Ashley stopped at the adjacent door to her dressing room. "Phillip," she barely knocked before pushing it open. "Why are you trying to drive me crazy?"

"What did I do now?" her co-anchor queried

"I'm the star of this show, right?"

"Right," Phillip humored her.

"So, you get to verify the facts before we go on air, right."

"Right again."

"So, what happened with the Kansas story?"

"Oh, that? Well, a little oversight but don't worry about that. Our public wouldn't know a wrong stat if it bopped them in the head."

"That's not the point now, is it? The hounds out there are waiting for us to screw up so they can sit their fat behinds in our chairs. Do you know that we are the only two black people together on a show? Do you want that to change because they decide you can't read more than a teleprompter?"

"You're right again."

"Great. Please, don't forget to check the facts for Monday's story…segment three. It's one of Rose's. I don't have to tell you how unreliable that gasbag can be at times. I'm meeting her after our taping for another half-baked story."

"Honey, all you need to build our stories is a half-baked tip from Rose."

"I know! That's why I keep telling you this job is damn nonsense. Pure shit."

"And this shit is always at the top of the ratings."

Ashley rolled her eyes. "That's because our audience is barely literate."

"Right," Phillip said slipping into his midnight blue jacket.

"To be honest Phillip, I don't think I can do this nonsense much longer." Ashley flopped down on his couch.

"You've been saying that a lot these days. Ahhh, ahh," he pulled her from the chair. "Don't get comfy; we're on in a few."

"That's because I mean it," Ashley said rising and re-creasing the pleat in her skirt.

"I hear you. Really, I do but right now we have to go into the studio. Let's continue this discussion later."

"Are you sure we can't grab a bite at the Rooster tonight? Better yet, I'll cook you a fabu English meal!"

"Come on Ash, I told you not tonight. I've got a hot date. I'll come by tomorrow and we can have our movie night then. You'll have to rustle up something better than fabu English food however for that's an oxymoron." Phillip grinned, flashing perfect, dentally whitened teeth that shone brightly against his molasses skin.

"And who says I'm available tomorrow?"

"Me. Didn't you dump what's his face?"

"Sal. That's his name."

"Oh, you remember?" Phillip smoothed back his already immaculate hair.

"What do you expect me to do tonight?"

"Get a date Tweetie? Every man in this place would kill to look into those lethal bottomless eyes of yours." He ushered her down the hall.

Phillip was not only Ashley's co-anchor and best friend, he was her walker and it was a crying shame that her love life had been reduced to her "dragging him along." They had met on their first day at WNCB, both newly minted journalists with a similar outlook on the direction of journalism and the role they'd play. They had become fast friends that day and even faster friends when reality seeped in. They were the only two coffee beans in an entire glass of milk, and if they weren't careful, they'd sink right to the bottom of the glass.

"Phillip, you really suck and you're an awful friend. Just plain picayune and totally selfish."

"Guilty as charged."

The tapings were as usual trite. Three, back to back. A few hours later Ashley climbed down from the darkened ET set wondering how much longer it was going to take her to muster up the courage to leave this podunk job and city. Inching closer to the wall to feel her way to the door, it never ceased to amaze her that the moment the word wrap left the producer's mouth, the set became a ghost town.

"Every penny count," Quinton had explained.

"I'll be back at one sharp," Ashley poked Phillip as she prepared to leave for her appointment with Rose Bradley.

"How about 12:45 p.m. Give yourself some slack time."

"I said 1:00 p.m. Bye," she terminated the conversation before Phillip could counter with his usual acerbic quip. Phillip, in addition to being her best friend and muse, was her pretend "man" friend. On most occasions, he was enough.

"What's eating Gilbert Grape?" Quinton asked as Ashley blew by him.

"This goddamn job is making her crazy." Phillip mimicked Ashley throaty voice. "It's fluff, not worth doing."

"Pays the bills," Quinton said lumbering down the hall.

But Phillip was not convinced that paying the bills was enough for Ashley anymore and that thought petrified him. He was well aware that ET's popularity was more about the woman who lit up the screen in the chair next to him rather than his suave attire or the content of the show. And he was also aware that something was shifting.

Ashley Freeman was not merely beautiful. She was breathtaking, resplendent even and deadly, a combination very few men could resist. But more than Ashley's exquisite style and lethal emotions, and though one of the reasons people tuned in was for their fashion fix, it was how she had parlayed a "fluff" job into a top-rated show that had Phillip mesmerized. Having finagled his way into the seat next to her, he who'd fought to get out of the projects in Baltimore, had no intention of leaving her side. 'Walk in the footstep of elephants' was his motto. He smiled to himself, examined his buffed nails and headed for his dressing room. And what the hell was fluff about a $750,000.00 a year job for a four-hour workday?

• • •

Monday, September 10, 11:30 a.m., Philadelphia, Chestnut Street Buddakan Restaurant

Ashley would rather be dead than meeting Rose Bradley but alive she was as she slid into the empty chair across from the gasbag, removed her shades and gave her a big smile. It was not unnoticed that the women smelled of alcohol. "Rose, how are you darling?"

Rose Bradley looked her up and down. She approved of her sense of style and her good manners. She liked these blacks from foreign countries better. More confident. More cultured. Ashley's short, feathered hair framed her beautiful, oval-shaped face which in turn highlighted carefully arched eyebrows. The mustard jacket she wore was cropped just above the waist and worn over a fitted black skirt that flared around the knees in pleats. Her, tall, lean frame was set off by the black pumps that extended her calves and her make-up was flawless. Her sense of style and of self was top notch.

"Couldn't be better," Rose answered, opening her compact and checking her own face, now lined with age.

Ashley could hear Rose's mind working to understand why this black girl was so different. How dare she think her approval was necessary for anyone. Ashley abhorred the race thing in America. Not that it didn't exist in England but it was so crass, uncouth and ugly in America.

"May I get you a drink?" Ashley was already signaling for the waiter.

"Of course," Rose's smile smoothed out the wrinkles

over her lips. Snapping the case shut she said, "The usual."

Ashley ordered a Bloody Mary for Rose and Evian for herself. "Lunch?"

"Not today, I'm having an early dining with Eric Bennett," Rose said, namedropping a newscaster from a rival studio.

Bitch. "Let's get right to it then," Ashley said. "Wyatt Steel and Isabelle Rosenthal are my subjects."

Rose, a well-preserved seventy-year-old leaned forward in her chair. "My dear, what choices," she said in a hushed voice. "That beast of a man is an ill-tempered drunk. Hardly worth the words, but it's a fascinating story, really. Absolutely priceless," she continued, lowering her voice a notch.

"Really?" Ashley said mirroring Rose's conspiratorial countenance, lowering her voice to the level of hers.

"Absolutely! *Entertainment Times* doesn't pay me half as much as I'm worth for all the stories it does on my back. It's risky, you know, to keep giving you these nuggets of gold. I'm thinking of raising my rates," Rose finished, feigning interest in her too brightly painted red nails.

Rose, the widow of Dwight Bradley, a once prominent Philadelphian who died penniless, was now a fallen socialite. Rose's income now came entirely from dishing dirt on her friends. It wasn't what one would call paltry, but it certainly didn't afford her the grandeur of her former life.

Ashley smiled, taking a sip of water.

"Rose, you should talk to our people about that. I'll put in a word or two for you myself. You're invaluable to me," she lied knowing she wouldn't utter a single word about Rose to a single person at ET.

Believing in Ashley's good fellowship, Rose's diatribe on the Wyatt Steel drama went on for an hour. She didn't seem to know as much about Isabelle.

"I don't know how a man like that could have had four wives and now it looks like he'll have a fifth. Half his age! What do they see in him? It is unbelievable. If you can't make a marriage work after two tries one should give up."

Ashley shifted. She'd often wished her mother had gotten that very point. Three marriages later and still, in Ashley's opinion, Emily hadn't found the right man. It was bad enough to have an English stepfather and put up with the glances and stares at their school in England but when her mother met and married that Yankee man and again uprooted her children, America bound, that was the final straw for Ashley. She was the wise old age of eleven, impressionable, unforgiving and there couldn't have been a worse time to come to America. There was no Beatle mania welcome for them. Instead, they arrived in America in 1979 when the results of civil rights movement were still in translation. Affirmative Action was one of the results of the movement. Until Frederick, she really hadn't understood the true burden of blackness and all the rigmarole that went with it until he'd assumed, she was at Georgetown because of Affirmative Action. Her weariness about men and life was earned from living.

"I've been meaning to ask where in England you lived. My parents, you know, were English."

"Really? We lived in Leicester. The East Midlands."

"I think my parents were from the Midlands somewhere. Can't remember where exactly. Does Cardiff sound familiar?"

"Yes, in the U.K but that would be in Wales. You should try to find out more." Ashley pushed back her chair. She really didn't give a rat's ass about Rose's ancestry and her absolute ignorance. Cardiff in England?

"And another thing," Rose said wobbling to her feet. "You're such a good reporter. I think you should consider using your talents better than you are. Take it from an old woman, use your God-given talent before it uses you."

For once Ashley actually stopped her usual dash out the door to listen. "I'm going to give that some thought. Don't forget to watch the show Monday night…it's all about you," Ashley said as she walked the noxious woman to the corner to catch a taxi.

On the way back from her appointment, Ashley thought about Rose Bradley's comment a lot. She was wasting her talent. She knew that. When she'd graduated George Washington's journalism school the job market had been soggy. Her expectation of landing a job at CBS, where she'd interned every summer, didn't materialize. With the job market tight she was forced to take the temporary job at WNCB until something real came along. She never chalked not getting the coveted job up to the fact that in the age of civil rights resistance, she was black, female and maybe her worst enemy of all, her Leicester accent. Most African-American reporters were assigned to the ghetto beat and she was clearly not the perfect fit. Her friend Eilah, a black Swede of African descent at the New Yorker was always assigned to write stories on Africa.

But in her favor, times were a-changing and celebrity-hood was becoming a celebrity all on its own. When Ashley was offered the anchor position at an entertainment show, she grabbed it with both hands. ET, the show that peeled the skin off the lives of the epicureans ratcheted up in Neilson ratings and so did her paycheck and her popularity. Now, not even the mega checks she got bi-weekly could keep boredom at bay. Lately, she had been feeling that she was wasting her life and she was seriously considering transforming it one way or the other.

CHAPTER THREE
Amelie

Wall Street, September 10, 2001, 6:15 a.m.

AMELIE'S OFFICE ON the ground floor of the Waltman and Sachi Financial Center was a place of constant activity and heartburn. If her daily heartburn didn't come from her two muses, it came from her job. Every day, for twelve years she'd watched peddlers outside her window become millionaires dispensing antacids and aspirins. In the past nine months, since her promotion, she'd become their number one client. With the new pressure and stress, her life hit the pandemonium needle and Amelie found it harder and harder to work up the frenzy needed to be an A-class titan on the Street. These days, to be honest, she found it more engaging to talk to her Muse or to spontaneously break out in song, a habit of hers, especially when her nerves were frayed. This morning her favorite ditty 'Don't push me 'cause I'm close to the edge' popped into her head. And she was singing it out loud when she hung up the phone for the second time that morning. Today she was looking over the precipice of greed and playing reconciliator to Randy and her mother had not been in the plan. Their last alcoholic fueled brawl over five years before had finally put a nail in the coffin of their tumultuous relationship.

Oy vey! Amelie grabbed her purse from the bottom drawer of her desk. Fishing out a few dollars she sprinted outside to grab her dose of daily calcium—TUMS and a 'pep me up' Starbucks designer drink.

"Making any money today?" the drug peddler asked.

"I make money every day, Tony," she said draining the last drop of her double shot mocha latte. "How about you?"

"I'll be a millionaire soon," he winked.

"Yeah, I know."

Halfway down the cavernous hallway to her office, Amelie realized that the song in her head had changed to 'Dance with My Father Again'. Where that came from, she had no idea. If only she had a father to dance with. She'd dance with her Grandpa, she thought as she made it back to her desk. How she missed him. Amelie retrieved the report she needed for her meeting from the credenza. Rocking backward in her swivel chair, she flipped open the folder to the summary sheet to review the info she needed to know. Mortified that the cheat sheet on Greedham Corp. was not summarized on the front page of the report, her stomach started to churn, the acid lurching and swelling in her belly. Stop this she scolded knowing how much damage this stress was doing to her body. After all, the importance of Greedham's (what's in a name?) Corp. report, which was about robbing yet another billion dollars from unsuspecting clients, was not all that important. Seen it once, seen it a thousand times. Still, Amelie expected exceptional work from Raymond and for the second time in six months, he had not delivered. Amelie threw the report across her desk and felt smoke rising from the top of her head. She hit the intercom. "Raymond, come to my office immediately."

No sooner the handset made a crashing sound on the receiver the door opened.

"Damn it, Raymond," Amelie lit into him with true Wall Street venom, "what the bollocks is this?"

"My daughter had her first recital and I had to get out of here by six yesterday. Everything you need is there I just didn't get to summarize it."

"How many times do I need to tell you, leave the personal whining out of this office? Do you expect me to sit here and read all this shit to get the points? Now take this piece of crap and fix it. You have twenty minutes. A half-ass report like this could lose my clients millions of dollars and the buck stops with me. I can't make any damn excuses like you do, so when you don't do what you're supposed to, I have to go in there and wing it. And I have no bloody wings this morning. Got it? From now on I want the best of the best out of you or you're fired. You have no more lifelines."

Amelie watched as Raymond's naturally open and friendly face became hard as stone. He was angry and no doubt hated being treated as a lackey. "You know Ms. Mercer, I am truly sorry that the report isn't good enough but I'm not prepared to stay here all night when my family needs me. I have a wife and two children who barely see me as it is. I won't sacrifice them for all the money in the world. With that said, I don't think I'm cut out for this kind of pressure cooker and I would like to tender my resignation effective immediately." Raymond left the report on her desk and walked out of her office.

Amelie immediately felt a deep sense of grief. Who was she? Nothing about the person who spoke with such venom was familiar to her. She couldn't have been the woman who just spoke to a grown man as though he was an infant. She, who was a most fragile and congenial person had over the years been morphing into a despicable person. Who was she anyway? Twelve years in the lion's den had kept her too close to evil.

No wonder she'd been feeling rudderless lately. The more she pushed forward to become the barbarian emerging, the more her musical Muse waged a brutal war against the life she was living. Albeit a good one, it was not her authentic life. Instead of despising Raymond Larimore, Amelie admired the man who had calmly and respectfully left her office. He was a man living on purpose. Amelie rose from the desk and sprinted to the hallway. "Raymond," she called and he turned to look back at her.

"I am sorry," she mouthed. I am so very sorry."

"I know," he said

"What instrument does your daughter play?"

"Piano."

• • •

Picking up the folder on her desk, Amelie headed to her appointment. When she walked through the doors of the American Express Financial Building, hope spluttered, choked and then died.

"Good morning, Mrs. Mercer," the receptionist, a corn-fed cherub-faced beauty greeted her. "Your meeting is in conference room one. I'll show you in and then let Mr. Ward know you've arrived. May I bring you coffee? Tea?"

"I'm fine, thanks," Amelie smiled graciously.

The receptionist closed the door and left.

"Ms. Mercer." Amelie turned in the direction of a baritone voice coming from across the room. A brown-skinned man with a confident swagger approached her.

"Mr. Ward," Amelie moved forward to meet him, hand outstretched. He was about six-feet, thin, and well dressed. Horn-rimmed half-glasses were perched on a sharp, flared nose. "Cecil sends his regards," Amelie said, nodding to the young woman standing behind John Ward.

John smiled. "He called earlier. Said he sent his right and left arm to handle this job and that you're a real team player. That's a compliment coming from Cecil. I must admit it's an honor for me," he clenched her hand in a bone-crushing handshake. "Never thought I'd say this but I do prefer to deal with women who have climbed the corporate ladder. You tend to understand the drill and the game much better than we do."

Yep. As long as knickers fly over couches. Amelie shifted from one leg to the other forcing back a rising grin and trying to quiet her muse. John leaned in to whisper in her ear. "I must admit, a woman CFO intimidates me. And a black woman at that," he finished smiling conspiratorially.

"Relax, Mr. Ward," Amelie reassured him. "Corporate America filed down my fangs a long time ago."

"I know what you mean," he said, a resigned tone creeping into his voice. He eyed Amelie closely noticing that they were practically the same height. She smelled like roses and citrus and she had the most amazing eyes, light brown, flecked with green. She was quite beautiful. Not the obvious kind of beauty so prevalent in New York but a subtle allure he couldn't quite put his finger on. Her soft-spoken demeanor was intriguing in an industry where most upper-level women execs were armored under blue and gray double-breasted suits with hard faces. Amelie Mercer was a corporate anomaly, a woman of significant power and alluring femininity. She was not what he'd expected. "Well then," John said after a moment, "let's get down to business." He beckoned the woman behind him closer. "This is Judy Smalls. After we've reached an agreement Judy will draw up the papers." When he turned to Judy, she beamed. "I'll buzz for you after the meeting," John said dismissing her.

Amelie sat at the small, round conference room table as John took his position in front of an erasable board. He picked up a blue marker and began jotting down numbers. Amelie watched him surreptitiously from under her long lashes. He was well attired. The whiteness of his shirt rivaled hers and his cufflinks sparkled like agates. John's words were carefully chosen and spoken with deliberate modulation. The inflection at the end of each sentence, the tremor in his baritone voice, and the force with which he delivered his opening had a preacher's eloquence. "Cecil and I have come to an arrangement. I give you this deal and Waltman and Sachi donates 5% of the contract's value to a charity I head for underprivileged children. The deal," he pointed to the breakdown on the board, "is worth one hundred million a year. Half a billion over five years and would help to bring money to underprivileged communities." His rousing speech was meant to inspire compassion but Amelie quickly saw through the scheme, a simple kickback. She knew from her many years in business that those poor children would never see a penny of that money.

Disappointment, not only in John Ward but also in her boss Cecil, overwhelmed her. What a way to end a morning that had started out with such promise. Amelie tuned out John's speech; she'd heard variations of it for many years. Staring out the window at the passing clouds Amelie slipped further and further into herself until all she could hear was the rhythmic rise and fall of her own breath until her muse found her.

I told you this world was filled with crummy people. Rocking backward in the gray chair, Amelie forced herself to focus on the meeting. Annoyed as she was with her muses' poor timing, she couldn't help but smile at her irreverence. Encouraged by her smile, John continued.

"What I'm proposing is that Waltman & Sachi sign a contract with us for five years, renewable for another five, if all goes well. That could be a lucrative deal for us both, don't you think?" John paused, waiting for Amelie's reaction. When she didn't respond, he continued. "Cecil and I go back a long way. Since our days at Harvard."

Double talk nothing but double talk. Her muse interrupted. Amelie shooed away her muse, frowning.

"Something you don't like?" John asked noting the displeased look on her face.

Go on. Tell the crook what you really feel. He's a crook, don't deny it. Admit it, Amelie, we had better times when we played music. You know there has to be more to life than this. Amelie sat up trying to concentrate. Her head was starting to pound. It felt like there was no air in the room. Amelie was trying hard just to breathe normally as the walls closed in on her. She began an inaudible humming to compete with the noises in her head.

*Someday, when it awfully cold…*Water splashing into a glass brought Amelie back to herself. She blinked and shook her head fixing her gaze on John Ward, pouring himself a glass of water from the jug. John took a sip then looked inquiringly at Amelie.

"If, Ms. Mercer, you are on board with the rules of engagement we can conclude our deal within the week."

Amelie forced herself to smile.

"I think we are going to get along just fine," John said, placing his glass on the table, a grin on his face.

Her pesky muse, welcomed this time, screamed in her head. *Get the hell outta here.* In complete agreement, Amelie pushed back her chair but before she could stand, John was next to her chair.

"Do we have a deal?" He extended his hand toward her.

Amelie stood up and looked into his eyes.

Under her stare, Ward's smile turned uncertain. He reached for her hand, enclosing it in both of his, "I look forward to our alliance."

At this moment Amelie was being initiated into the secret organization of business overlords. A rite of passage for those deemed worthy. As part of the ritual, one was allowed to see, the extreme edge of success. Some were allowed to enter this world of immorality, shady deals, denial, gross excess, and greed. Standing before her was someone she did not want to become—another mercenary whose only allegiance was to the "Benjamins." The power of dead presidents! "Mr. Ward," Amelie said, her hand now balled into a fist at her side, and her shoulders squared. "I'm going to do something I'd never considered doing before today." Amelie saw satisfaction in John's eyes. "I'm going to give you a chance to redeem yourself."

"What do you mean, Ms. Mercer? Is the contract not big enough? Or is my percentage too low?"

"What I mean, Mr. Ward is that what you're suggesting is not only morally wrong but also illegal. I'd like to give you a chance to retract it. For your sake, Cecil's and mine and for the innocent people about to be screwed, I'll pretend I didn't hear it."

John took a step back in surprise. "My sister," he said, his tone changing. "Let me give you a piece of wisdom. Corporate America is not for those who believe that best practices and best prices are the roads to success. You'll never win if you're the only one in the room with integrity. Do you know what it feels like to always be on the outside looking in?" John's face turned ugly. "I got my Harvard MBA in 1956. Do you understand what I'm saying? It means

I'm good. No, I'm beyond good. But you know what I've found out after forty years in Corporate America, Ms. Mercer. No amount of astuteness, determination, ambition, education, networking or hard work will deliver what I'm offering your company. The only way to sidestep the corporate bureaucracy of making every top-notch minority senior executive a Purchasing Director, Minority Coordinator or Community Affairs Vice President is to use the power of one's position to play the game. I have the power to deliver this deal. With a five-year exclusive contract, your company and you will grow in leaps and bounds, and I will have the freedom to not pine over that fact that even though I am most qualified that I will never make it to the Presidency of Greedham. You scratch my back…."

"Please." Amelie held up her hand stopping him in mid-sentence. She couldn't abide another platitude. "I know Corporate America is no child's play for us, but what you're implying, besides being dishonest can never be a win-win situation. You see, John, what you're offering is disgrace and dishonesty at too high a price for our people."

"Look, sister, everyone does it. I mean everyone. How'd you think CEO's afford those big houses on the hill? Kenneth Lay? WorldCom? Why shouldn't we get ours?"

"My brother," Amelie returned the ethnic solidarity, "kickbacks are not my style. I believe in cultural responsibility and because I take it very seriously, I must decline your offer."

"Did Cecil know this would be your stance?"

Amelie didn't answer, instead, shaking her head at yet another corporate predator with no real power and worse and even well-dressed, no style. Gathering her purse and briefcase, she went to the door. Why didn't John see that the endpoint of this game was that he'd be the fall guy?

John watched the woman walk out of his office. He was disappointed.

• • •

Sad and angry that Cecil Stratford, a man she had respected for twelve years would stoop this low to exploit racial inequity was heart wrenching. Weight of uncertainty sagged Amelie's shoulders as she went into her office and closed the door. She sat at her desk in front of the computer. Her flawless sable-colored skin was ashen. As she sat behind her massive oak desk staring out the window, she yearned for a simpler more cultured life. For the longest while, she stared unseeing at the computer monitor. Today she would give herself permission to enter chambers of her soul long deserted. Schumann's *Fantasie in C major* no longer seemed impossible. Amelie's fingers poised over the keyboard. The blank screen stared back at her. She began to type, slowly at first, and then her fingers moved faster and faster over the keyboard.

Amelie looked at her computer screen. She had typed a letter of resignation from a seven-figure-a-year job, which came with a six-figure expense account, a luxury company car, a driver, a handsome yearly bonus, and a wad of stock options. But none of that mattered anymore. Before she could change her mind, Amelie hit the print button, grabbed the printout, and walked into the CEO's office. "Over and out," she said handing the resignation, still warm from the printer, to Cecil. "Over and out," she repeated watching a look of bewilderment spread across his face. At thirty-eight, an age when one should be rational, Amelie Mercer walked away from conformity. *Roger that*, her musical muse's voice answered. *Roger that.* She, like Raymond, had had enough.

CHAPTER FOUR
Randy

New York, Upper East Side, September 10, 2001

SHE LOVED DAWN. It was like a meditation waking up early and going to her sanctuary. Too bad this morning had been interrupted by Amelie and Lawrence. Dinner indeed! She scoffed. Donning her white turban, Randy stood in front of the mirror to skillfully apply her age-defying make-up. Who, would look back at her this morning she wondered? The chic East Side maven; the angry, lonely wife; the frustrated mother; the playful eight-year-old; the sad, broken little girl of thirteen?

Frantically wiping the steam-covered mirror with a backhand, Randy examined the tragic figure morphing into a forty-five-year-old woman who could no longer deny that genetic markers were marching into position. Her worn canvas, mildly creased with crinkles and spider lines around the eyes, winked at the breasts and stomach muscles giving into gravity, forming their own designs below her waist. Surrendering, as they say, to the inevitable rhythm of time, Randy tipped the glass to her lips and took a generous swig of vodka, smacking her lips as the heat spread through her body. A thump on the door made her move quickly to stash her contraband.

"Ms. Austin." It was Mensa, her housekeeper, nanny, friend, mummy, family matriarch and the only person she trusted in the world. Randy opened the door. Mensa's look is cross when she sees the glass. No point telling her its gargling water.

"I need to get going with the shopping if we're to have any dinner tonight."

Randy padded away from the door, her feet making a squishy noise against the tile. "Never mind all that today. We're doing nothing elaborate. Order in and call it a day. I'll go shopping with Richard for dessert."

"Mr. Austin won't…."

Randy cut her off. "Really Mensa, does anyone care what Mr. Austin wants. Now go along and get the house ready." Randy shooed her away. "I feel like Mango ice cream. How about you? That will be our contribution to dinner. Where is that greengrocer in midtown you told me about? The one with the best mangoes you always get?"

Mensa again looked disapprovingly at the glass in her hand. "Richard knows," she said ambling back toward the stairs. As a middle child, Mensa knew how to keep her tongue-in-cheek but that didn't stop her lighting a candle for her boss's soul. The woman was lost and unhappy in this life like someone had cursed her at birth.

• • •

Two-hours later, the black town car pulled up to the curb at 55th and Eighth. Croc-saddlebag slung across her torso, Randy Austin slid from her car and hurried into a corner store for a rare visit. Exquisite with an updated flip and head-to-toe designer garb, one could easily imagine she lived a life devoted to shopping, travel, tennis, and the occasional charity work. What one could never imagine was the solitude, distress, and torment below the surface of such elegance and that today was just another day in a life she dreamed of escaping. Removing her sunglasses, eyes that changed from light to dark-brown with the angle of the sun scanned the room. Randy strolled through the fruit stalls poking at mangoes which were rumored to be the best in the city. Nothing like the mangoes from Jamaica but better than most.

"No. No. Don't squeeze fruit, Ma'am." The shopkeeper ran over to her. "They delicious. Which one want?" The merchant began removing mangoes from her hand. "Two for three dollars. Today only. Special."

"Stop that," Randy, who hated to be touched, brushed the merchant away.

He stood firm. "No squeeze. No good other customers."

"All right. How much did you say they are?"

"Two for three dolla. Special."

"I'll take five dozen mangoes, those roses, the red ones, and a bunch of the pink," Randy pointed.

"Imported. Nice." The merchant smiled.

Randy handed him her black Amex card.

"No take card, only cash."

"How much," she pulled out her wallet, slid the card back in and checked for cash.

"Thirty dollars."

"Just a minute." She left the store and went to the car. "Richard, they do not take cards," she said disbelief peppering her voice.

"How much do you need?" he reached for his wallet.

"Thirty dollars. I'll pay my debt as soon as we get

home."

"Here you are," she shoved the money grudgingly at the grocer.

When he was finished packing her goods, Randy collected her bags and started to leave the store.

"Thank you, bye. Come again. Give you good service like today."

Randy flashed a perfunctory smile.

• • •

"I'm going to walk home Richard," Randy said, surprising her chauffeur, handing him the bags. Usually petrified, in a there but for the grace of God way, of coming within ten feet of alcoholics, addicts, and beggars with their sunken cheeks and far away eyes, Randy needed to clear her head, as only a walk through the park could.

"I don't think that's a good idea, Mrs. Austin," Richard tried to protest. God forbid if someone spat in front of her or blew their nose trajectory style as though throwing a javelin in the Olympics.

"Stop fussing. Give these to Mensa. We're having mango ice-cream for tonight."

"Yes, Mrs. Austin."

Randy headed down Eighth Avenue toward Columbus Circle. She loved the energy of Midtown. As she rounded the corner at 61st, headed for the park, the distinct smell of curry from Sapphire Bombay Indian restaurant again transported her to that place with buried memories. The rising need to resolve her unspeakable memories seemed pressing this morning. The universe it seemed had been conspiring for her to finally face her truth. Randy had smelled curry a million times in a city dotted with ethnic restaurants but today the odor stopped her dead in her tracks and for the first time in twenty-nine years she allowed herself to be transported back to the dreaded Sunday dinners in London where she had to sit across from her idiotic Uncle Joe. Until her ill-fated day, she'd liked her Uncle Joe.

Randy, a sullen but relatively happy child had never experienced the overwhelming sadness that had sent her to bed for weeks, brought scores of doctors to her bedside, and made her mother and sisters frantic and devoted. Uncle Joe's betrayal had taken away her childhood innocence, sending her spiraling downward to a place of suffering beyond comprehension. Randy had never permitted herself to think or speak of that dark moment that was best buried deep within. For years, she'd blamed herself for Uncle Joe's unwitting indiscretion and still to this day, had told no one of her defilement.

"What can I do to make you feel better?" Her mother had often pleaded, when Randy napped a lot, would not eat and at times was found nicking herself with a dull blade.

"You should have thought of that before you uprooted us and took us halfway around the world," Randy would scoff.

Imagined or real Randy's pain had cast long shadows and daily uncertainties over her family. When would she try to run away again…go into month-long depressions…hack at her wrists…disappear from school or drink too much? For Randy, the chaos had not been disruptions, just survival…an indifference to life that in fact, saved her life. Now too many years of surviving had morphed into a life with nothing but responsibility, rituals, and routines. Randy crossed the circle and entered the park. Her sadness, bordering on despair was suffocating. When would she leave, if not now? At that moment Randy desperately wanted to flee; maybe to Jamaica; to a little cottage on the beach with the beautiful rainbow, cascading waterfall and soft sand she so often daydreamed about. But an Italian villa ensconced between miles and miles of sweet, plump, purple grapes wouldn't be bad either. Or, she mused, perhaps Spain or Paris. She could probably get a job at the Prado or the Louvre. After all, she was an Art History major. A road trip across America, though less appealing, was not out of reach of her escape plans. A jarring ring interrupted her fantasy escape. "Hello," Randy said into the ringing phone she dug out of her bag.

Randy's life, which should have held such promise, had been standing in the same place of desperation, still very much the little girl from Leicester whose life so long ago, had irrevocably changed in only one moment. She was glad for the distraction.

CHAPTER FIVE
Ashley

Philadelphia, 5th and Market Street, September 10, 2001

"THERE YOU ARE," Ashley said pushing the speaker button on her steering wheel. No answer. "Okay, I'm sorry," she purred into the phone.

Randy was not pleased to hear her sister's voice. She stopped walking, her body assuming a defensive stance. "Why is everyone calling me today. No. I'm not going to dinner with mother and I expected you for lunch Wednesday and not a word from you," she said dryly.

"Didn't my secretary call? I asked her to. Last minute gig came up in South Beach. Fabulous that place. We'll have to go, just us girls."

"Since when do secretaries call sisters? They call wives." Randy's voice was edged with ice.

Ashley decided on another approach. "Guilty as charged. I'm so sorry darling. What's doing these days?"

"Right now, I'm walking home from the fruit stall. I was buying fruit."

"You were doing what? Did you say buying fruit?"

"That's right. Mangoes to be exact. Mensa is making homemade ice cream for Lawrence's confounded dinner party tonight. What can I do for you Ashley?"

"I'm so sorry about having canceled."

"Ashley, you didn't cancel; you just didn't bother to show up."

"Right. Hold on a minute, honey." The phone went silent.

Randy looked around for a bench. With none in sight, she decided to continue walking.

"I'm back. Randy?"

"I'm still here. You know it's illegal to talk and drive."

"Hand-free equipment on board," Ashley said. "Now, where was I? Ah, yes. I've rescheduled a New York appointment for next week, so will you please, pretty please, have lunch with me?" she begged.

"Ashley, when are you going to stop hustling people? For Pete's sake, I'm your sister. Out with it! What, do you really want?"

"All right, all right, I confess. I'm interviewing Isabelle Rosenthal and I happen to know you two are friends. Do you have any scoop, off the record that is? My source was really a dud."

"First of all, I don't have friends and second, how dare you?" Randy said icily. "After what you did the last time I confided in you, never again. From now on I'm sworn to secrecy."

"Secrets, my darling sister, are overrated."

"You'd better think again, missy. What so ardently escapes you and your fellow media propagandist is that secrets are a vital part of psychic health," Randy said, her voice rising an octave. "Fine, secrets are good," Ashley said in a calming voice. She'd sure as hell didn't want to push

Randy over the "edge." The truth was Randy had been over the edge for a long time but no one ever spoke about it.

"No, Ashley. Really! You should think about their importance before you go dissecting peoples' lives on national TV," Randy squeaked. "Facing truths can be complicated and sometimes keeping them as secrets can be good. Exposing secrets threatens the very existence of humanity. Secrets can become the structure on which lives are built. Seems you of all people should know this! Didn't you major in psychology?"

Not only had Ashley double majored in psychology and journalism, she had a secret that she and Amelie had kept for years. What she knew for sure was that secrets rot out the insides, hollowing out feelings and one's very soul.

"What's more," Randy rambled on, snapping Ashley out of her reverie, "Don't you know that some of the sweetest things in life come from hoarding secrets?"

"Can't go there right now Randy," Ashley said.

"Honey, for instance," Randy continued, ignoring her sister, "Bees always make their honey in secret. But isn't the end product a delight?"

"Please, Randy, no tangents today. Will you or will you not help me out here?"

"How about the preservation of culture and the knowledge kept safe in secret societies? The Rosicrucian's, the Bards, the Druids? The very habits we live by today had to have been kept secret for them to live. Or the secret love of Lancelot and Guinevere? Can you imagine a childhood without Lancelot and Guinevere?"

Oh, for heaven sake here goes loopy again. "Look, Randy, I've got to go. Hot date tonight. Philly's looking up," Ashley interrupted, "Are you sure you're okay? Is everything all right with Lawrence? June?" Randy was getting more and more into her histrionics and, just for an instant, Ashley resented her for the years she'd kept them hostage to her pain. How clearly, she remembered the day when Randy first, as they often termed it, lost her marbles.

• • •

"Mother, Mother," eleven-year-old Ashley had bolted into her mother's bedroom. It was a well-known fact that when their mother was in her room, behind closed doors, that the children were not to enter…but she had been scared…really scared.

"This had better be good." Her mother's voice had been muffled and the shock on her face quickly changed as she composed herself and tried to hide whatever it was on her nightstand in the closet.

"Mummy! It's Randy. She's in the loo and she won't come out. She's been in there since we got back from the playground and she won't let me in. I've got to pee badly."

"Oh, bloody hell," Emily, tired of her teenage daughter's histrionics stormed down the hall. "Randy you come out here at once!" She banged on the door.

Silence.

"Randy, you selfish little brat. Come out of that bathroom now!"

"Selfish," Randy sobbed. "You are the one who's selfish and you are not to be trusted. You can't even protect your own children. What kind of mother are you?"

"Open this bloody door right now or I'll break it down." Emily's voice was shrill. This was the kind of melee that made her want to take a drink.

"Then break it down, I don't care. I just want to die anyway," Randy lashed out at her mother. "Why did you bring us to this country? Daddy would have protected us from this strange place. Where is my Daddy? He would have protected us but you…you," the voice was pained "took us away from Daddy."

"Randy, what has gotten into you?" Emily demanded. Adolescence angst and hormonal instability she was sure but Emily knew it to be more than that. And she was to blame but right now she didn't have the energy for that thought. Adolescence was a time when a girl needed a father and it didn't help that she'd just been sacked by her second husband and was all alone again with her girls. It wasn't as though she didn't need love, she just never found another Bunny.

"I hate you. Go away. "Randy was becoming hysterical. "Go away. I wish you were dead."

Emily wavered on her feet. She didn't quite know what to do. "Ashley tell your grandfather to get the spare key for this bathroom. He'll know what to do."

When the key finally arrived and the door was flung open Randy was hovered in the corner, covered in vomit, naked, big tears and snot rolling down her face.

"What's wrong?" Emily's tone had softened at the sight of her daughter. "Is it your period? Honey, it's okay. All women…"

"Don't you dare touch me." Randy was furious.

"You ungrateful wench. After all, I've done for you. What I did was to protect us all. How dare you?" Emily raised her hand but stopped short of slapping her daughter across the face. By now the hallway was packed with the entire household. Ashley grabbed a towel and covered her sister who was shaking, her small body racked with tears.

After that day, there were many drag-down arguments between Emily and Randy. Ashley would flee to the park and Amelie would take refuge in their grandfather's room. When their mother had remarried two years later, for the third time, and again moved them across the ocean this time to America in the hopes of bringing stability to her girls, Randy's bizarre behaviors escalated and her relationship with Emily fractured in more places than Ashley cared to think about at the moment. Ashley had missed her sister's silly songs, which after that day was replaced by the total silence that came to be known as Randy's "spells."

What she did know for sure was that Randy coped the same way their mother did. They drank. Behind their impeccable dress and charming smiles was a liquid strength, Johnny Walker Black for her mother and expensive vodka for her sister.

• • •

"Okay, okay, Ashley relented, "secrets are to be kept secret. And, you're right. I am wasting my life. I know I'm not doing the most important job in the world and to be honest, I hate it but for now, it's what pays the bills but I'm gonna get out of this business, mark my words. I only wish I knew how."

"Just walk away." Randy had returned to her center. "Ash, I'm sorry. I didn't mean to insult you. Who am I to say a thing? I've been trying to walk away from my life for a long time. I was just trying for a meaningful conversation before our vapid, crass, moron guests arrive tonight"

"I take it Amelie and Robb are not invited. I feel your pain. At least Robb would add some joy. Believe me, I understand your frustration. I don't know how we're all carrying on without meaning in our lives. That's what's stuck in my craw too. I want to do something meaningful."

"Sounds like time for sister's lunch. How about next Wednesday?" Randy said.

"Yep, Wednesday. You pick the place. I'll call Tuesday. Will you call Amelie, or shall I?"

"I will."

Where her sister Randy was bonkers, Amelie was gifted. A classical pianist turned Wall Street baller. Ashley, being the middle child, had no real talent for the drama of Randy, nor had she the musical genius and affable nature of Amelie. And though she was the one with the extraordinary beauty it hadn't gotten her anywhere. It certainly wasn't enough to hold on to that prick Frederick or to get her out of the hellhole of Philly.

"Sounds like a plan. Now, Randy, how about Isabel Rosenthal?"

The phone went dead.

CHAPTER SIX
Randy

New York, September 10, 2001, 2:00 p.m.

RANDY HUNG UP the phone readier than ever to do a disappearing act. Ashley was insufferable at times. Waiting for the light at 61thStreet to change, she was lost in thought. Africa, Tibet, India. Now there was a real escape plan.

"Well, well, well, Randy Austin, walking! What's the world coming to?" Sheila Branford, her colorful neighbor sidled up. Sporting an orange silk scarf tightly wrapped around her neck she proffered, "Singing tonight. What are you doing out and about in this neighborhood?"

"Buying mangoes. Mensa says that greengrocer on 55th has the best mangoes in the city so I got some. I'm hosting another of Lawrence's dreadful dinner party tonight!" Randy sighed, pleased as always to see Sheila.

"Hmm," Sheila smiled, "You'll get through it as usual."

"Why don't you stop by after your performance? We'll just be getting started, I'm sure." Sheila shook her head. "Now, now, missy, you've got to watch those thoughts. Thoughts are powerful communicators."

"What thoughts?"

"The ones that wish Lawrence to have a coronary when he sees me."

"Sheila!"

"Forget it. You know Lawrence hates my guts. He thinks I'm… what are the words?"

"Strange, archaic, loony Diva," Randy prattled. "But that's what makes it all the more fun. Torture by friendship. Come on, let's have some fun with the suits tonight. Please come and save me," Randy pleaded.

"And Adrienne?"

"Bring her too," Randy smiled.

"We'll see what later brings. Got to scadoodle. On my way to rehearsals," Sheila said leaving behind a plume of breeze and the lingering smell of the musty fragrance Datura Noir.

• • •

"Mensa, I'm home." Randy poked her head out the living room window to look at the clock over the Slater building. Two-forty-five. She used to be able to see the towering clock from her bedroom window without craning her neck but now the glass edifice under construction threatened to obscure her view.

"Mensa," she called again heading for the kitchen, reluctance nagging at her steps. Until this new crop of young investors, she would never have considered leaving one of her famous dinner parties to chance. But now her most pleasurable task of supervising grand dinners of seafood brochette, succulent lobster knuckles, creamy corn with sugar snap peas and scallions, grilled marinated veal and lamb chops with balsamic and cherry tomatoes and the chocolate soufflé, would be wasted on unsophisticated barons. This new money group didn't require personally signed Gallagher's invitations but could instead be invited by telephone. Why she didn't serve chips, salsa, guacamole, and mojitos and call it a day was what baffled her.

Mensa was examining table linen.

"How many of these people are coming here?" Randy asked in disgust.

"Eight," Mensa answered, "Mr. Austin called for you."

"What did he want?"

"To let you know the number of people coming for dinner and to find out if you needed anything else."

"Huh," Randy said spinning on her heels. At the bar, she made a Vodka and Tonic and climbed the stairs to her sanctuary.

Mensa never said a word.

• • •

Eight o'clock came too quickly. Eight couples invaded the Austin's Fifth Avenue, Beaux-Arts style mansion, that overlooked the MET. Warm and welcoming to guests, the Austin's home with its massive circular staircase was impossible to enter without being awed. The living room was dotted with English sofas covered in Macondo Silks and flanked by chairs upholstered in warm Busatti textiles. A chintz-covered dining room set overhung with a Floridian Papp Candelabrum was exquisitely appointed. Priceless paintings covered much of the cream-colored walls but most breathtaking was the simple, gold marble fireplace crowned by a riot of flowers. As they took their seats, Randy observed the flavorless, overdressed jet set more closely. After three vodka and tonics, she found it hard to pay attention to much.

Pulsing his wife's displeasure from the way her eyes traveled past a speaker to a spot just above their head,

Lawrence, without uttering a word, communicated her need to be more graciousness. Randy plastered a smile on her face.

"Who's that new woman from Wharton? What's her name?" Lawrence asked.

"Julia Goldstein. A true barracuda," Sydney answered picking food from his teeth.

"Now there's a ball buster if I've ever seen one. The chick is made of pure steel. Made a mint on the Cartel deal," Craig interjected.

"That tops us old folks for sure. A girl at that," Lawrence laughed.

That was Lawrence's opinion of women, especially wives; little more than cosmetic essentials for successful men. Lawrence raised his glass in Randy's direction.

The night progressed far too slowly. Nothing, not the exquisite dinner or the beautiful Strauss could add spice to a dull evening where every conversation was about money. Randy turned to the cat eyed woman next to her. "How could educated people find such a narrow and vulgar topic interesting for hours on end?" she lamented. The woman looked at her and her feline eyes blinked in awe. "Oh," Randy said, "I suppose you have the yacht in Palm Springs, the house in the Hamptons, the little cabin in Bermuda right on the water huh? Sorry."

Randy shivered. She had nothing in common with these people.

"The flowers are beautifully arranged," said another purring woman to Randy's left who looked even more tightened and scary. With her long fingers and bright red painted nails, she could have been the scary witch of the west.

"Thank you. I did them myself. A hobby," Randy smiled with as much grace as she could manage.

"This is such a lovely party. You have an amazing home. And Lawrence is such a dear."

"That he is," Randy's voice was becoming shrill. "Will you excuse me a moment," she smiled, desperate to get away. In the kitchen, Randy mixed another vodka and tonic. She opened the freezer, filled her glass with ice and then added another flask of vodka. Damn, Sheila, she thought looking with disgust at the kitsch monstrosity that Lawrence had bought in Italy. It said eleven-ten. Randy unwrapped a Rocher from its gold foil and popped the chocolate into her mouth. Around the house, bowls of the stuff were stashed in secret hideaways right next to her "coping" tonic. Not that they mixed well at all.

"Are you all right?"

"Why do you ask? Don't I seem fine?" she answered coming back to the present.

"You seem a bit edgy. Maybe you should switch drinks." He was eying the glass in her hand disapprovingly and with exasperation. "What are you doing in here anyway?"

"Making coffee."

"Where is Mensa?" He looked around for their housekeeper.

"Getting more wine from downstairs."

"Let her make the coffee when she returns. Come back to the party. The conversation stalls without your brilliant contribution, my love," Lawrence said, as he kissed her cheek. Words stuck in Randy's throat. Why couldn't she tell him that she needed to be rid of him so she could claim what little useful time she had left for herself? She felt trapped, albeit in a gilded cage.

The doorbell rang.

"Who could that be?" Lawrence looked puzzled.

"Sheila and company," Randy said moving out of his arms.

"Damn it, Randy, didn't I tell you to get rid of those women? You know I don't like them."

Randy leveled him an icy gaze. "I'm now to be told who I can invite to my own home!"

"Randy! They are so…so theatrical and full of drama."

"As they should be." Randy swept pass him. Lawrence overestimated her patience with him. Words hurt her throat more than ever but, again, she swallowed them. She opened the door. "Sheila. I thought you'd never come." Randy threw her arms open and smiled for the first time that evening. "Hi Adrienne," she said, her eyes straying to the women next to Adrianne, "and who is this?"

"This is Adele. She came to my performance tonight and I didn't think you'd mind if I brought her along," Sheila said.

"Mind? My dear, never. The more the merrier," Randy winked, observing Adele, whose mass of curly hair spilled from a topknot in a messy array. The girl seemed oblivious to protocol and seemed quite comfortable in her Bohemian disarray even on the East side.

"Come in, let's go say hello to the pretty people," Randy drawled. She was feeling quite light headed by now…how much vodka…she mentally counted…three maybe four…

There was no reason at all for these women to be friends. Sheila, a robust Broadway Diva was dramatic and unpredictable. Adrienne, rail thin and blind to the fact that she was not gentry, complained constantly about the insufferable East Side women she so desperately wanted to be. Sheila and Adrianne were the only 'real' people in the Kaufman cancer society volunteer group of mostly upper-crust New York wives. And worse, they were the only single women in the group. Singledom was a rarity, if not an albatross around an East Side woman's neck who, if unfortunate enough to be divorced, was actively looking for the next MIT (Mogul in Training).

Lawrence, mortified at the flourish with which the women entered the parlor, saw to it that the party ended soon after their arrival. For Randy, the party had only just begun and she invited Sheila and her friends to stay on.

Sheila poured herself a glass of wine, floated over to the sofa and when settled in removed the ever-present scarf from her neck.

"Weren't those women a little overdressed for a dinner party?" Adrienne prickled.

"Shamelessly so."

"The class-challenged always are," Adrienne said. "No matter how close they get to wealth, there's always something that gives them away. Take Camille Redstone, for instance. It has to be her middle-class upbringing why she has hair cascading down her back. It's uncomely for a woman over fifty to have hair longer than shoulder length. I think it's in bad taste."

Randy poured herself a drink and thought Adrienne's comment scathing but understood.

Adele, who had recently met the women, sat observing the mismatched motley crew. She quickly summed them up. Randy, a classy woman wound so tight that she could be on the brink of a breakdown, Adrienne, an evil hater who would give anything to be a blue blood and Sheila, simply a cherub-filled with mirth.

"Eastside women, an uninteresting topic don't you think?" Adele smiled.

"No, darling. The one thing you can't say about snobs is that they are uninteresting. Exciting people, though I admit, loathsome, are actually fun to watch and very, very entertaining," Sheila sipped her wine, opined.

"I suppose. You have a great eye, Mrs. Austin. I love your art collection. It's superb" Adele said, nailing shut the gossip. "Mrs. Austin…"

"Do I look so ancient? Please call me Randy," she said averting her eyes. French people had no problem staring openly at others but the eyes that held hers made Randy uncomfortable.

"You are an avid collector, no?"

"They are my pride and joy. I probably shouldn't admit this," Randy giggled, "especially since I was an Art History major, but I have no pretense about art. I buy what I like, not what has resale value. I love finding the 'next good artist' and enjoy *L'arte pour l'arte.*"

"Ah, *oui.* A fan of the Aesthetic Movement."

"If that means I'm not big on tradition, then yes."

"Then a bourgeoisie?"

"Just a pretend one," Randy laughed. She hadn't felt so natural in years.

"Good. I don't like bourgeoisie but I think I would like you even if you were one."

Something in Adele's voice made Randy look up. She was smiling over the rim of her wineglass, her eyes dancing with mischief. She'd succeeded in averting the conversation from vapidity to intellectual.

"Don't say that too soon. I'm known to be a little wacky. Ask Sheila." Randy smiled.

"Ready to drive off a cliff wacky," Sheila raised her glass. "We love wacky."

"We are women of the arts…crazy don't scare us!" Adrianne's eyes danced with laughter.

Adele, Randy later found out, was a French painter of distinction.

CHAPTER SEVEN
Amelie

Connecticut, September 11, 2001, 5:00 a.m.

HEY, CHICKADEE. How's life this morning? It feels good to listen to yourself, doesn't it? I've been telling you for months to heed the call of destiny. It's been far too long since we've had fun. Her musical muse piped in. *Remember that night at Carnegie? We can do it again…this time no memory slip…I promise.*

'Go to hell.' Amelie sighed. That nag had woken her again. Along with him came the thunder that rolled around in her head until it had split her into two. Enters muse number two, the no no-nonsense take all prisoners tyrant. *'Get your arse up, Missy…we got work to do. You owe someone an apology. After yesterday's meltdown, you're gonna have to shape up.*

How could she face another day at Waltman & Sachi? Amelie was now wide awake, lying in the darkness looking up at the ceiling, her body tense. She covered her ears with both hands as though the racket in her head was coming from the outside. Sometimes she swore she was going crazy, schizoid even. The good thought was that she didn't have to face a day at Waltman because she'd quit.

Amelie eased out of bed, careful not to wake her husband Robb. The Persian silk rug caressed her feet as she tip-toed to the walk-in closet and slipped into a fleece robe. Skipping down the stairs two at a time she felt a surge of hope and clarity. Raymond's resignation and now her own had given her courage. For someone living with muscles tense for months, hope was welcomed and clarity was needed. Pushing open the built-in roller cabinet, meant to keep-stuff-out of her sight, Amelie plugged in the pot and brewed coffee. Mug in hand, she crossed the length of the music room, ran a hand over her cherished mahogany piano, and exited the sliding door that led to the garden she was proud to have planted herself.

The stillness of predawn was palpable. She stood silently looking eastward as street lamps faded to black and the sun, lethargic and solemn, was barely creaping through clouds. Careful not to disturb the tranquil dawn, she stepped gently onto the freshly cut lawn, deeply filling her lungs with dew-laden air. Somewhere in the distance, a lone car sped by, the sound dying away as it moved further and further, returning the morning to serenity.

The vestige of hope hanging in the air surged. Though a minor resolve in her fissured life, this unexplained hope implied a moment of peace from muses rubbing against each other like flint. As resolute as the hard-charging demon of business, was the tyrannical musical four-year-old whose demands were becoming increasingly relentless. One or the other had to be freed. Reprieve in sight, Amelie negotiated a cease-fire. Why she asked them, did she have to choose one life over the other? Why not both? Couldn't feelings of destiny and purpose accompany duty and responsibility?

With her muses in deliberation, Amelie stood a moment longer to soak in the beauty of fall. Her eyes followed the early morning mist settled on creeping ivies that hugged the chimney of her Victorian house. She loved this house. She just didn't love her life. Throughout the garden, small, cobalt flower buds peeped around low shrubbery and Jacobs's ladder climbed fences. The garden's perimeter was dotted with yellow and red tulip bulbs, the last for the season cautiously pushing up from the earth while above, little brown and jonquil-speckled birds flittered from tree to tree, singing their refrain. The birds, all on cue, had stopped their melodious tunes, taking off for new heights in nearby treetops. There was nothing more uplifting than the dawn of a new day.

Out of habit, Amelie had clipped her cell onto the sash of her robe and the machine on her hip began vibrating. Amelie looked at the number…her driver? He'd be picking her up in forty-five minutes. What the heck? Amelie hit the call back button. "Peter, there is no need for you to be here today. I've left Waltman…didn't Cecil tell you?"

"No, he actually called and told me to make sure I was on time."

"Well call him back. Tell him I quit." Amelie hit the end call button and threw the work cell phone into a kitchen drawer. That man was too cocksure of her. Well, he was wrong this time. Amelie sucked air through her teeth and headed back to the music room. She lifted the mahogany lid and played a fast arpeggio. Beautiful. She could hear her Grandfather's voice. A smile dotted her face as she tried to remember the little girl in the blue polka dot dress playing her first concert for the parents and students of Leicester Preparatory. She had loved it! She'd been three years old when she began playing the piano. Her grandfather, who she'd adored more than anyone else in the world had convinced her that she was musically gifted. He had taken her talent seriously and began teaching her the piano. Amelie closed her eyes and thought of her Grandpa, as she always did in times of uncertainty. His gravelly voice floated into her head.

"Your mother used to so be much fun. So alive and spirited. Drove her mother crazy." He'd say. "I don't know when all the spunk seeped out of her but life has a way of doing that. Let you and I get it back for us all through the music." Her Grandpa's had said the very same words so many times, she honestly believed music would bring joy to her mother. So, she had worked hard at the music because she wanted to see her mother happy. By five, Amelie, a budding prodigy was spending hours playing the piano. At seven, she had her first teacher to the distress of her mother. When she'd entered school in her new country of America, Emily forbade her from spending so much time at the piano. "This is a new country, honey. You need to pay more attention to your schoolwork. In this country everyone is bright," her mother told her. But Amelie played on. Her Grandpa had unleashed in her the love of music and at a young age, she was addicted to the rush of adrenaline that came with it. Amelie played on still for her mother's happiness but now more so for her joy. Leaving her Grandpa to placate her mother's angst, she lived for the music.

By the age of twelve, Amelie had been transformed. For her, making beautiful, soul-inspiring music had opened the doors to the universe she loved. *Four Seasons*, Vivaldi. She played them over and over until she'd captured their beauty and radiance. At thirteen, she'd mastered *Canon in D. Moonlight Sonata, Appassionata*, and at fourteen, Beethoven's *Cavatina.* Amelie adored her music lessons; her time of private conversation with the universe. The universe, which understood all things, including things her mother never could. The keeper of her feelings. Yes, music had been the friend she needed when her mother moved them from their beloved England to America. For Amelie, music had a way of reaching deep within her, mixing all tongues into one universal language, articulating inner thoughts and feelings that were otherwise ineffable. Her friend Music spoke a language beyond time and like her Grandpa she had come to know and converse with Bach, Liszt, Ravel and her dearest friend, Beethoven leaving behind the reality of her chaotic childhood.

At fifteen, music had saved her life once again, for it was then that expert fingers had played away the sorrow of her first lost love. The music lessened the misery of Ronald Studmire leaving her for Anne Strathmore. Chopin, Debussy, Mozart, and Rachmaninoff had been her loves that year. At sixteen when she had met Robb, she had gone home and played *Claire de Lune.* At nineteen, William's arrival, Amelie played *Prelude in G Minor* and at twenty when her beloved Grandpapa passed away, Beethoven's *March of the Dead* wailed, helping her pay tribute to the one person who had nurtured her talent and for whom she wanted his dream to live on. She played on. Music continued to soothe her distractions, heartaches, and disappointments and even now as she played, the noose of Wall Street fell away.

It was after her Grandpa left, that she began hearing her muses… the beginning of echoes of those who could never understand her choices. Without her grandpapa to encourage her too, opinions that used to pale in comparison to her musical muse had begun to seep in and take control of her mind. "What do you expect to do with this music?" Emily's words had worn her resolve away like water against stone. "You'd best think about getting a real job, Amelie," her mother had declared when she'd dreamed of graduate study in the classics. "Can you support yourself and that family of yours on music?"

"But Mummy," Amelie had reached out for her mother's hand, "Joseph Campbell says…"

"I couldn't care less about Mr. Campbell or his soup." Her mother had shrugged loose. "He can say anything he wants. He is rich. Got rich off tomato soup. Can you imagine?" She had said pushing her gently away as though Amelie's closeness threatened her sanity. Yet, Amelie had noticed something…a yearning lurking behind her mother's very careful mask.

She'd never bothered to tell her mother, that the Joseph Campbell of whom she spoke, was the renowned mythologist on destiny, callings and the essential need for one to follow their bliss. Amelie, tormented by intellectual musical giants, had often thought of running away from home, from her family and into the company of her most trusted friends. There, she'd smooth Paderewski's hair. Examine the joints of Rachmaninoff's hands and gallop off with Ravel. Today she would do just that. Back in the music room, Amelie decided she'd finally arrived at a place where she understood time and purpose. Linear time, past, present, and future all merged into one. All life's lessons dissolved into each other erasing time and space; leaving in its wake only memories—imprints of a past she no longer needed to understand but somehow wanted to. She touched a single key, then another and another and before long she was lost in her true world. A soothing new voice whispered in her ear: *Music my child. You were born with music in you. I've come to take you home if you want to come.* This new voice was that of someone she hadn't heard before and it wrapped around her in beautiful refrain, spinning about her a cocoon where she could dream again. Amelie closed her eyes and listened. Trust yourself. Start again. Go to the coda and start again. Only you and the music. Live my dream. Amelie was dancing on the keys of hope with the resolve that she'd made the right decision. Welcome home, the new voice she didn't recognize said. It was her own.

"I'm going to do it," she said to the wind.

• • •

"Good Morning, sweetheart," her husband Robb said dropping into a chair at the kitchen table.

"You're up early. Coffee?" She tapped the cup in her hand.

"Yep. Feeling better this morning?"

"Hopeful," Amelie said.

"Hopeful about what?" Robb emptied two packets of raw sugar into the cup she'd placed in front of him.

"Music. I'm hopeful about my music."

Robb furrowed his brow at his wife. "Huh?"

"Oh, never mind."

"Mind," he said. His wife was a great pianist. Solid, competent and passionate. To this day he never understood her decision to leave the world of music.

"Okay then. I've been thinking a lot about music. I might try out to play with an orchestra on weekends."

"That's a great idea."

"I think so. It'll give me some balance."

"I'm happy for you honey," he said as he pulled her to him and kissed her cheek, "anyway, you'd better get ready. Patrick will be here in 15 mins."

Amelie looked at her watch but said nothing. She hadn't yet told him she'd left Waltman. It was seven-fifteen a.m.

"I'm not going in today."

"Oh. You're taking the day off?" Robb said. "That's a first."

"Long story." Amelie headed to the foyer to get the morning paper. The large, highly polished foyer with its exquisite cherry furniture was welcoming. I love this house, she thought for the second time, as she opened the front door. Amelie did indeed love the house with its Victorian turrets and wrap around verandah from the moment she'd followed the realtor up the driveway. Though Robb said it seemed more suited to the South, Amelie had insisted it was the only house she'd live in. Number 4 Brunswick Drive. Her sister, Ashley, had about given up life's breath when she heard the address.

"The number four! Amelie, are you crazy? What do you want, a lifetime of sorrow and misfortune? Petition the city to change the number. I'm telling you right now, the number four is nothing but bad luck."

But for Amelie, number 4 Brunswick Drive had been nothing but a place of peace and tranquility.

"Am I going to have to wait all day for the long story?" Robb took the paper she handed him.

"Well…" Amelie stalled.

"How about some breakfast?" Robb asked popping some bread in the toaster. "Whatever the reason, it's nice to have you home. We can play hide and seek," he grinned mischievously.

"That could be fun." Amelie smiled right back.

"By the way did you get a chance to talk to Lawrence about the sponsorship for the show?"

Amelie, who would follow her husband to the end of the earth, took a deep breath. In their years of marriage, not once, had she lost her way with him. He was her one and only true love. They'd met during her first year at Julliard. She, studying to be a pianist and him a dancer. She was only sixteen and he was already twenty-one. He was fit, confident and talented. She was uncertain and searching. He'd walked into rehearsals where Amelie was working with her professor, Dr. Vlachenko on a score for his graduating dance piece. One look was all it took for Amelie and when Robb told the story it was three seconds before he knew they'd marry. After his rehearsal, Robb had come to her practice room. They had fallen into each other, and into each other's aura, they had found completion. The naturalness of their love had never scared them. Together forever was still today their reality. And as much as she adored him, she had no idea why she was to be the one to talk to Lawrence about sponsorship for his show!

Robb placed the toast in front of Amelie.

"Honey, why can't you just pick up the phone and call Lawrence?"

"I can. Just wondered if you had a chance to ask. You and Randy are forever on the phone. Thought she might have said something, that's all," Robb answered.

"Be serious. When has Randy ever cared about such things?"

"No *problema*. I'll call Lawrence today. Anyway, tell me what's going on with you?"

"I need to listen to my music." Amelie sat in a chair that faced the kitchen's glass-paneled walls.

"Come again?" Robb walked over to the coffeepot and poured another cup of French roast. Amelie slid open the glass door, took her toast and coffee to the kitchen patio and sat under the garden umbrella. "It's such a beautiful day. Let's eat out here."

Robb eyed his wife. No need pressing for an explanation, she'd tell him in good time.

"Robb, isn't the garden growing beautifully? It's almost the end of summer and it's still so lush. You know what's wrong with life today, Robb? We have no time. No time and no music. Music is all about time. We're killing the rhythm of life."

"And you're here today to make sure that doesn't happen?" Robb scratched his head. His dear, sweet, Amelie never had a straightforward answer for anything. Ask her a question and what you got back was a circuitous response that was never quite an answer. Yet, her soft and vulnerable side also had a strong resolve and he could tell it was in full play.

Robb sat beside her and waited for the other shoe to drop.

"Robb, my life is so meaningless."

"Meaningless? How can your life be meaningless?"

Robb had heard this all before. Nothing was meaningless about their lives. In fact, they had a perfect life. Not too poor to be disillusioned, nor too rich to be jaded. And after eighteen years of marriage, they were still madly in love. They lived in the best neighborhood, sent their son to the best school, ate at the best restaurants and made love as though it was always the first time.

"I can't go on like this," she paused and faced him. "I quit my job yesterday."

Robb turned to look at Amelie. Even with her proneness to whimsical behavior, she wasn't crazy enough to quit her job just like that. He didn't need this Amelie today, especially with work deadlines pressing down on him. There was the play to complete, the choreography to fine tune, the song to finish, the sponsorships to secure.

"What's going on Amelie? I seem to be missing something important here."

Amelie sighed and took a sip of her drink. "Robb, we moved out here to have a good life. To hear birds, sing and to breathe fresh air, to see our son run free." Amelie's ebony eyes were sad, a deep frown creasing her pretty face. "I quit my job."

"All right," Robb said calmly, "Come," he pulled her up from her chair and sat her on his lap. "Now tell me exactly what happened." She was having another one of her 'I can't do this anymore' attacks. They were becoming more frequent.

"Yesterday my best man quit because I had a meltdown. Then I had the worse dose of corporate double-talk; a kickback offer for the Greedham contract. Robb, I feel as though I was drowning. Then to top it off my muses are being downright belligerent. What else could I do?" she shrugged. "I quit and when I did the pounding in my head stopped and all I heard was music."

"You're pulling my leg, right?" Robb was stunned.

"Why do you always do that?" Amelie said.

"Do what? I know there's something else on your mind."

Amelie's eyes filled with tears. "You should have heard my musical muse. Amelie choked up. "She was warning me that I'd die with the music in me." When she couldn't go on Robb soothed her.

"There darling," he said rubbing her temple, kissing her cheeks as they gathered salty water. His beautiful wife had always been overly sensitive, a little too delicate for the real world. That was her gift. She felt everything and could translate those emotions into imitable beautiful music. With each stroke of his hand, the muscles of the soft, smooth skin on her face relaxed. She'd brought this on herself. He never quite understood why she'd left Julliard in the first place. It had been such an irrational decision that even today he had trouble with her explanation. He'd never met such a musical talent. No ordinary pianist at Juilliard; she'd been brilliant. It was that brilliance that made her a little crazy. Robb looked at the woman on his lap clutching to him for dear life. Very much the delicate little bird he'd met at sixteen, she hadn't aged to him at all. Crazy as a loon but he loved her dearly. "So, what now?" He kissed her beautiful hands. It was clear that she was seeking his permission to get away from the demands of life for a little while. She often needed those breaks and would insist that they travel to some far-off place at least once a year. If he bent just a little, she'd come to her senses and there would be peace again. "How about if we take off tomorrow, drive up to the cottage and go bike riding?" Robb hugged her closer to him. "How about it, darling?"

"Couldn't we make that a couple of weeks? Really Robb, couldn't we? Let's go away for a couple of weeks. Reconnect with ourselves and each other."

"In a few weeks we'll do just that but for now how about taking the day off tomorrow. Call and leave a message for your secretary?"

"Robb, I don't think you get it. I quit. I can't face turning fifty with an unfulfilled life. Every day on Wall Street is the same; immorality, the pressure to be dishonest and unbridled greed. There's no place for me in that world. I can't play the game any longer," she sighed.

"Okay," Robb said, knowing when to back down.

"My life could go on like this forever if I don't do something now. I had to leave, Robb. Truly I did, I had no choice." Something in her voice told him she was serious this time.

"But darling, how could you do something like that without talking it over with me?"

"It was a spur of the moment decision. What did you want me to do, excuse myself and call you?"

"Amelie…"

"I had no idea being married to you meant I had to consult you about a decision that was affecting me. I had a job and I quit. Isn't it my choice?" She pulled out of his embrace and got off his lap. "I can't go on," she said sadly, "I need balance, and I need my music." She bit so hard on her inner lip that she felt the blood ooze into her mouth. "I had to quit."

"Take all the time you need. But wait to make a final decision. Fifty for you darling is twelve years away Amelie," Robb pleaded.

"No Robb. I am done. I know I was born to play music. I have to try again," she said with finality. "Even mother admitted that yesterday."

Robb had never seen her like this.

"Really? Your mother?"

"My mother."

"Okay. Fine. Whatever you want. We'll go away. Where do you want to go this time? But you do know that the dream you're chasing is right there on 63rd Street."

"Oh, Robb." Amelie hugged him hard and let flow the river of uncertainty.

"There, their darling. It's going to be all right," Robb said, massaging her shoulders as they heaved.

Amelie straightened up, little bits and pieces of her body still cleaving to him. She nuzzled his neck, touched his lips tenderly with hers, and cradled his head to her breast. She didn't deserve him. At forty-five Robb was still so handsome. Stately, guileless and confident, her erratic behavior rarely fazed him. Her Robb. He feared nothing, not her hysterics or the uncertainty of the times. He had chosen the life he wanted with dauntless conviction and was willing to hold out until he had achieved his goals. How lucky he was to have grown up in a place and family that protected him and encouraged his dreams.

"So where are we going to find life's harmonies?" he asked wiping tears from her eyes.

"You aren't kidding me, are you, Robb?"

"Of course not, darling. In a couple of weeks. Just got to wrap up a few things."

"I thought Lisbon," she said excitedly. "I don't know why, really. Thank you, Robb." Amelie was kissing him when something crashed into the sliding door. Her body began shaking and beads of perspiration dampened her upper lip. All of a sudden there was a commotion…It seemed all their neighbors were pouring into the street.

"What's going on?" Robb shouted to their neighbor Faith, a single mother of two girls.

"Thank God you're here Amelie. Turn on the TV the World Trade Center has been hit."

Robb and Amelie ran into the house and turned on the TV. What they saw was too surreal to believe. She could have been there…on the street…life had spoken. On the floor of the patio was a stunned bird that had slammed into the glass door.

CHAPTER EIGHT
Emily

Florida, September 11, 2001

EMILY WAS FOLDING a silk shirt, preparing to wrap it in plastic from the dry cleaners. Every now and then she'd stop to listen to a report from the Today Show. She didn't much care for television except she'd watch her daughter's show every day. Not that she liked it one bit, but it was the only way she could see Ashley and it made her feel included in her life somehow. She'd hoped to stop in New York on her way back from her cruise but she hadn't heard back from Amelie. That didn't surprise her. Her children did everything in their power to avoid her, and rightly so. It was her fault. Emily laid the silk shirt on the plastic wondering why the hell she was going through this rigmarole. Robin, the Miss-Know-It-All in the travel group "The Dis-continents" had informed them that if they wrapped their clothes in plastic before packing, it would spare them the chore of having to iron them at their destination.

Well into their late sixties to mid-seventies The Dis-continents were a bunch of wealthy beauties who could still turn the heads of charming, plaid-pant clad men on the Golf courses of Palm Spring. At their ages, these women didn't mince words and most of them had long admitted that they had married for security rather than love hence the name of their travel group. The pleasure they could no longer pretend to have with their husbands was sought by visiting exotic locations around the world every three months. The only point of disagreement among the group was the name. "It sounds like incontinent," one geezer had objected but they all knew the group should simply have been called…The Dis-content or indeed the Incontinents. As she put the last perfect crease in the blue silk blouse Emily's mind contemplated the news they had received from the Doctor. Michael had an advanced case of prostate cancer. She had tried to cancel her trip but he had insisted that he needed the two weeks to process all the information and it would be best if he didn't have to worry about her too.

What would she have done without him all these years? Michael had known all along that there was only a part of her that he could have. He understood her and she him. They had been good company for each other. After she'd married him her children had been devastated but he had been a good man to them. The moment they left home they never returned and with their own hectic lives now they never visited. Emily shouldn't have expected more. She hadn't been the best mother. However, little they considered her, she knew the sacrificed she'd made for them. She'd given up the love of her life to keep her children and to save her unborn child. In hindsight, life might have been better if she'd stayed and fought for the love she deserved. The love, which still today comforted her when she felt lost and scared. The love that for her had never, ever died. If only her children understood what she gave up for them.

Emily stopped folding the blouse and sat on the side of the bed. What, she wondered, would her life have been like with Bunny? Bunny, with his wicked smile, even wickeder laughter, and lethal love. From the day she'd met him their destiny had been sealed. If only she had understood that. Emily smiled without even knowing it. An even if she had, for just a moment, she wanted to be wrapped in the warm embrace of Bunny's memory.

• • •

Jamaica, 1947

"Emily, Emily, what on earth are you doing!" her mother was clasping her hands to her head, the sight outside her sewing room window giving her an instant headache. Where the hibiscus, dotted with pink and orange flowers tapered, Emily was leaning over the fence chatting away with Mrs. Stewart's gardener.

"Miss Emily," Sadie came marching over to the fence. "Your mother says to come inside at once," she gave the young man a look of death.

"Why?"

"Emily. Don't make me crazy today," she yanked the girl by her arm and hauled her off to where her mother was waiting.

"Where did I go wrong with you?" Norma was hopping mad. "What daughter of mine hangs over a fence chatting up a gardener?" she'd said through clenched

teeth. "If I ever catch you chatting to that worthless boy again, I'll have Mable send his backside back to country."

"Mother! Trevor is not worthless. And what so wrong with me talking to him? I just don't get why you're so upset."

"Oh, shut your stupid mouth and put on this dress."

Emily grabbed the confounded dress her mother had been sewing for weeks on end and dragged it in on over her t-shirt and shorts. Like the stuffy room, filled with mahogany furniture, too dark for a tropical island and overstuffed chairs covered with material too hot for comfortable sitting in 96-degree weather, so too was the stupid, frilly, unsightly dress her mother wanted her to wear to a ridiculous party that had no bearing on Jamaica and Jamaicans.

"What's wrong with you, Emily? The dress won't hang right over your clothes."

Exasperated Emily slipped out of her shorts and pulled the t-shirt off through the sleeve of the dress.

"Go ahead. Rip it up. It's your waterloo," Norma tugged the dress into place and began basting the hem. "You can chat up a gardener but won't take time to look presentable for your future husband. And keep still!"

"Husband? Not on your life and hurry up," Emily sassed. "How much longer yu gwan take on this stupid getup? Look, Mother, I don't care what I look like tonight. I don't even want to go. I won't marry Stoddard and that's final." What she really wanted to say was I don't give a rass about a bunch of stuck up black folks trying to act like they came from England. Debutant indeed! Emily knew better though. Such back talking would surely earn her a good "box" across her face and the threat of washing her mouth with carbolic soap.

"You look nice," Joseph, her younger brother came into the room. "Nice," he repeated, hugging his sister and touching her dress as he skipped around her, his permanent, idiotic smile in place.

"Joseph!" Norma Tate had yelled at her son and as always, the child stiffened. "How many times do I have to tell you to knock on a closed door before you enter? Where is Sadie?" She began shooing him from the room. "Go and find her and tell her to get you ready for your bath."

"You look nice," Joseph kept repeating clinging to Emily.

"It's alright Mummy. Let him stay," Emily protested.

"No, he can't," Norma said prying the boy from his sister.

Joseph, Emily's older brother was born, as they say in Jamaica, not quite right. No one knew his official diagnosis, but Joseph had a hard time keeping his distance from people. As their mother often said, he was always invading people's personal space. Joseph looked at his mother, his round face etched in disappointment. He hid behind Emily as though she could protect him.

"Joseph, how many times do I have to tell you if you're closer than arm's length to somebody," her hand shot out in front of her, "yu too close," She said this for the umpteenth time as though Joseph could understand time and space. He stared at her, his idiotic grin long having turned to sadness.

• • •

The inaugural ball was to be her debut, her introduction to society. Anyone within miles of Emily knew from her blowfish face that neither Stoddard, her date, nor the night, was welcomed. When her name was announced Emily was pulling at the puffy green dress pinching her arms and waist, drawing a scowl from her Ms. Manners Mother. How anyone willingly consented to this charade was beyond her, yet here she was, a lamb to slaughter smiling all the way to the guillotine.

The hall was large and airy. French doors opened on all sides allowed in the cool evening breeze that brought relief from the day's sweltering heat, but Emily was still roasting in the puffy taffeta dress.

"Are you having a good time?" Stoddard asked, squeezing Emily's elbow as he led her toward the line.

"No, I'm not. Are you?" Emily said easing away from his touch. "This damn dress feels like an albatross," Emily snapped angrily at Stoddard for reasons she couldn't quite fathom. Maybe esoteric reasons like it was his transplanted colonized family that was to be blamed for these nonsense rituals Jamaican society people emulated. Along the pale blue wall of Devon Hall, Stepford debs, with fixated smiles, were lined up waiting for the future husbands, handpicked by their parents, to

sweep them away into the dance of death. At least, that's what Emily called it. Stoddard, to Emily's disappointment, had turned out to be a so-so man of weak constitution. Like all their peers, Stoddard Winkler had accepted, without a fight, the life his parents had programmed for him. If only he'd had some spunk. Fought for what he really wanted. From childhood, Stoddard, versed as his musical family in all thing music, had only one dream: to become a missionary in India using music to transform lives. Emily and her best friend Josie had promised to visit him there on their own travels around the world. Now here he was on his way to becoming a doctor, one of the two requisite professions for well-bred Jamaican society boys. The other, being a seat on the high court as a barrister of great levity. After the summer holiday was over, Stoddard would be off to England or Scotland, as well-to-do family's children often do to study medicine while she, Miss pinned debutante would wait by the window with a lace hankie. Not on your life, Emily thought dutifully smiling up at Stoddard.

"You bet," he answered. "I've been practicing my dance steps all day."

"I'm sure," Emily said, now barely able to look at him.

The band played Blue Danube. As Stoddard awkwardly spun her around the grand room Emily looked here and there…anywhere for distraction; Joy's jeering face, the crystal drops of the chandelier, the Wainscoting, the ornate framing of the pictures of people who'd enslaved them. She even looked down at her silly, frilly dress made of a material that had no relationship to the tropics. She wanted to scream. If the evening got any worse, she'd… just as she was about to choke her way through an excuse, Emily's eyes came to rest on a young, but manly musician. There was a confidence in the way he was strumming his guitar and mischief in the way his lips curled up at the sides. Seeming to empathize with her plight, he winked and flashed a piano-perfect smile. Now there's a real man, Emily allowed her gaze to fully rest on him. His smiled broadened. Emily smiled back before lowering her eyes. From time to time Emily would let her eyes find him through the crowd.

Not a minute too soon, a snappy Papiamento, a tribute to the fact that Jamaica, though a British colony, had a flavor and pulse of its own, vibrated through the room. The music of their African heritage moved even the bodies of the most reserved.

"Stoddard let's dance." Emily smiled at the shock on Stoddard's face.

"To that music? I don't know how!"

"Ah, just keep moving," she said, dragging him onto the dance floor. Emily was the only girl with rhythm in the room and all eyes turned on her. Pleased that her mother was sufficiently mortified Emily ducked through the crowd to get a drink from the bar when the band went on break.

The guitarist was leaning against the bar and she managed to work her way closer to him. "You play very well," she said.

"And you dance very well." A lopsided grin touched his lips. His dark, blazing eyes drank in her presence. "You sure know how to stir the pot," he smiled again. This time his entire face lit up and she gasped at how handsome he was.

"Can I buy you a drink?"

"I don't drink."

"How come I man don't believe that. You, never take a waters?"

"What business of that is yours?"

"Cause I and I is a curious man."

"Well, Mr. Curious man what I do is none of your business."

"Huh, we'll see about that. Just because mi no society man don't make me less of a man, seen. Me a man times two so don't play with me, little girl. You know dark needs light, don't you?"

"And you are cocky too I see." Emily smiled devilishly watching as Bunny Higgenbottom eased off the bar and moved closer to her. He was handsome, no question about it, right down to the slight bow of his legs that was not from third world scurvy but from pure almighty God's perfection. He was irresistible. Dark needs light.

Surprising even herself Emily said. "Meet me under the Almond tree at the edge of the lawn. Beyond the gates in a half-an-hour exactly after the party ends. No more no less."

"Why?"

"I want to hear your story. If I'm not there by then I won't be coming."

"And then what?'

"It wasn't meant to be," Emily shrugged, turned around, flicked her bangs from her eyes and sashayed off into the crowd.

For the rest of the evening her musician seemed to have been given over completely to his music. Every time she glanced at him, his eyes were closed and his body seemed transported to wherever the music took him.

• • •

Bunny, sat on a tree stump guitar slung over his shoulder. He'd been waiting for twenty-five minutes under the almond tree as planned. Twirling blades of grass through his fingers he wondered why he even bothered to get his hopes up about a society girl who only wanted to taunt him with her good looks before she left him in the wake of her dust. "Chu." He sucked air against his teeth, rising from the stump. He could tell from the way she swayed her hips that she was trouble, to begin with.

Sneaking up behind him Emily cupped her hands over his eyes. "Why do you have that guitar strapped on to you? Didn't think I'd show up, huh?"

"Yeah, man I know you bound fi come," he said casually.

"Liar!"

"Girl, I know you bound fi come." Bunny's hand lingered on hers.

"Don't be so sure about me and don't bet on me either," Emily said untangling her hand. "Now," she said more excitedly sitting on the stump he'd just vacated, "what's your story?" The up-curl had now been loosened and her thick black hair now fell softly around her face.

"Ratid girl, yu something else," Bunny shook his head. "But how yu expect mi fi tell you mi story when you don't even know mi name?"

"I expect that'll be part of the story, then?" Emily smiled. She loved his patois. The man was so authentic.

He'd cupped her hand then and placed a hand-full of almonds in them.

Emily stopped her mind abruptly. What good was hashing up old memories? The truth was that the older she got the more comfort she found in the memories. It was better to have loved and lost…she sighed…ripping some more plastic off the dry-cleaning hangers. Emily was about to put the last perfect crease in another silk blouse when pandemonium came over the wire. "This can't be happening," she covered her mouth, grabbed her chest and sunk to the ground. The World Trade Center had been hit? Her daughter Amelie worked on Wall Street as did her son-in-law. Emily felt wetness on her cheek. What had her aborted life done to her children? Opting to take the road most traveled, now in the twilight of her life, she had deep regrets and a lot of guilt about her children. Bunny, running, and denial had eaten away the years. "If any of my children are hurt, I'll never be able to survive." Ice clinked in her glass of amber liquid as she tipped it to her lips and drank its content in one swallow. "Michael, Michael," she ran toward her husband's room.

That very day Emily pulled out the rose scented stationary and began writing letters to her children.

CHAPTER NINE
Ashley

Philadelphia, September 11th WCNB-TV Studios

5:10 A.M. PHILLIP WAS EASING into his make-up seat when she burst into the studio. "Another day of shit but I'm still fifteen minutes early this morning," Ashley announced. They were filming a special report.

"Miracles. I love them." His co-anchor was forever pushing the dial on timeliness.

"How was your date?"

A Cheshire grin lit Phillip's face. "It's gonna be an amazing life. I can tell," he winked.

"Philip you are so freakin' stupid. So easily lead down the garden path," Ashley flicked his ear and flopped down beside him in her makeup chair.

"What the hell is that supposed to mean?"

"Exactly what it means. You-are-gullible-and stupid." Turning to her make-up artist, Ashley finally acknowledged the woman.

"Clare. Look what I have for you. People of color make up. I decided to do something about that confounded make-up you keep using on me that makes me look grey when I should be black. Here ya go…use these," she handed over an IMAN cosmetics bag.

Clare rolled her eyes, none too pleased with Ashley's antics of changing make-up brands. "Suck in your cheeks." Clare flipped open the compact and signed loudly. "This isn't masking enough."

"The point," Ashley said raking a hand through her short hair. "I have nothing to mask."

Mean ass bitch! Clare yanked her head harder than she had to.

"Oh yes, you do," Phillip said. "That evil tongue of yours should be bound with masking tape."

Indeed. Clare stifled a smile, yanking Ashley's hair once again.

"This is what I mean." Ashley glared at Clare. "Why am I in this freakin' dead-end job talking to morons about nothing, when I have the chops for world domination?" Though she dared not say it aloud, she was surely thinking, how could her only date option be with a man whose interest in women was subzero? That's why she cared about Phillip in the first place.

"Moron? You didn't say that." Phillip grimaced launching into a petit tirade. As Ashley listened to Phillip jabber on, she wondered. What if Clare knew that Phillip's new love interest was a Johnny and not a Joan? She was the only person at WCNB who knew his sexual preference. Their secret. She thought too of the secret she'd kept her entire life with Amelie that she wouldn't want to be paraded on national T.V. Randy was right, secrets are to be just that.

"Four mins to air." The runner appeared at the make-up station.

"That woman is an idiot. Who gives a four min call?" Ashley's hatred of the number four was irrational but legendary. Perhaps because it was at age four that her world became harsh and unforgiving. She was four and Randy six when operation escape Jamaica happened. As the story goes, she was uprooted from a stable family and taken to England. Ashley considered England her home. It was the only passport she had in her safe. Even if she remembered bits and pieces of life in Jamaica, what good was it to always live in the past? The more likely reason she hated the number four, however, was because she was four weeks pregnant when Frederick, the pig, (dog was far too clean and animal for him), splintered her heart. For a woman who'd sworn that unlike her mother she'd never waste too many body parts on a man, much less precious time, she hadn't seen Frederick McDermott coming. Not in a million years had she imagined herself falling that hard for any man.

They'd met late one night in the cafeteria at Georgetown University while both cramming for upcoming exams. Ashley, who had been falling asleep at her desk, had padded barefoot to the food dispenser to get some coffee. Only as she stood in front of the machine and dug through her pockets did she realize she had no money.

"May I?" He'd dropped a couple quarters into the slot. Black or white?"

She hadn't quite understood what she'd found interesting about a guy with an annoying nasal twang and dirty blond hair.

"Black," she'd answered. Frankly, she'd have preferred tea but the thought of tea from a dispenser was more than she could stomach. It turned out that Frederick was studying biochemistry and obviously figured out sight on seen that she'd be a good experiment.

Weeks later they were exploding and combusting and not in test tubes. God how she'd fallen hard for the charming, sexy, confident son of a Tycoon from Virginia.

"When will you come and meet my family and me yours?" Ashley had asked as they were sprawled on the carpet after a marathon lovemaking session.

"Meet our families? Ashley, what are you saying?"

"That maybe it's time we meet each other's family."

"Hold your horses there, honey. This has to be our secret. My family would never understand."

"Understand what?"

"That I'm going out with a black girl?"

"A black girl? Frederick, what do you mean?"

"Look, it's okay. We're in college so we can do this sort of thing. Experiment. My parents are old Wasps. They would never understand. America's racial history is complicated."

"You have got to be joking." Ashley jumped up from the floor. "Who told you that? Your daddy?" Ashley pulled on her clothes. "Isn't he the one fuckin' the help while your Mama is on the fainting couch?" She glared at him before slamming the door so hard in his face as she left that she might have broken his nose. The racial tensions inherent in their union hadn't seeped into Ashley's mind back then. That sucking on her titties might have reminded him of his wet nurse or that her golden-brown skin of the pancakes his "Aunt Jemima" could have caused him to have "knee" jerk reaction of lust. It stands to reason too, that since the helpers were probably the only people in the world who'd shown him any kind of love, he must have had oedipal feelings for his caregivers. So, just like that, seven months of bliss had turned into a nightmare. Their split finally nailed shut her heart and solidified for her that people were mean and evil. That included her mother for not conquering her shortcomings as a human, her father for letting her go and Frederick for the ultimate betrayal. The bastard hadn't even offered to go with her to get rid of his child.

"Keep still," Clare pushed her head to the left.

Ashley tried to sidestep the secret she'd held inside her heart but it was not willing to be silenced today. Amelie had stood at the foot of her bed.

"Jesus, Ashley, you look like hell." Even at eighteen, Ashley had a finely tuned sense of class and style. That she was looking "like hell" was a clear indication of the depth of her pain.

"Go away, Melie!" Ashley said, barely lifting her head from under the pillow.

"Stop acting crazy." Amelie was not one to mince words.

"Can't you see I'm trying not to jump out the bloody window? Get the hell away from me."

"I'm not moving until you come out of this room." Amelie crossed her arms.

"I'm not ready, please just go away," Ashley pleaded knowing how stubborn Amelie could be.

"How much longer can you keep this up? You've been in here all week. Please don't pull a Randy on us," Amelie warned, remembering when their oldest sister shuttered herself in her room for almost a month.

"It's my room and I can stay in here as long as I want," Ashley mumbled into the pillow. It wasn't as though she hadn't tried to get up. The centrifugal force of her grief kept her rooted to the bed. Her life was over. It was clearly her fault that Frederick had left her. She should never have told him something so serious as her pregnancy on the dreaded fourth day of the month. She hadn't believed it herself when she first suspected but she knew it nonetheless; she was no longer alone someone was living inside her body.

"I'm pregnant," Ashley had told Frederick.

Instead of sweeping her off her feet in joy, he had backed away. "I can't have a half-black baby," he had said, "My parents would kill me."

Ashley was devastated. Until then she had not paid much attention to colour in America. After all her mother had been twice married to white men whom she had thought of as just men albeit she liked neither.

For days on end, the only things that came out of Ashley's darkened attic bedroom were sobs and sappy music.

Though the youngest child, fourteen-year-old Amelie was not only the logical mind in the household, she towered over her sisters. Her piercing no-nonsense black eyes and the black, wavy short-cropped haircut and tamarind complexion made her seem altogether of a different gene pool than her sisters. Without question, however, Amelie held the esteemed position in the family as the voice of reason and of all the girls, she was the one who seemed least traumatized by the dysfunctional household. She always said it was because her music took her away but Ashley believed her confidence was because she was their mother's favorite. Amelie was the only one who could get their mother to reconsider a particularly harsh punishment or to get her to smile now and then. And it was Amelie who was never criticized, except about spending too much time on her music, punished, or yelled at unnecessarily by anyone. Though the older girls had often tried to plot against her, Amelie's complete devotion and genuine love of her sisters had spared her excessive sibling rivalry.

Amelie finally managed to push through Ashley's resistance. "Get up now," she'd yelled, yanking Ashley from the bed and dragging her into the bathroom."

"Bugger off, will you? What's it to you if I indulge in self-pity? Don't you understand? I'm dying. This pain goes on forever and all I want to do is die." Ashley yanked her arm free of her sister's grip.

"Well, it's time for this pity party to be over and for you to pull yourself together. Heartbreak is a hard road to travel but you can't keep this up." Amelie stood with her hands on her hips. "Come on Ash, I'll make you a nice cup of tea and I'll play away the blues for you."

"What the hell is that going to do?" Ashley yelled before crumpling into a torrent of tears. "How could he have done this to me?" Ashley wailed. "He was my world. Made me tall, bold, hopeful and pregnant," she wailed as the tears came faster, "I will never, ever go through this pain again. I trusted him Melie. If you can't trust the one you love, why love at all?" And even as she said the words Ashley had wished the phone would ring and that Frederick would be on the other end of the line telling her everything would be fine, validating that her love had not been in vain.

Amelie had never liked Frederick, had always said he was too suave, too white, and too American in an unflattering way. Men like him, she'd told Ashley, only had one thing on their minds; sexual conquest of the Massa's mistress. Ashley had no real appreciation for what she meant at the time but Amelie, who'd grown up in America, had a different take on race and prejudice. Having one's heart broken by a first love, the one who you gave your virginity to, was no easy heartache from which to recover much less to understand her plight as the continuation of a social experiment. For the love of your life to abandon you, after heating up the mirrors all over town because of a pregnancy was downright cruel. That alone in Ashley's opinion was grounds for murder.

"He'll call," Amelie had lied, and though it was not said it was fully implied that there would be no phone calls, no movie ending and that all Ashley had to look forward to, for months to come, was the excruciating pain of her first broken heart. And more painful than Frederick's abandonment was that now she'd have to kill her own child.

Amelie grabbed a handful of tissues and wiped Ashley's face. "Look, sweetie, I love you dearly and I don't want to be the voice of reason, but it's time to take care of this little business. Besides, if Mother finds out you're pregnant there won't be any need for you to jump out of the window. She'll kill you herself."

"It would take a miracle for Mother to even notice that I'm alive much less pregnant. The only person mother notices around here, is you."

"But notice she will if you don't get some sense in that bloody head of yours." Amelie always found a way to sidestep any conversations about being her mother's favorite. For that, she became devoted to her sisters and would try harder than anyone else to be nice.

Ashley cried for ten more days, later regretting that it hadn't been eleven, her favorite number. She scribbled Mrs. Frederick McIdiot one last time in the diary that had born witness to her pain. By the time she emerged from the darkness of her room, she was ten pounds lighter, armored and unforgiving of anyone with XY chromosomes. No man would ever treat her this way again and no man would ever settle in her heart. As far as she was concerned, she was alone in the world and alone she'd make a life for herself that would be enviable. Screw Frederick and screw the entire human race.

The day Ashley left the abortion clinic something inside her had died permanently just like the child she had carried. And on that day, she'd promised herself to never, ever allow herself to feel this way again. No man would ever hurt her this way ever again.

"Two minutes to air." Ashley backhanded a tear threatening to fall. The show today was about Secrets. Randy would like that but this nonsense show made her depressed. Ashley could care less about the latest parade of celebrity idiots who insisted on destroying their lives and whom she had to run after to get interviews of their secrets that somehow ended up in the *National Enquirer.* She'd just as soon hand them the tools of demise. She never really understood America's fascination with celebrities but she made a great living at pretending she did.

"Well here you are," Clare handed her the makeup."

"No, keep it here. I'll be using it from now on, that's until I need a new look."

"As you wish."

"Shall we?" Phillip turned off his cell phone that he'd been furiously texting on and eased from the chair.

"I hate this fuckin' job," Ashley whispered clipping on her mic. "I'm getting the fuck out of dodge soon. Wait and see. You're going to have to find a new anchor to stand up on dates."

"Shhh…the New Big Boss is in the house today," Phillip whispered as she settled in beside him on the studio set. He's in the control room."

"So?"

"He can hear us."

"Only if the intercom is pressed on both sides Dufus."

"And how do you know it's not?"

"Really?" Ashley deadpanned looking at Phillip pathetically. "Are you pressing the other end of the intercom, Mr. Brainiac?"

"Ah yes. There's that."

They ran sound checks before smiling into the camera.

"The top story today, bad boy Jay Buford has been arrested for possession of drugs as he left a swanky Beverly Hills Restaurant. I'm Ashley Freeman." Ashley flashed her signature megawatt smile. The camera cut to her anchor. "And I'm Phillip Stalin. Join us for this, and much more on another edition of Entertainment Times."

As soon as the show was done with segment one, Ashley yanked off her mike then turned to her co-host. "Such bullshit," she huffed.

Ashley who'd yet to meet the new, big boss was determined to *carpe diem*. Some guy called Melvadore Follette had recently bought the station. This was the opportunity if ever to transition. She hit the intercom and said, "Hello Sir, just wondered if you have a moment."

"Yes, Miss Freeman," the commanding voice came through the intercom. "Please come to my office after your taping."

"Yes, sir," Ashley saluted, climbing back onto the stage. She smiled warmly into the camera. "Good Evening and welcome to another edition of Entertainment Times."

• • •

After the taping concluded, Ashley reported to Mel Follette's office. As she understood it, Mel was short for Melvadore.

"Ms. Freeman," the acerbic receptionist winced as though her shoes were pinching her feet. "Mr. Follette is expecting you. Down the hall, first door on the left."

She was about to knock when the door opened. "How did you know I was outside?" Ashley stared openly at the aristocratic man on the other side of the door. She felt a sense of dis-ease deep in the pit of the stomach that portended double trouble. Ashley had fully expected an old geezer with a hook nose, balding head, tiny spider web veins invading his face and crooked teeth. The kind of reject who became rich just to get girls since it would have been near impossible otherwise. Instead, before her stood this tall, olive-complexioned, imposing man, dressed in a well-cut steel-gray suit and a French blue shirt with the letters MF embroidered on his sleeve. His jet-black shoulder length hair, cut in a European style curled onto his collar giving him the look of an ancient warrior. Melvadore Follette commanded the room with unmistakable authority. Ashley laughed inwardly at the street meaning of the initials MF and thought how appropriate it seemed.

"Let me show you," he pulled her into the room, closed the door and spun around. A slight but lingering accent hung in the air. Mediterranean maybe.

Scary MF. "Nice to see you're big on trust." A two-way mirror not only made him able to observe the entire studio from his office but also anyone approaching his office. Ashley's eyes followed the contour of the room avoiding all eye-contact with the deep-set eyes that gave her the once-over. The office was bigger than her entire condo. To the left was a garden, complete with a swing, and to the right, a massive glass desk. What the hell was this guy about? "What's with the garden?" Ashley asked strolling around the room touching several awards. She couldn't appear intimidated. To these types, that was the kiss of death. On the wall of fame were numerous pictures of MF and people who looked like oil barons…sheiks and the likes. And then there were his Emmys. A little intimidating to Ashley.

"I like beautiful things and nature," his ebony eyes followed her as she paused at one of his Emmys. "I should not display them…too obvious?" he said, his eyes crinkling. He was laughing at her, she could tell.

"You should. Where better than your office?"

"Drink?"

"Yes. Fruit punch," she said. It was her turn to mock his tropical garden. To her surprise, he went to the bar and whipped up a fresh, tropical fruit punch.

"Reminds me of home." He could tell she was mocking his garden.

"Right," she took the chilled glass. "I suppose you already know that I'm Ashley Freeman since you called me by name."

"I know everyone who works for me. Ms. Freeman, what can I do for you?"

He sat in the high back chair that was turned so that his back was to her. Unhurriedly lighting a cigarette, he took a deep drag on the filter and then turned to face her again. She didn't like that at all. It was ill-mannered plus she detested smoking. Ashley stared at him, her eyes narrowing. She took a sip of her drink and walked around the room touching artifacts and opening trinkets. When she'd circled the room, she sat in a chair facing him. MF waited. It seemed an entire minute passed before either spoke.

"I wanted to see you."

"I gathered as much. "It seems you're in no hurry to tell me what about though." He leaned toward her, his elbows on his desk.

"Sir, I've been with WNCB for years now. I took the job because the market was soft when I got out of grad school but I'm really meant to be a serious reporter. I'd like to be considered for more serious news. It's what I know. It's what I'm good at. I'm wasted in this job and I hate it. To be honest, I'd love to give the brats we cover a healthy overdose of Xanax, Vicodin, Heroine or whatever. Mr. Follette, I don't mean to sound ungrateful or to be rude. I love journalism and WCNB but I have been giving some serious thoughts to quitting. It seems a good time since the station has been bought."

"I see."

"I can't do the fluff anymore. It seems…well, let me put it this way. I'm having a harder time than usual being impressed by the brat packers rehab stories. Age maybe. People with needles in their arms, sad as it is, are not what I care about. I'm sorry to offend you but…"

"No. Don't apologize. I'm not in the least offended. I agree. The entire me-me world is on the verge of a nervous breakdown and I understand your need to feel more impactful."

"That's a great way of saying it. We're living with a lot of noise indeed."

"Yes, in a rogue nation. I'm glad to hear your thoughts. It makes my job much easier because I'm actually here to cancel your show," he stubbed out his cigarette, lighting another.

"OMG. No. Really? What about the great ratings?"

"They'll be back with the new kinds of programming we'll be doing. You say that you want to do serious news, so let me be the first to tell you that the hard news can be life-consuming, emotionally draining and dangerous."

"I know that," was all Ashley said.

"So then, consider your show overdosed. Let's put a needle in its arm as you said."

"What? I was…"

"Don't worry we'll give everyone ample notice. If they can't be transitioned at WNCB, well they'll have to find new positions elsewhere. But we'll offer a generous package to help them along."

"Am I fired, Mr. Follette?"

"That's what I'm here to decide."

"And…"

"I'll let you know."

As Ashley was about to take her leave Breaking News interrupted the news and the station turned into sheer chaos. The North Tower of the World Trade Center had been hit by a plane? "You've got to be kidding me." Ashley and Melvadore rushed into the hallway as Quinton came barreling down the hall. "We need every available hand on deck. We need all our reporters in New York!" Quinton said rounding up reporters.

"Quinton, I can do this," Ashley stood firmly in front of the producer, "I can do this. Just give me a chance."

"Okay…let's do this then…get out to the chopper now."

Before Melvadore could respond Ashley was halfway down the hall. This is my big break she thought as she bolted to the news chopper. She could never have imagined. By the time they arrived in Lower Manhattan at 9:45 a.m., the North and South Towers were ablaze. Ashley began reporting as soon as she left the chopper making her way closer to the site. She wasn't truly aware of the gravity of the situation, and she was hoping that this day, she'd do such a good job that Melvadore would have no doubts about her capabilities.

"This is a day of deep grief and mourning for America. It is also a day of unbelievable courage. As you can see behind me, fire and policemen are still rushing into the towers of the World Trade Center to search and rescue people trapped inside these burning buildings…this is a day that will change America forever. Today the world is witnessing the horror and destruction in Lower Manhattan as terrorists flew two hijacked planes into the North and South Towers of The World Trade Center. Here is what we know so far. At 8:46 a.m. this morning American Airline flight 11 from Boston carrying 92 people aboard deliberately flew into the North Tower of WTC at a speed of 470 miles. At 9:03 a.m. United Airlines flight 175 flying at 590 miles an hour with 65 aboard made a cataclysmic dive into the 84th floor of the South Tower. People are still piling out into the streets while others are trapped inside and many have perished…plumes of smoke are billowing from the twin towers…police are trying to move the crowd back as chaos reigns. At 9:38 a.m. another plane struck the Pentagon and it is believed that it was heading to the Capital or to the White House. It has crashed over Pennsylvania. This is truly the saddest day of my life. Ashley made her way over to a woman covered in debris. She instinctively hugged her. "Thank God you are safe. How did you get out?"

"I don't know. All I know is the building was on fire and they were telling people to stay put. There was no way in hell I was staying put in a burning building. I was on the 20th Floor. I just knew I had to get out…the stairwell was dark but we held each other's hands in a daisy chain until we were outside. I just can't believe this," the woman wailed as she was escorted away by EMS.

"The blaze from the South Tower is tremendous. People are jumping from the building and there is debris falling everywhere. This day that defies all logic is only getting worse."

As Ashley was in the middle of a sentence, she heard a thunderous noise above and looked up to see the South Tower folding in on itself. "OMG. The South Tower of the World Trade Center is collapsing. "Oh my God…oh my God," Ashley fell to her knees as the severity of what was happening finally claimed her emotions and seeped through to reality. "OMG, OMG." Ashley kept repeating, barely able to raise herself to her feet. Just then she saw a flow of people, shocked and crying coming out of the collapsing South

Tower and not three minutes later at 9:59 a.m. the South Tower collapsed. As the building collapsed toxic dust rained down on Lower Manhattan. "The South Tower of WTC has collapsed. Many lives have been lost today…and many more may be lost as this horrific day plays out. As you can see first responders, risking their own lives, are still going into the North Tower to save as many people as they can. We are seeing the best of America on what has to be one of the worse days in our history. "For those of you who have loved ones who you are desperately trying to find…we can only imagine how frantic you are. We know how hard this must be. If you have been trying to call the emergency center know that all the phone lines are jammed with over 230 million calls. Building 7, where the nerve center for emergencies is located has sustained damage from the collapse of the South Tower. In fact, falling debris from the South Tower had lit fires in WTC buildings 4, 5 and 6 which are also ablaze. WCNB is working hard to bring you minute by minute development so please stay with us for more coverage of this most horrific day. We are now being informed that some 6,000 airborne planes are being diverted and for the first time in our history, American Airspace has been shut down. This is a day that no American will ever forget and as the world watches the dust and destruction billowing over New York, they too, mourn our loss. The anguish that must be felt by every American tonight and the realization that our lives have changed forever, is ineffable. From this senseless and selfish act of terrorism so much has been lost. Our President has vowed to bring those responsible to justice."

By 10:28 a.m., Ashley was reporting that the North Tower was going down…again folding in on itself like paper. It was going to be a night of terror. For 48 hours Ashley reported the news nonstop. By the time her replacement came, she was drained and emotionally spent.

For the first time in her life, she truly felt American and she was beyond despair. Like every other American, her life would never be the same. "Lawrence," she heard herself whisper.

CHAPTER TEN
Randy

New York, September 11, 2001, 7:30 a.m.

"MRS. AUSTIN," Mensa voice came over the intercom, "Ms. Josephine is here to pick you up. Says you're expecting her."

"Bloody hell," Randy struggled upright sending a shooting pain across the front of her head. Too much wine, she should have stuck to her vodka. Red wine, no matter how expensive, always gave her a headache. Randy popped two aspirins and washed them down with a swig from the Pellegrino bottle on the side table. Jesus, it was already 7:30 a.m. Dragging herself to the edge of the bed, she clicked on the intercom. "Mensa, patch Josephine through, would you."

"Hey Randy," Josephine, who had no idea of the power of her voice, said between bites, "I'm in your kitchen doing something awful."

Randy wished the woman wouldn't talk with her mouth full. "What's that?"

"Eating a strip of bacon."

"Bad fats," Randy said, pushing back nausea that rose.

"Are you on your way down?"

"I overslept. Do you want to come up?"

"I can't really, darling. We were supposed to meet the others for breakfast at 8:00 am. Have Richard drive you down when you're ready."

"I can't make it today," Randy explained. "I have a meeting with the party planners for June's graduation. I completely forgot. You know how hard it is to get an appointment! Go on without me. Tell the others I'll see them next time." Randy's head throbbed even more at the thought of June's graduation. Lawrence would be puffing up like a peacock taking credit for their child's achievements. That ass hadn't even been at her birth and in twenty-one years he'd been to two parent/teacher meetings. At least she'd done that. If anyone had the right to puff up it was Mensa. Mensa, the third born and always the wisest child according to Ghanaian tradition had jet black eyes that missed nothing. She was as much a caretaker to the Austin's as she was a matriarch. Randy slumped back onto the bed contemplating her new day from hell. If she hadn't had so much to drink, she'd be well on her way to another day routine which started for her at 5:00 am. She deserved a break today she thought, crawling under the cover and pulling up the sheets. Seven thirty, she thought rolling over!

• • •

"Mrs. Austin. Miiiisss Auuuustin." Mensa had burst into her room at 8: 47 a.m. "Turn on the TV!"

Randy without rising turned on the T.V. by the remote that was buried under her covers.

"Look…look at this." Mensa was screaming.

Randy pushed her head over the cover and as she realized what was happening bolted upright. "What on earth." Nothing had ever come close to the horror that unfolded before their eyes. To confirm that this was not art imitating life, Randy sprinted from the bed and took the stairs to her roof-garden two at a time, Mensa close on her heels. The sky was filled with dark plume. It was in utter disbelief that they watched as a dark mass from the south flew over the Statue of Liberty and plunged into Tower Two of the World Trade Center at 9:03 a.m. The cataclysmic release of the Boeing 747 on impact, that later became known as the death weapon coming out of thin air, was beyond comprehension as they watch the Towers absorb the impact. "Bloody, striking hell," Randy screamed as Mensa broke into *Fante*. Surreal as the morning must have been for people around the world, to New Yorkers and Americans, the attack on the Twin Towers was not only surreal, it was galvanizing and ineffable. For many, it would be a final reality. For her, it was a now or never moment.

Lawrence worked on the 28th floor of Tower Two, but it was not his life that went up in flames before her eyes, it was her own. What if she had died on that day? What kind of life would she have lived? Her own survival dominated her thoughts. She was frantic and panicked for her husband's safety, yet, all she felt was a pervasive sadness that if she had died in that blaze all she would have taken with her was a life of pain and sadness. Randy sought refuge in the numbness that had been her life. The tears that were now wetting her cheeks in salty streams, had been tears of deep regret for the entire world.

New York froze as the stalwart buildings melted like icicles in the hot sun. The phone began ringing off the hook. Mensa, the amazing, had by now secured all the windows to prevent the pungent smells from entering the house. June, who had been the first to call was beyond consoling and was frantically trying to reach her father.

He was the second person to call.

"I'm fine," his voice was surprisingly calm. "I got out in time but I gotta help some people. It's going to be a long day honey. There is gridlock down here and the heavens are raining ashes. I'll get there as soon as I can. I'm fine."

"You should call your family in Ghana and let them know you are okay," Randy said to Mensa.

"They will not know of this thing. We have no television or phones. But I will write so by the time they hear in the north, the letter might have reached. "This is very bad."

"Oh Mensa," Randy said. "Very bad."

That day would force Randy to find a space in this world for herself.

CHAPTER ELEVEN
Amelie

Portugal, November 2001

FOR WEEKS NEW YORK CITY was transformed but like true New Yorkers, it bounced back under the clear and concise leadership of Giuliani. He looked and sounded like a man in charge while George Bush faded into stupidity.

Robb had been sure that 9/11 would have canceled their trip all together but Amelie was not hearing a word of it. Amelie was more insistent than ever that they just had to go.

"I am so relieved everyone is fine. I can't imagine what families of lost loved ones are going through. What can we do? Imagine Robb, I could have been one of those people. I could have been there. I tell you, instincts are God's protection. Let's take time while we have it. Tomorrow isn't promised." As much as Amelie despised Wall Street she'd reached out to every one of her co-workers and even her ex-boss.

• • •

Lisbon was not what either of them had expected. So here they were in Lisbon climbing what seemed like endless hills. The main square of the seaport entrance to the city, Rio Tejo, sat at the foot of Dom Joao VI, fiercely holding on to its past splendor. Old and new, jarring and laid back, the city had come alive before them on buses, trams and on foot. In Portugal life hummed along and America seemed far, far away. Robb and Amelie visited Alfama, Chiado, Cais do Sodre, Alameda, and Rossio. In Rossio, they were fascinated as they watched pastel and ochre buildings seamlessly fade into modern edifices. The only building out of place was the mammoth western edifice erected for Expo '98.

Robb stood at the top of the hill and waited for Amelie who kept stopping every few minutes to catch her breath. When she finally made it up to where Robb was patiently waiting, a smug grin on his face, she, was totally winded.

"You look breathless my dear," he teased kissing the top of her head.

"Shut up," she croaked collapsing against his chest.

"Why are you mad at me? You're the one who wanted to come to Portugal. Portugal has lots of hills to climb."

"And trams to get you up them," she said still gasping.

Having lost the coin toss to take the *Elevador* up the steep hill of *Rua de São Pedro de Alcântra,* Amelie was determined to make it to the top.

"All right, give me your hand." Robb wrapped his long fingers around hers.

As they walked the final stretch of *Rua de São Pedro de Alcântra* myriad interesting shops lined the avenue.

"Just what I need," Robb said, pulling her into a coffee shop. Amelie was happy to oblige. "*Dos café,*" he said to the barista hoping his Spanish would work. He didn't speak a word of Portuguese. Robb pulled out a chair and Amelie flopped down gratefully. "How about a couple of these,"

Robb pointed to the *broa de milho* which looked just like cornbread. The barista pronounced the name for them. When he realized they were Americano, he expressed his sympathies.

"Thank you," Amelie said before turning to Robb. "Yumm…these are delish," as she took another bite of the cornbread. What's your favorite thing about Portugal?"

"You."

"Besides that," she laughed.

"The cafés. Visiting Plato's grave. His poetry is even more alive for me now. And yours?"

"Everything. Roast suckling pig. Codfish and potatoes. I think my Mum would like that best. Now and then she'd make something called Ackee and Saltfish. It tastes like this Codfish and potatoes. My next favorites are the tram rides to Estrela, and to Belém, the Carriage Museum and the Mosterio dos Jerónimos. Thank you for this, honey." Amelie leaned over and kissed her husband's cheek. "I really love you so much."

"No more than I love you," he touched his lips to hers. "Ready?"

"Yes. I'm so glad we are going down the hill," she smiled. Re-linking hands, they canoodled every now and then as they made the trek back down the avenue. Halfway to their destination was a beautiful park boasting an amazing view of the sun cresting.

"Wow, look at that sunset, Robb. Let's just sit here and watch his majesty go down."

"That is a beauty. But it could be a her, no?"

"I don't think so. The Moon is a her. They are twin souls…like us."

The sunset spread a rust hue over the already vivid colors of Lisbon and there was a freshness to the air that made Amelie think of lilacs. This, Amelie thought was one of God's perfect moments. The wind was singing softly in the key of life as she rested her head on Robb's shoulder. Amelie squeezed her husband's hand. She had been spared to bring music back to the world. "Robb…"

"Huh," he smiled at her.

"Just listen to the world in harmony. It creates everything. Beautiful music, golden light, winds that whisper softly against your cheek and words of love in your ear. Can't you hear it, darling?"

"Ah yes. I'm glad we came. But tell me, darling, what are you going to do about the music?" Robb pulled Amelie closer.

"I don't know. I'm scared to even think about it."

"Scared? Amelie, you were the best pianist at Julliard. I never ever understood why you really quit," he said.

"Oh please, not that again. It's the same reason as always Robb. Carnegie. My memory slipped in front of thousands of people. How was I to face that again and again? Real pianists never fail."

"Nonsense. Even Schumann, I'm sure, had a memory slip"

"And look what happened to him, huh? Jumped out the window. My mother didn't help either you know. She never wanted me to seriously pursue a career in music."

"How well I know the baggage of others' expectations. Well, it's a good thing we are both stubborn. Can't let anyone else define our reality, so young lady it's time to face the music." Robb laughed at his clever pun.

"I'm ready," Amelie boxed his ear playfully.

"What does ready look like?"

"Scary Dr. Vlachenko."

As the sun sank slowly beneath the horizon Robb and Amelie slipped through the massive door of Solar do Vinho do Porto. The soothingly lit salon, with its overstuffed armchairs, was warm and welcoming. They found a tucked away corner, held hands and sipped glasses of a 20-year-old tawny Port. Amelie was happy about her decision to go back to music yet she was fearful. What if she failed? Well after midnight they strolled back down the hill. It was their last night of a two-week vacation. "Robb…" Amelie said looking at the man who was her best friend and lover, her confidant and her easy chair. Most women would kill to have her life yet she still agonized. How personal the journey of self-discovery?

"Yes, darling?"

"I want to listen to some *Fado* one last time."

"Now? It's midnight already."

"So, what? We don't leave until evening. Please, Robb."

"But Amelie we don't want to be so tired that we have to take a vacation from our vacation. Let's call it a night."

"Tomorrow," Amelie said sadly, "We go back to such sorrow. I'll be pining for the simplicity of this place. I hate the thought of going back. I don't belong in America, Robb. I belong in a place that understands no time."

"Time is time and belongs to the world. It's not going home that's the problem Amelie, its facing reality. You can't run away from life darling, you've got to face the music once and for all. Life has offered you a gift. Use it. Time has offered you more time. What are you going to do about that? Just think Amelie, you quit your job a day before the towers went down. Our story could have had a different ending. Darling just do it."

"I'm so scared." Amelie's body began a slight shiver. "What if I'm too old to go back to the stage? What if Dr. Vlachenko won't take me on?"

"Then you'll find a new teacher."

"Impossible. I can't go back to the stage without him! I'm not sure if I can do this at all, Robb."

"All you have to do is try sweetie. Give Dr. Vlachenko a call and go from there. No point talking yourself into failing because you won't try."

"I'm a failure, aren't I? I never finish anything I start. Why am I so scared of failing?"

"We're all scared of failing." Robb took her chin in his hand. "What you should be more afraid of honey, is not trying."

Robb had always understood her divided selves. Like her favorite madman Schumann, she too had her *Florestan* and *Eusebius*. "I'm going to give it another try, Robb." Amelie's voice was convincing.

"You're not going to try, darling, you're going to do it," he said, and then encircled her shoulders with his strong, protective arm. "Come on kiddo. Let's go listen to some *Fado*."

CHAPTER TWELVE
Randy

New York 2002

BY JANUARY, THOUGH resilient, lower Manhattan had become a ghost town. The horrific tragedy had crippled the city temporarily but it had risen on its crutches more united. It seemed normal life was just beginning to return and Randy had an appointment with the graduation consultant for June's graduation. Randy plodded through the sprawling white kitchen, onto the patio and down to the landscaped garden where an oval glass table was set for her morning coffee. The garden, a private vine-covered glass enclosed haven with a panoramic view, was awash in sunlight. The heaters were blowing at full speed, mixing with the bitter cold outside, rendering the room the perfect temperature. It was heaven to sit up in the sky sipping coffee and looking out over the still spectacular Manhattan skyline that would never be the same. Like the skyline, the tragedy sparked in Randy a new yearning to live life.

"Morning, Mrs. Austin."

"Good morning, Mensa," Randy greeted her.

"Breakfast this morning, ma'am?" Mensa asked bustling around the kitchen. Her braids were tucked neatly under a white cap and her apron, girded over her big body was without a single spot. Randy had never ceased to wonder how she accomplished that feat.

"Toast, maybe a poached egg. Any news I should know about?"

"June is coming today. She wants to go shopping for graduation."

Randy smiled. Did Mensa think she'd forget her daughter's graduation or for that matter that June would let her forget? "I remember. She'll be here at 3:00 p.m. I'll be back by then. Who goes shopping for a graduation five months away? Fashions will change by April."

"June does," Mensa said, satisfaction in her voice. She had taught her to be a planner.

Randy glanced at Mensa. She was a proud woman. African women always seemed so sure of themselves no matter what position in life they held. "What do you think I should get her for graduation?" Randy asked, avoiding Mensa's penetrating eyes, knowing full well that if anyone knew what June wanted it would be her.

"I've been trying to figure that out myself. Since she took up with that new boyfriend she hardly bothers to call. New love, I suppose."

"Can you find out?" Randy asked pouring coffee.

"Don't rightly know. I suppose I could ask her but why not just get her something from the heart," Mensa said more staunchly. "She'd like that."

"You're right," Randy agreed, buttering her toast. What heart? She'd been too wrapped up in her own drama all her life to know much about her husband or her child. June often complained that they might as well be invisible. Pets to scratch and de-flea now and then. Randy loved them the best she could.

• • •

"Mom!" The voice was just outside the dressing room door. "Oh, there you are," June Austin said as she burst into the room. Dressed in boot cut jeans and a fitted blue sweater, June was tall and slender. The twisted knot atop her head, dreads, gave her mother conniptions. Her mother, as always, was immaculate in an ecru pantsuit and crisp oxford shirt. Next to her June always felt like a bum. "Good, you're ready."

"For what, dear?"

"To go shopping. I think we'll start on Fifth and then go to Soho."

"But I didn't expect you until later. I have to meet the party planners this morning. You know how long it took me to get this appointment after we had to cancel?"

"How could you forget that I was coming home today? I rearranged my entire schedule and you forgot. I wanted to go shopping!" June huffed.

"I didn't forget June, I just thought you said you'd be here at 3:00 p.m." Randy turned to her daughter. "Isn't 21 a little old to be pouting, darling?"

"I had a change of plans," June said, pouting even more.

"Then you should have called. If later doesn't work for you, maybe we can still go tomorrow."

"Tomorrow I have plans. I can't go tomorrow. I came home today to go shopping," June said stomping her feet like a two-year-old. The polar opposite of her narcotized mother, June accidentally on purpose, pushed over an expensive bottle of perfume that shattered sending overpowering fumes into the air. Barely four months since

9/11 and all the unity had dissipated…blame was back stronger than ever. Bush was blaming Iraq instead of Afghanistan for all that happened to the World Trade Center and June was blaming her because she didn't use the phone.

"Mother you are so damn exasperating," June said storming out of the room.

"Oh dear," Randy followed her, "why do you always have to be so clumsy." She buzzed the intercom in the hallway for Mensa to send someone to clean up the mess. "Okay," Randy called after her daughter, "why don't you come with me now and we'll go shopping right after? It would be great to spend some time together and you can tell the party planner exactly what you want."

"Ugh! That doesn't work for me, Mother," June huffed again. "I'll come back on Sunday so just make sure you're here."

June flopped down on the exquisite couch in the hallway crossing her booted feet on the silk covering. Randy pretended not to notice. June looked at the woman in front of her. She felt no maternal attachment to her. Spending an entire day with her would be sheer punishment. "By the way, I need five thousand dollars."

"For what?"

"I'm going away with some friends to celebrate graduation. We're thinking Vegas for a weekend. My credit cards are maxed out and they need to be paid. Will you write me a check, please?"

"Vegas? Isn't that a little…"

"Downright sleazy. Yup. That's the idea."

"There are signed checks in the top drawer," Randy didn't bother to argue. "Fill in the amount you want."

June turned to leave the room and for a split second had the urge to tell her mother that she wanted her to care about her choices. She wished that she could tell her that she loved and needed her and wanted to have her undivided and unconditional love but the words didn't make it past her lips.

"So, Sunday then."

"Absolutely."

"Hey lady." June met Mensa in the hallway, a bundle of laundry in hand. She kissed her warmly.

"Hey, scallywag. When did you come in?"

"Just now."

"Hungry?"

"Yeah. What did you make?"

"I'll make you pancakes and blueberries."

"You're the best," June grabbed the laundry and kissed Mensa again. "I'll help you like old times. Mother forgot I was coming." She sounded dejected.

"Huh. That's not true. I told her you'd be here at 3:30 pm. It's your fault for not calling. You know your mother is precise. Every moment packed with something. Since you started seeing the boy…"

"Ethan," June punctuated Mensa's speech.

"You don't even call me."

"I'm in love, Mensa. Really in love this time."

"*Chu*," Mensa sucked air through her teeth, "I've heard that before."

"When do you think I should introduce him to Dad?"

"When Ethan lasts past two months." Mensa rolled her eyes.

CHAPTER THIRTEEN
Adele Bijou

Tribeca, 2002

ADELE BIJOU'S ADDRESS was in Tribeca. 13 Varick Place. Randy stuffed the paper with the address in her coat pocket. She bet Adele and De Niro were probably the only people left in Tribeca as the place was deserted. De Niro was on the case though, asking people to return to lower Manhattan. Ashley would have had a conniption if Randy had told her Adele's address. "1+3 =4." She could hear Ashley's ominous voice. "She's just asking for trouble." As the rickety elevator wheezed its way up to the loft, Randy smiled at the thought of her sister and her crazy obsession with the number four. She was also pleased with her idea for June's present; a painting from Adele. Relieved to make it to the top she rang the doorbell of the artistically painted door, re-slipping the paper on which the address was written into her pocket.

"*Allo?*"

"It's Randy Austin. Is it unforgivable of me to stop by unannounced? I was in the area meeting with my daughter's party planners and thought I'd drop by to look at your work, as I promised. I did try to call but my cell battery ran out of bars." She held up the offending machine.

"*Oh là.* I will never get used to Ame-ri-kan ways. Friends don't have to call to come over." Adele opened the door and greeted Randy, who withdrew ever so slightly from her touch, a kiss on each cheek. "It is nice that you come. Welcome."

Randy stepped into the loft. It was huge and eclectic. Too large for a single person. Randy guessed it to be about three thousand square feet, priceless in New York. This woman, she thought had a deep connection to herself. The loft was a hodge-podge of her world travels; African fertility seats, mahjong tiles set out on tables, a Ganesh altar, a Spanish mantilla draped over a manikin, French silks on chairs and American steel. Wow! Original, but far too chaotic for her sensibilities which required absolute order.

"How are you? I should have called. I'm sorry. I only just now realized how close…It must have been frightening."

"Ah, we do not talk about that horror. I just finally got that awful smell from my nose. It was horrific this close up. Dust and death. It was awful." Her voice was pained.

Randy shook her head. She understood death.

"These are amazing," Randy said distracting herself from weighty memories, walking over to the works that lined the walls. Works that should have been out of place in the shabby chic space, seemed only to complement. "Is this all your work?"

"No. Not all. I have many artist friends."

"Which ones are yours?" Randy asked examining the canvasses.

Adele pointed to several pieces Randy had already decided she liked.

"You came to see my paintings. Thank you."

"Yes. I wanted to see your style. If I liked it, I was going to ask you to consider creating a piece for my daughter's graduation."

"Ahhh…commissioned! Your daughter is very lucky." Adele's French accent floated in the air. "Would you like a cafe?"

"I've already had three cups. I'll take orange juice if you have it."

"Straight from the tree. Croissant?"

"I'm really sorry. I should have called first. My sister Ashley does this all the time and I'm usually furious with her, now here I am doing the same thing" Randy apologized again. Contrary to her normal formality, Randy could feel herself relaxing.

"Sit." Adele waved her over to a sofa. "I can't join you, my coveralls are splattered." Indeed, they were splotched with a kaleidoscope of dried and fresh paint.

"Thank you for being so gracious."

"Randy you can come by anytime. I'm not from New York so I like surprises. Now," she said as she disappeared behind a rattan screen which apparently was the kitchen, "tell me what you have in mind for your daughter?"

"I was thinking of something classic. Soft. Inspiring. Thought provoking. Something she'd be proud to hang in her first home. She's an intellectual," Randy laughed. "There's not an artistic bone in her body but she appreciates good art. My husband will probably give her a car or a trip to Italy or both. I want to give her something that can be passed on for generations. Something from the heart."

"This is good thinking. It was my mother who got me interested in painting when I was only so high." Adele emerged from behind the room divider and brought her hand to her waist. "We'd take our brushes, canvas, easel and a picnic basket with cheeses and bread to the park. Those were good years. "Find the shape, she would say. Paint the space and the light will follow. Push hard on the brush and sweep. See the work in your mind's eye." Adele had been given over to the memory. "My mother was a very good artist. Studied at Academies in Paris, Italy, and Spain before I was born. *O-range* juice," she placed a glass in front of Randy.

"Thank you. Do you still paint with your Mum sometimes?"

"No, she died when I was sixteen."

"I'm sorry."

"Why do people say that? When I die, I don't want people saying I'm sorry. I want them to dance. What kind of music do you like?"

"I'm not sure. I suppose classical mostly," Randy answered. "It is what I know most about I suppose."

"Boring. I like hip-hop. I'll play hip-hop now and when I'm dead I leave it in my last will and testament to play hip-hop at my funeral." She crossed the room to the old-fashioned jukebox player.

Shaggy began crooning. "You're my Angel, you're my darling, Angel."

"That's not hip-hop," Randy laughed. "Even I love that song. My Jamaican roots."

Adele clapped her hands. "Reggae. I love Bob Marley!"

For the first time in what seemed a lifetime, Randy completely relaxed, sinking further into the shabby chic sofa. The jukebox made a whirring sound.

"Isn't that bad for the CD's?" Randy got up and walked over to the stacks of CDs against the wall. "You have discriminating taste in music," she said flipping through the collection of CDs and old vinyl.

"Oh, this is an old thing converted to laser. When it warms up it will be perfect." Adele smiled. "When I was a kid, I wanted to be a rock star," she shared, pretending to play the guitar. "What about you? Did you always want to be a housewife?"

Housewife! Randy had never considered herself a housewife. A member of the social registers perhaps, but never, never a housewife! "No. I'd always pictured myself having a career in the arts," she heard herself say defensively. Did she really? She hadn't thought of what she wanted in life until just now.

"*Oui?* Doing what?

Randy thought for a minute then answered. "An art dealer."

"I knew it the first time I saw those paintings in your house. You would have been great."

"Yes. I would. I always envisioned having important clients from all over the world rave about my keen eye and refer me as the best purveyor of paintings. My gallery would be filled with the "next" Monet, Manet or Picasso from all over the world." Her voice was excited and she laughed, only half-joking.

"And why did you not do this?" Adele asked.

"First, marriage then the baby carriage. When my daughter June was born Lawrence's, career took precedence."

"So why not do it now?"

"Now?" Randy repeated. She must've lost her mind. Anyway, what was she doing telling all this to a perfect stranger? A career? She wouldn't know where to begin. "I'm too long removed from the world of art to seriously think I could open a gallery."

Adele waved away her excuse. "Ah, nonsense. It is, how

you say… like riding a bicycle. It is better to try than to regret a lost past. So, what if it is a mistake? Make amends and move on to the next remorse. That's life. Anyway, tragic stories make for interesting stories."

Randy looked up Adele. The midday sun had fallen golden and warm on her face. "That's an interesting philosophy."

"Come," Adele said, "I want you to see my studio. It is only there that you can really understand my work."

Randy followed Adele through the dining area, living quarters and her bedroom to the studio. How could she afford all of this? She was so young. Maybe she had a rich lover. Or she was probably an heiress? "Oh my," Randy, shuddered, "this view is…how can you…"

"It reminds me to live every day with purpose."

Those words resonated with Randy's new conviction. She was a woman on fire. She just hoped it didn't burn her up! Though reluctant to look out the floor-to-ceiling window, Randy found herself pulled to the portal. The crater below was enormous, like it had been struck by the hand of a God deeply displeased with the sins of His people. Fed up with the wickedness of the world He had created in seven days, He had roared mightily. In this case, destruction was at the hands of Allah. Holy Jihad. Below, yellow, Caterpillar rigs with giant arms silently protracting and contracting, pirouetted, depositing leftover debris in giant trashcans. Debris containing human remains and crumpled lives. Randy had never seen Ground Zero up close and personal. Hadn't wanted to. Hadn't wanted to burden her already heavy heart with such visions. This tragedy had forced her beyond "reason," making her cry out into the night and her dreams restless. Randy inched closer, forcing herself to look. Ground Zero made her shudder.

"You get used to it. Like everything else," Adele said.

In the airy studio, canvasses of finished and unfinished works lined every wall. Jars of brushes; filberts, fitches, glazing, lettering, among others, felt soft to the touch. Palettes of color, azure, Prussian blue, cadmium reds, yellows, oranges and the infamous vermilion lay waiting to create.

"Where do you get the subjects for your sittings?" Randy asked looking at the stacks of nudes.

"Oh, anywhere really. Friends. Family. Students."

"And they don't mind posing nude?"

"Why would they?" Adele knitted her brows, genuinely baffled.

"Well…"

"American prudishness and hypocrisy. The body wants to be appreciated like anything else of beauty not just used as a sex symbol or labeled, how do you say… ah, dirty." Adele turned to Randy. "Would you like to sit for me one day? I would be honored."

"You're too kind," Randy smiled. "Just this morning I was examining my gravity problems and their relationship to my upcoming almost half a century birthday. I'm sure you can find a much better subject."

"What is wrong with aging? Fifty is not old. I can't wait to be fifty. To tell the truth I look forward to the gravitational pull. Wrinkles offer a certain wisdom, no?" she asked winking at Randy.

"It's wonderful to be in your thirties, Adele. That's why you can romanticize being fifty. I can't imagine anyone wanting wrinkles. My sister, Ashley, just forty-three mind you, goes to Botox parties to get rid of minor wrinkles."

"But it's the truth. Really. Why would I lie? Americans put too much emphasis on age and looks, and on morality and conformity. We should be free to make mistakes. If we were more adventurous maybe we could learn to appreciate more of everything, life, love, art."

"Do you really live life the way you talk about it?" Randy asked. A curiosity was edging into her consciousness. She'd never met anyone like Adele, so young, accomplished, and free.

"I rarely calculate the consequences of my actions. I live as life presents itself, taking and giving in equal parts."

"That's amazing," Randy, said gazing out the window. She wished she were brave enough to live without consequences.

"You have to be more exciting, more daring, more in love with life. Then your husband will want you and you will want him again. It all begins up here." Adele tapped the side of her head.

Randy was taken by surprise. "Did I say there was a problem with my marriage?"

"Your mouth doesn't have to. Your eyes tell all. What secret do you hide behind those eyes? What disappointments? What pain and hurt?" Adele taunted.

"What are you talking about?" Randy bristled.

"Don't make me have to say it. The eyes are the window to the soul. I can see in your eyes that you are burying your life. I can see you are afraid to live. Come," Adele slid the scarf from Randy's shoulder, "Let's dance. I teach you how to dance for your husband tonight. How to drive him wild with desire."

"No, really, stop." Randy was now quite annoyed. This was really all too much.

"Yes, of course, if you want." Adele spun her around to face her. "Look right here into my eyes," she held her close.

Randy laughed nervously. She hated to be touched; she rarely even touched her own body. Not since her innocence had been shattered and the ghost had moved in to inhabited her body. Randy pushed the memory and Adele away.

Adele's hips undulated side to side. The spaghetti straps of her tank top fell off her left shoulder and she pulled the rubber band holding up her ponytail and her hair came cascading down like a waterfall from the messy upsweep. Randy wondered how anyone could be so unselfconscious.

Randy stepped back from Adele and smiled. "I'm not big on romance, Adele. I'm sorry I have to go. My daughter is coming at 3.00 p.m.," she lied.

"Okay, enough for now," she said as she stopped dancing, "but we try again next time until sparks light up those eyes."

"Not likely." Randy moved to the other side of the room.

"You know one thing about the past that seems to be a well-kept secret?"

"Can't say I do?" Randy was reluctant to engage in any further conversation or demonstration.

"When you shine a light on the past, it becomes like all other things translucent so we can explore its lessons and messages. In light mysteries unfold, the past dissipates and present answers are revealed. Don't you think?"

"I think you should have been a philosopher or a psychiatrist," Randy snorted, gathering her purse.

"Viola." Adele abruptly changed the subject pulling the cloth off her latest work. "A painter's eye must see everything."

"Oh, my goodness," Randy gasped, stepping closer to the large canvas of three women. Even agitated, the work took Randy's breath away. "It's magnificent. It's so very…"

"No…noo…don't…never," Adele stopped her. "In art, there is only one thing worthwhile and that is what cannot be explained."

"Georges Braque quote," Randy said nodding. 'Only novices and amateurs try to explain art. One either feels it or not.' Still, this reminds me of Renault's, The Three Graces. Have you thought of having a solo show? You're very talented."

"Now you are saying nice things," Adele's dimpled smile returned. Deep dimples that pinched her skin giving her a mischievous grin.

"And, why not? What do you think of the idea?" Randy pressed.

Adele waved the thought away. "I have an agent for that sort of thing. I hate business. I just want to paint."

"You sound like my sister Amelie. She really should've been only a musician. She went to the Juilliard at sixteen and then for some crazy reason ends up in business. She recently quit her job. Said her musical muse was becoming tyrannical. I hope she goes back to her art."

"I admire that. I admire people who are brave enough to follow their heart. The heart wants always what the heart wants and there is no reason it should not get it. We cannot hide forever from our passions."

"Except me," Randy said.

"Not if you dance. Not if you are brave enough to shine light into your dark corners. Wouldn't having a gallery give you the passion that makes you tingle all over as you did just now Randy?" The woman insisted on touching her, "Isn't it passion that makes people brave, bold and fearless?"

"Yes," Randy answered, surprising even herself.

"Then do it, Randy. Open a gallery," Adele said, putting her hand on Randy's arm.

"I'm not so sure anymore," Randy said, still unnerved by Adele's touch but didn't pull away.

"Only we can stop ourselves. You wanted to stop. Maybe for good reason but there is always hope. Greatness comes from pain and struggle and the promise is never better than the dream. Live now, Randy. Tomorrow may be too late." Adele said, finally letting go of her. "Just look outside that window. So," she said a radiant smile plastered on her face, "when do you need the painting done?"

Randy, confused by Adele's comment, stared at her. Adele stared right back. Randy knew deep down that Adele was right. Her one-dimensional life, barely showing any evidence of a sinuous rhythm, except perhaps in the lines at the corner of her eyes, continued on its path without variation. After a few moments, Randy finally answered Adele. "Graduation is in June, six months away. Is that enough time?"

Adele bit her lips, her eyes rolling upwards in thought. "Hmm, we'll see. No promises. But I will try. If I miss, you give it to her as a wedding gift. *D'accord.*"

"Okay," Randy laughed, totally charmed by Adele's insouciance and *joie de vivre.*

"I'll return in a week to see what you think."

Adele walked Randy to the door and took her hand in both of hers. "I like you, Randy. Come see me anytime. We talk more next time and you will learn to dance. I promise your life is only scary if you make it so." Then she frowned. "By the way what is a Botox party?"

CHAPTER FOURTEEN
Ashley

New York, 2002

TRAFFIC WAS BUMPER to bumper. "Can't you take the back streets," Ashley implored the cabbie.

"No back streets to your destination, lady. Might as well read a book and relax," the Indian guru suggested. "I can put meditation music on."

"No thank you." Ashley sulked from La Guardia all the way to the East Side where Mr. Follette had requested her appearance on Wednesday at 12 noon without, it seemed, a care for her after 2:00 p.m. request. She had not seen him since the day of 9/11 and nothing had changed at the station for seven months. The world that had gone on hiatus was just going through the motions.

A taxi barreling down on them was damn near riding on the sidewalk. The driver, horn blaring as though he had the right of way and this was his own private sidewalk lane, almost sideswiped them. The Indian cabbie rolled his eyes and inched over as far as he could. Yep, New Yorkers were crazy and New York was back.

Ashley had promised to have lunch with her sisters today but this 12-noon summons put a wrinkle in her plans. She dug out her cell phone and punched up her sister's number. "Randy, I have to push back our lunch date today. How about dinner? Can you check in with Amelie?"

Randy, used to her sister's iffy ways, simply bellowed at her. "Call when you're can commit to something and keep it. I am not available tonight."

Ashley held the phone listening to the dial tone. When did her sister get this ballsy? "Are your friends and family a pain in the ass?" Ashley asked the cabbie, tucking the phone into the side of her purse.

"The worst," he smiled.

No point getting an ulcer Ashley sunk further into the seat and unfolded the newspaper she had tucked away in her briefcase. Before she knew it, the cab was pulling up to a high-rise building. "You're here now." He checked her out through the rearview…a nice-looking woman.

"Great." Ashley scooped up her belongings and was about to open the car door when the doorman approached. She gave him her briefcase and fished out a hundred-dollar bill from her bag. "You know that family we were talking about earlier? We should get rid of them."

"I'm going to give that some real thought," he laughed.

"Let me help," Ashley stuffed the hundred-dollar bill into the cabbie's hand. "Use half to file divorce papers and the other for a cab ride to freedom," she grinned. As she swung through the revolving door at Fifty-first and Second Ave, the doorman greeted her.

"Whom shall I ring for you, Madam?"

"Melvadore Folette, please. 3505." 3+5+0+5=13; 1+3=4. Shit, the obvious dawned on her and she busted out laughing. His house number reduced added to the number thirteen.

And one plus three was FOUR. No fuckin' way. A bad omen!

"Who may I tell him is coming up?"

"Ashley Freeman."

The doorman buzzed the intercom and shortly turned to her. "Go right up," he replaced the black intercom phone, "He's expecting you."

Ashley rapped on the ornate heavy wooden door. It was immediately opened by a young man apparently of the same heritage as Mr. Follette.

"Please, come in. Mr. Follette is just finishing up on a call. He knows you are here but I'll just poke my head around." The man disappeared.

Ashley took the opportunity to look over the flat. The apartment was as handsome as the man she'd met… grand and confidently decorated. Enclosed almost entirely by glass, a set of French doors opened onto a patio overlooking the Hudson River. WOW! Ashley was impressed. People say one can tell the personality of a person by their décor but nothing about this residence suggested a foreign taste. Not the Spanish man she imagined him to be. Maybe Brazilian, Argentinean, maybe Moroccan. This apartment was all American grandeur. Ashley stepped out onto the balcony and waited.

Leaning back on the rail she took in the apartment from another view. A spiral staircase with a carved, oak banister ascended to a private heaven. The gigantic semicircular glass enclosed ecru kitchen boasted restaurant efficient appliances which would be of little use to her since she hated, with a capital H, cooking. But, the space, the style, the wealth, clearly was to her liking. Ashley pivoted to take in the equally breathtaking skyline.

"We used to be able to see the towers. I still don't believe they're gone," the voice behind her said.

"Gone but never forgotten," Ashley murmured. "Hello, Mr. Follette."

"Thanks for coming."

"Well, I did have to change around some stuff and now my sister is furious. It's the third time that I'm canceling our lunch date." It was not right that one person should get all God's best qualities Ashley thought looking at the man's face bathed in the midday sun. What? The thought caught her by surprise.

"My dear, I think it wise to get used to disappointing people. It's going to get worse if the hard news is your goal…no one will ever be able to count on you. One minute you're here and the next you're gone. Shall we?" He ushered her through the sliding door.

Ashley preceded him into the living room.

"Since I interrupted your lunch date, I can have Shar make you something."

"I'm fine thanks you. A glass of water will do."

He headed to the kitchen and she trailed behind him. "Shar, we'll have lunch in twenty-mins. Some water for the lady please."

Did he not hear her?

"I asked you here for two reasons." He ushered her out as Shar was opening the refrigerator and pulling out an aerated jug with lemons floating at the bottom. "I want to hear your thoughts on the new direction I'm planning to take WCNB and number two we'll talk about later."

Shar brought a tumbler and handed it to her.

"Thank you," Ashley accepted the glass and took two generous sips before she spoke. She needed to slow down her thoughts. "So exactly what do you have planned for the station?"

"Twenty-four-hour world news. News with no spin zone."

She is mesmerized by his face. Everything in symmetry. "Not like FOX, huh?"

"Definitely not like FOX. Rupert is a dangerous man. We've got to stop his aspirations for world domination."

"In principle, I love the idea. What journalist wouldn't? After all, journalism the world over is built on the same code of ethics, objectivity, and truthfulness and as a watchdog for the common man. I think, and have always thought, journalists are supposed to be impartial and above reproach. Not like now. What we've become are panderers to people with the most money. Honestly, I find it deplorable and abhorrent."

"As you should but let me correct you. Journalism in many countries is used to drive propaganda and to oppress. What's true is that it's dangerous business when the press is a pawn. That's a dangerous and slippery slope."

"Not only that. It's just so easy these days for a journalist to get caught up in believing their own press and try to become rock stars instead of journalists. What you propose is clearly the right thing to do but I'm not sure if the model is sustainable in America anymore. Advertisers will defect. And you know what happens to whistleblowers. Who would risk their lives and careers going up against the establishment's lies?"

"I disagree. What advertisers want are ratings. Eyeballs. Right? We can create tabloid television of a different kind, of a truer kind like America's Most Wanted that do society some good. Only our America Most Wanted will be the everyday crooks in the system. We are going to tell the news as it is. No more cloaked daggers for the American people. I want to expose the dishonest politicians persecuting prostitutes yet frequenting their beds, the homophobic right-wing pundit ranting about gays yet bending over in bathroom stalls, the judges who send sex offenders to jail who boot up their child pornography at nights, the wall street gambler who passes himself off as a financial advisor, the minister stealing from his own congregation in the name of God…these are the tabloid stories where reality is better than art. I will argue that the American people will tune in to see us clean up this rogue society. To get the real stories not the whitewashed, wag the dog news. If we have eyeballs, we have advertisers."

"That will never happen. The interest groups will lobby you out of business. The advertisers, you know, are the interest groups."

"I'm going to bet on the American people. We are going to be the pit-bulls of the news media. Offenders of the American people will be running from us like they need to win a marathon." His steely resolve only made him likable.

"It sounds like a grand experiment. One I'd love to be on board with."

"I thought so."

"How?"

"I'm a great judge of character."

Ashley smiled, a rarity for her. "That may be so Mr. Follette but I can tell you this for sure, I'll need a lot of refresher training, a lot of insurance coverage and a lot more money."

"Lunch is served," Shar said as he materialized at the doorway.

"Thank you," Melvadore pushed his chair backward. "Shall we?" he reached for her hand.

Ashley placed her hands in his, noting his long fingers yet again, and feeling a slight temperature rise at his touch. For some weird reason, her psychiatrist's voice popped into her head. She immediately distracted herself by taking in the well-set table for two. Everything was a deep blue down to the wine glasses. Once they were seated Shar brought out two pear and candied pecan salad with goat cheese. On a side plate were three Salmon a filet was done rare, medium and well done. Why hadn't he just asked her how she liked her Salmon? As though reading her mind, Melvadore said, "our culture."

"Which is?"

"A little mixed up. I'll tell you all about it later.... where were we? Ah, yes. I was about to discuss the second reason why you're here. I'd like to offer you one of the twelve positions on the re-org committee for WCNB. Think tanks, pragmatists, pessimists, optimists...everyone will look through different lenses...that means we can come close to objectivity. And, when we accomplish the job, I'd like to offer you a job in hard news."

Ashley tried all she could not to betray her excitement. The job she expected, but a member of the change committee, no way in hell. "I am honored, Mr. Follette. But are you sure? I don't have that level of management expertise."

"Management is nothing more than common sense and instinct. I'm betting that you have both."

"What of Phillip?"

"We'll see."

CHAPTER FIFTEEN
Amelie

Connecticut, 2002

"HOW ABOUT MAKING me breakfast this morning?" Robb asked as he got ready for work. He was enjoying having his wife home more than he ever thought possible. He just wasn't ready to tell her about William. He needed to brace her for his visit. He wished he didn't have to break the news to her but there was no putting it off any longer."

"Why would I do that? I've been waiting for you to help me plot my return to music and what have you done? Nada! Make your own breakfast."

Robb, who'd been working nonstop since their return from Portugal, had been of little help to Amelie about her future. "What is there to plot? Call Dr. Vlachenko."

"You think it's that simple?" Amelie snapped.

"Yes. Pick up the receiver and dial the number. I'll bet his number has not changed. People like that are rooted."

"I will but not this morning. Maybe tomorrow." Amelie sunk deeper under the covers.

"You have been saying that for how many months? Tomorrow never comes, darling."

"Sometimes it does."

"I have an idea what is so hard about this. Why not come into the city with me today and try to see Dr. Vlachenko?"

"Don't be silly dear. I don't have time today. Look, Robb, I know you're trying to be helpful but let me do this my own way. Please. He'll answer the letter if he wants me back."

"Amelie," Robb took her by the shoulders. "Didn't I go halfway across the world so you could listen to the music of your life? Didn't you just tell me to be more supportive? Now what? You're acting a little crazy and it's driving me crazy."

"All great musicians are crazy," Amelie hissed. "You do know Schumann killed himself, right."

"So, you remind me a million times. The solution is that either you kill yourself or get on with it."

Amelie's eyes flashed daggers. "That's really helpful and downright mean! I'm going to get there. I just don't think I'm ready. That's all," she snapped. Her voice softened and now she was staring at her husband with pathetic doe eyes. "I'll give him another week, maybe he's out of town."

"Oh, maybe the postman stopped off at the bar and forgot his load." He wasn't falling for the doe eyes gimmick!

"But the postman always rings twice."

"Not if he left his load at his lunchtime speakeasy."

Amelie rolled her eyes and flipped off the duvet. "I think I'll take a bike ride to clear my head," she said.

"Isn't clearing your head what Portugal was all about?" Robb was not getting trapped with double talk today either.

"Okay already. I'm going to get there," Amelie's voice was back to tartness. "When I'm ready!" She padded to the bathroom.

"Chicken," Robb called after her, answering his ringing cellular.

"Hey, Dad."

"Hey," Robb said.

"Why are you squawking? Did you tell Mom? Did she hit the roof?"

"Not yet." He took the opportunity to leave the room and head downstairs.

"Well, when are you going to tell her?"

"I'm trying to find the right time. Don't pressure me. I'm doing your dirty work. Honestly, I don't know how you could have let this happen."

"I'm sorry, Dad. I don't know either. I thought she was taking precautions. What else was I to do?"

"Take precautions yourself, stupid and how about you could have come clean four months ago. Your mother will be coming down in a minute. I'll tell her then and you'd better be ready for the call you're going to get buddy. I have to go."

• • •

Dressed in riding gear, Amelie grabbed a slice of toast from Robb's plate and flopped down opposite. "Who was on the phone?"

"William."

"And?"

"Do you want some coffee?"

"No. What did William want? Isn't he coming home next week?"

Just then the house phone rang. She'd taken to ignoring it. It had been more than seven months since her abdication from work and she was still getting calls. Everyone from her office had called, her staff, HR, her boss. This time when the phone rang, however, she bolted, just in case it was Dr. Vlachenko responding to her letter in which she'd put her number. Robb grabbed his keys, relieved that he could now tell her about William's debacle over the phone. He indicated with his thumb and pinky to his ears and lips that he'd call her.

The phone call was from the police officer's campaign fund. She hated the way they called for someone and when you say, 'wrong number' then they say, "…maybe you can help us.'' She pledged $100.00. Slipping on her riding gloves, Amelie went to the garage, unhooked the bike's handlebar, mounted it, clipped her helmet in place and rode down the long driveway towards Brunswick Street.

"Hey Jessie," she called out to her neighbor as she passed.

"Hey, Amelie. How are you today?"

"Just fine."

"I'll stop in later."

"That'd be lovely." Amelie prayed not. Jesse was a talker.

The uphill ride cleared Amelie's head, made her sweat profusely, yet unfortunately, she hadn't gained enough clarity to make a decision about her next step. Amelie could hear the phone ringing as she let the garage door down. She took off her helmet and hung it on the hook next to her bike and sprinted to catch the phone. She looked at the number scrolling on the LCD. Robb.

"Yes," she grabbed the phone.

"Hey there, girlie." Unable to stay mad at her man, she said, "Only yours. What's up, honey?"

"I need to talk to you about something."

"I know. I'm going to do better. I swear." It was indeed time to make a decision. Amelie knew that only too well.

"It's about William."

"William?" Fear crept into her voice. If there was anyone in the world Amelie would die for it was her pride and joy and her greatest accomplishment, William. "Is he, is he ok?"

"He's fine."

Pulling the elastic band from her ponytail, Amelie shook her hair free and relaxed a bit. "What about William then?" she said softly. In her gut, she felt something. But what? She was as close to her child as any mother could be and if something was wrong with William, she'd have intuited it.

"He's leaving school."

"Don't be daft, honey. He's got a year to go. Why would he do that?"

"Because he's getting married. Got his girlfriend pregnant."

"What? You've got to be bloody kidding me."

"I wish…"

"When did you know this and why didn't you tell me?"

"He called two weeks ago. I didn't have the heart to tell you then."

"And since then?"

"I needed to find the right time."

"There is no right time to tell me that my only son is ruining his life or that I've failed again."

"How is William's mistake your failure?" Robb was talking to a dial tone.

What the hell, she went into her music room. She turned on the stereo. *Gurrumul, Wiyathul* flowed from the airwaves. As much as she loved that song, she switched off the stereo and walked over to the oversized chair near the window.

What's with this bloody life! Why does this nonsense keep happing to her? What nonsense she wasn't quite sure but life was NOT in flow. What she needed right now was silence. How could William do this? Why hadn't he trusted her? Married? What about his life, his future, his indelible mark on the world? She thought back to Ashley's pregnancy dilemma. She was glad he wasn't a cad like that McDermott character but somehow, she wished he was not so honorable. Today abortions were no biggie. The girl, whoever she is, was getting an abortion and that was final. Of that, she was quite sure. Pausing in the middle of a thought came the realization that she'd never spent much time on things that affected her life personally. Why hadn't she questioned her mother about her dislike of music? Ask more about her father? What about her habit of plunging headfirst into decisions before evaluating causes or consequences? Where did that come from? Why did she often end up quitting a project when challenges arose? She supposed she should be proud that her son was not a quitter like her. That he hadn't gotten her coward gene. Amelie felt the tears pricking behind her eyelids. She wouldn't call him and berate him. She'd simply coax him into her logic. In fact, she wouldn't call him at all.

Overwhelmed Amelie sat on her window ledge and allowed the pent-up tears of frustration to flow freely. When she had no tears left, she showered, changed into her favorite jeans and a sweatshirt, and left the house for her daily routine. Since she'd returned home, she'd become a fixture at the local record store listening to music for hours on end, bolstering her confidence and talent in preparation to approach Dr. Vlachenko. Flopping into the overstuffed chair, her body hit the cushion with a thud and it responded by making a loud deflating sound. "Oops," she looked around hoping no one thought she was passing gas. The sales clerk smiled at Amelie then went about her duty of rearranging the stacks of misplaced CDs. Amelie smiled back and began flicking through record selections. What the hell was wrong with William? She was tempted to call him and give him a piece of her mind but she'd promised herself to stay level-headed. Today she'd let the music take her disappointment to a place of solace. She chose Mahler's *Symphony No. 6,* The Tragic.

"You've changed music today," the sales clerk observed, stopping in front of Amelie.

Amelie pulled off her headset. "Is it a problem?"

"Not at all, we love when customers enjoy themselves this much. But I'm curious. You've been listening to every rendition of *Fantasie* for several months now. I imagined you were practicing for your debut…but today you listen to Mahler…they couldn't be more different. Just curious."

Months! Amelie began to understand the level of her procrastination before finally answering the clerk. "I love Schumann. I did my studies on him. I once played *Fantasie* very well but it's been a long time. Today I got some very bad news. I was hoping Mahler could give me some clarity."

"Oh, I'm so sorry."

"Thank you. One day I hope to go back to the stage. When I do, I will play *Fantasie*."

"Oh, I know you will," the clerk smiled.

Feeling guilty at the implication of customers, Amelie bought ten versions of *Opus 17*. And Mahler's Tragic. "*One day, you're going to play the Hall again*," her musical muse chimed in. *So that was not a lie.*

"Shut the hell up," Amelie said loudly.

• • •

On the way home, Amelie stopped by the train station to pick up a schedule to New York. Maybe she should go back to work. Just resume her life where she left off. After all, if William left school, she may have to spend the rest of her life taking care of him and some hussy. *Which life?* Her musical muse slapped her on the back of her head.

CHAPTER SIXTEEN
Ashley

Bermuda, 2002

THE TWELVE NEWLY hired top brass at all the Follette affiliates were invited for a week of 'getting to know you' and deep indoctrination into the new culture and climate of WNCB. At their training facility in Bermuda these disciples, the guardians of media transparency and the new branding gurus of WNCB would hammer out their new strategy to deliver honesty in journalism. They were to go up against the increasingly irresponsible and ever-growing Fox channel, with its well-oiled platform that filled the airways with outrageous propaganda and wannabe media whores.

Most of the men and women of WNCB charged with the fierce fight for honesty and justice were longtime stalwarts of media…not only were they disillusioned by the new shock and kill media but they were academically prepared to give the American public the impartiality on which to base their decisions. They were news people because it was their calling not because it brought instant fame. Ashley was the only "lightweight" in the line-up.

The short flight from New York had been but a blip on the radar before they were landing. Ashley wondered how all the egos on the plane were ever going to get along long enough to accomplish their mission.

"Hey," Daniel Hobbs, a veteran hired from ABC sat next to her. "How do you figure into this equation?" He intimated her lack of experience.

"Being in the right place at the right time," Ashley said.

"I see. Well if you need any help…reach out to me," he scribbled his number on the napkin on her tray.

As soon as he left Ashley crumpled the napkin and stuffed it in the seat compartment." *Asshole.* A convoy from WNCB handled every detail of their entry into the country before spiriting them off to what was apparently called the 'compound'. The salty sea breeze that whipped through Ashley's hair was relaxing as they drove down the immaculately kept breezeways still displaying images of Queen Elizabeth. Her nerves were calmed. Ashley tuned out the various conversations that were happening around her with iTunes. Fifteen minutes later the car exited the main road and began a steep climb up a long, winding driveway that ended in front of a majestic house with backdrops of mountains and the ocean. Ashley felt a vague sense of belonging and a familiarity that she could not explain.

"Welcome to Landilow," voice after voice echoed as the WNCB party alit. The help, in full Up-the-Down Staircase regalia, numbered twenty-four. This was going to be some kind of pampering. Ashley hung back for a few seconds under the sculpted carport to take in the majestic house which had to be some 25,000 square feet. It was completely open on the ground floor all the way around its perimeter.

"Hello," came a throaty, accented voice floating on the breeze. Ashley looked up to see a gorgeous woman floating toward her in a fuchsia top, a chartreuse pedal pusher with a megawatt smile on her face. "Welcome to Landilow," she echoed. "From Melvadore's description, you must be Ashley. He didn't lie…you have amazing eyes."

Just then Melvadore, in tennis garb sidled up. He greeted Ashley with a robust hello and the other woman with a warm kiss that she returned three times. Cultural tradition, Ashley thought. Wiping her lipstick off his cheek with a handkerchief she'd whipped out of her sleeve, she moved inward to greet each guest with the utmost charm. "I hope your flight was wonderful. If you need anything, please just ask. We are here to make sure you are happy. WNCB loves happy employees," she said with a smile.

"I can't stress that enough," Melvadore echoed. "I trust you'll find an itinerary of activities and workshops in your rooms. Any questions ask Nemba, here," he touched the woman's shoulder.

Ashley averted her eyes. This man must have been sent by the devil to disrupt her peace. Her God wouldn't be that cruel. In the sunlight, Melvadore looked very much like a savior. "I will," Ashley said, glad to follow the woman and the other guests on a tour. After a short introduction, both Nemba and Melvadore disappeared, leaving the guests to be pampered by their two to one servants. Landilow, the sprawling 120-acre property with the most luxurious Danish beds, housed conveniences Ashley hadn't even heard of much less be privy to. Ashley, needing some alone time, chose to skip the welcome dinner and go straight to bed.

•••

"Slept well?" asked Melvadore Follette who'd snuck up behind her in the buffet breakfast line.

"Like the dead…the best I've ever had. From box springs to Danish beds, that's moving up. And you?" Ashley said, maybe just a little too acerbically, looking out from the massive gazebo to the pink sandy beach ahead.

"Very well."

"This is an amazing property." She filled her plate with fresh papaya of the deepest orange and pineapple of the yellowest yellow.

"And the perfect spot. Not too far from the US."

"Yumm," Ashley said, now distracted by the sugar-sweet papaya. She licked the juice off the side of her hand. "This is how fruit should taste. I remember this taste from my childhood."

"In England? I don't think so."

"No. I didn't go to England until I was four. Jamaica, where I was born."

"That explains why you hate the number four."

"I've never thought of that."

"Jamaica to England seems backward."

"Wouldn't know. Can't remember," Ashley said.

"You do remember. You remember the taste. The food is why I love the Caribbean. I stopped eating lamb, eggs, and oranges in America because they don't taste the same as at home. I think it was the oranges that made me buy this place." Melvadore popped a peg of orange in his mouth.

"It's not just the foods! I used to get so confused with spelling words the American way. Can you imagine what my journalism teacher said?"

He smiled. "I guess Papaya was your favorite fruit in Jamaica?"

"I don't know. All I do know is that these smells and tastes take me back there. To where exactly, I don't know.

My Mother never talked about home so for me it's just a place I was born."

"And you haven't visited the island of your birth?"

"No." Ashley's face held a quizzical look. Why hadn't she thought of that? Why hadn't she tried to find her father? That thought had never really occurred to her. "My mother always said we couldn't go back so I suppose I thought it was a place never to go back to."

Melvadore was about to say something, something that would have made their expatriation kindred when…

"Hello, darling." The toned, fit Mediterranean mien Nemba from the night before came up from the tennis courts and pecked Melvadore on the lips. "Couldn't wait on you for a game so I inveigled a poor, unsuspecting soul. Good way to see their stamina. It bodes well for what Melvadore is about to put you all through at WNCB," she said to Ashley.

"Nemba," Melvadore scolded, "you should try to let the guests win."

"Not on your life. What'd you say, Ms. Freeman?"

"I think one should win fair and square."

"See," the beauty grinned, as the sun started a sparkling dance on her white teeth.

"Are you looking forward to your first assignment?" The woman asked catching Ashley off guard. Ashley glanced over at Melvadore.

"Oh, I told Nemba that I thought your first job should be to the Middle East."

Ashley was a little miffed.

"Don't be mad, Ms. Freeman. Nemba, who believes all battles are won on the tennis court here, is my sister. I tell her everything."

"Your Sister?"

"My one and only."

"Yes. The one who took care of him and made him rich and famous. Join us for dinner tonight and I'll tell you all about it. I've got to run for now. I hope you beat him at a game." Nemba floated on. "See you at dinner tonight."

Ashley noticed how proudly Melvadore looked at his sister. "She is good at everything," he said preening. "I let her play all the new hires to see who will survive at WNCB. If they're not good at sports or gaming, they are usually not good for us."

"Maybe you shouldn't be telling me this. I'm one of them to be beaten," Ashley said. "Anyway, not to be disrespectful but if Nemba's playing is what you judge us by then I'll be okay. In my hay-day, she'd never get one set off me. Maybe I should just skip Nemba and play you."

"Sure, about that?"

"Yea," Ashley said confidently," feeling her killer backhand coming to life.

"You were that good, huh?"

"I'm still not bad, but yes I used to be that good. Unless you and Nemba played the USTA circuit, I'm sure I can beat you both."

"You don't want to say that. I'm a very competitive person on the court. Played Lendl once. I lost, but it was a great match."

"As I said, unless you played the circuit, I think I can beat you."

"Okay Miss Venus or Serena. Which one do you want to be?"

"Just Ashley. I can hold my own."

"Then let's make a bet. What do you have to lose?" Melvadore asked.

"The five pounds I'm going to gain this week."

"Good one. I never understand why women are so obsessed with weight. Anyway, meet you on the court at 1:00 pm." With that Melvadore headed in the direction of the new hires who were gathered like groupies at the breakfast table.

Ashley took her breakfast down to the pink shores that kissed Landilow on its eastward edge of the Bermuda Island. Back propped up against a sea-grape tree she savored the juicy fruits on her plate. Landilow was as serene and it seemed as unchanging as the people of Bermuda from what she could observe so far. Somehow Melvadore Follette didn't belong here.

• • •

1:00p.m.

"Where did you learn to play…when was the last time you played…you can call it off now if you want. Do you want to?" Ashley goaded.

"Forget the twenty questions and serve the ball." Melvadore Follette squeezed a mouthful of water.

"Fine." Ashley fished the yellow ball from her white pantaloons.

"Are you going to be fair or do I need to get a ref?"

Ignoring him Ashley threw the ball into the air, swung her racket behind her and served him an ace. She hadn't told him she was number one seed on her college tennis team at Georgetown and that she'd often envisioned Frederick head as the ball when she practiced serving. At Georgetown where she'd met Frederick and the place where he'd left her barefoot and pregnant, tennis had been her therapy.

"Beginner's luck," Melvadore scoffed.

"I'll take any luck," Ashley grunted as the ball whizzed through the air at lightning speed with a slice that spun in it mid-air.

Mel, swaying from side to side, his eagle eyes watching the trajectory of the ball as though he was calculating its angle of decent, was ready. With a powerful forehand, he returned the ball at warp speed.

Ashley was on the ball lobbing it to right court. "Point," she hollered triumphantly.

"You're good," Mel shouted across the court.

"I'm very good. You want to give up now?"

"Hardly."

Ashley was at the net. She hadn't even broken a sweat. It was Mel's turn to serve. This ball came whizzing off the edge of his racket at a speed of 110 and landed center court. Five-five," Mel grinned.

"Huh. You're better than I thought," Ashley grunted. Moving midcourt Ashley watched as the ball flew toward her, she returned it with a backhand so smooth that even Mel was impressed.

Soon it was advantage Ashley and then it was break-point for the game.

Ashley adjusted her headband, tightened her strings and threw the ball in the air. With all her might, she hit the ball watching it spin in the air in perfect trajectory.

Mel lobbed the ball.

Ashley was at the net in lightning speed and as her arm connected with the ball, she knew she had won.

A good loser, Mel was already walking toward the net.

"Well done," he seemed nonplused.

"Good game."

"What do I win?"

"Wanna grab a bite in town? I'll take you to the famous courthouse of Bermuda and then to my favorite restaurant.

It's legendary."

"I'd like that and yes, I'm famished."

Ashley watched him as he strode away. From the back, his erect figure looked no more than a man in his thirty's. It was only the graying hair and the sage eyes that remotely tip off his age. Deeply tanned, hairy arms swung his racket in mid-air as though he was trying to understand his losing play. Was she glad that she'd won! It was a good way to start her career. As a winner. And to be honest, he wasn't as much of an ogre as she'd imagined. Ashley found herself light as a feather and literally singing in the shower. Her life felt right. 'Finally found someone…' When she realized the song that came out of her mouth, she quickly stopped singing.

"We'll take the truck," he said to his driver. Now dressed in Bermuda shorts and a gauze shirt, his hair wet from the shower, Ashley was again struck by the fact that Melvadore Follette was indeed a man who defied age. As he approached, Ashley's fell into step beside him as they walked to the LR3 parked at the end of the driveway.

Ashley had never been to Bermuda but as they drove along it seemed familiar in more ways than one. The Queen on the money, Her Majesty's signs on the well-paved roads all made sense since the island was still a British colony. The Caribbean feel, though the island was not really Caribbean, reminded her of a past that was still a mystery to her. The LR3 pulled into a parking space before a large, airy two-story pink building flanked by beaches. Ashley's stomach grumbled as the smell of what would turn out to be the best-stewed chicken she'd ever had, wafted by. There was something comforting about the taste of the island food. Occasionally, when her grandpa complained about all the "damn potatoes" and that he wanted his own food, her mother would cook curried chicken and rice and peas on Sundays and she too would feel less lonely. The taste of the sweet coconut milk in the rice and peas brought back a flood of memories, and it struck her, as it did this morning when she'd bitten into the pineapple and papayas, that her mind housed memories not conscious in her everyday living. Seated on the balcony of the restaurant looking out over the bay, Ashley felt contented and calm.

Mel's voice interrupted her thoughts. He'd flipped open his cell phone that was apparently on vibrate and was saying. "We're at Pepperpot. No. I'll have Samson prepare food for everybody. Nemba is bringing the group," Mel said, his voice tinged with disappointment. "Samson," he shouted into the kitchen, "there are more people coming. Nemba wants fresh fish and lobster," he rose, pulled out five one hundred-dollar bills and placed them on the table for Samuel. "Send someone down to shore." Melvadore returned his attention to Ashley once Samson had left. He seemed to be studying her, his hand, jammed in his pocket, where coins jingled. It was a habit of his she'd noticed. "You must try the grape nut ice-cream for dessert."

"I will," Ashley said a dreamlike quality had seeped into her voice. "When I was a child, I used to love to hear the ice-cream man come passing by, his jingle-jangle bell making a racket. Mother would stop pruning her roses and give us a few pence to go chasing after him. He'd pretend not to see us but just past the gate he'd stop and smile broadly, his toothless grin a victory to us. I loved that the ice-cream, half-melted by the hot sun it would run down my arms. Licking it up was the best part of the whole charade." It was a memory that came from nowhere but Ashley remembered it with such detail, that she was sure she'd read it somewhere. "Until I heard the roosters' crow this morning, I hadn't thought much of Jamaica at all. Now, I'm having another *déjà vu* from the foods."

"I remember those damn roosters like it was yesterday," Melvadore said. "My cousin Abdullah and I used to laugh at how the rooster was always competing with the Mullah. We'd always sided with the rooster crowing our hearts out too."

"What country are you from?" Ashley said.

Melvadore put down the lamb chop and finished dabbing his mouth with a napkin. He said watching her closely as he responded, "Afghanistan." Ashley expected him to elaborate but he didn't. Watching him surreptitiously, she picked up her spoon, scooped a generous spoonful of ice cream, savoring the taste of the fresh cow's milk churned into delicious grape nut ice cream. It didn't take but a second before she was again appreciating the robust taste of island food. Afghanistan, she thought. She would never have guessed.

Later that evening, before meeting Melvadore and Nemba for dinner, Ashley donned a plush white robe and headed down to the property's spa. On the right of the spa was a cottage. The door was ajar and inside was Ashley could see Melvadore and Nemba deep in conversation, a large sum of money on the table between them. She was perplexed at the exchange but then realized that Nemba, who ran the operations at Landilow, was probably getting the month's infusion. She paused for a second to see if she could hear what they were saying but decided that eavesdropping was tacky and contrary to their reason for being on the island in the first place. She hurried on to her appointment.

"I see you have an hour's massage and a facial," Betsy, her young Bermudian attendant handed her a spa approved robe. Ashley changed and within moments was prone on the massage table. The soft nature music was unnecessary as just below sea waves were crashing against the shore, providing all the nature she needed. After pummeling her body, the attendant began applying age-defying cream to her face.

"You have very good skin," Betsy's expert hands massaged Ashley's face.

"Thank you. What exactly does Nemba do here on the Island?" Ashley asked out of the blue.

"She oversees the Follette properties around the world. As I understand it, they rent most of them out to tourists except Landilow. Mr. Follette keeps this as his offshore home. She spends most of her time in Europe though, not here."

"And does he visit often?"

"Once or twice a year."

"I see," Ashley said and though her journalistic antennae were acute she let the subject drop. Why would a man like Melvadore invest in a place like Bermuda? It didn't make sense.

"Would you mind if I listened to some of my own music?"

"Not at all," Betsy flipped off the music overhead.

Ashley slipped tiny Bose headphones into her ears. She felt anxious. There was only one thing to do when anxiety rode havoc in life according to her friend Marie. Meditate. She'd uploaded her favorite kumbaya for Ashley. Hitting the button on her mini iPod Ashley tuned into her Joy of Being CD. Sprawled face up on the bed while Betsy deep cleaned, exfoliated and then re-hydrated her skin, Ashley was desperately trying to quiet her mind. The voice on the iPhone began, encouraging her to relax her entire body, to take deep, cleansing breaths. Go deeper and deeper. Not five minutes later, however, Ashley was hitting the forward button. *Eschebo, Eschebo, Eschebo hum duri lari*, the unmistakable Balinese riff was far more soothing than her meditation CD.

She allowed herself to relax. It was a relaxed but curious Ashley who arrived for dinner in the quarters reserved for Melvadore Follette.

"There you are," Nemba opened the door to their private quarters set away from the main house. She ushered her out onto an open patio, an oasis of calm where a reflective pool was dotted with lanterns that twinkled on the water. The smell of sweet, aromatic tobacco wafted as she entered what seemed Melvadore Follette's safe haven. Infused with a spirituality that balanced the external with the internal; from the decorated archways to the mustard, red and browns pillows and Persian carpets so common even at dirt storefronts in Afghanistan, there was no question that Melvadore Follette revered his culture and his inner peace. A prayer rug was in front of the fireplace facing east. Under the porch, a table was set for seven. "We have some friends joining us. Melvadore will be right out. Drink?"

"Red wine, preferably a Shiraz."

"Coming right up."

That night she tossed and turned in her Danish bed.

The next morning, with carefully formulated questions she'd written after dinner, Ashley was hoping to find out more about their presence in Bermuda. At breakfast, however, she'd learned that Melvadore, Nemba, and the dinner guests had already left the island.

"I hope you've had a great couple of days to relax. The welcome committee has left and we, the evil ones, must now make sure that we can do the jobs we've been hired for," a senior HR personnel said, welcoming them to their first WNCB class. "What we are attempting to do will not be welcomed by our competitors. We have taken out sizable insurance on all of you. We advise that you make sure your life is in order.

We have an attorney on premises should you want to do a last will and testament."

The twelve change-agents looked at each other, each no doubt wondering who would be there tomorrow. As the HR man droned on about the most mundane, Ashley's mind strayed and her warning antennas buzzed.

CHAPTER SEVENTEEN
Randy

New York, 2002

WHAT FABULOUS LUCK it was having Adele as a friend. And to think she didn't want to have Lawrence's confounded party. After all these years Randy finally felt safe enough with another person to relax and to live a little. With Adele she'd found places and spaces in herself she never dared look for much less knew existed. With each new experience, Randy felt the corrosion of her life flaking away ever so slightly. They'd skated at Rockefeller Center, took in Off-Broadway plays, rode the horse carriage in Central Park and even once discoed in the village where Randy danced to hip-hop. Rusting memories were giving way to a glimmer of joy. Randy did an Egyptian head move as she danced around her room remembering their best time of all. Giddy from too much vodka, Randy and Adele had stumbled onto the stage of a Korean restaurant where Adele breathlessly rendered, the now famous American Idol winner Kelly Clarkson on the Karaoke machine. 'Some people wait a lifetime, for a moment like this…' Randy found herself singing along. That night Randy discovered her voice. What would June or Lawrence have thought if they'd seen her cutting up the dance floor or on stage singing her heart out? Walk Like an Egyptian.

From that night on Randy began thinking of Adele as her savior. She was smart and funny and free. Who knew living could be such fun! "You have become a good dancer," Adele laughed as Randy pranced around the room. Her home had become Randy's hang out.

A clock bell tolled as Randy was about to sit down across from Adele in her kitchen. "Oh, my Lord," she said.

"What's wrong? Did I say something?" Adele asked.

"No. No." Randy answered looking stricken, "I'd promised to meet my sisters in Midtown and I totally forgot. This is the fourth time we're trying to get together. Would you mind terribly if I came back at a later time? Ashley will be furious if I'm late."

"You don't have to be late."

"Come on, it's Midtown. This is New York you know?"

"Eh," Adele poo-pooed Randy's concern. "I'll ride you there. No problem."

"You have a car that flies?" Randy could not help the sarcasm.

"No. On my bike silly."

"A bike? Are you nuts?"

"It is good. A Vesper. You'll see. Come on," Adele said leaving the room, "have an adventure." Moments later she returned with two helmets and a glass for Randy. "Drink this, it will calm your nerves."

"Surely you jest?" Randy vehemently protested. "I don't think so." Yet in her mind, she thought freedom, escape, unconscionable, but fun. Randy took a sip of the clear liquid. Vodka. Minutes later Randy found herself sitting on the back of a motorcycle.

"Put your feet there," Adele motioned to the pedal and just hold onto to me around the waist."

Randy snaked her arms around Adele's firm, flat torso. "Goodbye life," she mumbled as she snapped the helmet flap over her face. Adele laughed, revved the engine and weaved her way in and out of traffic, squeezing through the narrowest gap between cars and leaving a cordon of cars behind. Randy understood why they wouldn't be late. From the streets, Adele merged onto the Westside highway and paradoxically, though petrified, Randy felt free and unencumbered.

"This is fun. No?" Adele's voice reached her through the air.

"I wouldn't exactly say fun, but I will say that I've never appreciated open space like this from a car."

"Or saving time and money too, huh?"

What in the world was she doing sitting on a motorbike in her $3,000 designer suit? The idiocy of the entire situation caused Randy to burst into hysterical laughter. Finally, she had truly lost her marbles. When they pulled onto the street of the restaurant, reality finally sets in.

"Don't even think about it. Go one block over. I'm too well known here to be seen unloading myself off a motorbike!"

"*D'accord.* Now you have time and it's a beautiful day to take a little walk, I'll go two blocks over."

The bike now parked, Randy alit, smoothed her hair and checked her face in her compact.

"By the way you look wonderful today."

"You don't look so bad yourself, Adele. Would you like to join us? It'll be good to be seen at Carmichael's. Who knows, someone might fall in love with you today."

"Someone rich and old I hope," Adele laughed. "Thanks, but not today...another time perhaps."

"Definitely. Thanks for the adventure and on time arrival."

• • •

"Now this is a first," Ashley pecked her sister. "You, on time and Amelie is not here yet!"

"Cut me some slack today, okay." Randy returned the kiss, barely. "I, unlike you, show up for dates."

"You got me there."

"So how are you, kiddo?" There was an air of aliveness in her sister Ashley had never seen.

"Really good. Bermuda was lovely and scary."

"How so?"

"My boss is a little perplexing, hard to read. Hope I can cut the mustard. So, what's up with you? You seem happy, Randy."

"I'm growing up."

"Welcome to Carmichael's." The, 'I'm-just-waiting-table until my next acting job,' waiter flashed his auditioning smile.

"There's one more in our party but we'd like to be seated." Ashley's said. "Away from the maddening crowd if you don't mind." Turning to Randy, she said, "Tell me about it?" She really had never seen her sister so animated. Before Randy could answer, Amelie came rushing up.

"I'm with them. Sorry, I'm late. I've had a trying few days."

The women followed the waiter to an inconspicuous room bathed in calming colors and lit to its patrons' best advantage. Amelie flopped down in an empty chair pecking one and then the other of her sisters' cheeks. Ashley beckoned the waiter over. "I'll have the vegetable platter and a piece of grilled Salmon on a different plate.

Also, a bottle of Chianti and two glasses."

The waiter turned to Ashley and Randy.

"The grilled sea bass and asparagus," Randy said handing him her menu. She wanted to order a vodka and tonic but instead said, "I'll have a glass of Perrier."

"I'll have the fruit plate with chicken salad," Amelie said.

"Amelie," Ashley asked. "What about your idyllic life is trying these days? Did Robb grow a beard or something?"

Amelie laughed in spite of her angst. "Welcome home Ashley, and Randy," she turned to her eldest sister, "you are positively glowing. Are you okay?"

"I feel okay. I don't know what you all mean," Randy fished a compact from her bag and examined her face. She looked okay, she thought.

"The kind of glow I'm talking about," Amelie said, "is coming from the inside."

"I have a friend who's showing me how to live."

"You are having an affair?" Ashley leaned in for the gossip?

"An affair? Are you crazy?" Randy scoffed. "No, I have a new friend called Adele, a French painter. She is crazy."

"Oh," Ashley lost interest though she supposed it was good for Randy to have a friend.

"What's the big news about your trying life, Amelie?" Ashley asked, hoping for a more interesting conversation.

"Which one first? That I still haven't called Dr. Vlachenko or that William is getting married."

"You've got to be kidding," Ashley said.

"On which account? Vlachenko or William. I wish every day that this entire life of mine was a joke. A dream would be fine too…but no…this shit is for real. I'm so mad right now and Robb's acting like this is normal. I just can't imagine why William would throw his life away like this."

"What about graduation?" Randy asked.

"Who knows, I am only getting the news secondhand. I promised myself not to call. He called his father first and not me. Imagine that!"

"What do you know so far?" Ashley was all ears.

"That this damn drama is about to get ugly. Apparently, this Kyla chick is quite a sensible one. Under different circumstances Robb said I might even like her. She has, it seems, refused to marry William unless he graduates but that's the good news. She's pregnant is the bad news."

"What are you going to do?" Randy asked. She didn't mean to feel vindicated but she did. Amelie, the great mother, and wife who often made her feel inadequate, not intentionally of course, but nonetheless, was experiencing failure.

"What can I do? Robb said I am only a vessel for William's life so I should stay out of it. Imagine that! Well over this dead vessel will that girl have William's child."

"Did you at least talk to the girl?"

"No. William is coming home later. I guess I'll get the entire story then."

"What about her family?" Ashley asked.

"Not a clue. I just hope…lord, I don't know what I hope." Amelie gulped wine.

"That's a doozie," Ashley said. "Imagine. You, a grandmother!"

Amelie groaned. "Talking about Motherhood. Mummy called again, trying to reschedule our canceled dinner. She wants us to come to Florida."

"What's so pressing? What on earth does mother want with us?" Randy's tone was resigned.

"I think we should go. Her husband has prostate cancer."

"Why the hell would we do that? He's not even our father twice removed." Randy scoffed. "Prostate cancer is highly curable."

"Not the kind he has," Amelie said.

"Well, he paid for our education if you need a reason," Ashley piped in.

"And look where that got me." Randy gave up on the Perrier and ordered a vodka and tonic.

"I really think we should go?" Amelie said.

"Hell no," Randy said, "I'm not going."

"At least we have a Mother even if she isn't perfect. She probably wants to make amends for all the shitty years," Ashley suggested.

"Is that what you really think?" Randy asked.

"Yes," Ashley answered. "When I was in Bermuda, I had memories of Jamaica and Mummy was happy then, remember?"

"No, I don't and I'm not ready to."

Ashley cut her off. "Randy everything isn't always about you. Since Bermuda, I've been thinking about our father a lot. We should take this opportunity to ask Mom. When was the last time we even thought of our father?"

"We haven't because that woman murdered him in our minds! She ripped our lives right out from under us and then shredded it. Now she wants to play nice, nice. Well, I'm not ready to play nice, nice."

"Can't we give her the benefit of the doubt?" Ashley asked.

"Well, when I take a trip to Bermuda and suddenly remember old times, maybe. Unfortunately, the old times I remember are not pretty," Randy flung across the table. "No Ashley, I don't feel that forgiving or reconciled."

On her lap, Randy's hands were busy twisting the bejesus out of the napkin.

"Com' on Randy, Mother deserves a chance," Amelie said, "And so do we. None of us are the best we could be because we're emotionally broken into a million little pieces."

"Only a million?" Randy's voice tinged with anger.

"Okay, okay. Enough! I can't wait for you guys to see my new apartment tomorrow. Try not to be late for once Randy?"

"I wasn't late today, was I?"

"You're right. I hope it's a new habit," Ashley's sarcasm sprinkled the air.

"You know Denzel lives in your building, right?" Randy said.

"Yummm. I can't wait to see that man in the elevator. I'll have to push the stop button." Ashley smiled, "but my boss is better looking though."

"Is that a crush I hear in your voice?" Amelie laughed.

"Crush or be crushed?" Ashley's eyebrows rose.

"Whatever. Don't think about it! Mixing business and pleasure is combustible."

"Don't you be daft, Ashley," Randy added her two cents.

Before Ashley could respond her cell phone rang. "Hello," she hurriedly answered not bothering to look at the dial. "Phillip…yes…wow," she looked at her watch. "Yep, I'll be there in 30 mins." Ashley hung up and said to her sisters. "Really gotta go. My friend Phillip is coming in to check out my new digs and help me organize this party that's driving me crazy."

Her sisters looked blank.

"You know, the guy who was my co-anchor on ET. He's at my apartment, in the lobby, waiting for me."

"Why do you have to have this party so soon? Why not wait until you are really settled?" Amelie asked.

"Why, why, why do we do anything? Because we want to, that's all. Don't start with the lecturing, Amelie."

"I wasn't…"

Ashley cut her off… "ehh…ehhh…don't explain."

Randy and Amelie rolled their eyes in unison.

"Let's set our next lunch date now. Two weeks from today. Is that good? I'm good for a visit with Mother. Randy, will you at least think about it?"

"Lunch, yes. Mother no."

"Is your driver waiting?" Amelie asked. "Maybe he could drop me at Grand Central."

"Of course," Ashley said dabbing her lips with a napkin.

"Then you two go on ahead," Randy pulled out her credit card. "I'll take care of this. I'll see you both tomorrow."

"Absolutely not. What are expense accounts for? Save Lawrence some money," Ashley insisted.

Randy felt pricked. "I insist, Ashley. It's my treat. We're celebrating your new job after all and Amelie's freedom," Randy said.

"All the reason to give this card a good work. Got to train bosses right from day one or they'll nickel and dime you to death. I'll be giving this Black Card a good work out I can assure you. Make sure they understand my worth and taste are not cheap. Hurry," she said as she slipped the card to the waiter.

CHAPTER EIGHTEEN
Ashley

New York, 2002

"WHO SAYS DREAMS don't come true?" Phillip was waiting in the lobby when she arrived. "This place is fabulous."

"Wait until you see inside." Ashley ran over to her dear friend. "You look divine." Ashley hugged Phillip so tight he could hardly breathe. "I thought you'd never get here."

"You? I've sat on more tarmacs at LaGuardia airport than anywhere else in the world. I'm not sure why that airport even exists! We actually got here on time but had to circle for one hour for air traffic clearance and then waited another hour for my bags."

"I'm hearing that loud and clear but I'm so glad you're here," she squeezed him even harder. "Hi Oscar," Ashley said to the doorman, who was already pressing the button for the PH. "This is my friend Phillip. He's going to be with me for a few days. Will you send his up luggage please?"

"I only have a suitcase," Phillip whispered.

"Go with the program." Ashley dragged him into the elevator.

"Girl, you hit the 'mudda' load." Phillip ran his hand down the solid teak elevator panels.

"You are next. I'm sure of it. Did you meet Mr. Follette yet?"

"No."

"You will," she said with confidence as the elevator whirled its way to the penthouse. When it finally stopped, Ashley punched in a code and the door clicked open. Stepping into the atrium, bathed in sunlight, she turned to her Phillip. "I've been dying to know what you think. First class, huh?"

Phillip, a true designer at heart had that eye. "OMG! Ashley, this is magnificent! What a view! I hadn't imagined that places like this existed in New York City. This is a palatial spread. I always thought people in New York City lived in closets but this, my dear, is fit for a queen. How much did this castle set you back?"

"It was a steal, at least that's what my realtor said. Six million."

"Well, Miss Thing, I think you have arrived."

"I have, haven't I?" Ashley squealed.

"Yes, dear you have."

"Come on," Ashley tugged at his arm pulling him behind her, "how is the Philly station?"

"Nothing without you, but I must say I'm enjoying reporting far more than when we did that fluff."

"Haaa. I told you. Come, let me show you to your room. I'll show you the rest of the place later."

It was Phillip's turn to squeal. "Just what I need," he said exploring his little alcove and his Grecian bathroom.

"I don't think I will ever leave this room," he said.

"You don't have to. Wouldn't that be the best! It's a little lonely tooling around in this big space. Anyway snookums (their term of endearment for each other) rest up, we have things to do. Feeling totally complete with Phillip by her side, Ashley went to the kitchen to prepare him a snack. They chatted until almost 3:00 a.m. that morning.

• • •

"Phillip," Ashley cooed pushing open the half-shut door. "Hey snookums, are you up yet?"

Phillip, not ready for the drama of her welcome-to-my-new-life party, was snug under his down comforter pretending to be fast asleep.

"Phillip, are you up?"

Why didn't this woman go away? Discretely he snuck a peek at the clock. It wasn't even nine a.m. Phillip groaned, rolled over and pulled the cover over his head.

"Come on lazy bones get your ass up!" Ashley said. This time the light blocking eye patch was pulled up all the way and there was no mistaking the glare.

"Get lost."

Don't you want to run errands with me this morning?" Ashley persisted crossing the room and sitting on the bed.

"No," he said, his voice peppered with annoyance.

"Pretty please?" Ashley pulled back the covers and got into bed with Phillip.

"I thought I'd be rid of being an errand boy. Listen, honey," he made room for her, "you have drivers and maids now. You live like a queen. Please go away and have the servants take care of your errands. That's what they are for, you know."

"I don't trust them. Not yet. Anyway, we have to be out of the house while they prepare for the party tonight so we might as well help out by getting out."

"Why?" Phillip asked, finally rolling over to look at Ashley.

"Because…just 'cause. Please, Phillip, don't make me beg."

"Girl, I'm not leaving this fabulous room or that gorgeous bathroom. I plan to be in here all week looking at myself in all those mirrors. I might oblige and come out in time for the party though," he laughed.

"I'll lock the bathroom," Ashley threatened, knowing much of Phillip's day was spent in front of mirrors.

"Oh, for heaven's sake," Phillips said sitting up in bed and sighing melodramatically, "I suppose I should buy you a house-warming gift."

"You're a pet." Ashley grinned, pinching his cheek.

"Oh, stop that," he swatted. "But, plum face," he pinched her cheeks back, "if you expect to be seen in public with me, you'd better do something with that hair of yours. It needs some perspective."

"Right away." Ashley jumped to her feet. At the door, she stopped. "I've been meaning to ask, how on earth did David allow you to come without him?"

"David? Who's David?" Phillip asked as though he couldn't remember his boyfriend.

"Oh. I see. Another one bites the dust. I guess he wasn't all that after all?"

"They never are. But you know that by now, don't you?"

"What's that supposed to mean?" Ashley frowned.

"Didn't you dump your last boyfriend in under a New York minute," Phillip laughed. Four weeks in a relationship was a long time for Ashley, who dumped men for merely breathing too much oxygen on her side of the room.

"Boyfriend? Hardly. Booty call was more like it. Which one are you talking about anyway? The one with the Black Card?"

"That would be him."

"Couldn't tell you where that man is. He was a big fake and I suspected, so was that Black Card. Do you know I never saw him use it once? He just kept pulling it out so I'd see it." Ashley rolled her eyes. "Phillip, I have finally come to the conclusion that the only men I can stand are gay men."

"Me too, girl," Philip grinned. "Remind me again what got him the boot?"

"He crowded me. And you know how crowds make me nervous," she smirked at Phillip. "Plus, all he ever talked about was himself."

"Vile." Phillip smiled. "Next time run a stake through his heart."

Ashley smiled at the visual. "I'm going to get ready," she said sashaying down the hall.

Phillip was ready long before Ashley appeared in the living room. "This apartment is spectacular in the morning light," Phillip said, resting his jacket on the arm of a yellow, silk couch covered by exquisite cashmere throws. Rays splayed on walls and mirrors. "How about a cup of tea before we head out?" he walked into the chef's kitchen and pulled open the cupboard. The signature cups and saucers were so neatly lined that he was afraid to disturb their order. "On second thought, let's grab a latte on the way."

"Okay," Ashley said traipsing behind him, as he got his jacket and headed for the door. He reminded her of a gazelle.

"This is so fun." Ashley looped her arms through Phillip's. "Like old times. What'd you say we catch a movie after our errands are done? I hear that new Indian movie is fabu and the theater is only a couple of blocks from here. The dance routine is supposed to be spectacular." Back in

Philly, on a Friday night, when neither of them had dates, Ashley and Phillip would rent the latest Indian movie and practice the dance steps with each other. "By the time we get back it'll be time to get ready for my par-ty," Ashley sang.

In the sunlight she was radiant. Phillip was always awed by the complete transformation of the casual Ashley to the public Ashley. Her mildly heated butter complexion was enhanced today with nude make-up and her cropped, feathered hair was perfectly coifed. Tinted lipstick frosted her generous lips.

"You look divine," Phillip said looking her up and down. "So how is your Guardian Angel Mr. Melvadore?"

"He acts nice but I suspect he's not a nice man when he doesn't get his way."

CHAPTER NINETEEN
Amelie

Connecticut, 2002

ROBB WAS BUSY unpacking groceries when Amelie got home. She walked pass him without a word.

"What did you want me to do?" Robb asked.

"Oh, shut up Robb. You don't seem to care that your son is throwing his life down the toilet for some two-bit hussy!" Amelie answered. "You'd better get used to grocery shopping 'cause your child and his baby mama will probably have to move back home and you'll have three more mouths to feed." She threw the train schedule on the counter. "I may have to go back to work just to afford them. So there, my problem is solved. I hope you're happy now."

"Why are you blaming me for William's decision?"

"Well …"

"There is no well here Amelie. William is the one who's about to screw up his life. I'm going to try to talk some sense into that boy today," Robb said. "I thought his favorite meal might set the stage."

"This isn't bloody theater, Robb. I can't imagine why you didn't just handle it. Help him get to the abortion clinic!"

"Look Amelie. We are William's parents, not his life. He chose and we have to respect that. He'll be here any minute. Yale isn't going away. He can always go back."

"Are you out of your mind? He cannot leave school. He's only twenty years old! What about his future? I had such high hopes for him."

"As I had for you as a pianist, but honey, not even your love for me could have stopped you from leaving the Julliard. Look, he needs to do this for whatever reason."

"That's not fair. I had reasons. William has no damn reason to throw away his life. He doesn't even have a damn student loan to pay back…that's how certain I was about his future. I know what I should feel Robb, but I don't and I'm not going to let our son ruin his life over some hussy."

Robb looked at Amelie who was now throwing salmon from the freezer into the sink. Salmon, all crispy at the edges, was William's favorite food. "350…cover it with foil for 20 mins and then put it on broil so the edges get crispy."

"His reason is real, yours was in your head."

"You…you…bastard." Amelie got her pruning gloves and went into the garden to get some St John's worth to make tea. She was going to need it. 1) Not to kill Robb and 2) Because William her beloved son, her pride, and joy, would be close to dead if he didn't listen to her. She just had to stay calm.

• • •

"Yo', Mom." William found his mother in the backyard snipping green leaves from the bushes and stuffing them into a canvas bag. Beloved went out the window as soon as she saw him. She had to suppress the feeling to whack him on the ear. Tall and stocky, William was a dashing young man. A full mustache had now grown in. Baggy jeans and a rumpled plaid shirt completed his attire. Around his neck earplugs sent pulsing music into the airwaves. How could he be getting married! And a father!

"What exactly is 'yo'?" The sadness in her eyes was obvious. "And how the hell is 'yo' an explanation for your deceit?"

He kissed her. She hung on to him. He was no longer her little guy. He was a man now. A man who would be a father!

"I'm sorry Mom. I was careless. I know how disappointed you are but I really was scared. I didn't want to let you down. Did Dad tell you that I was bringing someone with me? I knew you'd understand," he took her hand. "Is it cool, right?"

'Bling,' 'balling,' 'cool,' she knew cool, but the others were all new words added to her vocabulary by William. "No William, he didn't. But honey, listen to me, you brought that woman here for us to talk some sense into both of you I hope."

"Mom please don't make a scene. I know you're disappointed but I have to do the right thing. You taught me that."

"William, there is another way. You're almost done with school. Can't…ehh…"

"Kyla, Mom. Her name is Kyla."

"Can't Kyla see that this will ruin both your lives? We've never even met her before now."

"Mom, she the one. I know we haven't known each other long but she's the one. We didn't plan this but now that it's happened, I want to do the right thing."

"William…"

"Please Mom, just come in and meet her, you'll see. She's the woman you'd want for me, Mom. Come." He put his arm around her shoulder.

Kyla was sitting at the dining table talking with Robb when they entered the room. She stood as Amelie came through the door and Amelie grabbed the edge of the counter. She was already big pregnant. She threw a glance at Robb who apparently was avoiding all eye contact.

"Mrs. Mercer, it's a pleasure to meet you. I'm really sorry that we kept this from you for so long. I wanted William to tell you earlier but he was hoping I'd change my mind and that there would be no need."

Kyla was not the sort of girl Amelie would have imagined William to pick. She was tall and slender, milk chocolate brown and wore glasses. She looked more like the studious type than a party girl.

"And why didn't you?" Amelie's tone was monotone.

"Because I'm Catholic and pro-life."

"Kyla's parents are just as upset if that makes you feel any better, Mom."

"It doesn't. You're both just kids with your entire life ahead of you."

"We're not kids Mrs. Mercer, we're twenty. Young yes but not kids. I came today, not for your approval but to hope that together we can talk some sense into William. There is no need for him to leave school or to marry me for that matter. Because I made a choice shouldn't derail his life. I'm okay with my choice. As soon as I'm able I will go back and finish my degree. My parents are willing to help me. I love William and I'm honored to marry him but I'm also capable of taking care of myself."

Robb, who had been readying the salmon for the oven stopped and looked at the woman his son had chosen to marry. He understood why.

William was beaming, obviously proud of the way his girl handled the situation. Amelie was speechless. She wanted to kill Kyla for ruining her son's life, yet she couldn't deny that she saw why William loved her. "Dad, do you need some help?" William asked, relieved that the worse was over.

"Yeah, I think I could," Robb said. "You know my show opens tomorrow. Maybe you can take Kyla to see it."

"Hey, that's a good idea. My dad used to be a dancer," he explained to Kyla. "Now he mostly choreographs, writes songs and plays. My mom writes all the music to his songs," he said proudly to Kyla.

"Not all dear. Just some," Amelie said, incredulous that he'd never mentioned this to his wife to be before. What on earth did they talk about if she hadn't known that already? She looked again at the woman whose belly carried her first grandchild. The thought made her head hurt. Where was her baby boy, she thought, looking up at the strapping young man in front of her?

"I'd like to go," Kyla said smiling. Her voice was strong and calming as she smiled warmly at William.

"Then it's on. Dad, make sure you leave us tickets at the box office."

"Wrong. You're buying tickets, son."

"You're joking, right?" He looked at his Mom.

"I don't think so. Grown-ups have to take care of their own lives. Kyla, I'll show you to your room. I know you're pregnant but you'll have to have your own room in this house until you're married."

Kyla was suppressing a smile. It was more than obvious to Amelie that not only was she a match for William but that she loved him dearly. What more could a mother ask for than for a woman to love her son? "I totally understand Mrs. Mercer," Kyla said. "And thank you so much for the kindness you've shown me. We'll make sure our William graduates."

Amelie straightened her back, smiled at Kyla and ascended the stairs. This was indeed the kind of daughter-in-law she wished for.

"Hey Mom, William was shouting up the stairs. There's some guy with an accent on the phone for you."

She hoped he'd covered the mouthpiece. Dr. Nickoli Vlachenko had been Amelie's instructor and her biggest supporter at the Juilliard. A world-renowned pianist and foremost authority on Schumann with a repertoire longer than the legendary Chechenko, he was a no-nonsense kinda guy. 'One in a million! That's what you are, the one in a million pianist with this kind of extraordinary talent. And what do you do, your stupid girl. You threw it away when you left the stage. He had been devastated when his best student decided to throw away her promising career at the slightest set-back. Amelie was hoping against hope that he still believed in her 'gift.'

"Hello," Amelie took the phone from William giving the back of his head a good clout.

"Yes, Sir. Thank you so much." Amelie replaced the receiver and skipped around the room. "He'll see me on Wednesday."

• • •

At the corner of 64th and Broadway, in the gray stone building that housed the Julliard, Amelie was moved to tears. So much of her life had played out on this corner. After fifteen minutes casing out the apartment building next door, she got her chance to slip in while the doorman was helping an elderly tenant to her apartment. No point anyone seeing her being thrown out. She dashed into the stairwell and climbed the steps of the apartment building behind the

Julliard. For a while, she stood in front of the beige painted door trying to calm her breathing. The knock on the door of apartment 2C and 2D resonated. Back in the day, when Manhattan living was affordable, Dr. Vlachenko had purchased the two apartments and knocked down the adjoining wall so he could fit his prized concert-sized piano. Amelie wiped perspiration from her upper lip. She waited and then knocked again a little louder.

"Yes, yes, yes." Dr. Vlachenko opened the door. "Where was that confounded doorman this time," he yelled.

"Assisting an elderly woman, Dr. Vlachenko," Amelie's voice faltered, "do you remember me?"

"Did you hear that I had gone senile? What a stupid question. Come in. Come in," he threw back the door and stepped aside. "And you're one minute late!"

"Thank you, I was knocking for one minute," Amelie smiled as she fixed her gaze on the man in front of her. His hair was now completely white but other than a deeper furrow in his forehead from frowning too much, he looked the same as he did when she'd walked into his office to tell him of her decision to leave music. Amelie entered the familiar room. Wall to wall bookcases were stuffed with leather-bound works of Homer, Virgil, Milton, Shakespeare, music books, biographies of musicians and Dr. Vlachenko's own text on Schumann. Artifacts from around the world, including a marvelous Cherry Blossom Chinese fire screen that had been her favorite, filled the room. To Amelie, the hand-painted screen symbolized a rebirth and renewal and somehow harmonized all the various periods and cultural pieces in Dr. Vlachenko's apartment. The 2,700 square foot space, however, was defined by the incomparable, gleaming, ebony, 9' 5" Bösendorfer, its lid open to full compliment. The Austrian piano, the finest and most prestigious in the world, was renowned for its extra bass keys, solid spruce rim, a tone unparalleled and keys firm to the touch. It was second to none. Wherever he played in the world, Dr. Vlachenko demanded a Bösendorfer. If one could not be guaranteed his personal piano would be shipped at the host's expense. At sixty-eight, Dr. Vlachenko still traveled the world playing as dexterously as he had at twenty-three. It had been with deftness and privilege that Amelie had first played the prized piano. They came to stand silently in front of the piano, Dr. Vlachenko looking expectantly at Amelie. "Dr. Vlachenko, I came here today," Amelie stammered, "to ask if you would consider teaching me again?"

"For what reason? What do you want to do with the music this time? You'll only quit at the first mishap."

"No, no," Amelie said shaking her head. "I'm sure I know what I want to do now. I want to play professionally."

"Are we talking about the same music? Ms. Freeman, for me, there is and has only been music. Music and Wall Street do not mix."

"I'm Mercer now," Amelie said softly.

"Mrs. Mercer, I don't teach without a purpose. The endpoint of my purpose is to create great musicians. I am not an entertainer."

"I know that, Dr. Vlachenko. I do want to perform. I'd like to go back to the stage."

"So," he puffed on an unlit pipe he'd retrieved from an ashtray. "You've finally come to your senses, have you?" He said nodding his head, "Why do you think you are still good enough? You are old now. Less flexible. You've probably lost your touch. With age, memory is uncertain. What about your confidence?" he peppered turning away from her to look out the window. Before she could answer he said, "I may not be able to do anything for you. Music is not what it used to be Mrs. Mercer. A concert pianist is no more than a dinosaur these days. Why bother?"

He turned back to look at her.

"Because I must," Amelie said softly. "I've never stopped playing, Dr. Vlachenko. I play at least two hours a day and I still get regular instructions from a good teacher. Mary Hendon. You remember her? She was your student too."

"Good enough, I suppose, but I suspect you can teach her a thing or two," he winked. "Well," he lit the pipe, "let's see. Sit down," he ordered her to the Bösendorfer. "Play *Fantasie in C major.*"

Knowing this was the first thing he'd asked, Amelie had practiced relentlessly, five hours a day, and committed to memory every pianist interpretation of *Opus 17*. But, could she do it? Amelie walked over to the piano and ran her fingers along its smooth finish. Her Steinway, albeit a superior instrument, was not Dr. Vlachenko's.
Her fingers tingled. She could do this. She'd spent her entire life living music not to speak of the pedagogy. She had taken every conceivable instruction, painful tests in, solfège counterpoint, music theory, and exhausting the finger-numbing recitals. They had to count for something. Amelie moved toward the piano. Her feet felt like lead weights. She pulled out the stool and adjusted it as Dr. Vlachenko got out the music. *Like riding a bicycle*, her muse chimed.

"Too low," he said pulling up a chair next to her. "How do you expect to play octaves fortissimo?" Amelie adjusted her seat.

"Ready?" he said softly and she drew strength.

Her fingers paused over the keys. Her eyes closed for a moment. Trust the music. Trust the memory in your fingers. She had played the piano almost every day of her life since she was three years old. This was her world. She could do this. She touched the keys. Andante, Allegro, Arpeggios, trill, fermata. She played, she didn't need to look at the page, she simply played.

"Good. Good. Very good for a financier but nowhere near excellent. You may no longer be good enough," Dr. Vlachenko opined. "Now," he said, "I am not sure if I'll take you on. If I do, you'll have to work damn hard on the interpretation, better the dynamics. I want you to dream this rather than play it. You have to work on conveying the music not just through the notes and the mechanics but through its inspiration. You have to use your back and shoulders more. Increase the tension in your arms. And your third finger is lazy. You have to use it to find the immortal spirit of the work. If we play again, I want beauty in this music, your spirit, and essence…and I want no shenanigans."

"I thought…" Amelie interrupted.

"You thought? If I want you to think my dear, I'll tell you. The last time you thought, what happened?" He shrugged his shoulders before continuing. "I am the teacher here. You are the one who left the stage and if, and I emphasize, if I take you on, I will be the only one capable of bringing you back to the stage and the only one with an opinion. Do not argue with me. If I say we work on the interpretation, we work on the interpretation."

Amelie was horrified. How could he be so unfeeling? Couldn't he imagine how she must feel? Did he think she was still seventeen?

"Why are you sitting there staring at me like a deer in a headlamp? I said we work on interpretation. You will find the full polyphonic texture of the music if it kills me, or you," he finished.

"Headlight." Amelie couldn't resist correcting him. Dr. Vlachenko hadn't changed a bit. She adjusted her chair and began to play again.

"Okay. The first movement. Deep lament. Restless. Lyrical. More. More rhythmic precision. More. Yes. That's good. Accent. Fortissimo here. More. When she was finished paying, he said, "That was just okay. I'll let you know my decision in a week." Dr. Vlachenko ushered her out the door five hours later. "Tell Robb Mercer he is a saint on earth."

Amelie smiled, pleased he'd remembered Robb from so many years ago. As Amelie made her way along Broadway, she felt rung out but never more alive. The honesty. No one in the world of business had incited in her such rage, such hope, such accomplishments and such satisfaction as Dr. Vlachenko and the music had done. Her heart was home and she knew it. She called Randy but got her voice mail.

• • •

"Where did you go so early?" Robb asked when she walked in.

"To the chicken farm."

"And did you cluck?"

"Piss off, Robb," Amelie was still furious with him and was giving him the "silent" treatment.

"What did he say?" He stopped joking and turned to her.

"That's for me to know and you to find out," she sashayed past him.

"Hell, no you don't," he grabbed her by the back of her jacket.

"He'll let me know in a week," Amelie said, throwing her arms around Robb's neck unable to keep up her "mad" charade. "I think he was pleased. I could swear he had tears in his eyes but he was awfully mean. He was back to his usual, "if I want an opinion, I'll give it to you myself." He's just the same. I'm not sure what's going to happen but I tried."

"Beats not trying."

Two days and there was no call from Dr. Vlachenko. Every time the phone rang, Amelie sprinted to catch it on the second ring but the call she wanted most never came. She'd been trying hard not to think of William. As much as she liked Kyla she was still hoping for a miracle. Maybe Kyla would miscarry…God forgive her. Life was sure leveled the playing field. She, the model parent who'd chastised Randy for being the worse parent on earth,
cautioning her about not repeating the cycle of dysfunction of their family; she who'd been so sure that June would run away from home with some brat "looking for love in all the wrong places" was going to have to "suck salt." One of her mother's many Jamaican sayings was coming to roost because it was her son who had mucked up the soup.

CHAPTER TWENTY

Randy

New York, 2002

THE GALLERY CONVERSATION with Adele and then Ashley suggesting that she save Lawrence some money made Randy obsessed with the idea of having her own work and her own money. For weeks now, she'd been mulling over her approach to tell Lawrence she was going to open a gallery. Her gumption arrived as she sat in front of her bathroom mirror. What was the big deal? She'd just show up at Lawrence's office and say, "I want to open a gallery." Just like that. Unbelievable as it seemed, it would be the first time she'd set foot in her husband's tome. Home was her domain and Wall Street was his. Randy's charcoal suit, crisp white blouse, simple silver necklace with matching earrings looked "corporate" enough. "Okay Mensa, here I go. What do you think he's going to say?"

"Well, first of all, you look lovely, and second, he'll probably say no but just don't take no for an answer."

• • •

Richard dropped her in front of the glass building. They had moved the office to 56th Street. "What floor again Richard?"

"Let me come in so security will know to let you up without a fuss." He put a card in the window, turned on his flashers and joined her on the sidewalk. They walked into the grand building, Richard and Randy's heels clicking against the marble in unison.

"Morning again John. This is Ms. Randy Austin. Mr. Austin's better half."

"You're going up with her?"

"I'll take her to the right elevator bank," he said leading the way, Randy close behind. Halfway down the hall, Richard stopped. "The 50th floor," he said, reaching over to press the call button.

Randy interlocked her hands, pressing them in front of her to release nervous energy. Her speech was well prepared and she'd memorized it. She hoped Lawrence didn't interrupt her because if she missed a line, she might just lose her courage. As she got off the elevator on the 50th floor she came face to face with a double mahogany door with the letters AUSTIN, INC engraved in gold letters. Randy took a handkerchief from her sleeve and mopped her brow before pushing open the door. The command center of the executive suites of Austin, Inc. was lavishly decorated and spelled success in every piece of furniture, accessory, down to the highly polished mahogany panel on the wall. Deep gray carpet muffled Randy's steps as she entered the office where the décor, she thought, was more suited to a luxury hotel than an office.

"Hello," Randy said to the woman at the desk.

"Hello," Sabrina answered, looking at the regal woman in front of her. She was surprised that someone was let up without a call from security. "May I help you?"

"Yes." Randy's mood was chipper, "I'd like to see my husband. Will you tell Lawrence I'm here?"

"Mrs. Austin?" Sabrina gushed, recognition spreading over her face. She didn't quite expect her to be as attractive as the airbrushed picture on Lawrence's desk but she was, in fact, prettier and magnificently dressed in a charcoal pantsuit, with an exquisite silver necklace dangling just below her breastbone. "I'm so sorry Mrs. Austin, you just missed him. He must have been going down as you were coming up. Was he expecting you?"

Randy ignored the question. "Did he say where he was going?"

"No, ma'am. I think he went to a late lunch. He had an appointment that ran way over but he should be back in a half-hour. May I get you a drink? You can wait in his office if you'd like?" She must be Canadian, Randy thought, an American would have said can I get you a drink.

"No. Thank you. I'll see him at home." Randy was disappointed. She'd been so ready damn it. Not to talk about having to draw on every bit of courage to show up this morning. Damn that man, he's never there when she needs him! Deciding not to waste the morning, she stopped by their favorite place, Andiamos, an upscale restaurant gourmet store, for a few delicacies. Tonight, she'd be extra nice to Lawrence. She would arrange a candlelit dinner of Dijon salmon and asparagus tips, and lots of brandies. Then she would ask him about the gallery.

As she was walking through the store, she thought she heard Lawrence's voice coming from behind the lattice that separated the market from the restaurant. She walked to the lattice and peeked through.

"Not tonight." It was Lawrence! Through the partition, she could see her husband and a woman who'd been a guest at their last dinner party.

Randy's heart began to race. Surely, she was overreacting. Lawrence had many female clients, it was normal, she rationalized. Yet, she was far more affected than she'd ever imagined considering she'd dreamt about her freedom for years. She should be elated to have a reason to leave but somehow, she felt betrayed. Randy turned on her heels and left the restaurant. She'd always known that Lawrence's wealth was a magnet for gold-digging women and she never thought she cared. Randy dashed from the store and jumped into her waiting car. She knocked back a quick drink and instructed Richard to take her home. "Mensa. MENSA!" Randy screamed as she threw her suit jacket on the couch.

"What's the matter?" Mensa came running from the direction of the kitchen.

"That man was not there! Not in his office! Do you know where he was? Having lunch with a 'client'. What kinds of clients do you think needs night visits! Bring me up a bucket of ice."

"No. I will not. Don't even think about it. Anger puts you in a different space. Best not to drink right now. Let me make you some coffee."

"If I wanted some damn coffee, I'd have asked you for coffee. Now get me some ice!"

"You're going to have to get it yourself," Mensa said retreating to her kitchen.

"One of these days I'm going to fire you," Randy pushed pass Mensa.

"Fine with me. I wasn't hired to babysit a grown ass woman." She walked back toward the kitchen.

"But Mensa, he was cooing to a woman…one of them who was here having dinner at our last party."

"Randy," Mensa usually called her boss Mrs. Austin but that was just a formality, she was more mother to this girl-woman than a servant. "I know I'm the helper but sit down, child, I need to say something to you."

"You are not going to scold me again for being a bad wife and mother, are you?"

"No, I'm not. I want you to call your mother. Only she can set your life in a new direction."

"You've got jokes?" Randy scoffed, "Why would you say that?"

"Whatever ails you, make you drink and lose yourself is in your childhood. Who better than a mother to release her child from childhood?"

"How daft." She waited for Mensa to respond. When she didn't Randy said, "I can't Mensa. Honestly, I can't."

"You must child. Really you must."

"I can't. Leave it alone," Randy shouted.

"Fine, if you want to handle things as always, go on drink yourself to death. Here is your ice."

"No thank you," Randy stomped out of the kitchen and up the stairs. She had a refrigerator in her room. Damn them all. She slammed her bedroom door so hard it reverberated. She was well on her way to being sloshed when she heard the familiar voice and the racket on the stairs.

"Randy. Randy, RANDY." Lawrence came bouncing up the steps. She didn't answer. What the hell was he doing home at this time of day? The bathroom door flung open and he stood in the archway looking at her holding the tumbler of vodka with concern. "Are you all right?"

"Why do you always ask me that?"

"I thought there was an emergency. I hurried home. I was worried sick about you."

When she didn't answer, he walked toward her. "What's going on Randy?"

"What do you care?"

"Randy…" Lawrence's voice took on his 'I-don't-have-time-for-this' edge.

"I don't want to talk about it Lawrence, or to you for that matter." Her favorite song popped into her head. *No night so long that you can't find the day.*

"Talk about what? Tell me what's wrong?" He took her by the shoulders.

"You. You're wrong. You've always been wrong." Randy said pulling out of his grasp. "And you always make bad choices. First, you chose me as a wife, your silly man." *Call on me like you used to do I still can show you who you are.* The tears were falling now.

Oh, here we go again. "Randy, what on earth are you talking about now?"

"We are talking about you. You who weren't even there for your daughter's birth and now you're acting as though…"

"Randy," Lawrence interrupted the incoherent tirade. "You're mad about something that happened twenty odd years ago?"

"Yes. Twenty-two years ago, to be exact." Randy gait was wobbly as she pushed pass Lawrence. "Aren't you tired of this sham of a life, Lawrence? Why don't you just divorce me?"

"Okay," he grabbed her arm, spilling the vodka. "What the hell is going on here?"

"I don't need to be taken care of anymore." Randy threw the half-empty glass at him. Randy had never loved Lawrence like he loved her but she needed to be "taken care of," or so her family thought. On their wedding night when she had lain trembling and lifeless beneath him as he took her "virginity" she had cried buckets, soaking him and the bed sheet in the process. When his gentle arms had closed tightly around her, she had felt calm and safe but no more in love and she knew this man was never going to own her soul. Randy thought of the man she was now crying over. There were no golden memories. No claps of thunder or bolts of lightning moments in her memory and though she had never loved him nor had she ever grown into any grand passion for him, she had become dependent on his predictable love for her and the amazing life his wealth offered. She had tried, really tried to be a good wife to Lawrence but she had failed miserably both as a wife and as a mother.

"What the hell is going on here?" Lawrence ducked the glass and again grabbed Randy in a vice grip. "You are drunk, as usual, but what's different?" He was pressing her arm hard.

"Don't raise your voice at me, damn it. You can raise your voice to your floozies but not to me." She tried to snatch her arm out of his grip but failed. "I saw you with that woman today. I heard everything. You're a low life, and with your own friend's wife. How could you?"

"Is that what this is about? The woman I was with today? Gale is a client, Randy. She doesn't want her husband to know what she does with the money he gives her. That's it. Most of these young wives don't last three years. They have to take care of their future when the marriage ends."

"Let go of me, Lawrence."

"This is what I do Randy. It's what provides you with this house and those fancy clothes you wear."

"Please," Randy's tone was pure acid, "don't be smug."

"Why do I have to go through this every time you get depressed, disappointed or drunk? Why did you jump to conclusions? Why didn't you just ask me?"

Embolden by the alcohol, Randy said, "Because I really don't give a damn. I've never given a damn and I've had it up to here with you, your vulgar friends and your ego. I've really had enough." The alcohol and sedative were making her head spin and her tongue loose. Randy fell against Lawrence's torso. Her head was really spinning.

"If I were with Gale, it would serve you right. Why would you care anyway? You don't want me. You never have and you can't even pretend anymore. You're frigid and cold. You've been that way since the day I met you. I thought after June's birth your maternal love would kick in and that I would benefit from your finding a heart. How wrong I was. What do you want me to do? Yes, I have had many physical affairs to keep being married to you but I assure you Gale is not one of them."

"How dare you? Fuck you, Fuck you, FUCK YOU, Lawrence!"

"That's exactly what you should have been doing all these years. Maybe I wouldn't have strayed. Marriage isn't only about pretenses and shopping with the money I earn. It's about love and caring. I haven't left you, have I? Even after all the shit you put me through. I've always and will always, for some crazy reason, love you."

"You're absolutely right, Lawrence. About everything. About me and about you. But marriage shouldn't take away life for either of us. Like you I need my own life apart from us. I want to open an art gallery."

"What?" Lawrence was stunned.

"You heard me. I want to open a gallery. That's why I came to your office."

"But you know nothing about business. I bet those idiot friends of yours are responsible for this."

"That would hardly matter. It's what I want."

"And if I say no," Lawrence finally let go of her, "what are you going to do? Will you disappear into the bedroom for months on end, drinking and taking sedatives?"

"That'll be damn well better than giving parties for those Neanderthals on Wall Street. Those days are over. Do you hear me, over! I'm no fuckin' social clerk or a sex object. You've never once asked me about my interests, never!" Randy had become hysterical her finger wagging in his face. Lawrence, who'd had never seen her this angry, grabbed the finger threatening to poke out his eye.

"Look, Randy. Why don't you go and see Dr. Sody before this thing gets out of control again?" Lawrence soothed.

"Why don't you go and see the village idiot yourself. Maybe he can give you some pills to keep your dick in your pants! I want a gallery or I want a divorce. You chose."

Lawrence turned on his heel and left the room.

Grabbing the silver frame off the mantle Randy smashed their wedding picture against the wall. She wanted to rip the whole damn pretentious place and her pretentious life apart. She hated this, hated it when he touched her, and today she hated him even more than she hated her life. It's not that she didn't suspect his affairs, she hadn't had to face them up close and personal. With the thought of a new life, her own, seeding in her head, and her new and only friend Adele, Randy no longer wanted any part of the pretense her life had become. Back in her sanctuary, Randy splashed vodka over ice cubes. She opened the medicine cabinet and took another Xanax, washing it down with the glass of vodka. She wasn't hiding from the pain of Lawrence 's philandering. Today she was hiding from herself. She was one messed up chick! "Damn you!" she screamed at the mirror, "Damn you!" She downed some more vodka. If she could stay in this bathroom for the rest of her life it would suit her just fine. A few minutes later the drugs and alcohol took effect. Relaxed she could now get through the rest of the day and the disappointment of her coward's life. Experience had taught her that pain only lasted until the numbing took over. She climbed into her bed, tucked herself between the coverlets and began her journey… *The earth was soft and fresh as it sifted through her bare feet. The double rainbow in the sky arched its way into nowhere. Along the footpath, a great waterfall gushed and seamlessly cascading down, down, down, down into the lake becoming one as it meandered to only God knows where. It was a place of respite. A place where God must have walked to make it so beautiful…a place Randy often dreamed of and wished for.*

CHAPTER TWENTY-ONE
Melvadore Follette

New York, 2002

"I AM SO SORRY I missed your party. How was it?"

"Necessary and good. I think all the men who weren't so sure about me as a choice felt better. Six million has a way of doing that. That was all the chatter I heard. I'm sorry you missed Phillip."

"I'll make it up to him. Promise." His eyes twinkled. "Sit down, we have a serious matter to discuss. It seems you have wished yourself into a hard news job. Our man in Afghanistan has been airlifted out."

"Afghanistan!"

"Baptism by fire. I always thought the Middle East should be your first real assignment. Do you think you could handle it? It could be your lucky day or your worst nightmare. One thing is for sure, it's a shot to get out of that management chair you keep saying you hate so much and hit the ground running. Find out if the hard news is really for you once and for all. This is as hard as it gets. It'll be quite dangerous and you can say no."

"No…no…this is great news!" Ashley said without hesitation. "This is fantastic. As an intern when I was on the news desk, I went to a shoot-up in South Philly…not exactly the battlefield but I'm very interested and confident that I can."

"Great. Then let's get the paperwork done."

"What does that mean?"

"It means you'll have to sign an additional "war zone" contract with us today. I'll also need you to speak with our psychologist and medical director before you can be confirmed for the assignment. Dr. Hagar will be waiting for you when we're done here and you'll see the med tomorrow after you meet with HR."

"Okay on the psych, but I'll need a week to have my attorney give this contract a look over."

"No time for all that. You're going to have to trust me. If you want to realize this dream of yours, it's now or never."

Ashley looked at Mel for a long time. He wasn't joking.

"But why do I have to sign today?" She pressed.

"Because your assignment starts tomorrow right after you get medical clearance. And I have to leave the country today so as I said it's now or never. I have arranged for a seasoned crew to fly with you and I'll have people on the ground waiting for you. You must follow the rules of engagement to a T. If you want out, well bring you home. Just say so."

Then it all happened so quickly. The next morning, donning her, I-don't-take-no-for-an answer suit, Ashley headed to the Human Resources office of WNCB, determined to push back her departure date by a day. There was no frigging way she was getting on a plane to enemy territory with no experience on the fourth day of any month. What kind of coincidence could that be? It was an omen! Her tirade had been abruptly halted by the marble in front of her who was sculpted to look like a woman! The cold blue eyes didn't even flinch at her request. Rochelle Marble, what's in a name, was the CHRO of all of Follette's enterprises. She had been brought over from one of Melvadore's other company. She'd been with him for years. Ashley could see why.

"Didn't Mr. Mel say this was an emergency?"

"Yes. I…"

"An emergency has no wiggle room, Ms. Freeman, so why are you here?"

"Well…"

"Please don't waste my time."

"Ms. Marble I know this is the opportunity of a lifetime. I'm very excited, really, I am. It's just that…"

The battle-ax cut her off again. "I wasn't for this idea, to begin with, but Mr. Follette seems to think you have the talent for serious journalism and need it on your management vitae. You've always been looking for the big story. Well, this is it. Your lucky day! What will it be, Miss? We can definitely try to find someone else if we have to, but I thought this was all settled," Miss Marble informed, planting the idea that petrified Ashley even more than traveling on the fourth. "Take this with you to Dr. Cromwell. Make a right out of this office, down the hall, fourth door on the left. Then report to your team. They fly at 4:00 pm."

"What's with this malarkey," Ashley groaned, another four. Was she to die in Afghanistan? Even the most frightening thought couldn't deter Ashley from what she had waited years for; her big break. Right then and there, she had sucked it up, put on her charming face, took the folder and walked out the door. Her big girl panties felt way too big!

• • •

So, it was the fourth of June 2002, at 4:00 p.m. that Ashley Freeman, who did nothing of importance on the fourth day of any month, nor did she stay in hotel rooms with the number four or had any relationship with anything remotely close to the number four, stepped onto the tarmac where WNCB's private jet was waiting to take her to the killing fields of Afghanistan. This was her big break, an opportunity of a lifetime and even though she fought hard to suppress her fears and bias and she was petrified. She'd never been on a private plane either. At eleven, when her family had boarded BOAC America bound, Ashley had been fascinated with the silver knives and forks, the little lights overhead and the pretty pillbox hats the Stewardess wore. Back then just being on the plane itself was an adventure but there was hardly a thing fascinating about flying these days, not even in first class.

The G5 cruised at 47 thousand feet, almost at the supersonic speed of Mark 9. Custom made, it supplied every convenience down to the gilded bathroom. Ashley felt adventurous all over again and like on her BOAC flight, explored the mysteries of the supersonic iron bird. Grandeur or not, the reality was that she was on her way to the Middle East to a possible death sentence in a place she could barely locate on a map. Some bloody fate! Not exactly what she had in mind to catapult her to fame and fortune. Ready to try for some much-needed sleep, Ashley pulled down the window shades, put on her eye-mask, and slid her chair into the bed position. Sleep eluded her as her mind kept replaying the falling bodies through time and space. Three thousand lost. Images of 9/11 swarmed in her head. How could she possibly do an unbiased story?

Ashley was wide awake when the pilot announced their landing in London where they would layover and refuel before an early morning flight to Kabul. The idea of being in her favorite five-star hotel, The One Aldridge, was a temporary solace. It was always comforting to come home. As Ashley sank into the feathered bed for what might very well be her last night in a swanky hotel, if not on this earth, she said The Lord's Prayer. On the plane by six a.m., Ashley gathered her crew for a last meeting. "Let's go over the rules of engagement for this trip," she said, looking at each crew member. "It's imperative that we are on the same page at all times. Above all, remember we are Americans in a hostile country. No matter how testy you are or how you may feel about these people who have caused such terror in our country but let's not be insensitive." She turned to her two bodyguards, giants by any standard. "On location don't ever lose sight of me. Always keep your eye on our translator but don't crowd us. I want these people to forget that you're there." The two men nodded. Next, she briefed the film crew. "Film everything. From the moment we get off the plane until the moment we leave."

Things did not go exactly as planned. First, brewing thunderstorms grounded the plane for two hours. Then the G5 had to circle for one hour over Kabul before it was allowed to land on the rubble that doubled as an airport. She and the crew were literally propelled by the sheer maddening crowd into an even more chaotic scene. Because they were American Press, customs officers confiscated their camera equipment before ushering them into a room where each person was interrogated. Two hours later they were allowed to leave, their equipment escorted to the waiting guide.

Outside, a local man approached Ashley. "You journalist from America," he said in halting English, holding a picture of the crew. "I am Hag, your guide. Come." He led them to the all-terrain UAZ-469 Russian jeep especially made especially for the Afghani war, instructing his colleagues in their native language, Dari, to load the equipment onto the back. He ignored the hand Ashley outstretched instead bowing deeply. Only later did she understand that a woman could never touch a man in public. Ashley took the front seat and the others crowded into the back of the jeep cramming the equipment between them.

"We go to hotel now. Early morning, we go to some towns and villages. Later we take horseback to mountains. Then we go to refugee camp in Peshawar."

"Who gave you our itinerary?"

"Mr. Abdullah. We meet him later. He's in contact with your men in America."

Shacks, mud-brick houses and seas of ragged people; women in tattered blue burqas, men in dirty tunics pushing their wares, and starving looking children, were the sights on the way to the hotel. Ashley felt like she'd stepped into a time warp. She was unprepared for Afghanistan and feared greatly that she was unprepared for the job.

The deep sense of horror in the air over Kabul left her in anguish and fear. Fear in a place like this was her enemy and Ashley dug deep to steel herself against the sight of the bombed out, ravished country that was so beyond her comprehension and reality. To appreciate that such devastation could actually exist in the world much less in everyday life was her new reality. Ashley dug, deeper like an actor in a challenging role and found all the instances in her life where distancing from emotions meant survival. She'd sat in silence beside Hag as he pulled the car into what appeared to be a parking lot. Ashley realized that her imagined death might not be that imagined after all. There was such sadness in the world as only men could cause, Bush not excluded! This was life in Afghanistan. America was momentarily under attack, this was a way of life for the people of this country. The jeep pulled up to what was left of The Intercontinental Hotel. It bore scars of war.

"Only yesterday happened, but other side is good. You fine here." He carried her luggage into the hotel, a mortified Ashley trudging behind. Hag made his way to registration and returned with a porter. "What time do you want pick up for dinner?" He handed her the room keys. "I have nice place for first night. Show you Afghan hospitality and you meet Mr. Abdullah. Please dress appropriately. As woman, you need to cover your arms, legs, and head while here and most especially if you go into a Mosque."

"I will. Thank you Hag. Shall we say dinner at about six?"

"Evening prayer. Seven-thirty."

Hag waved goodbye and soon the jeep was gone. Standing in the bombed-out lobby, Ashley didn't know where her center was. She felt disoriented and as affected as she had ever been in her life. She dispensed the keys to her crew.

• • •

Hag arrived promptly at seven-thirty. They drove a short distance to a tiny restaurant where bread was cooking in an earthen oven. Above the slabs of wood propped up on stilts that served as tables hung haphazard light bulbs that lit the dim room. The streetlight filtered in through the uneven windows that dotted the room. The walls were an uneven blend of whitewash and brown soot from oven smoke. Chain smoking men sat around scooping food with flatbread. Like Hag, she and her crew followed suit and removed their shoes at the mat by the door. Ashley was the only woman in the room. She had indeed dressed as Hag suggested; her head was covered with a scarf and a long sleeve magenta pantsuit covered her arms and legs. She gagged slightly as she stepped into the restaurant. The sweet smell of tobacco mixed with the spices was cloying and she quickly made her way over to an open window. Wow, Ashley thought as she looked up at the sky, what an amazing starry, starry night!

"Welcome," said a man in a white caftan as he approached them. "I am Abdullah. Welcome to my country." His english was excellent. It was clear that he'd been educated outside of Afghanistan.

"Thank you." Ashley smiled lowering her eyes, "I'm delighted to meet you."

"You are very brave woman to come here."

"Equal rights thing in America, you know." Ashley was surprised at the man's cultured manner. Somehow, she'd always associated the word primitive with the Middle East.

"Yes, I know all about that. I was educated at Columbia University in New York City."

"Really? If you had a chance to escape this daily reality why did you come back to this?"

"This is home. No other place on earth can be. This is where I want to die. Here among my people. I hope they become yours too after this visit. "Please," Abdullah beckoned her toward a table set with a large teapot and plates of sweets.

"How have your people been managing?" Ashley asked Abdullah.

His dark eyes turned somber. "We do the best we can. Here in Afghanistan survival is the daily goal. We are simply glad to see the sunset. We praise Allah for giving us another day with our family."

"What do you mean?"

"We can't control the time of our death, especially now. Death can find us in so many ways: from a bomb, or a Taliban gunshot wound, from stepping on a land mine in our own farm. We live every day as the last."

"I see," Ashley said not understanding at all. "Abdullah, do you think I could interview some families who have lost children, husbands, and fathers in this civil war? I would also like to talk to some of the children too to find out why they become radicals."

Abdullah smiled. "That is a western word. We are not radicals. We want peace like everyone else but we cannot…" his voice trailed off.

"Cannot what?" she urged.

"We are a country with traditions. We have a culture that must be preserved. We have a religion, Islam, which is as important to us as your Christianity is to you. Why must the western world try to eradicate what they don't understand? Why can they not respect differences? Much of what you hear in America is propaganda. We are a peaceful people if we are only left alone to be peaceful."

"Your 'peaceful people' killed three thousand Americans." Ashley couldn't stop the reporter in herself. "How is that peaceful?"

"All of Afghanistan is not represented by the Taliban. Americans and Russians killed millions of Afghanis. To be exact 1.7 million and another 4 million fled to Peshawar. They lost their homes and their country. America used us against Russia and then abandoned us. America is responsible for the rise of the Taliban. America has no loyalty or respect for any country but America. It might just fall under its own weight. History tells the truth. Any nation that loses its moral compass and declines in virtues is on its way to destruction. "We," he said proudly, "must have courage even in the face of danger. One life for the salvation of a people is nothing."

Ashley was horrified at what she saw as dogma but was

aware that what she actually felt was a surprising mixture of disdain, sympathy, and respect for Abdullah. She was impressed with his honesty and his commitment to the country of his birth. He was like any red-blooded American, a patriot. This new reality, and how it too made sense, frightened her. How can one nation inflict such horror on another? The conversation abated as steaming plates of kabob and flatbreads were brought out. Over dinner, she got an education on a country that before 9/11 she barely knew existed. "You are in good hands with Hag. I promised Melvadore that I would take good care of you."

"You know Mr. Follette?"

"He is my first cousin. My father and his father were brothers."

"Really?" Ashley said.

• • •

The silence over Kabul was shattered by a deep, mournful cry. The sound so frightened Ashley that she bolted from deep sleep into alert wakefulness. In her haste to take cover under the bed, she knocked the travel clock to the floor. It was four-forty-five a.m. Ashley, though fairly well traveled, had never been in a Muslim country and it was only later that morning as she described the ear-splitting noise to Hag that he explained it was a warble, the morning call to prayer by the mullah. Over the next few days, Ashley realized that the morning call to prayer was also a call for the Kabul roosters to crow the city into action. Somewhere in the recess of her mind, she remembered the roosters' cock-a-doodle-doos in Jamaica and the fact that soon after their morning alarm the maids would arrive for work. Children, she'd suddenly appreciated, do remember much sooner than adults imagined, yet until now, this memory had never been triggered. By 6:00 a.m. Kabul was alive with the street vendors preparing for their day of trade.

As they ventured over dirt roads, through parched desert and arid mountains, passing cemetery after cemetery littered with promised lives now snuffed out, passing even more cemeteries that will forever bear testament to the horror of more than thirty years of conflict in Afghanistan, Ashley's whole world, as she understood it, began to collapse. This morning, her seventh in Kabul, she stared almost unseeing at the mud houses lit by gasoline lamps, and rows and rows of tents that were being used as schools. As their jeep bumped along the rough terrain to visit a school on the outskirts of Mehtar Lam, Ashley was adjusting to life in a war-torn country. Mehtar Lam was the region where many of the suicide bombers came from.

"Will they let us in you think?" she asked Hag as the raggedy school tent came into view.

"We see in a few minutes," Hag said pulling the jeep over the side.

Ashley jumped out and waited until Hag joined her.

"Don't push if they don't want to answer," he suggested.

They made their way around to the back of the tent. Ashley was surprised to see children laughing and playing outside and couldn't help but wonder how a life, reduced to such sadness and simplicity, could still be filled with hope and joy. Ashley entered through the flaps that served as doors and sat quietly on the dirt floor lit by a single naked bulb, to listen to teachers who had no hope of ever being paid, teach children to read and write. Hope indeed, was still very much alive here. Hag greeted the teachers, mostly females. There were back and forth exchanges before he beckoned Ashley to join him.

Hag translated Ashley's questions betraying no bias.

"Why did he do it?" Ashley had asked AliBibi, the burqa clad mother of a suicide bomber.

"Because he could not stand the suffering of our people. Two generations lost. No more tears left to cry. Eyes dry," she said offering Ashley strong, black tea. "My son died a martyr for his people. Our young people, they know only war. But even if peace comes, so many are already dead. Our boys do the right thing. Always fight for freedom. With this war, our voices will be heard. Never crawl on your knees while you still have the strength to walk."

Ashley and AliBibi held each other in parting. They rocked back and forth and mingled tears. Ashley, a privileged woman beyond her wildest imagination, an English American at least by her passports and AliBibi, a grieving Afghani mother in a mud hut who would probably never leave this country. Yet, behind the veil, they were the same.

By nightfall, the pitch-black sky was magnificently lit with a blaze of stars. They had also reached the border of Peshawar and the team was handed over to the Military where tankers kept vigil over bunkers. They were fed and given sleeping bags for the night. The soldiers watched her over dinner. Finally, a young soldier from North Carolina came over. "What would make you come to a place like this?" he asked.

"I don't know," Ashley said and she was being honest.

• • •

Wrapped in her sleeping bags deep inside the bunker Ashley covered her ears from the constant firing of mortar, another horror that intruded on everyday life and she cried openly and unabashedly for the sights and sounds over Kabul. Afghanistan had given her a panoramic view of her own life and she was beginning to despise the smallness of her world and how inconsequential and self-absorbed she really was in the scheme of things. And as she watched the brave women who lost their children to a heinous war, she felt abject sadness and anger at America's myopic view of the world. Crossing the Pakistani border into Peshawar, where so many well-to-do Afghanis fled to escape the leveling of class by war, Ashley watched in horror as refugees, no matter how wealthy, waited in lines for three or four days just to get border permissions and rations of bread. In the City of Flowers where not a shred of a garden could be seen, Ashley was heart-broken to see three and four-year-old orphans forced into begging scraps of bread in order to survive. As she watched those with so little share what they had with those who had nothing, she knew she was losing her heart of steel. That night Ashley begged Hag to call her friend, Phillip in America on the satellite phone they carried. She needed something or someone to anchor her to another reality. "How can I possibly tell this story to America? It is so brutal," she was in tears.

"Tell it as you see it," Phillip encouraged. "Come home darling, it's time."

Ashley settled herself on the makeshift bed. She would leave this country in a few days. Her life would never be the same. What would President Bush feel if he visited Afghanistan and saw what she had seen up close and personal and not from a diplomatic convoy? That was her last thought as she fell into a fitful sleep.

• • •

Back in Kabul at the Intercontinental, as far she was concerned, a10-star hotel in comparison to some of the places she'd been over the past four weeks, Ashley gathered her belongings. She could not deny that she was glad to leave Afghanistan, yet she was sad to leave the people. She was, however, absolutely sure that the person who had arrived four weeks earlier, was not the same person returning to America. She was a reporter at heart. Mel had been right…he knew her, it seemed, more than she knew herself.

CHAPTER TWENTY-TWO
Randy

New York, East Side, 2002

RANDY CALLED EVERY commercial realtor in Manhattan looking for a Chelsea space to open her gallery. After her final realty call, she made one more.

"Adele, its Randy. Can you have breakfast this morning?"

"For you, of course, but what you really want is to see the picture, no? Graduation is in a week, no?"

"I want to do that too, but right now I want to talk about something else. Lawrence will back the gallery. I've lined up a few properties to look at. Will you go scouting in Chelsea with me? Are you near a computer?"

"I can be."

"Then go to this website and check them out. I'll meet you say ten-thirty a.m. at the Starbucks near the Chelsea Hotel. Corner of 23rd and Seventh."

"I'm thrilled for you but I don't do Starbucks. Meet me here first. I'll make nice French breakfast. French women you know don't get fat so it will be healthy. We chose the properties you want to see and we go together."

"This is so exciting. Now we can get busy with plans to open a gallery."

"Ah, I don't open galleries. I paint."

Finding interesting spaces and hiring architects and builders who would bring her vision to life was something Randy was looking forward to. Feeling more alive than she'd ever imagined Randy left the house and by 10:00 a.m. she was rapping on Adele's door.

"Allo." An unfamiliar, nattily dressed woman opened the door.

"I'm sorry," Randy said turning to leave, chiding herself for being absentminded, "I meant to knock on the next door."

"You are at zee right door, Randy," Adele laughed. "It is I." The voice, smooth like aged scotch, yet gravely as a newly paved driveway was Adele's. Randy peered closely at her.

"Adele? What have you done to yourself? You look amazing."

"I'm looking always bad so I got dressed for breakfast and to celebrate zee gallery. You like, no?"

"No smock. No jeans. No boots. No glasses. And your hair! You have beautiful hair." Randy was truly stunned at Adele's transformation. Her usual casual, messy upsweep, now thick and curly was hanging loosely around her oval face. Baggy T-shirt and jeans or paint splashed coverall were replaced by a Thierry Mugler pencil skirt and fitted jacket, her stunning and gorgeous womanly figure filling out every seam. French women indeed had no body fat! The air was spiced with French perfume. Adele would definitely be an asset to the gallery, Randy thought. Allure and art went hand in hand. She bet there'd be a lot of dirty old men ready for her allure who would buy lots of art.

Adele laughed at Randy's expression.

"Oh, I was just thinking that you're going to knock the socks off our customers, and we'll get the best rent from our realtor. You look *magnifique*," Randy said.

"*Merci, merci,* Adele thanked her, ushering her into the loft. "But you know I am no good businesswoman. I am just a painter, so keep that in mind."

"So, you say. I'll wait and see."

"Tell me. How did you get Lawrence to agree?"

Randy's eyes clouded. "Guilt."

"Works every time," Adele said. "I'm sorry."

"Don't be. I've known about Lawrence's dalliances for years. Now I can use them to benefit me."

Adele moved the conversation in a different direction. "I think I'll show you the painting for June before breakfast." She headed to her studio. "I hope you like it," she said pulling a drop sheet off the canvas on her easel.

"Oh, my," Randy's hand went to her mouth. "It's beautiful and so clever. The painting was a charcoal sketch on paper of a young girl on the verge of womanhood, open and unfinished as though waiting for life to fill in the rest.

"It is beautiful," Randy repeated. "Truly magnificent! But do you think it's a bit…"

"I was worried you'd say that. Maybe it is too assuming. But it is a young woman's transformation. That she is, no?"

"It's just perfect. Like a rose opening up to the morning dew. It is perfect." Randy took Adele's hand in gratitude. "Thank you. Will you come to her party and unveil it for her?"

"I can't?"

"Why not?" Randy asked, surprised.

Adele pulled her hand away from the painting and turned her back to Randy. She and Randy had become great friends. They were like schoolgirls together. Laughing and sharing secrets and dreams. "I just can't!" Adele said lighting a cigarette. "Come let's have café."

"You can. You must. I promise the party will be a great deal of fun," Randy said trailing behind her to the dining room. "I can't wait to see Lawrence's face. Ha, I will trump his gift."

"Funny no, how we start life with expectations and end up with disappointments?"

Randy was confused. "What are you talking about? June, I assure you will not be disappointed. I know June would love to meet the person who did this amazing painting. It'll be the best gift."

"I wonder if that's true?"

"It will be," Randy said. "Lawrence is going to give her a trip."

"Randy, would you mind terribly if we shopped for something else for June? We have time. I finished the painting so fast," Adele said. "I am not pleased with it."

"But why?" Randy said. "It beautiful, honestly."

"Because I really want this to be the first painting in our gallery."

"Then for sure, you'll be my partner in the gallery after all?" Randy was overjoyed.

"Yes. If this can be the first painting we show."

"Don't be silly. You'll do ten times better than this."

"But they will never be this. To be honest Randy, I didn't paint this for June, I painted it for you."

"Me?" Randy laughed.

"Yes, you." Adele came to stand in front of her. "I painted you as I see you," she touched her face, "On the verge of womanhood."

"I've been a woman a long time," Randy laughed.

"Are you sure?"

"What are you talking about, Adele?"

"Can't you see that I'm in love with you, Randy?"

"What?" Randy backed away. She must have misheard her. "Adele, you don't know what you're saying."

"I know exactly what I'm saying. I said I love you. I just wanted you to know that. You don't have to do anything with it, but for the gallery is it a problem?"

"Look, you're tired. Rushing the painting took a lot out of you. Adele, I'm married. We're women…"

"Married but not in love. *Law'rence's* love will never reflect the light in your heart or the love I feel for you. I know your love. I painted you as I saw you, unfinished and searching. Why haven't you ever let it out, your desires?"

"Adele! Stop it this minute!" Randy said, her hands going to cover her ears, "This is crazy."

"Love is crazy, Randy," Adele said. "I have studied love my entire life. There are three levels you know," Adele said moving toward Randy. "The love of self is third, the love of family is second and the love of Eros is first. It is that irrational love that is forbidden and without boundaries."

"And damaging," Randy said backing away from her.

"To whom?" Adele asked raising a brow.

Randy's words were filled with suffering. "To the victim." Her eyes filled with tears. "Adele, I thought we were friends. Why would you betray our friendship this way?" Randy asked.

"How can love be a betrayal?" Adele asked.

"You don't love me," Randy snapped. "You just have no boundaries for your lust." Randy turned to the window. "Do you know why I live my life this way?" Randy asked, detaching herself from the moment because it was necessary for her survival. "When I was thirteen, my uncle raped me in my own home. I've had to live with that memory and shame my entire life. He was someone I trusted. I've suffered at the hands of lust more than anyone ever should. At least he was the village idiot but you…"

They both stood in silence. Then Adele said, "I am so sorry. Why didn't you tell me before?" She reached out to Randy.

Randy pushed her away. "I have never told anyone and I shouldn't have to tell you to protect myself from a friend. To survive I had to forget. That's why you can't do this, Adele, because a lack of control can alter lives forever." Randy turned toward the door. "I have to go now. I'd like to take the painting. I won't be back." Randy reached into her purse for her checkbook. "How much do I owe you?"

"I'm so very sorry. I would have given my life not to betray you. But Randy my love is not a betrayal…it is honest and kind…haven't you ever wondered what true love feels like?" Adele asked.

"No, I have not. And I don't intend to find out with you," Randy said firmly.

"Let me show you, Randy," Adele said softly.

Randy backed away. "On second thought I don't want the painting. I want no memory of you, ever."

"Don't be afraid," Adele said coming toward her.

"Don't touch me," Randy yelled, "I hate being touched. I fuckin' hate you. I thought…I thought…we were friends, Adele and you betrayed my trust," Randy said angrily starting to cry.

"I didn't mean to fall in love with you. I would never do anything to hurt you. I want you to let me love you. I want you to be free for once in your life."

Randy felt a pain deep inside her body. Why did it always have to be her? "I trusted you. I trusted you," she said reaching the door. The look on her face was one of utter disbelief. Randy tried to speak, but words, as always failed her. She searched her brain for an explanation of why the people she loved betrayed her.

Adele reached for her and broken, Randy stepped into the circle.

"I can never love," she whispered, "and I will never be free. You were my only friend."

Adele reached for Randy's hand. "Everyone needs love."

Randy shook her head. "But we're women. Love can only happen between a man and a woman."

Adele held tightly to Randy's hand. "Ah, western poppycock. In India, women are taught the Karma Sutra. They learn to please their husbands by first learning to please themselves," she whispered.

"We are in America," Randy says. "Lawrence is my only reality and I chose him a long time ago."

"Isn't that the reality you wanted to run away from? You must allow yourself to feel love, to be loved," Adele said pulling Randy close.

Randy's body went rigid. "Let go of me, Adele."

"Look at me," Adele ordered, her breath against Randy's cheek. "Tell me you don't want to know. Tell me you feel nothing."

Randy tried to speak, but words again failed her. She searched her brain for an explanation of what was happening to her but was overcome by Adele's honesty. When Adele held her tightly, kissed her face and stroked her hair she did not resist. Finally, Adele's lips found Randy's, their breathing heavy and desired, the room warm and consenting. Surprisingly Randy felt alive with a passion completely new to her. Even more surprising was that she wanted Adele to love her. But who would she be afterward? Her world would shatter. Randy tried to shut down the compelling feelings but for the first time in her life was unable to silence her desires. Closing her eyes as Adele's kisses became more demanding, Randy finally surrendered, responding with matched passion. A passion so strong it threatened to overwhelm them both. Randy allowed her spirit to rise, being as much an observer as a participant. Adele's lips were velvety against hers. The hands that pressed her body close gently caressed her as they slid her out of her jacket.

"I love you," Adele said cradling Randy in her arms.

"Don't say that," Randy pleaded, hiding her face in Adele's shoulder.

"Let's go look at gallery space," Adele said simply.

"I'm not going anywhere with you," Randy said getting dressed.

A gale blew against her face as she stumbled down Varick. She felt sick, wretched and wanted to vomit. Dear God why? Why did you take my friend away? She could never see Adele again. Never! Only then did Randy realize that tears were rolling down her face. Mixed with the black mascara it hit her white blouse and left a dirty stain. Ashley was right, they were all broken into a million little pieces.

CHAPTER TWENTY-THREE
Amelie

Connecticut, September, 2002

AMELIE HIT HER stopwatch. It was an unseasonably cool morning and she was moving at a nice clip. Today she'd run a five-minute mile around the neighborhood. Running in Central Park was the one thing she missed about New York. She pulled out her earplugs and shouted a satisfied, yes! Racing back to the house she headed straight for her beloved piano soaking sweats and all. She had it, that feeling, that ineffable but certain feeling that she was ready. She could play *Opus 17* in her sleep. Every note, every beat, every feeling Schumann must have felt when he wrote the song about his hopeless love for his wife, Clara. In a single moment, years and years of study had clicked into perfection. And her muses were nowhere in sight. Dr. Vlachenko had called on his return from Austria. They had been playing together now for several months. As she dressed for her lesson, Amelie's hands play imaginary keys. She had the feeling. The Interpretation. The difficult octave leaps in the E-flat second movement. Indeed, she had captured the serene, passionate climax of the music. She couldn't wait to get to Dr. Vlachenko. She would wow him today. Amelie hummed to herself as she locked the door and headed for the city. She looked sophisticated but professional, her pretty face accented with make-up. On the train, Amelie's fingers played out music as her mind focused on holding the notes in her head. From Grand Central, she hopped a cab to Dr. Vlachenko's apartment.

Dr. Vlachenko was unusually cheerful. His unruly gray hair was neatly brushed and shone with Brill cream. He was wearing a crisply starched white shirt with a paisley bow tie and unbelievably, there were no smudge marks on his glasses. Today he reminded Amelie of Einstein. Something was clearly up but she didn't know what.

"I have a special treat for you today, *moya dorogaya*." His Russian accent was heavier than usual. "I had it sent all the way from Russia, the Black Sea, so we could celebrate."

"What are we celebrating?" Amelie asked following him into the kitchen. He only called her dear in Russian when he was angry or excited. Something was definitely up.

"Tea. I made tea. Special tea in a real *chainik*. *Zavarka*. Not too much. Just enough to make you relax. It has a narcotic effect you see. When prisoners get unruly in Russian jails, they gave them undiluted Zavarka to calm them down. Come, dear, come," he said impatiently, waving her closer.

"Dr. Vlachenko," Amelie said anxiously, "what are we celebrating?"

"Your performance at Carnegie Hall," he answered, pouring hot water into his *chainik*.

Amelie froze. She couldn't move a muscle. Did she hear him correctly? She couldn't have. "But I'm not ready," she finally said, softly, "I can't leap as well as I should from the first bar."

"Oh yes, you can. You have learned *Fantasie* better than Schumann himself!" He waved her words away. "We have a lot of work to do. We have to develop your repertoire. Bach. Schubert. Vivaldi. Brahms. Intermezzo in A minor will help with the leap and arpeggiated tenths. It is good practice. Maybe some Rachmaninoff. He has astonishing leaps and hand crossing in some of his pieces. Who other than Schumann do you want to play?"

"Dr. Vlachenko," Amelie's fingers were drumming against his beloved piano. "I really don't think I'm ready. Maybe with a symphony one day soon, but…"

"My dear," he patted her hand, "you are ready."

"Why didn't you ask me first?" Amelie scrunched up her face, torn between fear and elation.

Vlachenko frowned. "Isn't this why you came to me? That was enough asking," he handed her the pot of tea and a plate of tea biscuits signaling the discussion was closed.

"How did you arrange Carnegie Hall anyway?" Amelie asked, taking the tea and plate as if in a trance.

"My dear, one does not spend a lifetime in the New York music world and not be able to arrange such things. Frankly, it was easy. There were so many people who still remembered you from years ago. You were the biggest promise to us all." Dr. Vlachenko clasped his hands in delight. "Drink up and let's play," he said glancing lovingly at the Bösendorfer.

"When?"

"Now. As soon as you drink the tea."

"I mean Carnegie?"

"November twenty-seventh, 2003. We have lots of time."

"That's only a year away."

"Year and two months," he corrected.

"Can I get back to you on the date?"

"It's already set. You can only not be there if you are dead," he said shrugging, and then he turned to the piano.

Amelie followed. She trusted Dr. Vlachenko. He had been the only teacher to stimulate her creativity beyond its boundaries, he should know if she was ready. Together they gave each other the best of their gifts. They played five hours a day. At three-thirty, every day they went to a late lunch in the neighborhood.

"You were good today. Almost like Nadia Boulanger. Tomorrow we try *Toccata*." Dr. Vlachenko opened his New York Times and began reading.

"Thank you," Amelie said looking down at her menu without really seeing it.

"Did you know that Sviatoslav Richter could reach the 12th note and play the last chord of *Toccata* without arpeggiation?" he asked not looking up from his paper.

"Dr. Vlachenko," Amelie said looking at the man she loved so dearly, "Schumann was a madman and so was Richter."

"Aren't we all, *non compos mentis*," he smiled. Today I am having a Panini."

Amelie lamented that she hadn't driven into the city. The thought of sitting for an hour plus on a train with so many people around her was not pleasing. Today she needed space and solitude. *Not again you, stupid girl*, her annoying business Muse chided. *This is what you wanted. This is what you gave up our life for. Music.* After lunch, Amelie said goodbye to Dr. Vlachenko. It was four-forty-five. She unclipped her cell phone, turned it on and scrolled down to Robb's number. Heck, it was easier to just dial the number but her fingers were stiff after five hours of playing.

Amelie opened and closed her left hand, trying to relieve the pains shooting down her arm.

"Hey Robb," she said when he picked up. "Where are you?"

"Forty-fifth. What about you?"

"Seventy-second. Just finished. Can I come and watch you? Did you drive in? We can go home together."

"Okay, Amelie. Out with it. What's wrong?"

"I'm going to play at Carnegie."

There was silence and then Robb asked. "Are you joking?"

"I wish I were," Amelie said sighing.

"Oh, darling. That's wonderful. That's absolutely wonderful. Come down. We have to celebrate. Can you keep yourself busy for an hour while I finish up? I'll take you to the movies and dinner after I'm done. Then we can drive home together."

"I'll get the tickets and meet you at the Sony Theater on 68th."

"Honey, I'm so proud of you. You deserve this. See you soon. And honey."

"Yes?"

"Call William."

"Why? Is something wrong?"

"No. I mean call to tell him your good news."

• • •

Amelie sat on the bench in the median at Columbus. She'd spoken to William almost every day since the unfortunate incident. She'd reconciled his decision and truth be told she actually liked Kyla and her parents. Everything had been worked out. They had made the best of a bad situation. They'd marry, Kyla would stay home until William graduated and then she'd go back and finish her degree. She couldn't believe she was going to be a grandmother in four more months!

"Mom," William answered the phone on the first ring. "How did you know I needed to talk?"

"I didn't. What's wrong William?"

"I can't go through with this thing. I'm not ready to be a father or a husband."

"But William, it's too late for regrets. Kyla is due in four months."

"We broke up. She's moved out."

"William! What did you do?"

"I told her I was too young to get married. That maybe we should give the baby up for adoption."

"Are you crazy? Why on earth would you do something like that?"

"Because I'm scared Mom. I don't think I can do this. I'm only twenty. I'll be ruining my life."

"William calm down. You should have thought of all of this before."

"Mom…please no lecture. I'm dying here!"

"Well, I suppose we'll have to bury you. Number one, no grandchild of mine will be adopted and number two you are no coward. Have you told your father about this?"

"Not yet. He's going to disown me. I know it but Mom, it was Kyla's idea to leave…now I don't know."

"Come home William, we need to talk. You don't want any baby mama dramas."

CHAPTER TWENTY-FOUR
Ashley

New York, 2003

IT TOOK THE BETTER part of a year for the transition at WNCB. The management and programming team had worked around the clock to roll out what they considered rock solid programming. Ashley, with her real-life combat experience, had garnered a great deal of respect from the doubters and was well respected. When she proposed that she should anchor a weekly Monday night show, everyone agreed that she'd make it work. The unveiling of the new station was soft. People didn't know what was going on. As the weeks rolled by, however, the media industry caught on and all hell broke loose. The assault on the stations was merciless. The attacks only served to sharpen Ashley's canines. She was a deadly pit-bull, to begin with, and they hadn't seen nothing yet. Made for the job of shredding spinmeisters, she delighted in exposing the ruthless and the pretenders. So far, her weekly show had the best rating at the station. People with dirt under their nails who should have avoided her like the plague knew that it was imperative to get on her show if they were to maintain any credibility. No matter how much media training they had, Ashley would annihilate them, taking them by surprise with questions their media people never would imagine possible. Ashley had a knack for research that made people spill the beans. Ashley dropped the heinous notes on the desk. Those Rover boys were despicable. Assholes! She would crucify them. She pushed the button to her voicemail on the way to hanging her jacket in the closet. If she hadn't been trying hard to be angry about the threatening note she'd received, she'd have laughed at the message on her voicemail. Phillip, next to Mel, was her worse critic.

Her favorite messages were Phillip's weekly blow by blow on the rights and wrongs of the show and tips on how to make the show better or her voice more effective. Did that fool realize that she had the best-rated show on the station! "Yesterday's show was lousy. What were you thinking? I thought you were a hotshot. How could you let that pompous ass trip you up?" the first message began. It was the next voice on her machine that she turned her attention to, however. Melvadore Follette. They hadn't seen each other since her return from Afghanistan when he'd met her at the airport. Something had triggered in her that night when she saw him standing on the tarmac with his eyes burrowing into her. She had felt him, inside her heart. And when he insisted on taking her home, she did not have a single fight in her. It is so good to hear your voice…the thought caught her off guard. She' been glad for the distance. It was a Godsend that he'd left the country right after her meltdown even if she'd questioned his judgment about not overseeing the revamping of the station. Guess he really trusted his team.

"Wondering if you have a moment for me this evening. I'm in town, in fact, I'm in my office. If you get this before, hum…let's say 4:00 p.m., come on up. If not, I'll catch up with you tomorrow. By the way, I think I should have your cell phone number. Didn't want to ask HR for it. A spontaneous smile flashed across Ashley's lips. Lies…she was tingling all over. What the hell was wrong with her?

She dialed his office.

"Hi, it's Ashley."

"I know who it is. So glad to hear from you…can you come up?"

"I'm afraid not. I have an appointment. What other options?"

"My house. Tonight, for dinner. I have a few friends coming over."

"Great. What time?"

"8:00 pm."

"Wonderful, I'll see you there."

"Not if you don't know the address."

"Mr. Follette, I've been to your home before."

"No, this one…write this down. 1 W 72nd Street. PH."

No way. He lives in the Dakota, too! "Got it," Ashley said. "I'll see you there then."

• • •

It would be way too banal to describe Melvadore Follette's Penthouse in the Dakota…let's just say it made Ashley's Royal Palace the maid's quarters. Ashley did everything in her power not to gawk. She was no street urchin and she had been to some of the most fabulous homes of brat stars and socialites but she had never been in a home like this. Melvadore opened the door himself. "No problems finding the place?" She could tell he was humoring her.

"Funny." Her smile was plastic.

He helped her out of her coat. There were a few people milling around, including his sister Nemba. The in-foyer elevator opened again and Melvadore greeted his guests with the customary three kisses of Afghanis. Speaking to them in their language, Dari, he smiled at something the man said. The couple, in traditional garb, acknowledged Ashley and went on to greet the other couples talking to Nemba.

"Ashley!" Nemba greeted her, "How fantastic to see you." Kiss, kiss, kiss. Meet our dear friends Mr. and Mrs. Shapoor Zadran," Nemba said. "Ashley was in Afghanistan last year."

"How did you like our country?" a portly man, in a white and gold salwar kameez and a matching kufi asked. Probably real gold Ashley thought. His wife, smiling by his side, nodded her head.

"It was a life-changing experience."

"Yes, for most people. It's so different from the propaganda, no?"

"Very."

"I hope to go back one day. Come sit and tell me everything."

"Shapoor," Melvadore guided Ashley to the next group. "You cannot have her to yourself tonight. Well not until she's met, everyone." Melvadore took her from one group to the next, the number totaling sixteen. She had wet cheeks when it was all done. Ashley could not help wonder why he had invited her to such a dinner party.

"Dinner," Nemba announced. Ashley had expected hordes of support staff but none were in sight. They all filed into the dining room and sat wherever. No name cards…just grab a seat. Soon the conversation turned to Afghanistan.

"I was just trying to imagine what it would be like to live every day as the people in Afghanistan do," Ashley said.

"It wasn't always that way," Melvadore said. "The Afghanistan of our childhood was pure magic. "I love my country," he said, a sadness creeping into this voice.

"That was not all you loved," a man, introduced as Prince Anwar said.

"I know but I loved the palace more." Melvadore wagged a finger at him. "Remember that courtyard that stretched the length of the palace?"

"Hah, so much mischief. It had more back staircases to wander around than rooms in the palace. It made hide and seek especially fun," he winked.

"Ashley," Nemba tried to bring perspective to the conversation, "Melvadore and I were born in Kabul. Our father was forced to leave the country because of his progressive views. We were exiled to Spain."

"I sure miss those summer days," Melvadore said. "Ashley, I'm sure you can attest to summers in Kabul. Brutal but I loved it."

"You were the only one," Anwar said. "By noon, most Afghanis were behind drawn curtains hiding from that heat. It helped that we were some of the lucky ones to have air conditioning and a pool house to splash away the heat."

"Do you remember our *dini* teacher?" Melvadore started laughing. Ashley had never seen him laugh. His entire face was transformed and she could well imagine the impish child he must have been.

"*Dini*?" Ashley said knowingly, "The Muslim creed that teaches the ways of Allah?"

"Every Muslim child must do this. I guess it's like confirmation in Catholicism and Bar Mitzvah for Jews," Anwar said. "Most of the Mullahs who were hired to conduct our lessons would be so glad to get inside our house. More often than not, they'd come to sleep off the heat rather than instruct us."

"Melvadore," Anwar's wife, a woman quite a bit younger, said, "are we here for dinner or are you going to bore this lovely Ashley with yours and Anwar's memories?"

"Did Ashley tell you she saw Abdullah?"

The woman perked up. "How is my brother?"

"Apparently, as mischievous as ever," Melvadore interjected. "It was Abdullah who would inveigle us into climbing the hills behind father's compound and sneak into the forbidden cinema houses in town. Our instructors wouldn't dare tell on us because they'd be busted. It was risky but we got a thrill out of it."

A single help appeared with a seafood broth. All the conversation ceased as he ladled soup into each dish. Anwar said something in their native language and Melvadore answered. When the servant had left, Ashley encouraged Melvadore to continue his story. She had no idea why she was being given this level of access but she was truly interested in Melvadore's story.

"Okay. So, one day when it was just too hot, Abdulla and I shed our disguise in the theater. Unfortunately, one of my father's friends recognized us and escorted us home. From that summer on, we had to travel with father to faraway places as he drove the countryside to go on official business. At first, Abdullah and I hated it and I remember how petrified I was of driving along the Khyber Pass, the famed Silk Road into Peshawar."

"Oh my God," Ashley said. "I mean Allah," she smiled. "Those mountains touch the sky on one hand on and on the other, is nothing but treacherous precipices. I was so scared to look down and would cover my eyes until Hag said we were in the valley."

"It's like that in Switzerland," Nemba said. "Precipitous drops everywhere you look.

"This was worse." Ashely insisted.

"Not even close," Melvadore said. "Back then we'd stop at the colorful, chaotic bazaars and roadside restaurants for food and fresh fruits."

"I'm afraid not much of that is left now," Ashley said, shaking her head.

"What is it like?" Nemba said softly.

"Devastated."

The Afghanis exchanged sullen glances.

"That's why we must take our country back!" Al-fared said. "These Americans have destroyed Allah's land."

"How about the Russians? If Allah wanted them to have oil, he would have given them Afghanistan!" Anwar said.

"They wanted oil and all I ever wanted was to fly a kite," Nemba said.

"Foolish man, your father," Al-farad said. "He would not have been deposed but for that."

"I'm to be blamed," Nemba said.

"Nemba was the apple of my father's eyes." Melvadore had no malice in his voice. "When she came home from school, she'd sit with him for hours in dialogue about politics, something I was never interested in. Those innocent meetings were the beginning of the end of my father's rule. Because of Nemba, he wanted to modernize the society and give equal rights to women. He himself had studied at Oxford where he met my mother, a budding feminist. Education was a big part of her life and there was no way a child of hers, even in Afghanistan, would be forcibly ignorant. The Parchami officers in Kabul had other plans for the country."

"Enough!" Anwar said, "Let's forget about the past.

"But how is my brother?" the woman leaned over to Ashley and asked again.

"Proud and committed," Ashley answered.

Melvadore looked at Ashley. He had chosen right.

"Let's talk about WNCB." We have reviewed the line-up and we are very pleased."

"But you must be careful, Ms. Your job of exposing the underbelly and the corrupt will be more dangerous than the one you did in Afghanistan. American power will not cede easily. Watch your steps carefully," Prince Anwar proffered.

"I'm ready," Ashley replied, not entirely sure she meant it.

The rest of the dinner was a pleasant affair. As it turned out the group gathered were the money people behind WNCB.

CHAPTER TWENTY-FIVE
Amelie

New York, 2003

IT WAS MONTHS before her performance yet already her face was plastered on posters and advertisement throughout the city. Amelie pulled out a folder with every insert from the New York Times and any other publication that mentioned her performance. Amelie Mercer, Pianist, Enrique Gamba, Conductor, November 27^{th,} 2003 at eight p.m. Tickets $25-$88.

Today was the first rehearsal at Carnegie. Not that she hadn't been walking up and down 57th Street just to see her picture and name on the marquis, for she had. She, Amelie Mercer, would be playing at Carnegie Music Hall and people would pay up to $88 to see her perform. Unbelievable! Overcome with jitters, Amelie's stomach made a loud groan. She was famished. Across the street, her eyes caught the neon sign of the Hard Rock Café and she decided to have the biggest milkshake and the largest slice of mud pie she could find before heading to the hall. Since there would be no Thanksgiving celebration in her house this year, she could spare the calories.

"You're late," Dr. Vlachenko said. "The orchestra has warmed up three times already. "Are you ready, Diva?" He smiled.

"Yes, but I'm only a few minutes late," Amelie observed.

"Late is late. Let's get on with it then."

As much as Dr. Vlachenko commanded, Amelie could not take her seat at the piano. She paced up and down the stage. She hadn't remembered it being this massive. She cast her eyes upward at the acoustic ceilings and marveled again at how beautiful the space was. Center stage was a grand Steinway, its lid fully extended. She sat in front of the piano, jumped up, and sat again this time running her hands up and down the keys in a fast arpeggio. Her wrists hurt. Her fingers were numb. The pressure too great, but worse was that eerie déjà vu feeling. Twenty years. She hadn't been on this stage for twenty years.

"What are you waiting for?" Dr. Vlachenko said impatiently.

Amelie raised her hand dramatically. "Begin," she instructed the orchestra.

For a moment she froze. "Begin," Dr. Vlachenko voice commanded and she did.

"You call that playing? Horrible. Simply horrible. What are you doing?!"

Amelie started again. After hours and hours of practice, she was insistent that the orchestra changes the arrangements in the second movement. "I'm telling you. The second movement has problems, especially…"

"It is perfect just the way it," Dr. Vlachenko cut her off. "You are just not playing it perfectly." He groaned. "Don't tell me, Amelie, that I made another mistake."

"I think…" It was the sugar rush from that damn milkshake!

"Stop thinking!" Dr. Vlachenko said firmly. "Just play."

"It's time to get out of here. We have nine months to get this right. This is enough for today. Amelie 9:00 a.m. tomorrow. Right back here!"

Amelie was scared to death. "I can't do this."

Dr. Vlachenko took her in his arms. "You can, Amelie. You are the music. The best ever at Schumann. Be what the music wants you to be. What it demands. Stop trying to control everything. And for Christ sake remember what brought you back to it in the first place. The music will take you where you need to go. Trust it. Live it. You can do this, and you will."

"No, I can't."

• • •

Amelie was near implosion. This was becoming too real and she was a nervous wreck. She paced, sat, paced and sat some more in her home studio. She opened the lid of the Steinway and closed it again. She must have been crazy to think she could have a solo career at her age. She made tea, ate sorbet and made more tea. Her mother's voice kept ringing in her head. "Why wastes your time. What can you do with music?!" Then her Grandfather's. "Don't worry child you were born with the music in you." She was not sleeping again.

"If you don't take this, I'm going to clobber you." Robb handed his wife a sleeping pill and a glass of warm milk. If you keep pacing up and down, you'll wear a grove into the carpet! By the time you get to Carnegie, it will be shredded to pieces. "If you don't get some sleep you will be inviting disaster. Come on honey, what can you be scared of? Robb sat her behind the piano. This instrument is your friend and loves you as much as I do. You control it…Trust it and trust yourself."

"I think I'll take a bath," Amelie took the pill, put it on her tongue and gulped a mouthful of and milk. "I…" she looked at Robb never finishing the sentence.

"Amelie, have you ever asked your mother why she didn't want you to play? Is there a rational explanation?"

"I don't know."

She did not show up the next day. She had done it now…her musical career was dead.

Dr. Vlachenko had expected her to call in sick the next morning.

CHAPTER TWENTY-SIX
Randy

Lower West Side, 2003

RANDY STOOD STIFFLY, unable to find words. She wanted to appear calm and unaffected but she was nervous. Though she wished Adele hadn't come she couldn't deny her racing pulse at seeing her.

"Why are you here?" Randy had asked her into her office. The woman was without question crazy for showing up at her gallery opening and hour earlier than the gathering would arrive. It had taken almost a year to get the gallery open and she had not seen Adele since their…she couldn't even think about the unfortunate moment.

"I wanted to be here. I was hoping we wouldn't leave things the way they were," Adele said, touching Randy's arm lightly. Randy shrank from her touch. Adele dropped her hand. "It's all right if we can't be friends. I can understand what you're feeling. I'll go." Adele had turned to go.

Hating to see her leave, Randy stammered. "In time I'd like us to be friends but not until I'm stronger. Really, I do. Anything else, however, is in the past."

"But why?" Adele asked, turning back to her.

"Why? Because I'm not gay that's way. Because I can't live as you do. Because I am married. Have you ever considered that you are not gay either?"

"Is that what scares you, Randy?" Adele smiled. "I'm not gay either. I'm just in love with you."

Randy voice was now rising. "What you did was wrong and I'll never forgive you."

"Calm down, Randy," Adele begged.

"I don't want to calm down. I want you to go now. I don't want you here when the doors open."

"What do I get…"

"Are you blackmailing me?" Randy's eyes narrowed.

"Randy. Don't insult me. You're so entirely provincial."

"You are despicable." Randy put distance between them. "Forget that you know me. I don't even want to be your friend. I wish I'd never met you."

Adele's eyes narrowed. "You don't know me at all. But I respect your request and I'm happy to be your friend, whenever you are ready."

Randy shaken tried hard to get back to center before her guests started arriving. How dare she. In all her anger, she realized how much she missed their friendship. If only…she was forced to discontinue her thoughts when the first patron arrived. The gallery opening was a stunning success. She had really wished that Adel, who had encouraged her to open the gallery could have shared this moment with her but there was no way she was ready to see her. Why, why did she have to betray their friendship? Despite everything, seeing Adele had unsettled her and Randy found herself at Adele's flat. She wanted more than anything to share the success of the evening with her and maybe it was time to set the record straight and move.

• • •

Randy was leading a double life. Her life with Adele had become an obsession. It was becoming increasingly difficult to be in the same room with Lawrence and Adele, who was now her partner in the Gallery. The last straw was Adele's insistence that she made a choice between her and Lawrence and the blow up that ensued. What was she thinking? She was the one who'd restarted the affair and now she could not continue. If she had to make a choice, she would not be able to do it. She was used to keeping secrets but this secret was about to unhinge her totally. That was when depression found her. Then anger and finally hopelessness. Randy had been locked in her bedroom now for two days. No one, not even Mensa was welcomed. She had nothing left in her. Not for Uncle Joe. Not for Adele. Not for Lawrence. She padded to the bathroom, opened a new bottle of 'nerve' pills and got her stash of vodka from its hiding place and went to her study. Huh, what the hell did she have to do in a study but study the bottom of her empty glass? What use was there continuing her life? She'd made a mess of everything. For two days Mensa was turned away. On day three Mensa used her universal key to let herself into the bedroom. "Miss Randy," Mensa sat on the side of the bed. "I brought you some broth. Let me help you get it down."

"I don't want it," Randy knocked the bowl of soup off the table where Mensa had rested it, broth splashing everywhere. "Oh Mensa," Randy sobbed. I can't go on." She popped a valium and knocked it back with some vodka. With her friends, vodka and Valium, a deadly combination, life was not so painful. Randy closed her eyes and Mensa waited until she'd dozed off to trade out the Valiums for a placebo and replaced half the content of the vodka bottle with water. Randy was so high she'd never notice. After twenty-one years everyone in the Austin's household, she had Randy's blue moods down to a science but this time Mensa recognized something new. She left the room and placed a call from the kitchen.

"Mr. Lawrence, please. It's urgent." Mensa said into the phone.

• • •

Nothing was working Randy thought as she again staggered to the bathroom. Even her drugs and alcohol had failed her. This time she pulled out the eyebrow shaping razor. It was on the cold, hard tile that Mensa and Lawrence had found her covered in her own vomit, barely breathing, a pool of blood gathering at her left wrist.

"*Dihos*. What are we gonna do?" Mensa wailed.

"Call Dr. Sody now." Lawrence lifted Randy to the bed. He examined the gash on her wrist. Not life-threatening. Still, he applied a make shift-tourniquet by ripping out the sleeve of one of Randy's silk shirts. Slapping her cheeks and wiping her face with a cold cloth he spoke softly in her ear. Mesa handed him the phone.

"Martin, it's Randy," Lawrence said into the phone. "It's bad this time. Need you to come by. Need to keep this quiet." Dr. Sody, Lawrence's best friend, arrived 15 minutes later. After stabilizing Randy, he followed Lawrence into the study.

"What was going on?"

"I have no idea," Lawrence responded as he paced.

"Something out of the ordinary triggered this?" he asked.

"Nothing. Nothing I can think of."

"C'mon Lawrence. Something had to have happened. Be straight with me Larry, it's the only way I'll be able to help her."

Lawrence passed a nervous hand through his hair. "I swear I don't know."

"Okay. Let me be blunt. Are you having another affair?"

"Affair? When am I not having an affair? Be for real, Martin?"

"Just asking. Anything out of the ordinary you remember. Think."

"Oh, Lord." Lawrence's face went ashen. "This is a stretch and would really be PTSD. A year or more Randy came by the office to talk about opening her gallery. I wasn't there. For hours after that, no one knew where to find her. She'd even turned off her cell phone. I came rushing home. She had been drinking and lit into me about not being at June's birth and about seeing me with a woman that day. Gale Hawthorne. I was helping her hide her money but Randy would not believe me. That's the truth. Martin, I swear women are crazy. They make up their own reality. You know Randy has always been a little paranoid. I bet she may still think I am having an affair with Gail, but why would she have a break now?" he said, meeting Martin's eyes. "Why now?" he repeated, "almost a year ago."

"She's probably going through the change," Martin said. "She's how old? Forty-seven or so?"

"Forty-seven. Forty-eight in a few months."

"Yep. That's it. Be patient. Things will get back to normal. Now," Martin said, "I'll refer her to John for some hormone replacement."

"Will that make her better?"

"I'm sure a little, at least physically. The emotional stuff is another matter. I need to put her in the hospital for a few days because of this suicide attempt. The next time she tries to cut her wrist she might succeed. Plus, Vodka and Valium is a death wish."

Lawrence nodded his head. Randy was no stranger to instability but she'd never tried suicide before. Lawrence arranged for her to check into a private clinic for a week. They'd simply explain her absence as another of her blue moods if necessary. Since June was away and Randy was allowed to have her cell phone, no one had to know where she was.

Randy refused to leave her home. In the days that followed, though all substances were removed from her reach, her mental state got worse. That was when Mensa decided not to honor Lawrence's orders to tell no one.

• • •

Adele tried to reach Randy without success. Maybe she was pushing too hard. She'd give her some space.

CHAPTER TWENTY-SEVEN
Ashley

New York, Midtown East, 2003

ASHLEY'S STOMACH WAS in knots. She popped in an espresso pod and pressed the half cup button. On her way back to her desk she was pondering last night's get together. She couldn't shake the fact that her presence at Melvadore's dinner party involved more than met the eye. She looked at the Caller ID, it was Mensa!

"What's wrong?"

"It's Randy."

"What's wrong with her this time?" They'd actually gone an entire year without an episode.

"I think she's quite ill."

"Ill? What kind of ill?" Ashley asked. "The usual?"

"No, Miss Ashley. This is worse, I haven't seen this before."

"Why didn't anyone call?"

"Because Mr. Lawrence wanted to keep it personal. He's been trying to get her to go to a hospital but she is refusing. I shouldn't be calling but I think it's serious."

Mensa had only hung up a few minutes before Ashley dialed Amelie. "Randy's been shut up in her bedroom for a week."

"A week? I'm on my way over."

"I'll meet you there." Ashley's voice was calm.

• • •

The doorman waived the sisters in…pressing the elevator button…Amelie rang the buzzer to the house.

"Who is it?" Mensa was on the intercom.

"It's Amelie and Ashley, Mensa."

"I'm so glad you're here." Mensa yanked opened the door.

"What on earth is going on? Why is this different?"

"She tried to cut her wrist?"

"What! Why hasn't she been taken to the hospital?"

"She refuses. The doctor wants her to go to the hospital but she refuses. She's not eating and she's not letting anyone into her room, not even me."

"Do you have a key?" Amelie asked, making her way to Randy's room.

"Yes, Ma'am. I've used it to peek in on her every night, sometimes twice."

"Is she drinking?"

"I been diluting the vodka, but she'd drinking and popping pills. Dr. Sody came again yesterday. He wouldn't give her any more pills, insisting that she be admitted."

Mensa let Amelie and Ashley into the magnificent bedroom, with its attached green room and glass enclosed sitting room. All the curtains were drawn. A disheveled Randy, reeking of chemicals appeared asleep.

"This is so *déjà vu*," Ashley said. "Let's try to wake her up."

"I was thinking I'd play for her like old times. It will rouse her gently."

"Great idea."

As Amelie went to the piano in Randy's sitting room Ashley took a seat on the bed of their eldest sister. The imitable mastery of Amelie's music wafted.

"Hi, honey," Ashley whispered as Randy stirred but didn't awaken.

"Randy, its Amelie and Ashley. Will you wake up sweetie?"

A groan left Randy's lips.

"Randy," Ashley shook her by the shoulders, "its Amelie and Ashley."

This time Randy's eyes fluttered and she slowly came to awareness.

"Hey honey," Ashley said softly, "where have you been?"

Randy tried to sit up. "On Rainbows. Is Amelie playing?"

"Just for you, sweetie. How do you feel?"

"Awful. Why are you both here?"

"Mensa called. Said you've been out of it for a few days."

"And?"

"Well, you know, it was more than usual."

"Hey, Randy." Amelie heard the voices and came into the room. "How are you, honey?"

Randy pushed up to a sitting position. "Just coping with my life, I guess," she whispered.

"How about a bath?" Amelie asked…her sister reeked.

The beautiful bathroom was musty but the light flowing in still made it a spectacle. The regal, once proud orchids, however, were now at half bowed in grief. When Randy was dressed, the women decided to lunch together in her sitting room. The table was set with milkshakes, lamb burgers, gorgonzola salad and an assortment of teas and coffee. Before Randy, Mensa placed a terrine of chicken noodle soup.

"What am I going to do?" Randy whispered, tears wetting her cheek. Life had all been too much. Uncle Joe, Lawrence and now Adele were way too heavy a load for her.

• • •

Emily, Florida

The call from Mensa startled her.

"I'm breaking all the rules," Mensa said simply, "But your daughter needs closure. I think it is you that holds that key. If Miss Randy continues like this, she will leave this earth sooner rather than later."

"What has happened?" Emily slapped the table. Damn, she was such a coward. It was her secrets and her pain that had cast shadows over her children's happiness. God knows her life has been a true Shakespearian tragedy but hiding from oneself never works. Things have a way of growing when buried, either inside as cancer or outside as unbearable scandal, and worse, personal destruction. She'd spent a lifetime dancing with personal destruction, in the process, damaging her relationship with her children, maybe now truly destroying her daughter Randy. It was because of her sad life that she'd robbed her children of their confidence and their feelings of belonging; things only a parent can give.

"What do you think I should do, Mensa?" Emily pulled out her desk drawer and fingered the pink envelopes she'd tucked away almost two years ago now. She'd never found the courage to send them. Once she knew her girls were fine, she'd decided to handle one trauma at a time. Michael's cancer it turned out was unusually aggressive for prostate cancer and had rapidly spread to all his vital organs. Within months, he'd been gone. Emily had sent word to her children and admittedly had been hurt when none showed up for their step-father's funeral. They had their own lives to attend to. Amelie son's wife had given birth. Ashley had been in Afghanistan and Randy, had been planning for her daughter's graduation. None of her friends in Florida even knew she had children! She couldn't imagine having to explain their absence. They, fortunately, had been very supportive. The Dis-Contents were her only source of joy.

"I don't rightly know, but you have to do something," Mensa said. "I have to hang up now but I beg you to do something to ease Ms. Randy's pain."

Emily picked up the letters. She went to her library and placed a call to her travel agent. By day's end, four airline tickets had been delivered. Slipping a letter inside each of the FedEx envelopes along with the airline ticket, Emily sealed the envelopes, got in her car and took them to the nearest FedEx station.

• • •

New York

The mailed smelled flowery. The scented stationary announced itself before Ashley actually she saw it. Sniffing each piece of mail, she pulled from the stack a FedEx envelope. Recognizing her mother's handwriting she ripped it open and pulled out two envelopes. One rose-colored scented addressed to her. The other was an airline ticket. Ashley tore open the rose-colored envelope. The soft linen paper inscribed with a fountain pen. The few lines in the middle of the paper read; 'I need to tell you all the truth but

I must do it on my territory.' It was dated 9/11, 2001. This is why their mother had wanted to meet them.

Inside the FedEx envelope was another note: 'Please join me in Jamaica. I have enclosed a ticket and will provide accommodations.' Ashley rested the letter on the coffee table, picked up the phone and dialed her sister. "Amelie, its Ash. Did you get a letter from Mummy?"

"I did. It was dated 9/11, 2001. She's been trying to reach out to us for two years."

"I'm going to conference Randy…hold on the line."

"Hey Sweetie, how are you feeling this morning?"

"Are you calling about the letter from mummy? "If you want me to go, I'll go," Randy tone was resigned. "Classy woman, huh. Ticket and all."

"Can you be okay with this, Randy? We'll be together as always," Ashley said.

"Honestly, I don't know," Randy answered. "Part of me wants to put the past to rest but part of me wouldn't be alive without holding onto the anger and someone to blame. I really don't know if I can."

"I think we all need to do this…none of us are living our bliss," Amelie chimed in. "I'm scared of my own damn shadow. And I hear voices to boot. I'm going back to the stage in a few months and I need to understand my fears."

"She's been trying to reach out for two years. Before Michael died. I feel so badly for her," Ashley said.

"I'd like to say the same," Randy said, "but I can't fake what I don't feel. But, isn't it just like Mummy to always be in control of everything!"

"Randy what if we could see father again," Ashley said. "Isn't that's reason enough to go."

Randy couldn't deny the warmth in her heart at the thought of her father.

CHAPTER TWENTY-EIGHT
Family

Jamaica, 2003

THE GIRLS HAD NEVER quite felt heat like this and for sure they didn't remember it. Randy, hiding behind Jackie O shades spun her hair into a French roll and tucked it under a cap. As appropriately as they had dressed, in shorts and pastel summer shifts, each was hastily backing off articles of clothing and donning caps and hats as they stepped onto the asphalt tarmac from which vapors of heat rose to greet them.

The customs hall, to her relief, was air-conditioned. Randy accepted the plastic cup that the swaying women offered. They were dressed in head wraps, colorful plaid skirts, and blouses, their bodies swaying as they sang a Jamaican ditty she recognized, "Carry Mi Ackee…"

Randy that's your song," Amelie beamed. "It really is a song."

"Cultural identity in action." Ashley reminded her sister of the schooling they got back in England…this and other Jamaican ditties being the basis of their cultural schooling.

"Then I was right, huh. If I hadn't sung you those songs you wouldn't recognize them now, would you?"

Emily saw her daughters and nudged Joy. She was overjoyed. Nattily dressed in a marigold sun dress, having arrived an hour earlier, Emily was waiting with baited breath for the arrival of her girls. She wasn't sure they'd show up but there they were.

"They're here," Emily said to her childhood friend beside her.

"I see Mother," Ashley said.

A distinguished looking woman was approaching them. The woman was about the same age as their mother, though she seemed fit and alive. She was holding Emily's hand pulling her forward. Emily felt proud of her daughters…they all looked marvelous. In the sophistication department at least, she'd done well.

The woman, in a white linen suit and wide-brimmed straw hat, was smiling broadly as she approached. "Hello," her voice was sunny and sweet to the ears.

"Hello," Amelie was the first to respond, and then Ashley and Randy in unison.

"I'm Joy, your mother's best and oldest friend."

"Hi," Emily, said, reaching out to each of her daughters. Amelie and Ashley allowed themselves to be kissed but Randy extended her hand. Randy had not seen her mother in years, not since their last blow up some years before, the details of which she could no longer remember. What struck her most was how very much they looked alike. Drunks, Randy thought, have a certain look. Randy sipped the rum punch the women had given her. She needed it.

"You all look so fine and dandy. What a way it feels good to see you all back home. Never thought I'd set eyes on you girls again," the woman in white said.

"Really," Ashley said, "I don't quite remember being here."

"But here you were my dear, with ponytails and plaid ribbons. I have pictures. Now you are such sophisticated looking ladies. And you Randy are what we call 'put together' here in Jamaica."

Well, Amelie thought…roots…somewhere here she had roots. The woman turned to Amelie and smiled again. Sadness crept into her eyes. "I have wanted to meet you in person all these years. This may be your first visit to Jamaica but this is your home."

Amelie was puzzled.

"Okay Joy," Emily said, "enough gushing. We have a lot to thank Aunt Joy for, Emily said in explanation. She saved our lives. Where's the luggage?"

Joy beckoned a skycap. A porter, in a khaki suit and red cap, came rushing.

"Take the bags to the van you loaded up before."

"Yes, Ma'am."

The girls decided to go to the Cambio while Emily and Joy climbed into a minivan.

"Those are some beautiful children," Joy said, regret edging her voice.

"Yes. On the outside." Emily answered.

• • •

"Where we going, Miss Joy?" the driver unintentionally interrupted and Emily was glad. She wasn't ready to tell Joy the entire story of why her children, especially Randy were cool toward her.

"To the country house as soon as the girls get here. Maybe we should stop for lunch before heading out," Joy said.

"No Ma'am. Mable's planning a big lunch, she'd be upset."

"Ah yes. And who in their right mind would want to upset Mable? She's a tyrant," Joy said to Emily.

The skycap arrived with the luggage. Amelie and Ashley climbed into the second row of the van and Randy the third. Aunt Joy handed the porter a wad.

"Ladies, off we go. Carlton will stop and get us refreshments but Mabel will be livid if we stop for lunch. It's about a two-hour drive. Everybody okay with that?"

"As long as we can get some bottled water, I'm fine," Randy responded.

Amid farm animals and around winding roads with harrowing drivers, the minivan made its way to "country".

"I don't believe these drivers!" Randy was white knuckled as she slid from one side of the van to the next. Out the window, the scenery was out of a magazine…lush vegetation, blue, blue sea, and cerulean sky. The musical rhythm of the language as her mother and Aunt Joy talked was soothing, though she could barely understand a word. The low bass and drum line of the song that kept repeating 96 degrees in the shade -no joke- on the radio was hypnotic. She was nodding off when Carlton pulled up to a shack by the side of the road.

"Anybody for patties to tie you over?"

"No man, we don't want to spoil we appetite. Just bring us something to drink," Joy said.

Carlton returned with bottles of spring water and a few bottles of what he called aerated water. With each requested he twisted the bottle cap and handed the drink of choice to his passengers. Carlton was quite the host. Everyone opted for water except for their mother and Aunt Joy who opted for something called cola champagne.

An hour later the van began a steep climb up a winding road where the embankment was a steep drop into never land. The engine sounded like it would conk out at any moment. Randy was petrified that the entire van would slip back down the hill and over the precipice but it spluttered along under the expert navigation of Carlton.

"Wow, look at that? How amazing. It's like driving along the Silk Road from Kabul to Pakistan," Ashley said craning her neck out the window.

"Oh, Oh!" Amelie covered her eyes. She was deathly afraid of heights. "Stop leaning out that window, Ashley. You could tip the balance of the van. Tell me when we've passed this place." She buried her head in Ashley's lap.

"When did you become a physics major?" Ashley bopped her cowering sister.

"Look down there Emily. This is the exact place where Bunny's car went off the hill," Joy whispered pointing to an 'ess' curve along the steep precipice.

Emily looked away. "No. I don't want to see," Emily replied. She didn't want to see the spot that claimed the life of the only man she'd ever loved. She didn't want to make real a memory that she'd kept at bay in her make-believe world all these years. What if she looked? Could she feel Bunny's spirit? As the van chugged along Emily stifled tears. Joy was sorry to have brought it up.

"Where in hell are we going anyway?" Ashley said looking out the window as lush vegetation swept by.

"To Jamaica's most beautiful parish. Portland. I thought it would be nice if we went out to the sea and grotto. Kingston is too hard and ragged for your first visit home after all these years," Joy said.

"It was the sea that took us away from home. I'm sure it has memories of so many lives. Why not bring us back some old news," Randy said, adjusting her hat to the glare of the sun.

"A didn't think of that. But I suppose *yu* right," Joy responded nodding.

"Get up off me now," demanded Ashley pushing Amelie's head from her lap. "We're back on level ground."

Amelie peeked from behind her hand. The death drop had turned into the most beautiful scenery. Amelie took in the sights and sound of the island and her heart, if not her eyes, definitely knew this place. Finally, after what Randy called eternity, the van pulled onto a winding road that ascended steeply into the sky. Carlton, the driver pulled up to a rambling old house. The acres of land were littered with fruit trees and a yellow ropy vine covered the hedges. Carlton brought a stool to the sliding door to assist his passengers.

"I've never seen a vine like this," Amelie a pretty facile horticulturist said.

"It's called a love bush. A parasite really, much like love, *nuh,*" Joy laughed. "It grows anywhere and only takes a little attachment to start strangling its host."

"This place is spectacular." Ashley alit the van and spun in all directions.

Randy refused to be helped as she climbed onto the stool. All she wanted to do was to get inside from the confounded heat and get herself a real drink. The property was magnificent and the house was indeed beautiful and airy. Striking hand-woven rugs atop imported marble floors gave the place a palatial feel as they stepped into the open foyer. Newly renovated with every modern convenience, Emily wondered how Joy had been able to afford this by herself since she'd never married. Granted her parents were very well to do but she'd never imagined the woman would become a "Czar" in her own rights. Emily remembered the house as being beautiful but it had been so spruced up, she hardly recognized it. Emily walked down the driveway and cut across the lawn to the little pool cottage. Even the old cottage, where her life had begun its end looked sparkling and new.

"You've done marvels with this place," Emily said walking back toward the group.

"Yes. A real proud of it, man. Did the redesigns myself. A went to design school and all in New York but that place so damn cold I run back home as soon as I was done. Imagined we were in the same country and didn't know. Anyway, let us get out of this heat, *nuh*." She ushered her guests into a large room where the air condition was blowing at full speed. Joy's artifacts, collected from years of travel, were proudly displayed around the room. She'd been to six of the seven continents of the world.

"You'll all hungry. We can lunch now *yu nuh*," Joy said, "I bet Mabel has made a fine welcome lunch for *unuh*. George," she waved over the yardman, "tell Mabel to get the ladies some drinks and take this luggage upstairs for *mi nuh*? Bamsy knows where everything should go." She then turned proudly and said to her guests in the Queen's English, "So welcome to Port Antonio and to Whispering Corner. They call it that because at night you can hear the sea whispering. Obediah, Emily you remember him, says it's the souls talking among themselves when they take a swim at nights."

"That man *caan* still be alive?" Emily said.

"No. He left us a few years ago. But I bet him out by the sea chatting up a storm. If I know that man, he must hang out at Loud Mouth Corner, the only noisy place in the parish. For most of the time, it's quiet around here, except when Obediah preaching," Joy laughed.

The girls were silent. They had never seen their mother with a friend and certainly, they had never seen the peace in her that they saw today or heard her new language, patois, which was quite a surprise to them.

Randy, despite herself, warmed to Joy.

"After lunch, I'll take you into town," Joy offered.

"Joy, Aunt Joy," Randy corrected herself. (She didn't remember the woman at all but she remembered that one must address their elders with a title) "I don't mean to be brash, but we're not here on vacation or to sightsee. I have to be back in New York, Amelie has a concert soon and Ashley has a weekly show to do. I'd like it if Mummy could just get to the point of why we are here."

"And what is waiting for you in New York?" Ashley said.

"That's none of your business," Randy snapped.

"Now, now," Aunt Joy butted in, "let's not get ahead of ourselves. Let's have ourselves a nice rum punch and enjoy lunch first."

Amelie cleared her throat. "Water is fine for me," she said, "but rum punch is better if you have it."

"Better? My rum punch is boss and legendary on this island. It's all about the fruits."

"You have to try Aunt Joy's fruit punch. You've never had fruit punch until you have Joy's, fresh from all the trees on this land," Emily said walking over to the window. For a moment she stood looking out at sea.

Ashley thought of Mel and his office orchard. A smile lingered on her lips.

"Thank you," Emily said taking the glass Ashley handed her. "This is the place where it all started." Emily looked old for the first time in her life. Her shoulders slumped and she walked slowly back to the chair she'd vacated a few minutes before. Folding her hands in her lap she looked at each of her children.

"*Mek* all that wait 'till tomorrow," Joy insisted. "Today we catch up on each other lives.

The past ain't going nowhere. Welcome home." She lifted her glass. "For real."

• • •

Randy asked to be taken to her room, instructing George to bring her a glass of ice.

By dinner time, rested and filled with her elixir, Randy was able to fit in with the moment. They passed the evening listening to Aunt Joy gush over the island she loved dearly.

CHAPTER TWENTY-NINE
The Truth Reveled

THE NEXT MORNING, Ashley was up at the crack of dawn, awakened by the rooster's crow and the birds' tweets. She felt tears prickle her eyes. This was where her life had begun but she knew nothing of it. Who was she really? This morning she'd go down to the beach and try to remember this beautiful island from which she came.

• • •

Braaah, raaah, the tinny sound of the bell from the early morning milk delivery man sounded. Randy bolted upright, a smile dimpling her face. She was shocked that she was actually smiling as she listened to the lilting voice of the head cook negotiating with the milkman outside of her window. The patois soothed a long-forgotten memory and she found herself trying to mimic its cadence. "Man, don't bother *mi* nerve *dis* here morning'. *Mi* already told *yu* we 'ave plenty visitors today so a need five more pints than usual. How about *yu* only charge me *fi* four since you overcharge *mi* last week for the bad tasting yam *yu* sell me?"

"Miss Ruby *yu* forever trying to rob a man. Pay *mi fi de* five *bokkle* a milk and mi bring *yu* a nice breadfruit to roast later on and a whole heap of Bombay mangoes *tu*. I know how *yu* love *yu* Bombay mango."

"Last time *yu* promise me Bombay mango *yu* bring me some stringy with a whole heap a worms."

Randy couldn't help but laugh out loud at the banter. It could be weeks before she actually saw one of her neighbors in New York. She wondered too if she would have been as isolated and alone in Jamaica as she had been in England and the United States or would the easy, unpretentious rhythm of life in Jamaica have healed her wounds more quickly. She sat back down on the bed and wondered why from this wonderful beginning had her life had gone so wrong.

• • •

Amelie's eyes flew open and her ears immediately tuned into the musical rhythm of life in Jamaica. The clanging of pots, the birds, the bells, the chatter and humming of the water, the entire place seemed filled with the sounds of music. She rose, drew the curtains, opened the window and inhaled deeply. The sun had not yet commanded the island's day and a wonderful morning breeze slipped in. Under her window, a stalwart woman, her rotund girth pushing hard against the apron around her waist, was scolding a man on a bicycle.

"Don't you come here tomorrow without *mi* five *bokkle* ah milk."

"Would I do that to my *bunununus*?" The man grinned, his gold tooth catching the morning sun.

The woman sucked her teeth and waddled into what must have been the kitchen.

She could live here she thought. She loved the cadence and the rhythm.

• • •

Emily was up before everyone. She too was listening to the island of her birth wondering how her life took the turn it had. For love, she had given up all this, yet love was not what she got back from the children to whom she was practically estranged. At seven a.m. she ambled to the kitchen. Joy was already bustling about, Miss Ruby none too pleased.

"Here you go," Ruby said as she handed the women two cups, "go take in some fresh air until de breakfast ready."

Joy and Emily made their way to the verandah with their morning cocoa.

"Just like I remember it." Emily sipped the creamy cocoa, "Oily and gritty but oh so good."

"Let's take the children down to the grotto…*mek* the wind and water carry the *story yu gwain* tell them, children, today," Joy said to Emily.

"Joy," Emily teared up, "I never thought I'd see you in this life again."

"See. One can never predict life. No bother worry about how the children will react, just tell *yu* story…bam! Me wish me had children to tell any story to."

"Why *yu* never marry?" Emily asked Joy.

Joy sucked her teeth. "*Chu*, me wasn't born fi no man *mek* me mad. An if me di marry how you would find me? Me would have someone else's last name."

Emily laughed. "All I can do is to tell them the truth. It's up to them after that but they deserve the truth."

• • •

One by one the girls (women) came into breakfast. Joy knew it had been a good idea to postpone the storytelling until a little bit of Jamaica had seeped into them.

"Good morning," Joy smiled. "I hope you slept well. We've got plenty food this morning. Miss Ruby went to town with this breakfast. Help yourself to anything your hearts fancy."

"Where is Miss Mabel?" Randy asked.

"Her day off today. She only came in early to sort out the delivery."

Randy and Ashley went for the island foods and Amelie filled her plate with eggs, bacon, and fruits. Emily and Aunt Joy chose breakfasts of roasted breadfruit and mackerel.

"Mumm," Amelie said. "These eggs are really tasty. What's in them?"

"Island magic. Nothing. No hormones. No antibiotics, just good old free-range eggs," Aunt Joy said.

"Aunt Joy, what does the word *bun…bonnynaias*…I can't exactly remember…maybe *bunnunnois* mean?" Randy asked.

"It means sweetheart. Was that man bothering Ms. Ruby again? She likes him right back."

Emily looked at her daughters as though seeing them for the first time. Amelie was curious, Ashley was going with the flow and Randy as usual, distant. Except for the "very few occasions," she'd not spent much time with her girls in years. Did she even know them now? Unable to wait for the ocean and wind to carry her story, Emily began talking when everyone was seated.

"I didn't know what else to do," she began. "I was always a hardheaded child. Hard-headiness and privilege don't mix well because it makes you bolder than life will allow. Bunny was everything I wanted to be. Free, adventurous and bold. With Bunny, I had stars in my eyes and love for the whole world. I met him the night of my debutante ball. He was a musician in the band. He would never have been accepted by my mother. Being a musician was no career for well-heeled children, only something one did for sport. My mother had already fought that battle with my daddy who, though music was his first love, became a doctor. But Bunny was not even middle class so he was free to do with his life as he pleased. Being a lawyer or doctor was not a choice.

"Bunny and I became inseparable after that night. We'd meet every day under an almond tree and he'd always have a fistful of almonds for me. "One day he had no almonds. 'Buttercup,' that's what he called me… I have to go away. The band just booked a six-month gig around the Caribbean." When Bunny spoke the Queen's English something was serious. He always spoke in patois, something I was never allowed to do. He was the most authentic man I had ever met.

"I'm coming with you," I'd blurted out. The world beyond Kingston, Jamaica was calling loudly.

"Not if you want to come back to this island," Bunny shook his head. "Your *Mada* will kill us both."

"Not if I'm your wife." So, we eloped. "I never thought life could be more exciting. Cuba was the place to be in those days. The mix of world cultures was staggering and I immediately knew that I'd found the authentic world that complimented my spirit. Night after night, I would sit in the lively lounges and listen as Bunny's music filled the air. As the Jamaican, Son Latin and African Bueno Vista rhythm mixed, not a body was still even as they spilled out into the street. And later in the pitch-black of the night in our little cottage Bunny and I would sit under the stars and he'd play only for me. Those were magical nights. After six months, not even the Caribbean twilight and bacchanal nights could dampen the reality of being a musician's wife. I wanted to come home but the tour had been extended. I wasn't cut out for life as the wife of a musician on tour. Worse, the constitution for poverty was not in my blood. Wanderlust wore off fast. I left Bunny on tour and came home.

Back then I thought eloping was the only solution we had and I never wrote to my mother to even explain. I'll never forget the morning I got back home."

"Boy that Madda of yours was one hard woman." Joy shook her head. "You'd think no matter what, she'd be glad to see her only daughter."

"She wasn't happy to see me. Daddy told me the night I came rapping on the door to wait 'till morning to tell Mummy I was home. He'd obviously told her before I did. The next morning, I was going to the take a shower when Mummy came down the hall.

'Mornin' Mummy.'

Mummy barely looked up, passing me, her own daughter, in the hallway without a single word. Like I was a ghost…long dead. You'd have believed she didn't even know me. Not even an ounce of shock much less joy, that I'd come home. But my brother Joseph, poor little thing, he was born funny, was so happy."

Randy looked up from her plate. She never ever thought of her mother as a woman, much less a woman in love? It had never crossed her mind, either that her mother and the poor bastard Uncle Joe also needed their own mother's love and care.

"So, what happened? Start from the beginning Mummy," Ashley said.

"Back then things were different. It was the Jamaica of 1952. I said mornin' Mummy again and she just kept walking."

"Norma. You don't hear your child speaking to you?" Daddy who was behind her said. She ignored him too."

"Mornin' Daddy," I said, tears spilling down my cheek.

"Mornin' darlin'." Daddy pulled a kerchief from his pocket and wiped my face. He was more than glad to see me and gave me a big hug right in front of Mummy as she passed us in the hall, still without a word. Daddy, you see, understood wanderlust."

"Don't mind your mother, she'll soon come around," he'd said.

"How you put up with that woman so long?" I asked him.

"Because *mi* love her bad, bad."

"Enough to give up everything you ever wanted?"

"But look what a got instead. You and Joe-Joe." He pinched my nose and shoed me along. Daddy wanted to be a musician but his family and Mummy put a stop to that quick, quick, so my running off with a musician was unforgivable. It was a rough time for me as a young girl because neither Kingston nor Mummy welcomed me back, not even with arms shut. With grit, I suffered the harsh whispers levied on a woman fallen from grace. Mummy was completely devastated by the gossiping of her backbiting friends and was forever picking a quarrel with me. Six months after I got home, she asked me to move out. "Two big women don't belong under one roof," she'd said when I wouldn't hide under a rock or back down from her spiteful arguments. I was just past my eighteenth birthday…we graduate high school at sixteen back then and I'd never worked a day in my life. I decided to get a job and that's how I met Joy. I went to work for Joy's parents. They owned a flat and I was able to stay there.

"I was so glad my mother let us move in together. Oh, boy, did we have some fun." Joy continued the story. "On Saturday nights, your mother and I would make our way from one party to the next. She could dance like a fairy. Light on her feet and very sexy. Remember how taken Gregory was when he saw you dancing?" Joy smiled at her friend.

"Gregory," Emily said, a far-off voice sounding in her ears. "That was where I met Gregory, your father, a Brit of Jamaican heritage. He was a dashing man with impeccable social grace and family wealth. A newly minted barrister and Oxford scholar, he was assured a life of success and comfort in Jamaica. He'd come to oversee the legal affairs of a sugar factory, a British firm back then. Maybe because he was new to the Island or because he was a world-traveled man, a little girl's wanderlust didn't seem outrageous to him. I was encouraged by his understanding and began thinking of him as my savior. I imagined that marriage to the most erudite bachelor on the island, one who studied in England at that and not at a second-rate American Institution, which according to Jamaicans was not up to par, would force my mother's forgiveness as my mother would never disassociate with the wealth and class that Gregory represented. One night he offered to fetch me a drink. The drink made me bold. "I hope you're glad to come home," I said when he asked me to dance.

"Home. Yes, I suppose it is home, isn't it? The way my mother and father talk lovingly of Jamaica I've always felt it was home. I had to come and see for myself what all the fuss was about."

"And?"

'I like what I see, so far,' his eyes flattered me and I blushed."

"Blushed," Joy again interrupted, "girl, your face was red as a ripe tomato."

Emily smiled at the memory. "What you need is a good dose of Jamaican hospitality," I said to Gregory. My boldness rolled off the tip of my tongue like butter. Joy and I had found out the next day that a welcome party was already in the works for him. The extravaganza had been arranged for the upcoming Saturday so we quickly volunteered to serve on the gala's food committee. We didn't know how to cook one thing but Obediah, the local mystic in charge of the kitchen was there to make things right. In addition to his sweet cooking, he instructed us in what he called the "power of intention."

"Lawd, that man was a right stitch. I can still hear him now, 'If a husband you want then give 'im good food and a good dose of island love. After that sprinkle a *likkle* cinnamon behind 'im bed or 'im chair when 'im a eat cook food. *Ahoa.* For sure then, the entire matter wi done.'" Joy ended her Obediah impression.

Amelie was giggling. She loved this. She loved hearing about her Grandpa and now understood why he wanted her to play music.

"Wow, you sound just like him. Joy and I began to follow Obediah instructions to the tee."

'You really think you want to go through with this thing?' Joy had asked, adding more nutmeg to the bread pudding batter.

Emily laughed again at another memory.

Joy was laughing too. "She nearly killed me that day for almost ruining her chances."

"Joy," I had shouted said Emily, again picking up the story. "The man said cinnamon. If you spoil my chances with that nutmeg, I'm going to give you a good *thump*."

"Eh-eh. Then *weh* the cinnamon? Pass it to me, *nuh*."

'See it here.' Emily had spluttered in laughter as she handed me the cinnamon.

"And don't add too much either and reverse we spell," I warned. "I have to do something quick, quick to get mother off *mi* case. She's still whining about how I made her a social outcast with my trolloping behavior. This man will make everything okay and he's not bad looking, right? What you think? Him not bad, right?"

"Bad?" I didn't believe her. That man was fine like a good piece of potato pudding. Like curry goat and gunga peas…Good thing she saw him first," Joy said.

The girls looked at each other. Their mother had turned into someone else!

"Don't worry, you'll taste all them things before you go back home."

"In the sizzle of our sauces and the sweetness of our plantains," Emily picked up the story, "I had every intention of planting the seeds of love. If the legend is true that 'the way to any man's heart was through his stomach', I was definitely in the winning seat with all that food they cooked for that man. Our spices worked wonders."

Joy cast her eyes at the distant memory. "Remember how that man followed you around after that?"

Amelie was looking from one woman to the next. Who was this mother of hers? She had loved? And plotted and tried to please her own mother? "I can't imagine any of this," Amelie said, "it sounds like a fairytale."

"It's no fairytale mi love. Is true, true story," Joy assured.

"What happened next?" Ashley interjected impatiently. The journalist in her loved stories and made her a good listener.

"Gregory was besotted all right and though he did everything right, I found it hard to work up an ounce of passion for him. Still, I owed it to my mother to right my wrong and restore her place in society. When Gregory asked me to marry him, I stalled only long enough to finalize my divorce from Bunny. The day my divorce became final I cried for days knowing that, not only were my carefree and adventurous days over but that like my father, passion would no longer be a part of my life."

"That's why you married me off to Lawrence," Randy interrupted the story. "Because you think I could live your life. And that's why you married all those husbands?"

"Randy, let mother go on," Amelie, was wide-eyed.

"Our wedding day was grand. Seven years and two children later I had re-cemented mine and my mother's place in society and she was on the coveted social registry. Not a day would go by, however, that I hadn't yearned for the passion I had shared with Bunny and so foolishly gave up. With Bunny, no two days were ever the same but with Gregory life was predictable down to our once a week, on Fridays, "get together." I used to pray that Gregory was never triumphant at work otherwise our "celebration" on Sunday mornings was more than I could bear. I prayed long and hard for God to forgive me because from the good and stable I had thoughts of running away again."

"Ah feel so guilty about all this. It's my fault why you children had to leave home." Joy tone was somber now.

"No, it was not," Emily continued. "No matter how things turned out you saved my life that day when you forced me to accept that tea party invitation to this house insisting that the sea air would do me a world of good. Unlike my stuffy, unbearable social circles you see, Joy's parents were rich liberals from Lebanon who thought dividing people up by class was entirely unnecessary in a country whose people were descended from slaves.

"Before I got married, I used to be a fearless driver. I was the kind of person who would eke out every joy in life. You should have seen how bold and confident I was driving the curvy, treacherous roads from Kingston to the country. The very roads we took to get here. I would drive up that Spur Tree like no body's business. Behind the wheel, navigating the ess-curves that climbed into those mountains and then down again in steep decline, I was fearless. That day

I was surprised to once again unearth the spirited child that was buried under layers of properness. Without you all and Gregory, I felt light as a feather."

"See," Randy again blurted out, "she's never really wanted us."

"That is not true." Emily got up and paced. "I was…"

"Go on Mummy." Ashley was on the edge of her seat. To say that there were jaws hanging open would have been an understatement.

"Continue Mummy." Amelie pleaded.

Emily hesitated. She looked at Amelie and drew strength from her. Her voice trembled as she began again. The voice that had told them of her bold driving became less animated. It was Aunt Joy who continued the story.

"Emily," I had sprinted toward the car before she could throw the gear into park. "I have a surprise for you. It's important that no one sees us. I took her by the hand and surreptitiously led her through the garden and down to the beach cottage by the grotto. Go in there, I'd ordered."

"What's in there?" Emily had asked.

"You'll see, I said more than willing to be a conspirator to my dear friend who was no longer even living. I was worried about your mother's deepening depression and wanted to see the light once more in her eyes."

As only two great friends could, her mother picked up the story as though it had happened only yesterday.

"I pushed open the cottage door as cautiously as Joy had spirited me off and poked my head inside. I didn't see any surprise. Then I thought. Why a surprise anyway? It wasn't my birthday and it wasn't hers. Joy was a real prankster and just as I was about to go find her a give her a good t(h)ump, I heard the voice that would lead me down the path of destruction."

"Well, well, well if it isn't my runaway bride."

My heart spluttered and I fell to my knees. I turned to find Bunny lounging in the doorway, a lopsided grin on his face. "Thanks for the Dear John letter," he goaded. "Did you suppose I should have understood?"

"Bunny," I'd stuttered so bad I bit my tongue. "What…what are you doing here? When did…oh Bunny, I'm so sorry." I stared stone-faced at the wall in front of him unable to make eye contact. I felt real bad. "I'm so sorry about the whole mess," my voice had dropped to a whisper but my heart was galloping down Spur Tree Hill."

"Sorry? Sorry don't buy back heartache," Bunny had said. "I will never forget the look on his face. It was one of hate, love, desire, unbridled passion and fear.

"I'm so sorry. What else can I say but forgive me? I was too young. Way too young," I pleaded.

"What's to forgive? Kismet is kismet. It felt right. We acted on it. When it was gone, we let go. Or rather, you let go so I had to."

"I hope it was easy to let me go after such a betrayal."

"No. Not one bit," he said, and I swear he was about to cry.

"Thank you. You really look great Bunny and still as handsome as ever. I'm so…"

Before I could utter another word, Bunny had covered the distance between us and reminded me what passion was. I didn't know what to do. All I know was that my heart didn't want him to stop."

A sob escaped. All eyes looked over at Randy who was, without shame tearing up?

"What's wrong?" Amelie asked her sister softly.

"I might never have known such a love," she allowed the tears to fall. "Imagine, I might never have known such a love." Randy's tears fell even faster as she thought of how she felt the same forbidden love for Adele. And she cried that she had forbidden any love for Lawrence because of her fear of men. She and her mother were the same. "Excuse me," she rose from her chair and went to the bathroom.

"Maybe this wasn't such a good idea," Emily said wiping her own tears on a hankie she pulled from her sleeve.

"I didn't mean to hurt any of you it's just that life can be so unfair."

"Life is life," Joy handed Emily a box of Kleenex. That hankie up the sleeve business drove her bonkers.

Randy had composed herself and was back at the table.

"Maybe we should stop for now," Joy said.

"No. I want to hear the whole story," Randy insisted.

Amelie rose from the table and began clearing dishes.

"Dear don't do that," Aunt Joy said, "Ruby will be livid."

"Where was I?" Emily asked.

"He had just come over to you," Amelie offered.

"Ah yes. 'You are so beautiful', Bunny said as he pushed me away, his gaze fixed on my face".

Starved for affection, I was holding on to him as though I'd never again let him go. I begged and pleaded and shamelessly blurted out. "How could I have left you?" I went on and on about how young and foolish I was all the time holding on to him for dear life. Then I started with alliteration. "I was so stupid. So self-centered, so selfish, so…" That man was as attractive to me then as the first time I had met him at my debutante ball. The same dark smoldering eyes that had winked at me from the stage as Stoddard, my date, dragged me around the room, pierced my very soul that night. Bunny, you see was the base musician in the band."

Amelie gasped and an erratic movement invaded her body knocking the pitcher of orange juice to the floor. "Sorry," she said her body forming sweats beads all over.

Aunt Joy beckoned for someone to clean up. "Let's walk down to the grotto," Joy said but Emily was on a roll. Joy suspected that if she stopped, she'd never start again.

"Bunny was a funny man too. Like me, he loved to laugh and cut up. "Hey…hey hold up a minute." he'd covered my mouth with his hand. "Leave me some adjectives *nuh* man. How about spoilt, sassy, and sugarlicious."

"I'm one big alliteration of S for stupid," I'd cried burying my face in his broad chest.

"Ya man. *Yu* all them things but I still love you."

"And still love being impossible too I see."

"Ya, Man. Once impossible, always impossible, just like you, *nuh*?" Bunny had unleashed his accent which was music to my now British weary ear. I swear that was the moment that I knew my life was over but Bunny got serious all of a sudden."

"How *yu* doing Emily?"

"Okay. I'm married now with two beautiful children. Girls."

"That's nice man but I mean how are you, really Emily?"

"Miserable, frankly," the words blurted out. They were honest words that I should never have spoken but talking to Bunny, my soul mate, it was the only thing that I could do. "I've got the life I never wanted," I said. I became more composed now and pulled back a distance.

"So, Buttercup, you didn't find happiness in the creature comforts you were searching for, huh?" Bunny asked.

"It was fun for all of a minute. But as you know the dream is usually better than the reality," I'd answered.

"It wasn't for me." Bunny lasered me with an unwavering gaze that burned through my heart but sent chills down my spine. My whole body caught fever after that and I was afraid. I was surprised that Bunny, now a Doctor of Philosophy in music had returned to the island, after studying at The Royal College of Music, wasn't all over the papers, but as he often said about that. "What kind of news is a country boy coming home going to make?"

Emily, embarrassed looked at her toes. "I loved Bunny and I wanted a little bit of our dream to come through. I wish I could take it all back now, but back then, all I could think of was maybe we can go forward and have our dream and our lives at the same time. When I asked him if there was any chance he'd want to tell his story on a stroll through the garden he'd said, "Sorry Buttercup, I'm married now too. Our stories have gone in different directions but I had to hold you one more time. I really hope we can be friends," he'd touched my face tenderly. "Come on, Buttercup, let's go join the party. I'll introduce you to my wife." I felt a knife in my heart.

CHAPTER THIRTY
Old News, New Freedom

"SO, YOU DO KNOW how we feel?" Randy snapped. "Lost, lonely, afraid."

"Now, now Randy," Ashley warned.

"Now, now nothing," Randy snapped pushing Ashley away. "Isn't it about time we are all honest. It's all well and good that she lost her love but it's because of her why all our lives are fucked up. It's because of her why you can't commit to a man, why Amelie ran off the stage at Carnegie Hall twenty years ago and why I'm a drunk. It's okay for all the chips to fall on this table. If we are being honest, shouldn't we go all the way."

Amelie was catatonic. None of her sisters had yet grasped what she had heard. Amelie who had made herself small in corner asked the obvious that had seemed to escape her sisters. "So, Bunny was my father." Her voice was so small that only the wind had carried it. The silence in the room was deafening.

"Yes," Emily said staring at her folded hands.

"He played music," Amelie said. "He was the musician."

The rest of the conversation became a blur to Amelie who was lost in the obvious. She was a half-sister. She looked at her sisters and now understood why she'd been the one who was so different. She was Emily's and Bunny's love child. Her entire life had been a lie.

"Mother, did it dawn on you to stop getting married and pay attention to your children?" Randy choked.

"That not fair," Joy jumped in to defend her friend. She couldn't listen to Randy another second. "Your mother was miserable with Gregory. She needed to try to create a home for you all. He would have killed her if she stayed here. I know I was wrong to reintroduce her to Bunny perhaps but nothing can come in the way of true love; Not, I'm afraid, even children. If she didn't leave this island, by now all of you must understand that she'd be dead."

Randy thought of what she'd have to give up to be with Adele. Would she ever be brave enough to choose love? And did it really matter? Her only child probably felt the same way about her as she did her mother.

"You are right, Randy. I was spoiled, entitled and hardheaded. There is no righting my wrongs but Bunny and I could not be apart for long. The day I found out I was pregnant with his child he asked me to leave Gregory and marry him. I couldn't do that. I told him maybe Gregory would think it was his child and that I could just stay married and we continued as we were. He refused. Wouldn't have any of it. I finally agreed to tell Gregory and ask for a divorce and he agreed to tell his wife. We would marry again. Gregory refused to even listen to my request for a divorce. He was furious and called his family in England and told them he was sending me to get an abortion. I was young and stupid and I was petrified of raising three children on my own. If I didn't go, he'd make my life a living hell and if I had an abortion, I'd lose the only man I have ever loved. I went to England as my husband demanded but I never returned. Joy was the one who helped me. She sent me to her sister in Leicester. The only thing that connected me to this new land was the letter of introduction from Joy in my purse."

"Joy," Emily reached for her friend's hand, "what a dear and faithful friend you are. A true Joy to the World indeed. Had it not been for you, I would have been out on the streets of London months pregnant with two kids in tow."

"Chile that was nothing."

"It was a good enough life," Emily patted Joy's hand. I lived for Wednesdays when Bunny's letters would arrive. They were filled with the excitement of Island news and the promise that he's soon be leaving for England and we could all be a family soon. Emily pulled out a stack of papers from her bag…they were yellow with age. Joy noticed that each was dated and stacked accordingly. Emily handed the letters to Amelie.

"The first Wednesday Bunny's letter didn't arrive," Emily continued, "I had a bad feeling in my soul. It was so disheartening I cried for hours. All kinds of thoughts went through my head. Maybe he'd found someone else. That night as I sat in the living room with Aunt Clarissa I wanted to die.

Aunt Clarissa had a telephone that never rang. Nor did she use it as it was too expensive for everyday use so it sat on the little mahogany table like a big paperweight with eyes, reserved for emergencies. When the bell peeled nearby neither of us realized at first what was happening and keep looking at each other and out the window to see what the ruckus was about. It was the black machine rattling and shaking."

Finally, I said, "Aunt Clarissa, I think it's the telephone."

"Yes. I do believe so," Aunt Clarissa walked over to the heavy black machine and picked up the receiver. After a few words, Aunt Clarissa said, "It's Joy. She wants to talk to you."

"Man, that was one of the hardest things I ever did," Joy interjected.

"What's wrong? What happened to Daddy? Mummy?" Amelie asked.

"He had a horrible accident. His car crash on Spur Tree Hill while he was on his way to play a session with a guy called Bob. The legendary Bob Marley as we now know him."

My life ended that day and everything beyond that is pretty much a blur. I began drinking to dull the pain. I drank to forget, I drank to cope and I drank to escape. Three years later my mother died. They said my mother died of shame."

"So that's why Grandpa and Uncle Joe came to live with us," Amelie said.

Emily nodded her head.

At first, the Jim Beam was just conversational, a toddy in my tea now and then to help with the pain. Then for some reason, it became a friend, dropping by on lonely afternoons.

Randy said sarcastically, "After all that heartache why didn't you just give up on men altogether? Did you ever think of us once, Mother?"

"You were all I ever thought about. Every decision I made was because of you all."

"But in the end, you didn't make the right choices, did you mother? Because everyone left you. Didn't they?"

"Randy," Ashley and Joy shouted at the same time.

"There comes a point when we have to take responsibility for our own lives, no matter what. That's why we're here, isn't it?" Randy spat.

"To find the information we need to take responsibility for our lives, not to punish mother," Ashley said.

"You know Randy, I've made many mistakes. And yes, I've made bad choices, but I never abandoned you."

"You didn't? What do you think you did, Mother?" Randy, emotionally exhausted flopped down on the sofa. "Sometimes I wonder what life would have been like if I had never left Jamaica. If Uncle Joe hadn't been so cooped up so he had no other outlet but to…"

"To what? Uncle Joe. What?" Emily's eyes widened. "What does he have to do with this?"

Randy's face twisted in scorn.

Emily's hand flew to her mouth and her eyes widened further with understanding. "Did he do something to you? Is that what happened to you at thirteen? Why didn't you ever tell me?" Emily's heart was beating so fast in her chest she thought it would burst.

"Because you weren't there mother," Randy hurled venom, "You were never there."

"I'm so sorry, Randy."

"Isn't it too late for that now, Mother?"

"You got to be kidding me?" Ashley blurted out. "Crazy Uncle Joe? Jesus Randy. What the…why didn't you…Randy what? She went over to where her sister stood and held her close. "How could you have kept such a secret all these years?"

"Because secrets sometimes protect," Randy said. "They protect the fragile and fester into something worse."

Emily sat catatonic, tears streaming down her face. She wanted to hold her daughter and ask for her forgiveness but she was not able to move. It was all too much. Amelie walked slowly from the room her shoe heel pulverizing gravel as she headed down the path to the boathouse. She had been living all these years without really knowing who she was. She pushed open the door of the little cottage. Tears spilled down her cheek as she entered its cozy interior. This, she sat on the four-poster bed crowned with a sweeping mosquito net, could have been where she had started life. Her father was a great musician. Her grandfather was a musician. That was in her DNA.

• • •

Randy finally understood. "Poor Amelie. To have to learn this now."

"It all seemed so right back then not to tell her. But I know now how wrong I've been." Emily finally spoke. "I am so sorry. I am so very sorry."

Ashley looked at her mother. They were all damaged human beings. Damaged by secrets. "Is our father still alive?" She asked, the entire morning feeling too surreal for her.

"Very much so," Joy said. "He still practices law at the courthouse in Kingston. I don't know if you would care to see him but it could be a good idea"

"I should like to meet our father," Randy said finally pulling herself together and leaving the room to go to find her sister, Amelie.

"Wait for me," Ashley said, following Randy down the gravel path.

When the girls had left the room, Joy turned to Emily and said. "You mean Joseph?" Joy's voice rose in timber. "Little, crazy Joseph?"

Emily said grief-stricken. "I can't believe all these years Randy kept this secret to herself. The poor thing. If I had been a better mother I'd have known. I'm so sorry." She began weeping all over again.

"The past is past," Joy said. "You did the best you could and you are doing the right thing now."

"I know that but just look at what the past created. My children hate me."

"Don't take that on. Look how close they are. This is all a shock to everybody but we can find strength in this. I'll get Junior to drive us to Kingston. They have a right to know their father."

"I too owe Gregory and apology. But I will wait until after the children have seen him. I won't go with you."

"I understand." Joy said.

"Joy," Emily said. "Do you think God was punishing Bunny and me?

"Not the God I know but I don't believe in those things. But look at it this way, sorrow comes from living. It's a part of the life God must have intended."

• • •

Amelie was lying curled up in the bed. Ashley and Randy climbed into the bed on either side of her.

"Are you okay?" Randy asked, surprisingly placing an arm around Amelie. "I'm so sorry that we had to find out this way Amelie but what difference does it make?"

"I mean really," Ashley said.

"All the difference in the world. I would have understood the voices in my head and listen to my heart. I'd never have left the Julliard. I would have had the confidence to be the pianist I was supposed to be…I would have heard his voice and not mothers when I had that memory slip." Amelie sat up and she reached for her sister's hand. "Oh Randy, how could you stand the pain?"

"I didn't feel much. Alcohol took the load away," Randy said, tears glistening.

"I can't believe we didn't even suspect something," Ashley said. "How could we be so unconscious?"

"What a burden. How do you think mummy feels?" Amelie asked.

"I imagine really bad. Uncle Joe. Who would ever…anyway, since all this is old news let's sleep here tonight and, in the morning, early we go to the grotto and wash off old news. What'd you say?" Ashley said.

"I'd like that," Amelie high fived her sister. "But how could a family keep such secrets," Amelie sniffled. "How?"

"Because, as a wise sister once told me, secrets are sometimes protection," Ashley said reaching for Randy hand.

"But they wear you out. To be honest I feel like a weight has been lifted. I even feel I can understand mother a bit more." Randy said.

"What happens now?" Amelie asked.

"Tomorrow Randy and I will all go to meet our father. Will you come, Amelie?"

"No. I don't think so. To him, I am a secret. I am really a total secret. Are you guys mad?"

"Mad? Are you bonkers? Nothing could have changed our bond as sisters. No matter her many secrets we all kept," Randy said. "I swear I feel ready to wash away this shit," she too high-fived her sisters.

"Do you think I was conceived in this room?" Amelie inquired.

"It's a pretty darn nice room," Randy said and the sisters busted out laughing.

"Better than the room I got pregnant in. At least she didn't get rid of you like I did Frederick's child," Ashley said. "And they were really in love. Amelie, you are a love child and they were married once you know so you are not a jacket child."

"You were pregnant?" Randy said softly.

"My secret," Ashley said.

• • •

The children had not expected to learn about their fathers in the way they had, neither had they expected to walk into the minefield of emotions that revealed secrets so long buried. Yet, somehow the light breeze that flowed through the beautiful room brought new clarity. There was a rap on the door before Aunt Joy entered. She was holding a tray with cups and a teapot. "Not even duppy can compete with this cocoa. One cup and you will fall asleep like a baby."

CHAPTER THIRTY-ONE
Ashley

New York, 2003

BACK IN AMERICA Ashley's life had resumed its breakneck speed. Jamaica now seemed so far away under the demands of her daily realities. Meeting her father for the first time since she was four, learning the stories of where their respective histories began and parted, centered Ashley. Her father was an amazing man and was obviously where she got her superior brain. She looked forward to getting to know him better. Over the past couple years, she'd faced some sobering realities and she was all the better for them. She slipped on her jacket and aloud she said. NEXT.

Ashley added rock star status to her already rocketing career at WNCB. Her Special Report *Two Sides* was focused on Arkansas, which included an interview with former President Clinton who happened to be in town, was a megahit. Clinton, a most charismatic figure, overshadowed his faults with his over the top charm. Ashley's feeling was that there were two Bill Clintons…and that was the crux of her story…to show the public charmer and the less attractive private side of Bill Clinton. Even after the show America still paid homage to the wildly popular ex-president, but her work got a lot of praise. To be frank she hadn't yet met a person who didn't have two people living inside them! But Melvadore was right, after all. People would make their own decisions but giving the information on which to base their decisions was important. Just as he predicted, advertisers swarmed.

An astute and pernicious reporter dead bent on exposing the message manipulators, Ashley knew that her strength was her ability to compliment but not coddle, to expose but not judge. On her weekly show *Two Sides*, she'd set a new standard for the competition. People were fleeing from repeat and negative journalism to hear something fresh and thought-provoking from her show where there was no spin, no talking heads, and no sound bites. What everyone had expected as the kiss of death, turned out to be Ashley's biggest trump card. Her piece, *The South*, in which she explored the dark history of southern states with empathetic and journalistic integrity, earned her the trust of America. Melvadore said her piece on Afghanistan was going to solidify her star in the galaxy. Ashley felt warmth come over her as she thought of Melvadore Follette. He was a man true to his word. Indeed, he was going to make her a star. She'd know that the moment she walked out of George Bush's White House. She hadn't quite understood until now that Melvadore Follette was personally guiding her career and training at WNCB.

Ashley walked down the long corridor toward Melvadore's office. She wished she could have surprised him but the confounded one-way mirror was an enemy of surprises.

"Hey." Melvadore seemed ecstatic to see her. "You're back just in time. How was your trip?

"Really eye-opening. I went to Jamaica for the first time since I was four. I met my father." *Why was she telling him this?*

"No kidding. What was that like?"

"Liberating."

"How were the fruits?" He smiled.

"Mmmmm. Good."

"Wonderful. I have a favor. From now on you need to let me know your exact whereabouts."

"What? Even if it has nothing to do with work? I don't think so?"

"I think so. You haven't noticed anything out of the usual, have you?" He seemed concerned.

"Is something going on I need to know about?"

"No. I am just being cautious. Your stories could make some people uncomfortable and ruffle a few feathers. Just wanted to ask you to be observant of everything."

"I will. That's really nice of you to be concerned about your reporters. I'll keep you posted if I anything out of the ordinary happens. Why am I just in time?" she asked. Something lurked ominously in her mind at his question.

"This," he said handing her a folded paper.

Ashley glanced at the memo. "Nooooohhh. You don't mean it."

"Yes," he said. "He's never, ever given an interview. Certainly not in recent history. I think it's a good idea to disappear for a minute anyway. Our rating can't get any higher on that bad diet stuff…let's raise the bar a bit and show some good people. America has always been fascinated with Royalty. Let's give them a story."

"Oh, my!" Ashley rushed over to stand in front of him. "Rainier? For real? The Principality of Monaco. I've always dreamed of going there.

"After Monaco, you will cover an event in Cannes, Paris then back home. *D'accord?"*

"Cannes," Ashley repeated excitedly. She'd always wanted to go to Cannes too. "Cannes?" she asked realizing then that it couldn't be for the film festival. "We aren't talking about May here. What's happening in Cannes?"

"You're so banal. All Americans know about Cannes is the film festival. But you know it exists 365 days a year, don't you?"

"Don't patronize me. Plus, I'm Jamaican," Ashley shot back.

"Then don't act provincial. We leave October 5th."

"We?

"Yup."

"When do we return?"

"On the twenty-first. The twentieth if you want to miss the swanky parties.

Ashley murmured. "Three weeks. This is an amazing opportunity."

"I thought so," he leaned over and pecked her on the cheek. "I missed you," he said putting on his jacket. "I have to be downtown in twenty minutes. "Text me your number. And, if you need to talk about anything, I'm around."

Ashley touched her cheek. She felt warm and dreamy. When she finally recovered, only then did she realize that she hadn't bothered to ask him why on earth was he going to Monaco with her? By the time she got to his doorway, Melvadore was already turning the corner of the hallway. Her questions remained as brainwaves but she made a mental note to ask him the next time she saw him.

• • •

It had been any normal day when he had approached her about doing a documentary for the third-year anniversary of 9/11. It really wasn't an Afghanistan story, it was a story about tyranny and humanity. She had traveled to places she hoped never to see again; Cambodia, Rwanda, Somalia, Syria, Lebanon, and Israel. "I want you," he said, "to be aware of everything around you. Everything. Is that understood? I'm putting you out in the killing fields of the world and you will be in harm's way much more than is visible to your eyes. Your next assignment will be here in the U.S. It could prove more dangerous than most. It's the last part of the story that we need to finish your special on the *Cost of War*."

"And where am I going?"

"For an interview with Bush," he'd said undaunted.

"George Bush?" Ashley said dropping her shoulders dramatically. "What on earth could we accomplish with that? His ratings are plummeting after Iraq. Do you think people will tune in?"

"America has been at the forefront of many wars. They cannot be left out of a story on the *Cost of War*. This is not a story about Bush. It's a story where the face of tyranny sometimes wears a smile. No matter where in the world tyranny is, the end result is always destruction. On this assignment, you have to be as careful as everywhere else. Power the world over does not cede easily. And America is a superpower. I'm getting you a partner and companion."

"What? I don't need a babysitter."

"How about a big brother? That Phillip of yours will be on this story with you."

"Really? That's fantastic. Does he know?"

"Not yet."

Phillip was going to be over the moon. The conversation concluded, Ashley skipped down the hall. Shucks, she turned around, she'd left her phone on Melvadore's desk and she again forgot to ask why he was accompanying her to Monaco.

Melvadore's door was open. He was on the phone, his back to the door.

"I don't think that will be hard to do," Melvadore was saying to the party line. "Check on operation ED. Sharvhab is in Bermuda with Nemba. What else do you need?"

"Ahem," Ashley cleared her throat.

"Did I forget something?" Melvadore looked at her nonchalantly.

"No. I did. My phone."

"Ah," he grinned.

"Thanks," Ashley said retrieving her machine. As she walked back down the hall, she wondered what Operation ED was about. She was awed by this man and if she were honest her heart fluttered every time she was in his presence. Give unto Caesar what belongs to him. "Quit," she said loudly, hastening her pace.

• • •

Bush's Afghanistan/Iraq switch was prime fodder and would raise dander. From the moment she got the assignment Ashley went into full tilt. Phillip was the first to arrive at the assignment. Ashley pulled up right behind him. As she approached him, he grabbed her and planted a kiss on her forehead. "I love you," he said. "Simply adore you. Thanks for the recommendation."

"Are you ready?"

"Nevermore." He pulled out a notebook filled with facts Ashley didn't even know existed. "Who's a serious ass reporter now," he slapped the notebook in her hand. They spent the morning in a little coffee shop pouring over the notes and planning their clever strategy. Ashley was the only one allowed inside the private offices of the President. Bush was the first American sitting head of state Ashley would interview and she was as nervous as a newborn kitten. Between clearance, security, press people and fact checkers, Ashley had been up for almost twenty-four hours. Though getting to the President was like getting into Fort Knox, when she finally arrived for her interview she was treated well. She would interview the President of the free world in his private quarters, a place off limits to every other reporter before her. She could tell they were sucking up.

While Ashley was setting up for the interview, Condoleezza Rice walked by to have a word with the President. The woman was all that and more. Gracious and stylish she acknowledged Ashley with a slight bow. "Make us proud and be gracious," she said to Ashley as her erect and controlled body disappeared down the hallway. Ashley, now fully acclimated to her adopted country understood, without a doubt, what was being said—make us proud—don't act like the rest of them, assimilate and be gracious meant don't bait the President. It pained her that someone so powerful and so brilliant didn't understand that uttering those words meant she had been mind-controlled, hypnotized and lethal.

The session was the best she'd done yet. Bush was mush. She actually liked the man whose wide eyes reminded her of a child. The man had no clue why he was in the oval office and she got the impression he thought it all a game he had to win to gain his father's approval. He'd failed so much before. Still, she liked him and found him to be open and fun.

"Well?" Phillip asked as she came up to the waiting car.

"Our President is childlike and believe it or not fun."

"A child with dangerous toys," Phillip said.

• • •

Ashley flew back alone leaving Philip to anchor the B roll with the team.

Melvadore met her at the airport, again. "Welcome back."

"It's good to be back and it's good to see you, Mr. Follette," Ashley, said, surprised that he had come to meet her at the airport, again.

"How was it?" Mel said taking the lightweight luggage she carried.

"Unexpected. He's truly is affable. Do you always meet your reporters at the airport?" she asked.

"Never. I just couldn't wait until tomorrow to hear about your interview. Can I get a first look at the tapes?"

"I don't see why not. Ask the cameramen to set it up for you."

"Nah., I think we'll do this on our own. If you'd let me, I'd love to help you shape the final piece."

"That would be amazing," Ashley said. "We can begin tomorrow if you want, but right now I've got to get home and climb into bed."

"Great. I'll drive you home. Look, Ashley," Melvadore held her by both shoulders. "Please be careful. Don't say anything on your home or office phone about anything. He reached into his pocket and handed her a cellular phone. "If you need to talk about anything work related use this, and," he handed her another phone, "on this one you talk only to me, anytime and anywhere. They are burner phones."

Ashley swooned. What was this man doing to her? But what was all this about?

"Level with me. What's going on?"

"I am only taking extreme precautions. What we are working on is tantamount to a weapon. I just want complete security of the information."

"Okay." Ashely dropped the phones into her bag. The white one for work and the black on a private line to her boss!

• • •

For four days, Melvadore and Ashley worked intensely and in private on a special, they came to finally name, *The Other Side of Reality*, the special, was scheduled to air on 9/11/2004. This story was going to set America on fire. When they thought they had the tightest product, Melvadore, who showed more emotions cutting this special than she had ever seen in him, sat back and laced his hands behind his head. "This is the best work we have ever done. What do you think?"

"You're a genius. I had no idea you could even do basic editing much less final cut. I would never have thought to merge these stories together.
It's share genius. I hope the American people will be as amazed to see the complete picture of war around the world and the decisions behind wars."

"Oh, I don't think anyone will be pleased, but this is a story that has to be told. There are journalists trying every day to tell the true story of war, some even willing to give their lives so the truth can be heard. This is our tribute to them. Thank you."

"No. Thank you! I'm privileged that you chose me to bring it all together. And you're absolutely right. People must know the terror of war and understand that war is not only about what happens to the people who die, but what happens to the people who live every day with war. The President's people will be quite annoyed I'm afraid and I'm sure we're going to get some heat on this."

"Clean up your personal business. Make it squeaky clean if there's anything to take you down because they will find it. Trust me, they'll be looking into your background after this airs with a microscope but my dear you will be a star. By the way, I've arranged for you to have a chauffeur. Don't settle into a routine, vary your day and only call from the cell I gave you."

"You're scaring me. Is get the feeling there is something going on I don't know about?" Ashley looked up at Mel and held his gaze.

"We are only being proactive. Truth is scary. We are messing with the Shadow Elites and believe me; their arms are long."

Melvadore's brilliant merging of footage from her Iraq, Afghan, America and Darfur and many others with interviews from political heavyweights of those countries was indeed going to cause a media frenzy. She would do what he said. She'd be very careful.

The next day Ashley, all excited, was busy gushing on the phone to Phillip about their masterpiece. "He's an expert. I have never seen anything like it."

"Ashley, I think you're in love with this man. YOU think a man is a genius?"

"Phillip don't be daft, I'm just saying." What was she saying? Did she feel…could she really be… "Anyway, I think he might bring you to New York. You were a great shadow."

"Now I'm a shadow. I'll be a monkey's uncle!"

"Okay, that's it. I am done talking to you."

The knock on the door startled her.

"Hold on," Ashley said into the mouthpiece of the cell phone he'd given her.

Mel pushed his head around the door. "Got a minute?" Ashley motioned him to the couch. "I'm just finishing up with Phillip."

Melvadore motioned for her to hand him the phone. "Thanks for taking good care of her in D. C. You guys did a superb job. Let's plan on meeting in New York when I'm back late October. Ask my secretary to get you on my schedule," Mel said handing the phone back to Ashley.

Ashley was beaming. Her Phillip was going to move to New York, she could feel it.

"How may I help you?" Ashley was aware of the little flutter at the nape of her neck. It was her sign. Always portended caution was needed.

"Came to pick you up so we could see the final, final product. The color is fantastic, the music is amazing and the little touches have made a world of difference. We should also figure out our plan of rebuttal for it will surely come. I'll order in and we can watch it in my home theater in Westchester. I have an idea I'd like to run by you."

"I didn't know you had a home in Westchester."

"I'm afraid there's a lot you might not know about me, Miss Ashley. If you care to, you could spend the night. It has eleven bedrooms," he added hurriedly when he saw the shock on her face, "or I'll have the driver bring you back when we're done. We should also discuss Monaco."

• • •

On the way out to the country, as he called it, Mel, who chose to drive himself, played Habibi music. Ashley found herself tapping her feet to the riff she too had become used to in Afghanistan. The downbeats reminded her of reggae. Mel sang along his warble a comfort to her ears. The house in Rye was amazing. Like Landilow, it offered all the conveniences one could ever imagine except for pink sand and blue skies. On the first floor, beyond the library were a set of frosted wooden paneled door that leads to a full-blown theater. On the way into the theater, a concession stand was fully stocked. Ashley filled a bag with popcorn and stuffed a twizzler and two bags of M&M's in her purse.

"I'll get some wine," Melvadore opened a concealed bar on the left panel of the theater. "Red, white or rose?"

"White, please." Ashley sat in the middle of the mid-row. "If this were my house, I'd never leave this room. I'd spend my entire days watching Indian movies."

"I love Indian movies. If people lived and fought as they did in Indian movies the world would be a better place. No matter what happens in life there is always a dance. Do you want to eat while we watch the movie or later?" Melvadore asked.

"I'm okay with popcorn for now."

Melvadore popped in the DVD and settled next to Ashley. For the next hour, they were riveted by the images unfolding on the screen. The piece started with a straight interview with President Bush. As Ashley's questions turned to the war in Iraq, images of Afghanistan filled the screen and through clever editing and interspersed interviews they showed the bait and switch tactics of the Bush administration to oust Saddam by inferring that Iraq was responsible for the World Trade Center catastrophe. The piece was expertly cut to show the devastation of insurrections, weaving in the civil wars around the world, showing them as the tyranny of men who failed to look beyond their own egos and need for power. The piece was powerful. Ashley wasn't quite aware of the moment when Mel's fingers slipped through hers, maybe it was when tears fell or when her spirit soared at the indomitable human spirit of the people on the screen, but as she closed her fingers over his she was very much aware that at that moment, they shared a special bond.

"Why are you crying?" He encircled her shoulder.

"Three days, can you believe it, three days Afghani children waited for food in a Peshawar refugee camp. And all they get is stale bread and water."

"Yes," he said a pained look on his face. "I know how hard it is for most of the world to simply survive."

"Do you remember the Afghani woman on the cover of National Geographic? I saw a million such women, their eyes full of hardship but also hope. AliBibi is in every third world country being destroyed by war and civil strife.
And the mothers of the young men who have died. Unbelievable courage. I always said if I'd had a son, I would never let him fight in a war but now I understand that one life is nothing when it means saving an entire culture."

"I think you're going to win an Emmy and we're going to make some enemies," Mel said.

Aware that they were too physically close, Ashley rose to get another drink. "Do you really think so?"

"Without a doubt. I'm very proud of your courage and your honesty."

Ashley was not sure if it was courage or honesty that drove her. Was she any less power hungry than these men who caused war? Was she starting another war with this explosive and uncongenial piece? Was it a manipulation of journalism? Should they have gotten permission from the Whitehouse to use the President's interview this way? Would she be forced to leave the country or have her life torn to shreds by CIA and FBI operatives? What had she done? What had Melvadore done? If the piece offended the government, they would paint him as a radical and make his life a living hell. Ashley turned to Melvadore and she had never quite felt as much respect for another human being. "No matter what happens," she said softly, "I will always stand by you. This is really good work and this is the truth that all journalist should strive to tell. We did nothing wrong."

"Thank you," Melvadore leaned over and kissed her cheek. "I chose you because I saw the courage and conviction of honesty in your eyes. I'm glad to know that you'll stand by me no matter what happens. There may come a time when that will be necessary."

This time he held her face and kissed her fully on the lips.

Ashley rose from her seat as though in a trance. "I think if it's okay with you I'd like to go back to the city now," she said.

"If that is what you wish."

• • •

"Hey, there."

Ashley was at her desk bright and early. She was nursing her coffee and replaying her first kiss with a man that made her ready to give up her steely edge.

"Hey," Ashley was jarred from her reverie.

"Hey," she said looking appreciatively at the man in her doorway.

"You are ruling the world, Missy. I am proud of you."

It was Quinton, her former producer on ET.

"Hey, Quint. It's great to see you. What are you doing here at this time of day? You're usually gone by 9:00 a.m., aren't you?"

"Yep, but I had to come by to see you, Ashley, I've always been proud of you. Keep up the good work."

"I owe a lot of it to you, Quint," she rose and walked over to where he stood. "Let's have dinner soon."

CHAPTER THIRTY-TWO
Randy

New York, 2003

RANDY, DESPITE HER reluctance to go, loved Jamaica. Her spirit felt whole as though she had never left. When she was finally face-to-face with her father, every memory of him flooded her head; the candies at lunchtime, the bedside stories, and the picnics in the park and she had clung to him, in a deep embrace.

"Why didn't you try to find us?" she'd asked.

"I did. Not a day went by even to this day that I did not try to find you all. I tried darling. I really tried."

When her father put his arms around her, it was as though the whole world was right again. Randy returned to the US determined to make up for lost time. One thing she realized in Jamaica was that she could stand on her own and she was not afraid. Nothing like knowing the past to move forward. She wasn't just some step-daughter to faceless men. She was her father's child. Her lineage was rooted in stalwart, fierce and accomplished people. She could do this and she would do it. She would face reality head-on. She pushed open the door to the Gallery she hadn't been to for months. She'd hired competent staff, as she knew that from time to time, she would have been gone on long buying trips and that Adele was never going to be in the gallery full time.

"Hi."

"Adele. Adele? What…what in heavens are you doing here? I thought you only came in on Wednesday's."

"I've been dropping by more often since your absence."

"Then there is no need for you to stay. Please leave now before Mr. Sandler arrives."

"Just like that. Is that all you have to say to me after cutting off all communications?"

Randy stood stiffly, unable to find words. She wanted to appear calm and unaffected but she was nervous.

"I'd like you to go now," Randy said. "It's over."

"I'll wait for you anyway."

"You'd be wasting your time. Let's talk about a buyout of your shares in the gallery," she went to her office and shut the door.

• • •

Randy reached for the bottle of vodka. After Jamaica, she'd thought she could keep her drinking under control, but some habits die hard. Seeing Adele had unnerved her and after the first drink became ten and when the walls began closing in on her, she called Dr. Livingston.

"I need help," she said into the phone.

"I'll make arrangements, Mrs. Austin."

Next, she called Lawrence. He was relieved when she told him, "I'm checking into rehab. Dr. Livingston has found me a place he thinks will be good for me."

"It's a good decision, Randy and it's a good time. When do you go?"

"Tomorrow. Could you drive me out to the center, please?" Randy asked.

"Of course. I'll cancel my appointments. You are being very brave and I know everything is going to be all right," Lawrence said, "I'll come every day and anytime you want me to."

"Once I check in you won't be permitted back for the four weeks I'm there."

• • •

When Lawrence kissed her goodbye, he could tell that Randy was acting brave and it was all he could do not to take her home with him. But he had to give them this chance and hope that the woman who came back to him would be the wife he'd hoped for, for so long.

The center was the best money could buy. Large airy rooms, cheerful hallways, and first-class food. The only things defective about the place were the people and even they were first class defects. The floor monitor spoke in a deep monotone, robotic voice as though she was the one whose brain was faulty. "I-will-check-on-you-every hour. When-I-am-not here, your-other-monitor-will-be-Pamela. We-will-provide-anything-you-need-except-what-is-prohibited. Shall-I help-you-unpack-or-are-you-okay-doing-it-yourself?"

A lanky brunette was picking away the skin of her thumb when Randy entered the room. She barely looked up.

"Hi," Randy said.

"Hello," the bag of bones answered.

"I'm Randy Austin. I'm your roommate. I hope you don't mind."

"First time here?" she asked.

"Yes. You?"

"My third."

"I see." Randy didn't feel encouraged.

"I'm Lauren. I'm an anorexic, bulimic and a cocaine addict."

Randy was taken aback by the girl's admissions to a perfect stranger.

"I'm…I'm…"

"Don't worry about it. They'll help you figure it out. They are good at diagnosing what ails us here."

• • •

Wakeup call was at 6:00 a.m. and with all the activities on campus, one would believe it was midday in Manhattan. The routine was rigorous and structured. The first week Randy welcomed all the attention she was getting from the doctors, nurses and even some of the first-class defects. She also appreciated the first-class facility with every convenience of a five-star hotel, if not better. Apart from not being able to sneak her vodka at nights this was going to be a cinch. By week two Randy was climbing the wall. "What happens here?" she'd snap to the attendant. She badly needed a drink. "Is this all there is. God, I need a drink," she said frantically scratching her arm which was itching something terrible. Her five-star hotel without a bar was becoming a nightmare.

"I think it's time to see a counselor."

After breakfast that morning Randy was taken to meet with a counselor named Dr. Franklin Ditmar.

"How are you feeling this morning Mrs. Austin?" he asked. Dr. Franklin Ditmar was about thirty-five. He seemed happy to see her.

"Agitated. I need a drink. I want to go home."

"Huh." He sat back in his leather chair. "Tell me exactly what you are feeling."

That night Randy was climbing the walls. She paced and paced and emptied the refrigerator of fruit juices. The next morning it was a disheveled, puffy face and hands shaking Randy who turned up to see Dr. Ditmar.

"Hi," Dr. Ditmar greeted her. "You seemed tired this morning," he said. "Rough night I see. Tell me how you feel right now."

Randy lowered herself onto the chair and passed a hand over her eyes. "I have no feelings. I might as well be dead."

"I know."

"I doubt it," Randy said.

"You're wrong. Fifteen years ago, I was sitting where you are. Confused and hopeless. Know that the one thing I do know is what you might be feeling, right now." Dr. Ditmar handed her a cup of coffee. "The next few weeks will be rough. I can't lie to you, it will be the worst thing you'll ever go through. The good news is that it might be better than most because you went an entire two-week before showing withdrawal signs. And the better news is you will get sober. Randy this might well be the hardest thing you'll ever do in your life but if you want to get better, you're going to have to go to places that scare the bejesus out of you. All I ask is that you keep a journal and that you allow yourself the depth of the pain. If it is time for you to move on from the rut Mrs. Austin, you'll have to accept that to fail, to make mistakes, is going to be a part of this process. But remember to err is to be human. Over the next few weeks, you will discover secrets inside you that fuel your fears. To face them and make them your friend is your goal. I will be using hypnotic therapy on you today to help you go "there" on your own when it all becomes too much. Ms. Austin…"

A bad case of nerves overcame Randy and immediately she began fidgeting trying to escape the dark, cavernous memory that came marching into her mind.

"Go there," she heard Dr. Ditmar voice far in the distance.

'Courage…live…die…Randy struggled to surface from the memory pulling her under. She was sweating and crying…Please don't…she kept pleading. Uncle Joe, please don't."

Dr. Ditmar did not interrupt and he allowed her to feel the pain as the memory washed over her. Randy was now in the corner curled up into a ball. "I don't know why…I don't know why he chose me…I must have done something to lead him on. I should have locked the door." She clung to Dr. Ditmar as he encircled her. It was enough for today and quite a breakthrough.

"Tonight, I want you to write a letter to Uncle Joe and to anyone else who you feel have let you down. I am going to prescribe something to take the edge off for tonight."

Randy, now lucid, felt embarrassed that she had lost such control. The following day she did not go to therapy. Instead, she wrote letters. Randy stuck a pretend thirty-seven cent stamps on the envelopes and walked to the corner mailbox at the end of the property. She opened the flap and pretended to mail the letters. There was a letter to her Mother, Uncle Joe, Lawrence, June, Mensa, Adele, Amelie, and Ashley and her dad. She was not supposed to mail the letters but she was to go through the motion of stamping them and going to the mailbox. That they said was therapy. What her letter writing revealed to Randy was that there was a difference between what Uncle Joe had done to her when she was thirteen and what had happened between her and Adele. She had allowed what happened with Adele, even wanted it. Who was there to blame for that? She also understood that Uncle Joe was a lonely and sad man who had been abused by his mom and the only person who had paid him any attention was her and her grandpa. He misunderstood and not being in his right mind he was probably unaware that what he did was wrong. Randy stood looking at the acres and acres of rolling hills. The air was crisp and it was reviving to be up in the mountains. She had been at the center now for four weeks and these were the first letters she had completed. She turned back in the direction of what was now her home, letters still in hand.

For several hours Randy walked aimlessly around her room straightening pictures, watering the orchids that Lawrence has sent up, weeping and dying for a glass of vodka. Her stomach ached, her hands trembled and her skin was clammy but much less than they were before. She'd long passed the first bout with DT's when she'd wished for death rather than the pain. As overwhelming emotions, brought out through therapy, threatened to overwhelm her, Randy felt the need to shut down. She went to the medicine cabinet and took out the bottle of sedatives that had only two pills that Dr. Ditmar had prescribed for when things got too bad, then decided against it. Problems do not go away unless they are resolved. What was the point of simply numbing the pain, if it never gets resolved? Randy slammed the cabinet door. Live…courage…die. She thought of June, her father, and even her mother. She wrote a letter to June.

After breakfast, Randy, now dressed in her usual impeccable style, went to Dr. Ditmar's office. He welcomed her in his jovial way, handing her the usual cup of coffee and complimenting her on her attire.

"I didn't want to drink today," Randy said as she flopped down in the chair of inquisition. "I didn't take any sedatives last night either and I had a good night."

"That's definitely progress?"

"Am I ready to go home?"

"Not quite, but I'm pleased with your progress."

"What do we talk about today?"

"Anything you want. How about what your life will look like when you leave us?"

Randy's eyes sparkled. For the entire hour, she spoke of her vision for her gallery. There was one thing that had to be done. She needed to buy out Adele.

• • •

It was late October when she walked back into the home she'd left four-weeks before. She had decided to surprise everyone. She was glad she didn't have to miss Amelie's recital. If it had come down to that she'd gotten a day pass.

"I missed you bad, bad, bad Miss Randy," Mensa's broad smile greeted Randy as she walked through the door.

"Mensa," Randy rushed over to hug her guardian angel. "I missed you sooo much. How are you? The house? June? Lawrence?" She had actually hugged someone!

"Everything is fine. You hungry?"

"Thank you, Mensa, but no," Randy said smiling. "I'll lie down for a bit. We'll have a good chat when I get up. I can't wait to hear everything. And Mensa removed all the alcohol from the house."

"Already done, Ms. Austin."

"Even my secret stash?"

"All gone," Mensa said.

"Mensa, what did you have planned for dinner tonight?"

"I was thinking of chicken."

"Make Mr. Austin's favorite, filet of sole. Have that shop you call send some up fresh. Let's have dinner at about eight."

Upstairs in her private quarters, Randy sat silently letting the new person she'd become readjust to an old life. She was glad to be home. The first person she called was Amelie. "I'm home."

"Oh Randy, that's fantastic. How do you feel?"

"Never better. Ready to help in any way. I can't wait for your recital. How are you feeling?"

"I can't lie. I am a wreck."

"Hang in there."

"Randy," Amelie said. "I am so very proud of you."

"Thank you, Amelie."

Next, Randy called Ashley.

"Who is big and bad," Ashley said.

Finally, she Adele. Randy listened to the ring, contemplating if she should leave well enough alone.

"*Allo.*"

"Adele, its Randy."

Adele put down the brush in her hand. "*Allo,* Randy. What a nice surprise. How are you?"

"I'm fine and you?"

"*Je suis malade.* I've been better," she shrugged.

"I'm sorry to hear that."

"But I'm painting so I'm fine," Adele said.

"That's great. Are you well enough to meet me for a late lunch?" If this is a bad time…"

"Where?" Adele jumped at the suggestion.

"Tribeca Grill."

"Why not come here?"

"I'm afraid I can't do that."

"What time?"

"Two-thirty."

"*D'accord.*"

"Are you sure?"

"I'm sure."

Randy was intentionally late. As the cab rounded the corner, she pulled out her compact, powdered her nose and patted her hair into place. Her olive-bronze complexion was pallid. She could see Adele from the doorway drumming her fingers on the table and nursing a glass of wine. She looked amazingly beautiful. Randy's stomach did a series of flips. Adele saw her and waved.

"What do you think of his work?" Adele asked as Randy slid into the chair the maître'd pulled out for her.

"Whose work?"

"De Niro's. These are all his or his Dad's," she waved a hand around the restaurant.

"Really? If they are his, he's a better actor than a painter," Randy said.

"Hmm, I kind of like them."

"How are you?" Adele asked. "You look great."

"Never better but for a slight headache earlier. It went away when you called."

"That's good."

"I thought I'd never hear from you again."

"The thought has crossed my mind." Randy felt an unexpected pleasure being with Adele. She poured herself a glass of water. "I was away."

"Away?" Adele smiled.

"Yes. In rehab. I came back only today."

"Wow. How was that experience?"

"Intense but the place was beautiful."

"And how are you doing?"

"So far, so good. I'm here partly because it is my therapy. I have to apologize to all the people who I've hurt and also because of the gallery." Randy was trying hard not to notice the fading twinkle in Adele's eyes, or the smooth skin above her scooped neckline.

"I'm listening," Adele said solemnly.

"I am sorry about everything. I was being selfish and needy."

"No, you weren't." Adele put a hand on Randy's arm. "I felt your pain."

Randy snapped moving her hand away from Adele's touch. "Please let me finish."

"Have you decided on a lunch selection?" the waiter asked.

The women looked tensely at each other across the table. Adele's eyes were pained while Randy's were filled with sadness and perhaps even loss.

"Could we have another minute?" Adele asked the waiter who promptly turned and left. Adele's eyes were moist. She opened the menu but didn't appear to be reading it. Her tears disarmed Randy.

"Please don't do that," Randy said, "We have to be over. All my life I've been trying to deny feelings. To me, they were the enemy. What happened between us was nothing more than an escape for me. Another place to hide but it did set me on the path of discovery." Randy was gentle. "I have to find my own way for once in my life. You can't be a part of that journey and you can't be a part of my gallery."

Adele was silent. The women stared at each other.

"Maybe when the dust settles Adele, we'll be able to understand. What I know for sure is that I need to get my life in order. It's time to get it right or give up altogether."

"Is that really what you want?"

"Yes."

"Then I have no choice. Do you mind if we skip lunch?"

"I don't mind at all."

Randy watched Adele leave. She signaled the waiter and ordered lunch.

• • •

Mensa did a marvelous job setting the table on the enclosed balcony off her bedroom. Though it should have been a cooler night, thanks to El Nino, it was a perfect night for a twilight dinner. Randy tried on three outfits before she decided on the orange satin blouse and fitted black pants. She dabbed her lips with a gloss, her cheeks with rouge and her wrists with Escape.

"It's okay to go now Mensa. I'll handle it from here."

"Everything is in the warmer. All you have to do is serve it."

"See you tomorrow," Randy said.

"Nite ma'am."

"Goodnight, Mensa."

Mensa retired to her quarters.

• • •

Randy poured a glass of sparkling water and sat on the patio. It was indeed a perfect night. The phone was ringing in the distance but she allowed the machine to answer it. She hadn't had a drink in four weeks and though she was tempted, she held her ground. She was proud of her willpower. And if overly challenged, Dr. Ditmar had given her some Antabuse tablets.

"Is that you, Lawrence?" Randy asked when she heard the bouncing footsteps on the stairs.

"It's me. I'm coming right up. Can't believe you didn't tell me you were coming home." His voice was getting closer.

Randy put the glass to her lips and drank the water in one gulp wishing for the first time it was vodka. She had to do it. "I'm on the patio."

"Hi," he said, kissing her cheek. "It's so good to see you, Randy. Do I have five to take a shower? I'm so glad you are home."

"Have a glass of wine first. Shower later. It's only us," she said.

"You look beautiful."

"Thank you. I thought it would be nice to have dinner together. It's been a long time since we've done so."

"Well…this sounds really nice," Lawrence said a quizzical look on his face. "Let me take a quick shower. I think I need to feel and look as good as you do." He wondered if she was going to ask for a divorce. She was, it seemed to him, way too calm.

Randy got up, turned on the stereo and music filled the room. "Dance and let your husband desire you." Adel's voice floated around in her head. The dance of death Randy thought.

Lawrence dressed casually but nicely, re-joined her on the patio. "I said it was gonna be one helluva day today and it was. If this market keeps sliding there'll be a lot of people jumping off high rises," Lawrence somehow wanted to avoid the conversation he felt was coming.

"Will we be?"

"Of course not. I've never seen anything like this though. I don't even think Black Monday was this bad, ordinary people losing a lifetime of savings. The market is definitely not for the faint of heart."

Randy placed a tureen of vichyssoise, along with a salad, on the table. On the warmers were sautéed sole and grilled asparagus.

"You look really swell tonight."

Randy smiled and cupped his hand to her face. The unmistakable smell of sex had been washed away.

"Hungry?"

"Starving actually." What was all this about Lawrence felt nervous? He had never ever thought of leaving his wife.

"Yes. Sex does that, doesn't it? So," she sat opposite her husband. "How was it?"

"What?"

"The sex?"

Lawrence looked away. "What are you talking about?"

"Please don't start lying, Lawrence. When you came in you smelled of sex. That and her perfume."

Lawrence felt his chest constrict. How could he deny it? Damn Whitney. He'd gone to break it off for the umpteenth time but as always, she'd cried and begged him not to and then she'd stripped down to her high heels.

"Randy look…" He started…

"Please," she held up her hand, no details. "Don't explain. What is a man in your position to do? Soup?"

As they ate Randy told him about her experience in Rehab. Lawrence was surprised she hadn't gone on about his infidelity, then again, she could care less what he did as long as he didn't touch her. After dinner, Randy cleared the table and placed the dishes on the breakfront. Mensa would deal with the rest in the morning…she went to the stereo and turned the music up a little more.

"Shall we?" She moved into his arms. Pavarotti and Tracy Chapman were singing a duet, "Baby Can I Hold You".

Lawrence was speechless.

"Well?"

"You, want to dance?"

"Yes. Do you mind?"

"Not at all," Lawrence pulled his wife into a slow waltz. This is what he had waited for. He closed his eyes as she cradled her head in the crook of his arm.

"It's over," he whispered.

Randy nodded, "so is mine."

Lawrence pulled back to look at her. "Your what?"

"My affair," Randy said nonchalantly.

"I know…I'm so glad Randy. Maybe now we can really try?"

"Oh, I don't mean my affair with Vodka. I mean my affair, affair."

Lawrence pushed her gently away. He'd heard somewhere that suicidal people become delusional, overly attentive and affectionate before they offed- themselves.

"Honey, are you okay?"

"I'm perfectly fine. We are just discussing our affairs. Yours and mine."

"What's going on here?" Lawrence let go of her completely. Is this your idea of a joke?"

"What do you mean, Lawrence? "My affair was no joke. Was yours?"

Lawrence brought his fist down on the breakfront, harder than he'd expected. The tureen splintered on the floor, green liquid splattering everywhere.

"Symbolic." Randy looked at the jagged china. "Splintered just like our marriage."

Lawrence turned a deep hue, ran a hand through his balding hair. "Randy, men do that kind of stuff. Especially middle age, who are stressed and have no sex with their wives! But you know I'd never leave you." *What did she expect!*

"If you can do it, why can't I? I'm definitely middle-aged and very stressed and clearly not having sex with my husband."

"Because you are a wife and a mother for one," Lawrence yelled.

"I'm sorry Lawrence. I don't blame you. I know what a stick in the mud I've been and I don't blame you one bit. And I didn't do it to spite you or to get even. But…"

"Who is he?" Lawrence demanded.

"She," Randy said filling her glass with more water. She was losing her nerve and prayed for strength.

Lawrence's leaned against the table. He was in the grips of frightening anger. He paced up and down the patio. He broke two more dishes and then the wineglass.

"I hear that *Oo-Pah* trick really works," Randy said as another plate splintered onto the floor.

"I told you to stay away from those women." Lawrence began shouting, "I should kill you."

"No need. I'm leaving you, Lawrence. Our life together is over. It's been over for years."

"You're leaving me for a woman?" It seemed all the anger left him and he slumped into a chair. "A woman," he repeated staring out into the distance. "This woman," Lawrence asked, his voice hollow, "do I know her?"

"It doesn't matter, Lawrence. I am not leaving you for or over a woman. I am leaving you for me. We've known for a long time that our marriage was over. Why should we keep up the charade? Why not try to find some happiness in what's left. Why would you stay with me? I have been a terrible wife."

"I've never even thought of being with another woman other than for sex."

"I am so sorry," Randy cradled her husband. "I am so sorry to have robbed you of so many years. But let's stop here. June is all grown up and has her own life now. We can do this right and we can do this gracefully. I know we can. That's why I wanted tonight to be special. I wanted you to know how much I appreciated you not leaving me. You are a wonderful husband and I want you to have at least one wonderful memory for our twenty-three years together."

"I can't live without you, Randy. What am I supposed to do?" Lawrence pierced his wife soul. "Is it better with her than with me?"

"I'm no judge of that," Randy said. "I've never made love of my own choice. I'd like to do that Lawrence just once. Would you?"

Lawrence was crying. He couldn't believe any of this was happening. Was she really going to kill herself? He gathered his wife into his arms and said. "I'd love that very much."

As they laid in each other arms, Randy was glad she found peace and she hoped her husband had found a little part of her. "I'm going away Lawrence. I'm going to find Randy. When I return, I will understand better what my life will be about."

Randy looked at the man she'd lived with for twenty-three years. His jaws were tight and his right thigh kept jerking up and down. Randy couldn't believe her confession about Adele had caused him so much pain. Lawrence's concern, however, was genuine and at that moment she wished she had loved him. He was deserving.

"Thank you, Randy." Lawrence felt like his world had just ended. "Thank you for being so gracious. When are you leaving?"

"I'll wait until after Amelie's recital and then I'll go." You just need to reshuffle the deck, Doctor Ditmar, at Cedar's Point had said. Go back to the place where life stopped for you and make your life whole again.

CHAPTER THIRTY-THREE
Amelie

Connecticut, 2003

AMELIE RESUMED HER practice. She had her day so structured she could barely think. All she could do at nights was fall into bed almost comatose. Under her brutal schedule, the news that should have rocked her world was swept up in the tsunami of practice. No flourish accompanied her mother's confession that she was an illegitimate child or that Ashley and Randy were her half-sisters. She had not even told Robb the entire story yet. One thing that could not be ignored was the nagging of her new muse that would not go away…it was worse than her two muses combined and finally, she could no longer put off the nosey ninny. The letters her mother had given her were still at the bottom of her pocketbook. This morning, unable to ignore her nagging muse any longer, Amelie locked herself inside her music room and retrieved the letters. With trembling hands, she removed the first letter from the envelope and unfolded it with care. Tears welling in her eyes.

She was holding something that her father had touched. She cleared her throat and began reading, her voice tiny.

My Sweet Buttercup,

Not long now my darling. Edwina finally recapitulated and we are divorced. I'm working on a post-Independence Day project with some fellow musicians. Jamaica catch a fire for sure. As soon as I 'm done releasing the country from Colonialism, I will join you in the land of the oppressor. How are the girls?

The second letter was obviously a stenciled copy of her mother's response.

Bunny that is wonderful news about Edwina. I only pray she doesn't hate me too much. The Lord must know why he gave us this challenge. Everyone here is fine. This place is cold and damp and if I didn't find this wonderful bakery in Brixton where I can buy my hard dough bread, I think I'd have gone mad. I swear, even the restaurants there serve beer and milk like at home. I have enclosed a picture of Amelie. She is chubby and crawling now. That little ivory thing sticking out is her first tooth.

Always, Emily

• • •

Dear Emily,

I bet I know that very restaurant. Don't eat too much bread and spoil you figure, yu hear. Mi daughter is as beautiful as you. Yes man, she will have many ivories to tickle…See those fingers? She is going to be a musician, just like her father. See Emily, we can't hide from the genes. Talking about that, I am writing a song for some youth called Marley. The guy is a prophet man. Been playing with his band on weekends. Lots of fun but I have enclosed a picture so that you can see me in my high life with tails and all. I love this new music bad…bad but for you, I'd do anything. Suppose you could still love me as rude boy musician?

Bunny.

A tear fell on the paper. Amelie dabbed it up quickly and wiped her eyes. The next letter she held so that even if she cried, the tears would not destroy her father's words.

Dearest Bunny,

You are as handsome as ever and as hardheaded. How can respectable artist play music in a rum bar at nights? Anyway, how long now do you think? I 'm cutting out all the names of the music festivals in England, all the colleges, and music related stuff so you can have them when you get here. There is a Schumann concert tonight. I am going with the children. You'll still have to wear you high life suit when you get here, I'm afraid! Well, I suppose you know that…But if you decide to come and join a ragamuffin band in Brixton. I promise I'll still love you…Give Joy a big kiss for me. I owe her a letter. The girls are doing well and we miss you.

Amelie gasped at the word Schumann. Her father loved Schumann. Tears were now flowing unabashedly and she did not try to stop them. She opened two more letters. Her mother must have had every intention of giving her these earlier or why would she have written the letters on carbon copy paper?

Dear Emily…

The days are long without you. I miss you and I can't wait to meet my daughter. Do you suppose Randy and Ashley will accept me as a step-dad? Are they still taking piano lessons? What about you? I miss you all…Bob is a true genius…but even him can't keep me away from you…another month at the most and I will be holding you in my arms…

Amelie tried to imagine her father's life. He seemed like a great guy from the letters. He was a man who'd given up his art to be respectable and for love. She had given up her art, too, for a different reason but still succumbing to the pressures of those who could never understand. Now inside of her something was growing. Something strong and bold and affirming.

• • •

It was the last week in October and the weather was beginning to cool down. After the scalding heat in Jamaica, Amelie welcomed the season change. Pulling on a light cardigan Amelie went to stand in front of the mirror on the wall of her music room. Alongside it, she held up a picture of her father, whose most noticeable feature were the long fingers crossed on his lap. Amelie held out her hand examined her own long, slender fingers, turning her hand over and over again. She had his eyes too. Deep, smiling eyes. She put the picture in her skirt pocket when she heard Robb's keys in the door. She quickly closed the door to her music room.

"Yooohooo. Honey, I am home. Amelie."

Robb, who knew her like a well-read book, passage, and verse, was aware that something out of the ordinary had happened in Jamaica. He also knew he'd find her in the music room. When he opened the door, she was staring at her hands.

"Something wrong with your fingers? Are you in pain?"

"Not that I know of. Just wondering why God gave them to me if I can never realize my dream."

"Why are you talking poppycock again? Amelie, when people are afraid of success, they unwittingly sabotage their dream. Look how you made up the story that Dr. Vlachenko would never see you again. Now in a month or so you'll be playing Carnegie Hall. What are you planning to do this time?"

"Or Robb, the explanation could be that if you have no roots you have no wings. What about that?"

"Roots, huh? Well, roots they're overrated."

"No, they are not. If I'm going to fulfill my destiny, I had to find out who I really was."

"Fair enough, now what?"

"I was just checking out my features when you came in. My hands in particular. Mummy said not only was I the spitting image of my dad, I have his fingers down to this little tuft of hair on my pinky. What do you think?" she handed him the only picture she had of her father.

"She talked about your Dad?"

"And much more, I'm afraid."

Robb waited.

"My father was a musician turned college professor. And Ashley and Randy are only my half-sisters."

"Come again," Robb said, easing his body on the piano stool next to her.

"I'm illegitimate. Their father is not my father. My father was my mother's first husband but she ran off and left him and then became pregnant for him while she was married to Randy's and Ashley's dad. He, apparently was an amazing musician, imagine that. He played five instruments but his love was base guitar. His name was Bunny Higgenbottom and he played with Bob Marley. But he was a classical pianist and guess who his favorite composer was. Schumann."

"Wow," Robb cupped his chin, "But wait. Technically, you're not illegitimate. This Bunny Higgenbottom was your mother's first husband, right? They just did it backward."

Amelie drew her eyebrows together. "That is so true."

The point seemed to make Amelie feel somewhat better. "Can you imagine a name like Amelie Higgenbottom? Sounds like a character out of *My Fair Lady*," Amelie scoffed.

"Wrong continent."

"No dear, Jamaica might as well have been England. The colony thing, you know."

"Point taken. But it wouldn't matter. I'd still have changed your name to Mercer. What did Ashley and Randy say when they found out? I can't imagine that any news could change a thing between you sisters."

Amelie didn't answer right away. "My bombshell wasn't the worse. Randy told mother what happened to her at thirteen. Our Uncle Joe molested her. Poor Uncle Joe. He was not quite right which makes it worse. Randy took good care of him too."

"You're kidding."

"Wish I was."

Robb reached for Amelie's hand. "The entire thing sounds heavy."

"Not as much as I thought it would be."

"I'm sure it's better to know than not, right?"

"It sure explains Randy's behavior over the years and it sure explains my silly musical muse. I'm not alien after all."

"Huh, I wouldn't go that far," Robb gave her a tight squeeze.

"I don't think anything can change our sister bond, ever."

"I know that to be true."

"You know what I need right now, Robb. Amelie slipped out of her skirt.

"What are you doing?" he busted out laughing.

"Showing you what aliens do to humans when they get cheeky." she winked.

"If you'd told me before that you were an alien and that your family members were Martians, I could have been a much happier man a long time ago."

Amelie pulled her husband to her. "Tell me human, how did I get so lucky?"

"Wanna find out?"

• • •

"Oh, Jesus." Amelie woke with a start.

Robb stirred and pulled her close. "Wanna do it again, alien?"

"Holy shit, I missed the train. Dr. Vlachenko is surely gonna can me now."

"He'd never do that. He wants this as much as you do. He waited his whole life to find another him…you are that for him, Amelie. Get dressed I'll drive you over."

"Truth that. Jamaican saying," Amelie explained locking lips with her friend, husband, and lover. Her body stirred but she could not stay.

She was still late. Dr. Vlachenko kept her waiting for a full fifteen minutes. He barely looked at her when he yanked open the door waving her casually to the music room and returning to his phone call.

Amelie sat at the piano and stared at the instrument. She began playing softly. Her eyes closed as she felt inside of her the music. Through the music, she connected with her father. She told him her story and listened to his. She felt a soft touch, a hint of a feathery breeze against her nape. She played on and inside of her she knew that the something missing had been returned. When she looked up Dr. Vlachenko was leaning against the door.

"You are the best damn pianist in all of New York. Too bad you have no discipline." He walked toward her. "I've dreamed all my life of a student like you. With you in the world, I knew the music would never die. You are the secret vessel, the conduit between past and present. But you are squandering your gifts with all this emotional doubt…gifts passed down through generations only get perfected in a few. Tell me…are you ready?"

"I am ready," Amelie said, "to accept my gift as the vessel to my eternity. I am ready to be all that you ever imagined I could be and more."

"Then my dear, find your own way home."

CHAPTER THIRTY-FOUR
Ashley

Europe, 2003

THEY DECIDED TO DO the trip backward. First Paris, then Cannes and finally Monaco. Paris was Paris, rife with ceaseless strikes, but Cannes was a true fairytale and certainly the liveliest pleasure port in the Côte d'Azur. Though it was not the film festival, Ashley hobnobbed with celebrities and power brokers in attendance at an exclusive celebration thrown by Prince Albert. She enjoyed every bit of the VIP treatment lavished on the jet set. From private screenings at the Palais des Festivals to shopping on the exclusive Rue d'Antibes, there was never a dull moment.

On the nights when Mel had late meetings and she was free, she'd dine with fashion celebrities on *Soupe au Pistou* and *Salade Niçoise* in the elegant La Belle Otéro restaurant of the Carlton Intercontinental. Or, she'd simply sit, with great contentment, on the balcony of her rented apartment looking out on the sea and the islands of Lérins. Her scenic meditation was interrupted by a knock on her door. She padded through the suite and answered the door. "You're finished early," she said.

"Yes. We leave early tomorrow for Monte Carlo." Mel said, his business concluded in Cannes. "Are you ready for your close up?'

• • •

The following day a stretch Mercedes picked them up for the trip to Monaco. The scenery and winding roads were incredible. The smells of herbs, fields of lavender and good country air were calming. They barely spoke as Melvadore slept on and off. He must have been very tired. He had been very busy in Cannes. Ashley, snuck peeks at him but mostly watched the scenery passing by. This was entirely surreal and she'd pinched herself a few times to make sure it wasn't a dream.

"Have you been staring at me all the way?" Melvadore stretched and looked at her through half closed eyes.

"No. Why would I do that when the scenery outside is far better?"

"You wish." He reclosed his eyes.

Ashley, who'd dressed to the nines, was unprepared for the steep climb up to the Grimaldi, Palais du Prince once the driver let them off at the foot of the hill as no car could go further. Unabashed, she pulled off her shoes and handed them to Rolon, the driver who followed behind. In New York, she'd rather have died than consider such an option but Monaco was as clean as the heavens above.

"I can't imagine what it's like to live like this," Ashley said, "What a Cinderella story."

"Until Princess Grace's tragic accident, it was indeed such. So, you see, even Cinderella stories sometimes have bad endings. Grace's death was a tragedy. I miss her."

"You mean you knew her?"

"Why, of course."

"You did. You really did. How come?"

"The circle, I suppose. My parents. The fishbowl of the wealthy is quite small. Shall we go up and see Princess Grace's tomb?"

"Yes, I'd like that." Though not a travel ignoramus or the ugly American, Ashley felt quite provincial next to the supremely, worldly Melvadore Follette.

"Tomorrow we'll have lunch with the family. Today we take in the sights."

• • •

Later that Afternoon.

"That's as much of my money as Albert is getting from me," Melvadore said pulling her away from the slot machine.

"They own the casino too?"

"They own pretty much everything in Monaco. Come on let's go to the center of town. I want to show you something."

Now back down at the square, after losing a few thousand Euros in the Casino, Melvadore and Ashley decided to spend the afternoon window-shopping along the golden circle of the Grand Piazza. When they got to Joaillier's row Mel pulled her into his favorite store.

"Unbelievable," Ashley exclaimed at the size of a yellow diamond on display in H. Stern's window. "I've ever seen a gem that big outside of a museum."

"My wife said the same thing the first time I brought her here. Let's take a closer look?" Mel said, hitting a discreet buzzer.

"Your wife?" Ashley was shocked but more so by the

gnawing in her heart.

"My ex-wife. We divorced fifteen years ago."

"Monsieur Follette, welcome. Good to have you back." The doorman smiled, "It's been too long."

Ashley did the best to hide her disappointment that Mel, as she had come to think of him, had never told her he'd had a wife. Then again, he hadn't told her much of anything!

"Miss Isabel was here only last week."

"How much money did she spend Gustav?" Melvadore asked, a smile creasing his face.

Gustav smiled and stepped aside for them to enter.

Inwardly, Ashley was fuming as Mel chatted away to the attendants in French. Isabelle. Who the hell was that? Did this man have a woman in every port?

"Let's have a look at this diamond. Do you want to try it on?" Melvadore asked Ashley.

"No thanks," Ashley who striding toward the door though she felt like running, said over her shoulder.

"I thought you liked the ring?" Melvadore said trailing behind her.

"I do like it. But, why do I have to try it on? That's entirely unnecessary. Outside where she could breathe again, Ashley added, "You should have your Isabelle try it on? Remember what they say, happy wife, happy life, and diamonds make wives happy."

"Isabelle? Isabelle is my sister."

"Isabelle is your sister? I didn't know you had two sisters!"

"I don't. Isabelle is Nemba. Her real name is Isabelle Follette Zahar. Nemba is my nickname for her. I'll tell you that story one day."

"Oh Mel," Ashley grabbed his arm. "Why didn't you tell me that in Bermuda?"

"Because it didn't come up! I guess then that I should tell you that my Islamic name is Al-Shahid Melvadore Follette Zahar."

Ashley interrupted him before he could finish. "I'm so sorry. You don't have to tell me anything. I'm acting silly like some crazy girlfriend." She took a step backward letting go of his arm.

"Why not be silly? I actually like that you think of me that way. As a boyfriend?"

"I don't really care. Honestly, I don't. It's just…" Ashley recovered returning to her brusque countenance. "What I meant was I…oh never mind. We should go." Ashley had forgotten what a neat feeling it was having someone to talk with or to have someone who somehow seemed to belong in her life. Was she falling for Melvadore Follette? Nah. No way! They'd just been spending too much time working together. Artificial feelings and transference. Satisfied, but not convinced with her rationalization, Ashley said, "Mel I think it's time to go home." There was mild panic in her voice. Now she was calling him Mel! She needed time to process what the hell was going on with her.

Instead of retreating, he closed the distance between them and cupped her face. His touch silenced her and for a brief second, she rested her cheek in his palm. Coming to her senses, Ashley yelled, "Now. I want to go now." Quickly turning away, she headed in the direction of the car.

Inside the car Mel said. "Did you know that when you're frightened your nose twitches?"

"Please," Ashley laughed out loud. A nervous laugh. "Don't try it. It'll be hard to get me to fall so easily."

"It's true." Mel was not confused about what he felt for the woman beside him. From the moment she'd said she'd never leave him, he had fallen hopelessly in love with her.

Moreover, she was the woman who seemed to understand him best. She was the woman he needed.

• • •

Back in her hotel suite, Ashley quickly went to her room, kicked off her shoes and flopped down on the couch. What the hell was the matter with her acting like some country idiot? Exhausted she sprawls out on the salmon sofa without covering it with fresh towels or whipping out her purple UV light to do cleanliness inspection. Seven stars or not she knew what went on in luxury hotel rooms. "I need a drink," she said out loud but was too tired to get up.

"Cote du Rhone," he held up a bottle, "or something else." The voice came from the doorway.

"What are you doing here? How did you get in?" Ashley bolted upright.

"You left the door open, but if you don't mind that drink sounds great."

Ashley was too exhausted to fight. "I thought Muslims didn't drink?"

"They don't advertise it."

"Right. I know at least five Afghanis who could drink you under the table. When we couldn't find bottled water my guide, Hag gave me vodka."

"Leftover from the Russians, I'm sure."

"Still alcohol."

"Don't say that too loudly. You could have a man killed."

"Do you still miss Afghanistan?" Ashley asked

"Every day."

"Surely it's safe to return home by now."

She waited for him to answer but he didn't. At the bar, he was clinking ice cubes into glasses. Ashley stretched out on the couch, her eyes heavy.

"Why are we here?"

"I can make you a star," he finally said, handing her a glass. Mel took a sip of his wine. He watched her over the rim of his glass.

"Am I ready?"

"More than ever."

Mel sat on the sofa. Ashley was keenly aware that she wanted him closer. In fact, the thought struck her like a bolt of lightning; she wanted him close forever. Close so he could talk to her while she took out her rollers in the mornings. Close so they could fight over the bathroom when they got ready for work and most definitely close at nights so she could curl up in his arms and feel safe. Close so she could experience what her mother had given up her life to experience. Love.

Melvadore's cell phone rang. He got up from the sofa and went to the opposite end of the room and began speaking in Arabic as easily as he had spoken in French earlier. Ashley could not understand a word but the look of concern that crossed his brow deepened. Melvadore walked from one end of the room to the other as he spoke rapidly into the phone. She could make out Nemba's name and nothing else. Within a few minutes, Melvadore ended the call and came back to sit on the sofa.

"Is everything okay?" Ashley eyed him.

"Yes. Everything is fine. Why do you ask?"

"Well, you seemed worried and you're speaking *Dari*."

Melvadore took a sip of his drink. "I often speak *Dari* to my family. That was Nemba."

"Why didn't Nemba come to the States with you?" Ashley asked.

"She did. She still has an apartment in New York but prefers Europe and Bermuda."

"Bermuda seems like a really odd place for a person like you to have a business."

"*Landilow* is a faux business. It's a vacation home really. I rarely take people there. It's more for Nemba than it is for me. But it's convenient as it's so close to the US, it's a tax haven and you can't argue with the weather."

"Why did you get a divorce?" Ashley twirled the wine glass in her hand. The wine was exquisite.

"You're full of questions today. Are you trying to get to know me? I like that."

"I'm just curious." Ashley was flooded with feelings and immediately her antennae zoomed upwards and red warning sirens went off in her head. She had to consciously reprogram her thoughts which said flee.

"Bianca was tired of me working so hard. She found herself a nice prince with time on his hands," Melvadore answered.

"She betrayed you," Ashley said, knowing the feeling all too well.

Melvadore paused before he answered. "Betrayed? No, I wouldn't say so. It's human nature to want to be with someone you love. I wasn't the right person for Bianca but I think I might be right for you."

"If you make a commitment you should honor it.

If you don't that's betrayal in my book."

"Are you saying you've been betrayed? Or never loved?"

Ashley said. "I swore off love when I was nineteen years old. I'm was always a woman on purpose and love does nothing but derails dreams. It's not for me."

"Nineteen? Broken hearts are what life is all about at nineteen. That can't be the reason you swore off love," Mel said.

"That depends on the life one has lived before then. I come from a home where love seemed to cause nothing but destruction. Trust and hope. Isn't that the bases of love? None here." Contrary to the words that left her mouth Ashley felt little beads of perspiration trickling down her back and the embers that warned that if she acted, what was about to happen was no booty call.

"You can't let someone else dictate your life. Betrayal is fear and cowardice. The right love is inspiring and giving. You should try again," Melvadore said.

"That's what my psychiatrist says."

"Love can replace him too." Melvadore pulled her into his arms.

Here comes the pain was all Ashley could think about when she shouted, "Stop. Please stop," she pulled herself away from the embrace.

"Your nose is twitching," he leaned over and kissed the tip of her bewitched nose.

"Please. Let's just be friends. Really, Melvadore I can't go there again," Ashley said moving out of his reach.

"But you've never been here before. I can assure you."

A pain shot down Ashley's arm and she was convinced she was having a heart attack.

"What happened that made you so scared to be loved?"

"As I said, love is for people who trust. I have a very hard time in that department. In fact, I don't have that in me at all. Childhood conditioning that's all."

"But when we become grown, we put away childish things. Anyway, you are lying." He twitched his nose.

"No really, I'm not. Melvadore," Ashley jumped up from the chair. "I think I'm having a heart attack," she said rubbing her left arm. "I'm having a pain…"

Melvadore pulled her back down to the sofa. "Maybe you are. But not the one you think you're having. Why can't you believe me?" he said sliding his hand down her back. "Have I ever steered you wrong?"

Ashley was about to protest when she felt his hand unzipped her from her dress. "Shall I change your perspective," his hand in the small of back paused.

Ashley's body was rising, singing and all too soon trembling under Mel's touch. "But I really think I'm having a heart attack," she whispered.

"Nothing I can't handle," he eased the dress down her body. "You are as beautiful as I imagined," Mel ran his hand down the length of her body. He pulled her to him and kissed the nape of her neck. For minutes he just rested his head in the cradle of her neck.

Ashley wondered what he was doing. Mel, eased her backward, his weight bearing down on her, he looked deeply into her eyes as his hand stroked her hair. Ashley blinked. She was petrified and had an idiotic grim on her face. She could feel it.

"What could be better than dying in the arms of the man you love? Trust me, Ashley," he said as the dark cloud over her heart faded to a glimmer of light.

The smile on Ashley's face faded too and then her eyes clouded. "Mel," Ashley said, her voice trembling as she spoke, "please, please I beg of you don't hurt me. I can only be brave without pain. I've worked my entire life to avoid this moment please…"

"What you're feeling is love, my darling. It comes with guarantees but not freedom. Let it be what it must." This time the other shoe dropped as Melvadore lifted her to the bed, and their lips met. He kissed her as none had ever done before and again and again made her cry out with joy. She had never kissed any other man but Frederick…sex yes…kissing no…kissing implied intimacy…she had been captured….

"Do you need me?" his breathing was uneven.

"I…I…"

"Do you need me?" He yanked her head backward arching her body. He covered her areola with feather touches. "Do you want me?" he repeated.

"I'm not sure…please…yes…I want you." Her voice sounded like a ventriloquist…her desire tingling every inch of her body.

"And do you need me?"

"Yes." Ashley heard herself say.

• • •

Melvadore was still sleeping when Ashley's eyes flutter open. She was butt naked in bed with her boss! She snuck a peek at him, studying in detail her sleeping Idol, Melvadore. So, this is what sex and love feel like? She liked it. Sitting on the edge of the bed she took in his physicality, the sharp nose, the pitch-black hair that
caressed his shoulders and the deep hue of his smooth skin. How old was he anyway? And, what had he done to her? Ashley felt the blood rushing into her face and was
embarrassed at the memory of how she'd begged him to do it again…and again. Sweet love. Was all this real? Was she really in love again after all these years? Could a love of such speed be real? What if he changed when they got back to the USA? What if…he finally tired of her? Ashley eased herself from the bed, deciding she was famished.

A strong arm tightened its grip. "Where are you going?"

"I'm a little hungry."

"Still hungry after all this?" he kissed her.

Ashley knew she was in love. Not in this friggin' life would she kiss a man much less kiss a man with after sex breath.

Melvadore rolled over to watch her.

She was, to her own surprise, not self-conscious at her nakedness. "I'm still hungry." She slipped from his embrace. Turning full frontal, she asked. "Where are we dining tonight? I might have to go shopping."

"We are dining here…so come back to bed after breakfast. We have an early flight tomorrow," Mel got out of bed and padded to the bathroom, his body firm and vital stirring her and she quickly dropped her gaze. She could hear him streaming and was so taken back that she sat on the bed in awe. She, Ashley Freeman, was in a hotel with a man who was in the bathroom peeing. She listened as the water came on and listened as he began a warble in the shower. She'd never been around a man this long after sex to appreciate sex's natural rhythm. Tears touched her eyes and she prayed, prayed hard that he would not betray her.

Melvadore, wrapped in a towel began splashing aftershave on his face. Where did that come from, she wondered? It was her room. She left him to take her own shower.

Today she would interview HRH Prince Rainier, III. This Ashley though was definitely not her life. Melvadore did not accompany her. He said he had errands to run and he'd visit with the family later. He arranged an additional driver for her. Ashley dressed conservatively and was on her best behavior. The Prince was gracious and forthcoming. When she left the palace, she had wings on her feet. Their interview had gone longer than she had planned and it was now nearing 5:30 p.m. She rushed back to the hotel.

When she returned Melvadore was coming through the adjoining door straightening the white bow tie of his Tuxedo.

"I see you took the liberty of unlocking the door."

"I did."

"Thought you said we were having room service?"

"We are."

"Then why are we getting dressed up? We could stay in our robes. It would make things easier," she teased.

"I don't think you want to make the maître'd uncomfortable, do you? How was the interview? Isn't the Prince princely?"

Before she could answer the doorbell rang. Mel answered it.

Ashley dashed into the bathroom for a quick shower and soon re-joined Mel. Not to be outdone, she donned a gold lame dress.

Hermitage, a haven of opulence was considered one of the most splendid hotels in Europe and lived up to its reputation with style and grace. Hotel Hermitage offered spacious suites which were more like a luxurious apartment. The private dining room opening onto a marble terrace overlooked The Harbour of Monte Carlo and The Prince's Palace. The terrace with its twinkling lights at night and by day, the turquoise waters of Monte Carlo was a memory she would not soon forget.

A sous-chef, maître'd, waiter and sommelier entered the dining room pushing in front of them a portable kitchen. The waiter handed her a single rose. "For Mademoiselle," he smiled, before placing an exquisite floral centerpiece on the white linen tablecloth. The lavish place settings were executed to perfection. Candles were lit and Mel and Ashley were seated for what turned out to be a seven-course meal which included, *Soupe de Poisson, Loup de Mer au fenouil, fromage tomme de chévre de Montagne, filet mignon* and bottles of Viognier. After the main course, the pastry chef arrived with fresh fruit sorbet and chocolate soufflés. After dinner, the table on the balcony was set with after dinner wines from the region. A virtuoso promptly took his seat at the ebony Steinway in the main suite.

"What music pleases, Madam?" he asked, liltingly.

"Debussy, Liszt, Bach or Ravel," Ashley answered, completely beguiled by the evening and the music of her childhood.

For two hours, while they drank and looked into each other's eyes and across at the lights of Monaco, Francois commanded the Steinway. Ashley was speechless. She felt like pinching herself but didn't want to wake up if she was dreaming.

"Mel," she said softly. "This has been the best day of my entire life." Tonight, she'd follow him to the end of the earth and certainly to the moon and the stars above.

"Good," he said puffing on a Cuban cigar the hotel had sent up along with a specially distilled bottle of perfume called Ashley.

Ashley removed the stopper from the perfume and inhaled. It smelled like the freshness of spring. Light, airy and unforgettable. She dabbed it behind her ears and her wrists.

"Shall we dance," he asked extending his hand to her. Ashley stood up. Unable to contain her emotions any longer she rested her head in the crook of his shoulder and soaked his expensive black silk jacket. "If I should die tonight," she whispered, "this day would have been worth being born for. I would have fulfilled my purpose in life."

"And what is that?" he kissed away her tears.

"Loving you, if only for one night."

"Isn't that a song? You know, darling," he pulled her close. "You said, and I repeat verbatim, 'do you think you can ever make me fall in love with you. Do you think you can change everything I believe in and know?'"

"I hadn't yet become fully human," she raised her face, and looking deeply into his inky eyes, she kissed him.

Mel beckoned the musician to stop. "Send in the Masseuses," he said.

"Masseuses?"

"Yes. We are having his and hers massage so we can rest well before our journey."

Ashley burst into laughter. "You're crazy."

"My mother always said that. She said it was from my father's side."

"You're kidding. My mother always said that to us."

"If that's not a sign," Mel laughed.

They went into the bedroom, dressed in the fluffy robes provided by the hotel and climbed onto side-by-side massage tables that had been wheeled into the room.

"Tell her what a great body I have," he instructed the Masseuse in English so Ashley could understand.

"*Magnifique*," the woman said and winked.

Ashley had a male Swedish masseur.

"Tell him," Ashley said, "that I am Halle Berry's only rival."

"Tell her," Mel continued but this time in French, "That I'd like her to marry me. Give her this."

The woman beamed at Ashley. "*Mademoiselle*." She handed Ashley the ring on a velvet cushion, "Will you marry him?"

Ashley jumped from the table, barely covering herself with her towel and ran to Mel. She looked at him for a full two minutes before answering yet there was no fear or doubt in her when she said. "*Oui*. Please tell him *oui*, *oui*. *Oui*."

• • •

Phillip rushed off the set to catch his ringing cell phone. The one Mel had given him to call them if necessary.

"What took you so long?"

"I was on set. Where are you?"

"I'm in the car waiting for Mr. Follette and I have to talk fast." Ashley was whispering.

"Why the Gestapo voice, Snookums?

"An intruder," Ashley gasped.

"Where? At your house now? When did you get back? Silly girl, call the police now!"

"In my heart."

"What? Ashley, what's the matter with you?"

"Mr. Follette," Ashley gushed. "He's invaded my heart and now I'm getting married."

"WHHHHAT! You're not!"

"Yes, I am."

"How the hell did he get in? Did he have a crowbar?" Phillip was picking his lip up off the floor. Never in his lifetime had he expected Ashley to marry a man. Since he'd known her, she had gotten rid of men as often as she changed shoe…sometimes within minutes of their meeting. The last fake, as she termed the guy who always flashed his Black Card but never used it, got booted for leaving a strand of hair in her sink.

"I wish I knew but I'm so sure," Ashley was laughing.

"Either that or that man must have been a locksmith in his last life. Oh, I'm so damn happy for you," Phillip said. "Where are you?"

"Monaco. Gotta go. He's coming."

"Who were you talking to?" Mel asked as he got into the car beside her.

"Phillip."

"If I didn't know that man was gay, I'd be jealous as hell. Now buckle up," he reached over and strapped her into the seat. She held his hand in place.

"How do you know that Phillip is gay?"

"His fingernails."

"Huh?'

"Oh, never mind. Now let's talk about how to handle the media once we get back."

"Hey," Ashley's voice was smoky. She was not interested in reality just yet. "When we are in the air, would you like to join the mile-high club?" Ashley began unbuttoning her blouse suggestively.

"Huh. I knew it! Once the river opens it flows to the sea. I can't wait." He kissed her, sliding his hand along her thigh. And he wasn't joking. Little did Melvadore know he'd unleashed the randiest devil in Ashley. They just couldn't get enough of each other.

Back at the station the following morning, Ashley burst into Melvadore's office, locked the door and begin undressing.

"This is a place of business, Ms. Freeman. You should control yourself."

"No one can see us, it's a one-way mirror."

"Are you sure about that?"

"I don't care," Ashley hurriedly dropped her skirt.

"Woman you're a temptress," his eyes crinkled before he said. "Follow me."

Behind the tropical garden was their den of ill repute.

• • •

Ashley hadn't told a single soul at WNBC, other than Phillip about her engagement to Melvadore Follett though the stares as she walked the halls of WNCB were an indication that the news had already reached the newsroom. She wasn't exactly hiding it as there was no way to hide the rock on her third finger left hand, yet she wasn't flaunting it either as she was still waiting for the other shoe to drop. Ashley decided however that it was time to tell her family. They were each so busy they hadn't had their sister lunch date as usual. She dialed Amelie.

"Hey, girl."

"How important is this call Ashley," Amelie said. "I'm running out to meet Dr. Vlachenko. I have rehearsals and I can't be late."

"I'm getting married."

"What? Did you say married?"

"Yep. That's what I said."

"Oh crikiey. Ashley that's wonderful." And then Amelie stopped dead in her tracks. "Who are you marrying?"

"My boss."

"No way. I thought he was just your boss."

"He was until last week. We got engaged in Monaco."

"Wow. Have you guys set a date?"

"Yep. February 16th, on my birthday."

"What? You can't plan a wedding in four months!" Amelie gasped.

"Of course not. I can't but I hired a full-time staff to do it."

"What's the hurry?" Amelie asked.

"I can't wait. I've waited my entire life for this man and I'm scared to wait too long in case he evaporates."

"OMG. This is amazing…just let me get through my concert and I'll plan everything for you. Have you told Randy?"

"My next call. I'd like to tell her myself if you don't mind."

Randy screamed so loudly on the phone, Ashely had to hold the receiver from her ear.

"I just can't believe any of this. You sly devil."

CHAPTER THIRTY-FIVE
Amelie

Connecticut, 2003

AMELIE'S CONCERT, only a week away, brought a flurry of activity to the household. William, Kyla, and baby Robb William Mercer had arrived three days before and were on their way to picking up Emily at the airport. Robb was dealing with the caterers who were hired for the pre-party since it was Thanksgiving. Amelie had been adamant that there should be no party but to no avail. Who knows if there would be something to celebrate? Amelie had been sequestered in her music room all morning. When the doorbell rang Robb answered it.

"Hey," Ashley and Randy sauntered in. "Is she crazed?"

"Beyond."

"Is Mother here yet?" Ashley asked.

"No. William and Kyla went to get her."

"Do you think we can disturb the Maestro?"

"Not yet. Let's wait until everyone is here. Let me hang those coats and I'll get you some tea. Randy, how is June?"

"She's amazing and she's so sorry she couldn't get back in time for the recital. She made a video of her journey that I'll show at the after party. What can we do to help?"

"Nothing. Aren't you going to show me the bauble on your hand? I heard through the grapevine that you are engaged."

"Old news," Ashley held up her hand for inspection. It was just over a month since she'd gotten engaged and she still could not believe it.

Keys clicking in the front door alerted new arrivals. "I think that maybe your Mother now." Robb pulled open the door.

"Aunt Randy, Aunt Ashley," William greeted his aunts. "How are you? Grandma," he called back to Emily who was walking up the driveway, "Everyone is here."

"Hi Mother," Ashley kissed her mother on the cheek. They were all inching their way back to love.

"Hi," Emily greeted her daughter.

"Mother," Randy, awkwardly embraced her mother. "It's good to see you."

"Same here." Emily held on to Randy as long as she could without it getting awkward.

"What do you think of your great grand?" Robb asked as he embraced Emily.

"You've got a beautiful daughter-in-law and grand-baby. How do you feel being a grandpa?"

"Loving every moment of it. You could have another soon."

"Really? Is Emily pregnant."

"Oh Lord no, but Ashley here is the next likely candidate. She is getting married right?"

Ashley squirmed. She hadn't yet told her mother. "You know me, Mother. I wanted to make sure this was going to work out. No need getting your hopes up."

"Congratulations. I'll pretend I don't know until you tell me."

"Let me go find Mother," William said.

Robb was about to stop him but decided against it. It was time to rouse Amelie. "Don't be upset if she is a stick in the mud. She was dead set on not doing Thanksgiving this year since it was before the concert. I had to put my foot down on this. She has been working so hard and I really wanted her to have a break and the support of her family before her big day. Plus, it'll take Amelie's mind off the obvious. She rarely came out of her cave these days, I hope she comes out now."

She came out ate dinner and went right back to her studio.

• • •

Carnegie Hall, November 27, 2004

November 27th brought with it a beautiful crisp day. The air was warm and fresh, the temperature a gentle 50 degrees. Amelie, who had barely seen the family at Thanksgiving was now anxious to make sure they had arrived on time and were seated in their reserved seats. "Is my family here yet?" she asked a dozen times.

"Almost everyone is here," Robb was pleased to finally be able to say that.

"Who is not here?" Amelie asked.

"Ashley and Mel. But I'll let you know as soon as they arrive. Go on now and prepare yourself."

It was 7:30 pm and Amelie Mercer sat staring at herself in the dressing room mirror. The free-flowing emerald green dress, cinched at her waist with a pavé pin, shone too brightly under the harsh theatrical lighting. The fluid material moved with every turn of her body. She felt sick. She should never have chosen a dress the color of vomit! The black dress with crystal spaghetti straps and a billowing skirt would have been better. Or the sleek lamé she had tried on five times. Anything would have been better than a dress the color of bile.

Amelie took a deep breath filling her lower abdomen. Pulling the air deep into her lungs, she dropped her shoulders in an exaggerated exhale. Slowly, she rolled her head from side to side pulling back a fallen wisp of hair. She sat still and willed her body to join with spirit. In her mind's eye, she conjured up Schumann and his wife Clara for whom *Fantasie in C major*, *Opus 17* had been written. Schumann's melodic rises and peaks so clearly could she hear them ringing out over Leipzig peppered with the syncopation, hemiola, and cross-rhythms, symbolic of his tormented soul. Vividly, she watched him slip into soft, sweet refrain before every so quietly passing into the darkness of madness.

"Fifteen minutes," Dr. Vlachenko, followed by Enrique entered the room. "You will be wonderful my dear. Play tonight only for the music," he added, seeing the stricken look on her face.

Amelie's heartbeat strummed loudly blocking out her thoughts. She was descending into chaos but she was confident. *Father, I will make you proud tonight.*

"Is everyone here now?" she whispered to Robb.

"Yes, they are here. "Break a leg, sweetheart," Robb kissed her tenderly and left.

• • •

"Are you ready?" Enrique Gamba, the conductor of the New York Philharmonic asked calmly.

She nodded. There were no words. And if there were, they'd have been absorbed by the cotton balls that filled her mouth.

"Let's do it, Amelie," Enrique smiled warmly. "And stop worrying so much. You are infallible and a wonderful interpreter of this music. You, my dear, will delight the audience," he patted her shoulder.

Amelie again sat in front of the mirror. She looked up at the picture of her father hooked to its corner. Amelie Higgenbottom. Amelie Francis, Amelie Mercer. Amelie Higgenbottom Mercer. She felt calm…she was almost sure she'd heard her father's voice… 'Good luck darling…I'm right here with you.' Amelie rose and took her place behind the curtains. "*That's my girl,*" her musical muse chimed in. Waiting in the wings, she watched as Enrique parted the curtain and stepped out to greet an eager audience. Before taking his place in the conductor's box, where his elegant, passionate direction would add ritualistic gravity to her musical interpretation, he winked at her. Peeping from behind the curtain, Amelie caught a glance of the hall. Every seat in Carnegie appeared occupied. Why had so many people come to see her fail? Beads of perspiration formed on her forehead, under her armpits and her palms. She took a deep breath as the orchestra began warming up the audience with Symphony No.2. "I am here too," the voice said. It was her grandpa.

"Dr. Vlachenko," Amelie began, as the orchestra's number came to a close. He motioned her to be quiet. He would not indulge her doubt. Fear crept up her toes, along her spine up to the nape of her neck. As fear enveloped her, she began to shake. Amelie felt a touch on her hand. She had thought it was Dr. Vlachenko but when she looked up, he was still across the room.

"Ladies and gentlemen," she heard Enrique begin his introduction. "Good evening, again. Our wait is over and you are in for an evening of exquisite mastery. For the first time in twenty years, please welcome back to this stage, Amelie Mercer on piano."

Amelie heard her name but couldn't move. She was seized in the grips of an irrational sense of terror. The Orchestra played. They would until she appeared at the curtain. It was happening again. She'd made a huge mistake. What was she doing here? Amelie looked fretfully at Dr. Vlachenko. "I'm so frightened," she whispered.

"I am here." Dr. Vlachenko smiled warmly at her. His smile seemed to free her. He believed in her. Her family believed in her. Her father believed in her. Her grandfather believed in her. She could do it. She knew she could. She wasn't going to let them or herself down. She believed in herself. Amelie took a deep breath, parted the curtains and stepped out onto the stage to thunderous applause. Unexpectedly her heart calmed as she walked to center stage. Amelie, a smile on her face, turned to face the audience and bowed deeply. She saw her mother first, then scanned the room for the rest of her family. After what seemed like an eternity, Amelie turned toward the Steinway D Grand concert piano and sat. Her heartbeat surged then slowed.

The orchestra began the first movement of *Opus 17*. Amelie's fingers poised in readiness waiting for her cue. She took a deep breath and nodded discreetly to Enrique. *You chose this life*, her Muse reminded her. *The life you always wanted. Now play.* That was when she heard it, the downbeat. Amelie's fingers struck chords without missing a beat. Her fingers took on a life of their own, as her music filled the hall. Her heartbeat quickened, her body tensed and adrenaline surged through her as the virtuosity of the piece overtook her. Amelie's body bent to the work, her face conveying the spirit of the music. Her fingers climbed through arpeggios and then slowed softly into ritardando to deliver flawlessly the march of the second movement. The convergence and complexity of the music, finally willingly subsided into a masterful exposition. She was in control. Her technical display was infallible. She would never doubt herself again. She was home and she knew it. She also knew that backstage, Dr. Vlachenko was smiling.

At that moment, Amelie released totally. Closing her eyes and trusting her memory, she allowed herself to be spirited away with the music. She was rising and falling with the second movement. Her hair stuck to her forehead with sweat as her hands moved gracefully and easily over the keys and the tension, well sustained in the pedal, expressed her phraseology, achieved the tonal color of the music, and shaped the melody, harmony, and counterpoint into beautiful ritornelle. She had gone there, her body, as well as the notes, interpreted the music. She drew vitality from the music. She was the music. And right beside her, her father and grandfather were smiling. She played on. She played for them all but most of all she played for herself. Her body lifted. Her music rose and her soul found
its place. Tonight, her playing was technically brilliant and flawless. As she shaped the interpretation of *Opus 17,* she searched for its sonority, its color, its mystery, its brio, and she'd found it. Schumann *Fantasie in C major. Opus 17.* The piece, thirty-three minutes long had come to an end.

The audience was on its feet. Thunderous, wild applause caused her to look up. Where was she? She looked out at the sea of people but saw no one. She stood up, bowed, and in an instant was behind the curtain. She was drained. She had risen out of herself and she needed a moment to come back. Dr. Vlachenko was hugging her. "You were beyond magnificent. Your playing is poetry in motion. You found something new tonight in the interpretation. Schumann would be pleased. Brava, Amelie. Brava," he was, unabashedly tearing up.

"Dr. Vlachenko," Amelie took her mentor's hand. "How can I thank you?"

"Don't you mean how can I thank you? Amelie, you were extraordinary, brilliant, genius."

"You are being kind."

"No, I'm not. You were extraordinary, brilliant and genius. Thank you," Vlachenko kissed her cheeks three times. "I pass my baton to you."

"I'm only that way because you're extraordinary, brilliant and genius. How can I thank you for sticking with me?" She was hugging him and she too was teary eyed.

"Now, now. You can't smudge your make-up. It's is only the beginning my *Moana*."

Amelie hugged him tighter.

"See you Monday morning," he said pushing her away. "We play Rachmaninov. I'm going to sneak out now if you don't mind. I've already had fifty mothers asking me to tutor their children."

"Any prodigies in the bunch?"

"I have no intention of finding out."

"Thank you, Dr. Vlachenko. Thank you so very much."

"Good. Good but I must get away now. I have *Zagrav* and cake for you at practice Monday. You can come at one o'clock instead of ten."

Amelie held on to his hands tightly, tears clinging to her lashes. "I owe you my life," she said softly.

The applause would not stop.

"You have to play more," Dr. Vlachenko pushed her back through the curtains. I have seen all I need to see. You have conquered your fears and the stage."

Amelie returned to stage. It was littered with bouquets of flowers, red, yellow, and white. She smiled at the audience. She bowed. She adjusted her seat and pulled down the mike.

"Thank you. Thank you all so very much. I have so many people to thank for bringing me back to the stage. My undying believer and musical rock Dr. Vlachenko. My grandfather, who started me on this road when I was three years old. My husband who as Dr. V says is a true saint. My family and all of you who are here tonight. Thank you. Thank you from the depths of my heart." Finally, her heart was home. Finally, an enrapt audience.

"This next song I will play is for my father who died way too young," Amelie said. "He was a gifted musician, a professor of Music who loved playing with the great Bob Marley. As I was made to understand, this was one of his favourite songs."

The riff to "No Woman No Cry" began.

Emily stared at her daughter, shameless tears streaking her cheek. How could I have stopped her from ever playing? Her father would be proud. So very proud.

• • •

When Amelie returned backstage Robb was waiting. He took Amelie's face in his hands. "You were wonderful," he kissed her smiling lips. "I'm damn proud of you, Chicken!"

"I could never have done it without you. Thank you for letting me find myself. Thank you for loving me in my imperfection."

Robb squeezed her to him, giving her another tender kiss and Amelie felt safe in his arms. "Robb."

"Yes, darling."

"Do you think it would be okay if we went home?"

"I thought you'd never ask. Everyone is waiting for us to arrive."

"Robb, do you know what I'm going to do tomorrow?"

Here we go again, Robb thought. "We're going to Italy after your practice?"

"No. I'm going to fill the house with roses from our garden.

"Beyond brilliant."

CHAPTER THIRTY-SIX
Ashley

New York, 2004

THERE WAS SOMETHING wrong about the morning. The ringing phone was relentless as Ashley, sitting cross-legged on the floor mired in wedding details stifled the feeling of being green in the gills. The queasiness was no match for the bristling hairs at the nape of her neck. "You'd think with all the money we paid those wedding planners they'd be on top of things! Thank heavens people only do this once or twice in a lifetime," she rubbed a hand across her nape trying to halt the flutter.

"Once for you, I can assure you, my dear."

"I don't know why I feel so blah," Ashley got up and headed in the direction of the bathroom.

"How about wedding jitters?" Melvadore planted a kiss on her forehead. "Tell me, Mrs. Follette…"

"Don't call me that until we are married. It's bad luck."

"I thought you were over that nonsense!"

"Old habits die hard." She smiled wanly.

Mel was right, she examined her neck in the mirror. Nothing. Wedding jitters turned to stress. Four months had zoomed by, but everything had come together nicely. Ashley was enormously proud of her family's efforts to make her day special, but it was Randy's efficiency that floored her. The woman had become her rock and was very much the big sister in charge. "Where did you learn these kinds of event planning skills?" Ashley had asked.

"Do you know how many charity balls I've been on planning committees for?" she answered. "Not to talk about Lawrence's dinner parties!"

"Ashley," Mel sat her on the bed when she re-entered the room. "There's something we have to discuss. I can't tell you everything yet but you'll have to trust me. Nemba, Abdullah and I have been secretly working on a project in Afghanistan. The fewer people know the better and the less you knew until now was important too."

"What kind of project?" He was finally going to tell her about Operation ED.

"The project doesn't itself matter at this time. In time. Just trust me. What you need to know is that I'll have to be gone for a bit. Is that going to be okay with you? Unfortunately, it'll be right after our marriage."

"I'm going to be your wife in 24 hours. When are you talking about leaving? You'll need to tell me everything. Let's agree to begin our life together with all our cards on the table."

"You're right. I don't have time to explain everything now but we'll talk when I get back from fitting my tux. About 4:00p.m. All our cards on the table."

"All our cards," Ashley said hoisting up from the bed.

Melvadore pulled her to him. "Never doubt how much I love you."

"Why would I ever do that?" She searched his eyes for the reassurance she'd find there.

"You shouldn't."

"I should be home no later than 5:00 pm. All cards on the table," she said sprinting to the bathroom as her stomach lurched with spasms.

When she came back into the room, Melvadore pulled her to him. "Let's be naughty one more time before we get married."

"What took you so long to ask?" Ashley kissed him and dropped her robe to the floor.

• • •

You would think everyone in her family was getting married. They all arrived at the fitting before she did. "I can't believe you are here. Is that a good or bad sign? Shouldn't the bride arrive earlier than the attendants?!"

"At least it's not the 4th damn it," Randy said. "Go get dressed."

Ashley stood on the pedestal for her final fitting while the seamstress examined her dress. It was perfect. It took the entire four months to have it designed and made. Flown in from Paris with its designer the night before, had put quite a strain on the seamstress to make final adjustments. But today, in her fitted oyster Duchesse dress, with its reinforced off the shoulder scoop neck dotted with Austrian crystals, Ashley looked divine. The Mikado silk headdress that flowed twelve-feet from a Swarovski crystal tiara edged in satin and lace ran the length of the little shop. "It is perfect!" the seamstress said clasping her hand. It is perfect. Just a small hem and we are done."

Slipping her feet into satin and lace sling-backs,

Ashley spun around and around in the mirror. As usual, with her extreme happiness came her extreme fear. Would Mel show up or would he desert her like Frederick?

"Be still," the seamstress snapped, her eyes rimmed in red from a lack of sleep. "Stop moving all around if you want me to get this done."

"I can't believe I'm getting married."

"Aren't you glad you waited all these years?" Amelie winked. "Mel is far more interesting than Frederick."

"Can you believe I was such a wuss?"

"Okay. You can move now. We're done. What do you think?" the seamstress asked.

Nervous, Ashley turned to her sisters. "How do I look?" she asked.

They too were on pedestals getting fitted in pale blue off the shoulder, satin dresses.

"You look divine," Amelie said. "You are music in motion."

"Divine," Randy tugged at her tight-fitting dress. Except for a slight bulge at her tummy, which was camouflaged with the swirl cut of the dress, she was pleasantly surprised at how good she looked.

"You two are so great together. And he's such a handsome man," Amelie said

"That he is," Emily said. "I still don't believe he's over fifty."

"It's love, darling. It makes us younger," Ashley suggested.

• • •

Ashley's cell phone rang. "Oh Lord, if this is another wedding call, I going to have a hissy fit.

These people call with the most asinine questions, every second on the hour.
What the heck did I hire them for if I need to be this hands on? I've already cut the guest list three times to give them less work to do."

"Three hundred and fifty guests are still too many," Randy said. "How do you know that many people?"

"Ask Mel." Ashley scrambled off the pedestal to find her purse. "Has anyone seen my damn purse?" Ashley started throwing clothes around. "Where's my damn purse?" she yelled.

"Here it is," Amelie said hoisting the oversized purse with effort. Ashley caught a look at herself in the floor-to-ceiling mirror. She was going to be a bride. Dear Lord in Heaven, tomorrow Saturday, February 16th, 2004 at 10:00 am she would be Mrs. Melvadore Follette. As Ashley grabbed her phone, she stared at the 10-carat Asscher cut rock on her hand. She was getting married! Unbelievable!

"You know," Emily came from the fitting room. "I have never looked good in yellow. My complexion is a little too pale. Do I look washed out?" Her relationship was growing with her girls and Ashley had consented for her mother to give her away. Emily had been pleased but, in some department, there could be no compromise. As the mother of the bride, Emily had made certain that she would stand out. The yellow, she had insisted would accent the blue and white to perfection but now she wasn't sure.

"It's too late for all that now so quit being so vain," Amelie warned.

"Why is someone wanting to look their best vain?" Emily asked.

"Mother!" Randy grunted.

"This is NOT about you, okay?"

Amelie stepped between them. Old habits did die hard. Around each other, as if in concert they were always on the verge of a mini explosion. Not with explosives detonating as before but with a mending of fences impatience. It seemed more of a ritual, a definition of who they were.

"Darn it," Ashley dug through the suitcase she called a purse. By the time she found the confounded phone, she'd missed the call. She pressed the call log and redialed the last number on the list. Sighing with gravity, she put the phone to her ear. All this hassle just to spend the rest of her life with the man of her dreams! She should have eloped. A year before, no one could have convinced Ashley that there was a man born into this universe who could make her feel this way.

"Hello," Ashley sang into the phone. "Yes. This is she…What? Speak up please you're breaking up…. Yes, Ashley Freeman. May I help you?" There was a pause. Ashley's face drained of all color. "No. He's not with me. Did you try his cell?" Ashley voice faltered, "or home?"

"We are getting an out of range signal on his cell. And his assistant has tried to reach him at all the usual places she tells us."

"What is it?" Ashley, what is it?" Amelie looked over at her sister.

Ashley beckoned her to be quiet. "Who are you?"

"This is Randall from WCNB. Mr. LaFlore, WCNB Canada is trying to reach him. Mr. Folette gave us your number as a contact. I hope you don't mind. By the way, congratulations on your marriage."

"Well, I wish I could help. He's probably at his tailor at this very moment," Ashley looked at her watch,

"fitting his tux? Knowing him he left his phone in his suit jacket. Give me your number. I'll ask him to call you. I should hear from him any moment really. In fact, I thought you were him. Thank you. Yes. We are getting married tomorrow," she reiterated…meaning stop bothering him on the day before his wedding.

"What is it?" Randy asked.

"Mel's Canadian station is trying to reach him. They are launching something or the other in the Canadian market. They've been unable to contact him. I'll try his cell," Ashley said dialing the number. No answer. She called his driver. "Where's Mr. Follette?"

"Haven't seen him this morning."

"What do you mean? Didn't you drive him to Valentine's?"

"No Ma'am. He told me last night he'd be driving himself around today. He joked that it would be his last day as a bachelor in his Porsche. Said he was going to buy a station wagon."

"Funny guy." Ashley hung up the phone. "Get my driver, will you Amelie. Tell him to bring the car around right now." Ashley was already shedding the wedding dress.

"Where are you going? Randy said gathering up belongings."

"This can't be happening." A pit landed in Ashley's gut. "This can't be bloody happening," Ashley's voice rose decibels.

Amelie rushed through the door to find Ashley's driver, Justin.

"Calm down, calm down," Randy said. "Don't overreact."

Ashley body began swaying. "I knew this would happen. I knew it," she said.

"Ashley, Ashley," Randy grabbed her sister's arm mid-air. "Nothing is happening. Mel has probably turned his phone off.

What are you doing?"

"I'm going to drive to Mel's tailor to tell him to turn on his damn phone."

"Shall I call the police to see if any accidents were reported?"

Ashley glared at Randy. "Why? Why must you go there?"

"I was just trying to cover all the bases. Sorry."

"When I find him, I'm going to give him a piece of my mind. How can you not have your phone on, on a day like today? How inconsiderate can he be?"

"Huh," Randy laughed, "welcome to married life. Shall I wait for the dress and bring it to the house?"

"Would you, please? Thanks."

"Where is this damn tailor anyway?" Amelie said.

Ashley called Ian, Mel's driver again to find out.

Fifteen minutes later they were pulling up in front of Valentine's. The discrete shop on Fifth Avenue was service by invitation only. Ashley rang the buzzer and a short, balding man appeared at the door. "Yes."

"Mr. Valentine. I'm Ashley Freeman."

"Yes. I know who you are. Melvadore is very proud of you. He carries pictures of you all around. He wanted me to find a tux that matched you. Imagine that. I've never had that request before."

"Thank God," Ashley whispered. "Would you ask Mr. Follette to come out for a moment, please? I'd like to see him."

"Ah, but he's not here. We were expecting him at two but he hasn't arrived yet. He's never late but a little tardiness today is expected, no? I suspect he's probably shopping for his bride," Renaldo Valentine winked. "He should be here soon. If you want you can wait."

Ashley stepped inside the immaculate showroom with its plethora of fine cloths. Over to the right was a waiting room appointed with Italian style furnishings.

"No. I won't wait but would you ask him to call as soon as he arrives? And tell him to please keep his phone on."

Renaldo nodded. "I hope you have a beautiful day tomorrow."

"Thank you."

Outside Ashley called Ms. Delaney. Nothing. She dialed the number on her call log, still nothing. She used the private phone he gave her to reach him anywhere, anytime. Nothing. Next, she dialed the Police.

"Were there any accidents reported involving a Porsche?" Ashley asked.

"Nothing is coming up. Wait a minute. There is something just posting about a black Porsche. Went over an embankment off the West Side Highway."

This couldn't be happening, tears were streaming down Ashley's face. Why God are you punishing me. She felt the meltdown beginning. "I'm afraid something might have happened to my fiancée. Please, I need you to check to see if you can get some information about that accident. He was driving a black Porsche, license plate CKX-5331.

A car matching Melvadore's was recovered in a ditch but was so badly burnt that not even the license plate was identifiable. Ashley's whimper turned to a wail.

"There was no one in the car, Ms. It was empty," the police informed when he called back. That night Mel never came home.

• • •

Ashley, in spite of her family's pleading, decided to show up at the church in her wedding dress the next day at 10:00 am.

Melvadore would show up! She sat very still in front of the mirror as Amelie helped her dress.

"You don't have to do this," Amelie pleaded.

"He'll be there." Ashley insisted. "It's as though you're accepting Mel's death and we don't know."

"If you believe…."

"He'll be there, damn it."

When Ashley and Amelie arrived, Father John, her friend, and minister came over to her.

"I'm so sorry, Ashley, Melvadore is not here."

"He will be…he will be…" Ashley's confidence wilted. "What am I to do now? Why did this have to happen now?"

They waited and waited.

"God knows all things," Father John reached for her hand.

"Then why would he take away the only man I have ever loved." The threatening tears slid down her face. "I…"

"Trust that He does know," Father John calm voice interceded. "Are you going to be okay?"

"I'm going to be okay." Ashley began wiping tears from her face. "I just can't be brave right now. She could hear AliBibi's voice and see in her eyes her dignity even in the face of the most trying challenges.

"Sacrifice is a part of life," she'd said.

"But how do you cope after a child sacrifices his life?" Ashley had asked.

'You just go through the pain. Stay there as long as it needs you and then walk back through it into the open air. The struggle goes on.'

"I have to stay in the pain until it's ready to release me." Ashley tried to smile. "You know, Father, love is a wonderful thing. People have known this for a long time, haven't they? "And they always will," he said squeezing her hand. "Love is a gift from God. It's a divine sacrament. Once you have experienced it you will be able to carry on."

"And I'll take his love with me and do something wonderful with it."

Beethoven's *Arioso Dolente*, a piano sonata depicting the journey through grief, was playing as Ashley walked over to her family.

"Darling," Emily held her daughter. "If I could take this all for you, believe me, I would." Emily's eyes clouded with her own pain, remembering how she felt that Wednesday when Bunny's letter never arrived and knowing she'd never hear from him again.

"Thank you, mother," Ashley she said before turning to her sisters. "I don't know how I'm going to go on but I will." It was then that she wilted to the floor, her white grown spreading out like a wing. "If you don't mind," she whispered, I'd like to be alone right now."

"She should see a doctor," Robb whispered to Amelie.

Instead of a day of joy, they were now in the house of sorrow.

"She'll be okay."

• • •

When Ashley was finally alone, she shed her beautiful dress. She needed the numbness to protect her from the pain. But most of all she needed to be away from the pity. It was then that she realized no one had called Nemba.
There was no question in her mind now that the car had been Mel's though the police refused to corroborate her suspicions.

Her phone rang. It was Phillip.

"I'm so sorry my darling," Phillip wished he could cradle her head in his arms. "Me too," Ashley's hollow voice quivered as she pushed down the tears.

"It took me a lifetime to trust and now look at what happened. It's as though God's punishing me…for…for…"

"Hush. Don't try to make sense of this. It's going to be rough but you must try to find happiness in the little things," Phillip said, "One day at a time. That's all you have to do."

• • •

The next day Ashley went to the Dakota, the home Mel called his headquarters. She hadn't spent much time in this tomb with its dark paneled walls and Middle Eastern décor and she'd forgotten how warm it felt. More than any other of his homes, this place reflected the true Melvadore. The strong aroma of tobacco hit her as she entered the front door. Ashley walked around the apartment. This was the place Mel had taken her into his trust. She felt the prickling tears as she made her way over to his desk. Papers littered the top and she wondered how he ever found anything. Her head hurt as she began the tedious task of sorting the papers into piles. Where to begin?

In plain view was a will. One that had been changed only two days before! Did Mel know something was going to happen to him? Was that why he wanted to talk to her? Did he suspect? Ashley picked up the Last Will and Testament of Melvadore Follette and began reading. To her surprise, he'd left most of his empire to her. Was he planning to surprise her? Ashley scanned the rest of the will. To his chauffeur and to Mrs. Delaney, he had left 1 million dollars each. But to her confusion and surprise, he'd left nothing to the only sister he had. The one who was as close to him as a pea in a pod. Ashley folded the will and put it in her handbag. Nothing was adding up. As she moved the mountain of papers, she saw a mahogany box pushed back to the extreme left corner of the desk. Inside was a letter.

> *Dear Aga,*
>
> We are no longer under the radar. Because of the tragedy, we are all being watched closely. We can transfer no more funds at this time. All projects are to be put on hold. No point in building what might be destroyed.
>
> *Alaikum Salaam.*

The letter, typed on plain white paper, was not signed and was dated almost two years previous. Was this a copy of something he'd sent? Who was Aga? Ashley's heart almost stopped. No way. Had Mel been an operative? A Mashoud? Was that what he was going to tell her? No wonder he wanted her to go to Afghanistan. He needed her to become a sympathizer. Was he intentionally killed?
Ashley dropped the letter as though it was fire. Mel knew he was going to die. "They'd killed him and made it look like an accident." Ashley wailed aloud. "They killed him. Oh Mel," Ashley fought back tears at the sound of his name. She had not said his name aloud since his death. But why three years later? Ashley dashed from the house. She took the letter from the box and placed it and the Will inside her purse. Something did not add up. She couldn't find Nemba. She even tried calling Abdullah. She had no idea how she got from the living room to the massive mahogany bed. She was so tired. So very tired.

Mrs. Delaney's roused Ashley from a fitful night. Her usually crisp, authoritative voice had been replaced with a gentle. "Good Morning."

"I needed to be here," Ashley said softly.

"I know."

"How can I ever thank you?" Ashley embraced the woman to whom she owed so much.

"It is not necessary to thank me. I should be thanking Mr. Follette for my life."

Ashley smiled, placing her hand on Mrs. Delaney's. "Thank you anyway," she said.

"What will you do now?" Mrs. Delaney asked.

"I'd like to schedule the plane. I need some time away."

"Can I get Lacy to pack for you?"

"Yes. Not too much. I won't need much."

Mrs. Delaney nodded. "May I say again; how sorry I am?"

"And may I say again, that I can never thank you enough." Ashley kissed the woman's cheek. "I'll send the plane right back and thank you for doing this for me. Can you ask my driver to come and get me in an hour?"

"Right away," Mrs. Delaney said leaving the room not knowing she was now a millionaire.

Ashley padded to the bathroom, pulled open the built-in hamper and stuffed one of Melvadore's merino sweaters in her bag. She grabbed his robe that hung behind the door and stuffed a few undershirts too, in her bag. Two hours later Ashley boarded Mel's G5 for Monte Carlo. Inside her suitcase was his clothing's. She took one of the V-neck shirts from the case and slipped it over her head. The smell comforted her.

• • •

Ashley checked herself into the same suite they had shared at Hermitage where he'd proposed. She ate the same dinners, listened to the same music, drank the same wine and watched the sunset. The pain weighed down and its jagged edges bore new wounds into her soul. She blamed the Americans. She blamed Afghanistan. She blamed the Spaniards. She blamed the entire world and then she blamed God. For weeks Ashley, devastated and forlorn, racked her brain for a plausible explanation for Mel's disappearance. She was now shut down to any emotion. How life had a way of explaining the unexplainable. She now understood what her mother had felt. She now understood love and pain.

Ashley sat on the balcony and wrote a letter to Mel on stationary she'd taken from his desk drawer. The sunset was magnificent and breathtaking. It was a moment when her despair and grief was so great, that she thought of ending her life. As she looked out at the surge of life on the streets of Monaco, she wondered if she would ever be able to feel again. When she finally put the pen down, she was aware of a new feeling. For several more nights, she wrote long letters to Mel. "Don't blame, she'd hear him say. Find the meaning. Find the purpose.

The next day Ashley changed from the smelly robe she'd worn for four weeks into a skirt and Mel's T-shirt. She could still smell, very faintly, his cologne. This was the point at which she knew that it would be possible to go on. That evening Ashley left the hotel for the first time and dined alone in town. On her return, she made a call. "Mrs. Delaney," she said into the phone, "I'm ready to come home."

"Rest them right inside the door," Ashley said pressing a hundred-dollar bill into the porter's hand. "Thanks a million. The other stuff you can bring up later."

"Is seven-thirty okay, Ma'am?"

"It's perfect," Ashley said stepping inside her apartment. She switched on the lights and inhaled her own scent. It was good to be home.

The platinum lighter on the center table was the first thing to catch her eye. "Oh Mel," she said, picking it up, rubbing the smooth surface against her palm. "I miss you so much."

Ashley sat on the sofa, realizing that what she had hoped a new beginning was very much a part of the past. Mail was piled high on the credenza. Dear, dear Ms. Delaney. To pass more time before heading to the bedroom, the place where memories of Melvadore would be everywhere, she grabbed the stack of mail and flipped through it.

The invitation was on white Gallagher paper. You are cordially invited to attend a "Night of Leipzig", Performance, by Amelie Mercer, Conductor, Enrique Gamba.

Again, it never ceased to amaze Ashley how life just goes on. She needed to find out if foul play was at hand in Melvadore's death…no one had ever found a body…and she would not bury her husband until she was certain he was dead.

CHAPTER THIRTY-SEVEN
Family

December Christmas, 2004

IN THE WEE HOURS OF the morning, the fireplace crackled, throwing yellow sparks into the air. Robb, untangled himself from the jaws of his wife's legs to throw more logs into the hearth. "Your son is upstairs sleeping and look at what you started."

"I finished it wouldn't you say," Amelie winked at her husband. "Anyway, quit being a concerned parent. I locked the door; the room is soundproof and your son knows all about love and its reward. You forgot you have a grandson upstairs?"

The house was festive with Christmas decorations in every room. This was, for the Mercer's, the most cherished of holiday seasons. Outside the ground was blanketed with snow that also clung to poplar trees and hedges. The entire family, except for Lawrence and June, were there.

Robb opened the curtains. "Come and look at this." He beckoned Amelie.

"So much for sleeping upstairs. Where do they get all this energy?"

"Dear, it's 10:00 a.m. Christmas morning."

"Point."

Robb pushed open a window.

"Throw it," William was encouraging little Will to release the snowball. He was just past his first birthday. Instead, Will brought the icicle up to his mouth and began licking away. His wife Kyla, was pelting William with her snowballs.

"To be so young again," Amelie said shivering turning away from the window. In the hallway, she bumped into Ashley.

"Morning."

"Merry Christmas…do you want some tea? "Amelie asked.

"Don't mind if I do. Where's little, Mel."

"I just fed him. He's with his grandmother. They are singing Christmas Carols."

"I see." Amelie smiled…inside.

"Did you see William letting that child eat the dirty snow?"

Amelie patted her sister on the arm. "Those buggers are more resilient than you and me…plus this is Connecticut, our snow is clean. You'll drive yourself crazy if you try to keep stuff out of Mel's mouth."

Ashley, who'd found out on her return from Monaco that she was pregnant was forced to abandon her plans to go sleuthing for Melvadore. She had even thought of going to Afghanistan but if what she suspected had any validity, it would be far too dangerous for her to go traipsing through the Middle East. Plus, she wanted her baby to be born in America. Ashley who'd spent months trying to find Nemba finally gave up reluctantly accepting the inevitable or even the obvious. Melvadore and his sister were dead or he and his sister had vanished into thin air. The thought of him just leaving her at the altar had indeed crossed her mind and that her worse fear had come true was unsettling. But she knew deep down he would never do that. No matter who was to blame for his disappearance or death, what was for sure was that her future was destined to have no Mel in it, she had a piece of him through her child. At her age it had not been an easy pregnancy but never for a second did she think of any alternatives. If he were dead, Ashley prayed to God every night that his body would be found so that she could make closure and give him a proper burial.

From the kitchen, Amelie watched with pride as William and Kyla made a snowman replete with a carrot nose and button eyes, and Baby Will again squealed with joy.

"How does it feel to be a grandma and a new aunt at the same time?"

"Fantastic. They are the best babies to have…the ones who belong to others."

"Good morning sunshine's. Merry Christmas." Randy swung through the kitchen door.

"Morning," her sisters answered.

The three sisters sat at the table with their tea. For a good while, they didn't speak…so much had already been said.

"It's like old times isn't it?" Amelie said.

Her sisters smiled… "All you have to do now is go bang on that instrument of yours and it will be old times."

"Great idea. That will bring everyone downstairs. I'll leave the door wide open."

"I'm surprised Phillip wasn't the first one down here," Ashley said.

"Let's go deck the halls with boughs of holly," Randy suggested, leading the way.

As hard as their lives had proven to be over the past year, it was Christmas. They were ready to let the world sing.

"I'm so sorry June isn't here," Ashley said.

"Her beau really wanted her to meet his family. I think he's going to propose. And, since Mensa was going to Ghana, June thought it a good time to go since, in her words, "Christmas wouldn't be the same without Mensa and her Dad. I can't get upset really because Mensa has been a mother to her all her life and her father was the one who showed her affection."

"It's a new day," Amelie said. "It's good that she spends time with her new family to be, we've had her for twenty-three years.

"I think you might be right about that. It's probably for the best. She has her own life now and she needs to leave our stuff behind."

"We all need to leave a lot of shit behind," Ashley said. "But hell, if it's not easier said than done."

"You can say that again," Randy agreed.

"But my sisters, love will prevail…no matter how hard things get or will get," Amelie said.

"I guess love is more resilient than any of us ever imagine," Randy proffered.

"I'd even venture, now that I'm in my old age, to say, Love, is all," Ashley added.

"The old part I'm sure of!" Randy laughed.

Ashley, who'd rarely seen her sister laugh, was surprised at how beautiful she was when her eyes lit up. "Mother," Amelie saw her mother coming down the stairs "We were just headed to the music room to signal all the lazy bones that this was Christmas.

"But I think everyone is up, except little Mel." Emily came into the music room. She then sat on the piano bench next Amelie and placed the baby monitor on top. "Do you know the Song of the Bells? She began playing.

"What…Mother…" Amelie had no idea her mother could play the piano. "I took lessons as a child and your father was my teacher later."

Amelie now understood the why of her mother's fear of her choosing music as a career. It was a knee-jerk reaction to losing her father. For only a split-second Amelie hesitated before picking up the melody an octave higher… "Noel rang out."

• • •

Later in the Afternoon.

"Randy, Randy, RANDY," Amelie, who was in the kitchen checking on dinner was yelled louder and louder with each call of Randy's name.

"Why do people feel they have to scream my name?" Randy said coming into the kitchen pondering if Lawrence was Amelie's teacher. "What? What on earth," she ran to aid her sister when she saw her bending into the oven. "What's wrong?"

"I need your help." Amelie beckoned. Her mitted hands disappeared into the oven and she pulled out a fat turkey. "Is that thing cooked?" she asked as Randy looked suspiciously at the bird she'd put on the stove top.

"Is that why you're bellowing my name? How would I know when this damn thing is cooked?"

Amelie shook her head. "Why did I ever think I could cook a turkey? It's the last time I tell you. Dinner is going to be a disaster."

"I've never even tried. I know how to supervise meals and menu's sweetie, not cook them."

"Did the gizmo in the breast pop up yet?" Ashley, who had come into the kitchen and overheard their conversation, asked. "That's an indication. Let me have the wing and I'll tell you for sure."

"Get out of here," Amelie warned, shooing her away from the turkey.

"Where's Mother? She'll know." Ashley said. "She was boasting in Jamaica about her Home Ec. skills."

"Right. Did you see the life those women in Jamaica lived? Their maids certainly shielded them for the chores of ordinary living. Didn't you notice how Aunt Joy called the maid from the kitchen to serve the lemonade that was on the table next to her?"

"Mummy's later life was not like Aunt Joy's. Anyway, she's resting. Said she wasn't feeling too chipper," Amelie answered.

"I'll go check on her," Ashley said. "It's time to feed Mel. Nothing like some good old mother's jugs." She jiggled her breast. "These things hurt."

"Little Mel will take care of that," Randy said.

"I have a question…but no attack, okay? Do you think we should have mother move closer to us?" Amelie asked.

The sisters looked at each other but no one said a word. Finally, Randy said, "Why don't we take turns having her stay with us for a while."

Amelie thought she would keel over. "Let's see what she wants to do at dinner," she said hurriedly said pushing the turkey back into the oven.

"What a blessing little Mel turned out to be for Ashley. The baby certainly helped her a lot," Randy said when Ashley was out of earshot.

"As the world turns," Amelie agreed.

"Her eyes are definitely brighter." Amelie threw her gloves onto the counter.

"She's turned out to be a real survivor," Randy said.

"Haven't we all?" Amelie asked and while they were on the subject of love and loss she added, "How's Lawrence these days?"

"I really haven't seen him. June said he was going skiing with friends in Aspen."

Stuffing her hands back into the quilted mitts Amelie asked, "So what now?"

"One day at a time I suppose."

"For all of us."

Amelie poured herself a glass of egg nog and Randy her favorite fizzy water. "I have something to tell you but I don't want you to be mad at me," Amelie took the moment to slip in her secret. "I've invited Lawrence for dinner. He came back from his trip early and he was going to be home alone." Putting an arm around her sister's shoulder, she said. "He's got a good heart, Randy. He's flawed, but who isn't? In the flaw department, we own a big slice of that cake. To understand sometimes is all love needs. Please don't be upset. He's family. You didn't throw me out when you found out I was a half-sister."

"It's fine, Amelie. Truly it is. It's Christmas after all."

"What'd you say we give the bird another hour?"

"How about some more Christmas carols while we wait?"

• • •

"Amelie," Ashley called as they walked into the music room. "Come here a minute."

"What's up?"

"Did you hear me playing that piano? I'm pretty good, aren't I? I thought little Mel should learn early." The baby as in a bed swing next to his mother.

"A virtuoso," Amelie rolled her eyes. Little did Ashley know the music room was soundproofed! "What I need to know from you is what did mother say about knowing when a turkey is cooked?"

"Oops. I forgot to ask."

Amelie shook her head. Smiling she said, "What earthly good are we as domestic women? To think three adult women can't figure out when a turkey is cooked."

"Apparently no good at all. We are good at other things," Ashley laughed but the laughter did not reach her eyes. This would have been her first Christmas with Mel. "Go ask Phillip. He'll know!" Ashley said.

Phillip, who was reading the paper in the library and heard his name floated through the open door.

"You rang?" He came into the music room.

"Do you know when a turkey is cooked?"

"You mean you don't?" He looked aghast. "Let me ask Calvin. He's the woman in this relationship." Phillip went to find his lover.

• • •

The doorbell rang.

"I'll get it," Randy said, happy to leave the turkey mystery behind.

She pulled open the door and was face to face with Lawrence. They stood looking at each other for a few moments. "Lawrence," Randy finally said.

"Hello, Randy. It's good to see you." He handed her a bag filled with gifts, then bent down and hoisted a case of 1985 Chianti Classio from the doorstep.

He looked well, Randy thought. A little grayer, a lot slimmer, but well. She hadn't seen him or Adele since her return to New York after months of traveling. Lawrence had offered to move out of their home until she was certain of her plans when she told him she was coming home. "Good to see you too," Randy smiled.

"Hey, Uncle Lawrence." William pressed flesh with his uncle. "See that snowman. He needs a bottle of that wine."

"I bet." Lawrence scooped him. "You're all grown up and you are a daddy now so why not! I can hardly believe this. I think you can definitely have some wine."

Lawrence was still so much a part of her family. Not only was he the father of her child, the investor for the entire family and Robb's good friend, if she had to be perfectly honest, she'd admit she'd missed him. Being away from him had been essential but now it was time to decide on her future.

"Hey, sport," exclaimed Robb striding into the room, his hand extended. "You brought any of that expensive wine that only you can afford?"

"I hear that Amelie's raking in the dough as a concert pianist. She may have to split this with me," he said indicating the case.

They both laughed as Lawrence followed Robb to the bar.

"You're just in time for my excellent playing," Amelie kissed her brother-in-law. "More Christmas Carols. Everyone. Into the music room."

"Lawrence looks great, doesn't he?" Ashley asked sidling up to Randy.

"Yes, he does." Randy's eyes followed Lawrence as he crossed the room to stand beside her.

"Oh, Come All Ye Faithful," rang out as people toasted the day with eggnog, wine, water and baby milk. A couple of hours later the bird actually looked golden and the thingamajiggy had popped up and Calvin had given his blessings that the bird was cooked.

"Dinner is served," Amelie announced. "Come one come all. William, go and get your grandmother."

I'll never grow up in this house, William thought running up the stairs.

"Lawrence, sit here next to Randy and you Rob over here. Let mother sit at the head and I'll sit next to Robb." Ashley was back to ordering people around.

Randy and Lawrence were the first to be seated as the others slowly made their way to the table. "You really do look well, Randy," Lawrence whispered once they were seated.

"So, do you."

"And how were your travels?"

"Amazingly enlightening. I can't actually believe I was gone so long."

"It felt like forever."

"I'm so glad I did it. In countries like India and China, it isn't easy to hide from oneself as it is in New York with its myriad distractions. I found the Ashram a true channel and challenge to my spirit. It wasn't easy but I had to go through it. There were a lot of tears as I peeled my onion. But, I'm on my way. You should try it." Randy spread her napkin in her lap. "And how are you and how's your business?" Randy asked. She was surprised at how easy it was to get back in sync with Lawrence. She supposed the grooves of twenty-four years didn't fade overnight.

"I've cut down a lot on my schedule but it's good enough considering the times. June was by the other day. She really looks great."

"How is she really doing?"

"As well as can be expected. She calls me every day and stops by on the weekends." Lawrence placed his napkin on his lap.

"It would be better for her if we were back together. Our home is big enough for two."

Randy looked down at her hands. "Let's not do this now. It's Christmas plus we can't we go back to life as usual?"

"But we could try moving forward," Lawrence said covering her hands with his. Randy didn't pull away.

• • •

Emily took a seat next to Amelie. She looked at her children and wondered what their lives would have been like if hers had not been lived in the margins. They were truly successful and now it seems they were all working hard to get whole. She regretted the pain her choices caused them, yet as inconvenient a mother as she had been, her children were okay and except for Ashley's tragedy, this had been a good year. At seventy-two years old, for the first time in years, she felt alive again. She closed her eyes as the prayers started. She thought of Bunny Higgenbottom. Bunny with the wicked smile and even wickeder love. He'd left her a most precious gift.

"As we give thanks for another year let us remember to live every day with purpose. We have all had to deal with disappointments but you know what? Life still goes on. Let us ask ourselves if we should die this very night would we have lived our best lives. If the answer is no, let's make 2005 our best year yet," Robb said raising his glass. "Merry Christmas to all."

Merry Christmas echoed through the Mercer's home. All was well.

EPILOGUE

WHEN ADELE OPENED THE Christmas card a letter fell to the floor. She unfolded it, her spirits sinking.

Dear Adele,

I returned from my travels a few months ago. It was a sobering and enlightening experience. I spent a month at the famous Ashram in India and another month in Peru. Whoa. Talk about facing demons! In Europe, I visited your esteemed City of Lights, took the Orient Express to Portofino and back before I took the Chunnel home to England. I went to visit my old home in Leicester Square and even stayed at the same boarding house my mother came to from Jamaica with my old and dear guardian Aunt Clarissa. The pain at times was unbearable but it was truly a time of renewal, forgiveness, and self-discovery for me. After England, I went to Scotland. Don't ask me why. Maybe because it was in one of the childhood rhymes that kept me sane. In Loch Lomond, like my favorite sonnets said, the hills are indeed purple hues and the grass greener than anywhere else I've ever seen. It was great to eat bangers again but I have to tell you I truly hated Haggis. I hope your time was productive as well and that you understood why I needed to go away. My time in China was also fun.

Living without my family was hard and sobering. I never knew just how much they defined who I am. Always my first thoughts were of them. Yet, I thank you for opening up my life to truth and honesty. I will never deny what happened between us and I will always treasure the memory of our friendship. But Adele, Lawrence, and June have been my life for so many years and in all honesty, they continue to be.

For my entire life, I have longed to feel the love that so many talked about but escaped me. You gave that to me when I needed it most. But sometimes even when we have choices, some doors should never be opened. Once opened, we will always know what was behind them, yet it is still possible to close them again forever. Neither Uncle Joe's nor your door should have been opened in my life. And though your love filled an enormous emotional void for me at a time when death felt more authentic than life, it is not who I am. With you, from your gentle touch to your open heart for once in my life I wanted to choose happiness over pain. So, Adele, be happy with the knowledge that you saved my life. Yet, even our delirious and unbridled happiness was soon replaced by guilt and a knowingness that I didn't belong …where this love required me to go. I guess when pain and loss weigh heavily on one's life any escape to find love can be rationalized.

What I discovered from my travels is that I can be happy outside the doors I have chosen with either you or Lawrence. Today, I have no need to hide behind my pain or guilt anymore. I am through with blaming and feeling helplessness to control my own destiny. I am, ready to own my happiness. The new me won't allow any pathology or my inability to forgive to cover my world in darkness. I have chosen…what yet I am not entirely sure but I do know that I have chosen life. I also do know that my natural love is for a man.

I had a date with Lawrence last evening. It was very pleasant. We have so much history and so many memories. Last night I spent the night at our home with him. It all felt so familiar. I don't know where it will lead but for now, we are moving forward with hope. It was only this morning that I felt truly ready to complete this letter to you, which I began months ago. I am sitting among my orchids and feeling a sense of total belonging…a true sense of purpose. At Christmas dinner, my brother-in-law asked:

If you should die tonight, would you have lived your best life. In 2005 that is my goal. I hope you make it yours.

I hope all is well with you and I still think you should open a gallery to show off your magnificent work. I have enclosed a check for "Destiny," the painting you did for June as a gift. Though it never worked out you did do the work. I want to repay you for your thoughtfulness. One day I hope we can meet again as friends. Thank you for showing me another part of myself and of life. It is a part of me that I no longer need to see. I have grown so much and have forgiven so many all because of you. One day you will make someone very happy. One day I know we will be friends."

Always,
Randy Austin

P.S. Sorry the card was late. A belated Merry Christmas to you.

Adele folded the letter and stuffed it back in the envelope. She traced the handwritten address with her fingers. Rising, she went to her studio, opened her writing desk and tucked Randy's letter in between the pile marked keep. She turned toward the painting she'd done of Randy and filled in the color of the lips. She entitled it:

You were my best life.

• • •

Ashley tucked little Mel into his crib. She wound up the mobile and watched as his lids got heavy. She went to the kitchen and made herself a cup of tea and took it back to her bedroom. Ashley stood for a minute looking out over Central Park, before pulling the curtains. She missed Melvadore but how lucky she was that she had his son. As always, she removed the phone he'd given her and placed it on the bedside table before climbing into bed. She had carried that phone with her everywhere for almost one year and it was the last thing she touched at nights. Just as she was about to turn out the light the phone began ringing.

She put the phone to her ear.

"Ashley. Hello Ashley."

"Who is this?"

"It's so good to hear your voice. I've missed you so much."

"Who is this? Mel? Mel is that you?" Who would play such a cruel joke?

"Yes, my darling it's me. I can't talk long but I want you to write this number down. I have so much to tell you. I'm so sorry about the wedding. It was the perfect cover and I knew you'd understand what I had to do. I'll tell you everything when we meet. Call this number tomorrow and I'll tell you where and when to meet me. Throw the phone out I just called you on…I mean destroy it too. Do not call on any other phone other than the one you'll get tomorrow. I can't wait to see you and our son. Please kiss him for me. Just know that I'm safe and we'll be together soon. I can't wait to finally make you my wife. I love you and I am sorry about the pain I've caused."

"You know we have a son?'

"I know everything darling…Everything."

"Where are you? I don't…where are you?" Ashley was crying hysterically.

"In New York. You can't say anything until the plan has been executed. Just a few more days my darling and all this will be behind us."

"But Mel, I can come now."

The phone went dead.

Ashley was awash in tears, she was crying, laughing, crying and laughing some more. What if this was a trick her mind suddenly jolted. She didn't tell a soul.

The next day had barely dawned before Ashley called the number Mel had given her. A strange voice answered. "Don't be scared. It's Abdullah."

"Where is Mel?"

"On his way to meet you. Fly to London. Check into Claridge's. Suite 908. Wait there for him. He'll bring you home."

"Home?"

"I am home. Why doesn't he come home to me?"

"You'll have a new home with Melvadore. He'll tell you everything when he sees you."

"Is he in trouble?"

"Not in the least. He's never been better. He knew you'd understand."

THE END